THE
LUCK
PARTICLE

Justin Hayward/Murray-Hayward Limited
http://theluckparticle.tel
Published by Murray-Hayward Limited
ISBN 978-0-9928585-1-3
First Edition

THE
LUCK
PARTICLE

J.K. Hayward

For Lisa, Matt and Kash, without whom
this book would not have been written.

"History is written by the victors."
Anonymous, attributed to Sir Winston Churchill

CHAPTER 1

Near Mayak, Crimea, Ukraine - August 2007

The man sat with his eyes shut, facing the setting sun. Whether he was aware of the beauty of the moment, with the impression of a fire burning far out into the ocean as the great orange orb sank into the sea, he made no sign of it.

Barely breathing, he sat cross-legged, on the end of the crusted and rusting pier platform. Jutting out from a secret alcove, long forgotten, surrounded by rocky, mountainous outcrops. A sailing craft big enough to sleep six people gently tilted side to side alongside the pier. Its main sail raised marginally, the canvas flapped every so often softly, in concert with the stays and the lapping of the small waves.

The air was dry, even this close to the ocean and at this hour of the evening. A stillness hung around the cove. The sand, hot and hazy, was motionless except for a little soft-shelled crab that tiptoed from where it had buried itself in the shade an hour or so ago.

All was quiet.

He took a long, silent breath in through his nose, filling his lungs, drawing the air in from his diaphragm to maximise his intake.

He held it for several moments.

Removing a Dictaphone from his pocket, he clicked it on, and began to talk.

"I am the Historian. If you're listening to this, either a copy has reached an unknown place in the world by some slim chance invisible to The Watchmen. Or, quite unbelievably, one man can change the world."

CHAPTER 2

Vienna, Austria - Tuesday August 7th, 2007

The report that had just hit his desk provided the first trace that things might be going awry after recent acts of intervention by his close circle.

BNP Paribas had just terminated withdrawals from three significant hedge funds, without authorisation.

It had cited a 'complete evaporation of liquidity' in the financial markets as the reason.

Many of Adnan Karvorkian's peers, both inside the group of individuals connected by a special bond as well as those outside, were surprised and damaged by this action.

That no one had been pre-warned within his cabal was especially egregious, given their connections and associated 'skills'. The situation was more than simply a little awkward.

The flashes of embarrassment caused in a few isolated incidents tore across complex interconnected investments. Deals, on-going discussions and a couple of significant projects imploded spectacularly.

No one was entitled to be surprised that some re-setting of the financial markets would happen. Given the bursting of the bubble in the sub-prime lending market the year before, in part forced by the actions of his fellowship, it had been inevitable. But this should not have affected those in in Karvorkian's circle. There were precautions to limit the ripple effect of the re-balancing to those who deserved to be reminded of their place.

No. Something had changed. It had to be an external factor. No one in their collective counsel would have deliberately caused this outcome. It was impossible.

Sitting in the near dark, Karvorkian's screen flashed financial market information in reds and greens (at this point way more reds than greens). He tapped a sinewy finger slowly on the mouse, pondering.

Accounting for all known variables, he sighed; it could mean only one thing.

That infernal machine was getting closer to completion.

His hand moved to the phone. He depressed the well-worn speed-dial button, lifted the receiver and waited.

Before the person at the other end of the line could even acknowledge him, he spoke.

"We need to convene. Please make the necessary arrangements."

"I understand. I'll do so now."

Karvorkian put the receiver back down without a word of thanks and resumed scrutinising the screen.

He was not yet perturbed. This type of thing had been going on for hundreds of years. At the same time, he was not careless enough to think that this was a blip, an anomaly or accident.

There was no such thing as chance.

A correction and a punishment. That was what was needed. But first, the situation required further analysis. To choose the appropriate counteraction to re-align the current situation to his coalition's interest.

They needed to bring back balance. By balance, of course, his definition was that of reintroducing the status quo. A situation where Karvorkian's close union of peers regained control.

As he shut down his computer he reminded himself of the mantra that had been guiding people like him for centuries.

"May you live in interesting times," he whispered, as he stood and stalked out of the room, now completely dark.

The screen ticked as it cooled, like seconds ticking away. It gradually slowed, giving the impression that time itself was slowing. Nothing could be further from the truth.

CHAPTER 3

The city of Geneva - Tuesday August 7th, 2007

For a city of around one hundred and seventy-five thousand people, Professor Ebhart Fenkhause mused, Geneva was possibly one of the most interesting petri-dishes in the world.

He remembered as he navigated the wet streets that it was the place which printed the first ever English version of the Bible. He saw a delicious irony. How could such a religious city play host to the European Organization for Nuclear Research? An organisation laser-focused on understanding a universe without a god?

Indeed, he mused, if ever there was a counter-balance to the Holy See in The Vatican, Geneva surely provided it.

In its relative infancy, a Count under the Holy Roman Empire ruled it. Now, Geneva was a global centre of finance. A rumoured one trillion dollars sloshed around private bank accounts, through transactions almost as shady as the Vatican Bank itself.

He wondered how the city managed to draw the first organisation which then led to the hive of institutions with globally-significant power bases swarm to its streets. The United Nations through to multi-national internet and telephony infrastructure organisations. Trade, transport, meteorology, medical and economic bodies. The breadth of politics and morality was incredible. If Geneva was a party, the guests were A-list.

Luckily for him, the Professor smiled, the chances of an actual party in Geneva occurring were slim to none. The place was almost as animated at night as the plastic owls placed around the railway generators to scare away rodents.

Professor Ebhart was single, a confirmed bachelor and married to his work. He ate, drank and slept science. If it was possible to forgo sleeping, drinking and eating, he would have happily spent twenty-four hours a day at CERN.

It was Ebhart's job, his mission, to lead the ATLAS team.

The team responsible for the detector critical in searching for and verifying the existence of the Higgs boson.

The God particle.

Every step he took, every minute that past, he felt a growing sense of closeness to that confirmation.

For a man of no religious belief, his strength of feeling in his work could have been described in a religious context as fanatical. His certainty in something so fundamental to his perception of the universe that was unproven by science made him who he was.

ATLAS was his church. Forty-five metres long, twenty-five meters high, and weighing about seven thousand tons.

He had even described it on the official website as 'about half as big as the Notre Dame Cathedral in Paris'.

His three thousand bishops were physicists drawn from thirty-eight countries. Universities and laboratories made up his one hundred and seventy-seven dioceses.

Every morning, he would go and pray at the altar of data. His white coat his cassock and surplice. He ate and drank of the body of work that created the future of scientific proof.

His work was beginning to generate a real sense of anticipation and a growing awareness around the world.

The recent switching on of the largest electro-magnet in the world generated strong press interest.

Eighteen years had passed since the start of development. Billions of Euros later, the Large Hadron Collider project was almost ready. Ready to delve into the answer of life, the universe and everything, to steal from the wonderful Douglas Adams. Ebhart had appreciated his work greatly when, in his youth, he had had the time to read fiction.

That he would live to see it switch on and begin to work caused Ebhart to have a profound sense of awe and mystery on a daily, if not hourly, basis.

Others were less inclined to feel so positive about this progress. The shifting of institutional power that it would inevitably cause if Ebhart was successful, formed a clear and present danger.

The intervention of those holding these views was currently not anywhere near his list of possible threats.

Ebhart trudged along the pavement, thinking about his current schedule.

One international organisation that had a presence in Geneva tracked him ever more closely.

It had no name, no offices and no tax returns. It did have one of those hidden bank accounts. Very useful for all types of emergencies that required surreptitious financial transactions.

Soon, it would strike. Hard.

Harder than it had in 2005. Its intervention then caused a one thousand two hundred-kilogramme cabinet containing electrical switchgear to fall on Miguel Salenca. With fatal consequences. The death remained unexplained. The internal report logged the incident as 'Personal Accident' in the Electronic Document Handling System. It sat in the database, gathering virtual dust. Unlike the real dust that gathered on the first place trophy Miguel had won in the individual unloading event at the recent French Forklift Championships.

There was no field, even had someone identified it sabotage as the cause, to record an act of sabotage like that on the form.

No, it would strike harder than on the twenty-seventh of March of that year. A cryogenic magnet support 'broke' during a pressure test involving one of the machine's inner triplet magnet assemblies. This was due to a 'fault' that had been present in the original design. A fault which had remained 'unnoticed' during four engineering reviews over the following years.

Further analysis revealed that it was a design flaw. Made as thin as possible for better insulation, the magnet was not strong enough to withstand the forces generated during pressure testing.

Again, someone filed an internal accident report. No mention of the possibility that a member of staff may just have manipulated the results to impact the core stability of the LHC.

Professor Fenkhause was completely unaware of who and what was about to attempt to destroy him.

CHAPTER 4

Near Mayak, Crimea, Ukraine - Tuesday August 7th, 2007

The Historian, oblivious to the twilight shroud draping itself around his shoulders, continued his monologue. Waves split gently around the struts on the pier.

He was now in the middle of a recent history lesson for his as-yet unidentified listener.

"Many holding extreme views think that the world will slip into a black hole when CERN finally utilizes the Large Hadron Collider. Few appreciate that it will have such an immediate effect on the world just by switching it on.

"On the twentieth of November in two thousand and six, CERN activated the largest super-conducting magnet in the World. This brought what some thought of as Europe's most important project one step closer to understanding how the Universe was created.

"There's a great deal of opposition to scientists playing with particles. Accelerating them until they smash into each other deep underground. Many despise the desire to dive more deeply into the resulting data. The aim of finding a god made of tachyons rather than of religious trinity scares them.

"But a tiny minority, fewer than twenty people around the world I believe, oppose scientists studying the universe at this level for a different reason. There are side-effects of what the scientists are attempting to do, which affect them. Even though those same scientists are unaware of the effect their work will have.

"Here's an example. You've heard of the butterfly effect? Well, I can tell you that, in less than a year, the sub-prime mortgage bubble will burst. We saw the start of it in July. Discussed in bars and broadsheets, we will be told it happened because it was unsustainable. The debt could not be re-packaged into new financial instruments attractive enough, that Governments had to step in and bail out the financial institutions. This will be fallacious. In actual fact, this financial merry-go-round can be sustained indefinitely with no intervention.

7

"No. What I believe will instead happened is the injection of a dramatic loss of confidence. This will be caused deliberately by a small group of people intent on creating a diversion. They will try to destabilise the liquidity of funds. It will have tremendous global impact, but its sole measure of success for them will be the amount of disruption caused to the research underway at CERN. All this will occur to maintain a secret that gives them power over everyone else."

The Historian paused, opened his eyes and shivered, finally perhaps aware that the night was drawing in. Momentarily stopping the Dictaphone, he stared for a while at the first star of the evening. He knew, behind the growing gloom, billions more stars lay, unseen. Only a fraction would be observable to the naked eye. Proportionally, a few more by using devices on earth.

Bringing himself back from his reverie, he clicked the Dictaphone back on.

"Why am I telling you this? To prove, if it gets to you in time, that I'm not a madman. I'm not a soothsayer, I'm analysing the data. The key to seeing what is going on in its true context is not to look for the cause or the effect. Instead, check for absence. Look for the unnatural spaces between events."

He thumbed the Dictaphone off with an audible click, emphasising with that gesture that he had come to the end of a chapter. He slipped the device back into his trouser pocket. He stood in one slow, fluid movement, as if he had been sitting for a few minutes rather than in that spot all day.

He nodded at the sea, lifted his head to the sky and saw that a few more stars had pricked the blackened indigo canvas. Like the stars' half-lives, time was running out to challenge those engaging in the biggest power struggle the world had seen for millennia.

CHAPTER 5

CERN, Geneva - Monday February 4th, 2008

Professor Fenkhause lived at a different speed than everyone else. Buried one hundred and seventy-five meters below the surface, he measured time not by the normal rising and setting of the sun. Instead, it was with paper. He mapped the progress of his life through his to do list. Crossing out and adding items and issues, counting down towards the switching on of the Large Hadron Collider.

He missed the turning of the year from 2007 to 2008. He was sheltered in academia within a city of riches and ample funding. He was unaware of the many turbulent events that were tipping countries and communities over the metaphorical edge.

His focus was on September of that year. His ambition was to send the first proton beam around the facility. To begin the process of dissecting the building blocks of life.

He had no idea that his progress had inspired the meltdown in the financial markets in January. The price of a barrel of oil was above one hundred dollars for the first time ever. Rising food and fuel prices were triggering riots in Third World countries.

His team continued their oversight of the one thousand six hundred LHC superconducting magnets. He had no inkling that his activity had caused the situation hysterical governments in many countries were trying to fix; taking over and bailing out banks deemed to be 'too big to fail', to prevent all-out implosion. Governments built consumer societies on the belief that, when its citizens went to bed at night, their financial security would still be tangible the next morning.

The response to Professor Fenkhause's diligent work was an attempt to decimate that decades-old belief structure in one day's trading.

The little time he spent above ground gave him enough understanding that time was still progressing routinely.

The nights and early mornings gradually were still chilly. But it was lighter every time he left his apartment and returned to the facility from the few hours' sleep he caught early in the mornings.

His awareness did not extend as far as his direct connection to the worst snowstorms in China for fifty years. Or the sixty-nine thousand deaths due to a seven point nine magnitude earthquake in south-west China.

Or the deadliest tornado outbreak in the southern United States for over twenty years.

Nor the four hundred and fourteen square kilometre of Antarctica's Wilkins Ice Shelf breaking off, putting the entire mass at risk.

Political disagreements inside CERN were always par for the course. They were never on the scale of the huge disruptions across the world from the Middle East through to Chad. Leaders were subject to increasingly widespread assassination attempts. Incumbents suddenly removed from office after years of corruption, the political will to see it through appearing overnight. Hell, even Fidel Castro stepped aside, albeit to elect his more progressive brother Raul.

Investigating the forces that shaped the universe, Professor Fenkhause had become a lightning conductor, drawing the focused wrath of unknown enemies. They were intent on preventing him from discovering something he himself had no idea that he was looking for.

Their frantic action had caused significant reactions. They affected the natural and man-made constructs everyone had become comfortable with.

The world itself and all on it were being influenced by a force that a scant few knew existed and fewer controlled.

Even the powerful have nightmares. Their fear was that their control was on the wane for good. The terror they went to bed with was that their loss of control would speed up exponentially if the particle accelerator were to perform its function to any decent level.

They were focused on any means necessary to achieve their desired goal.

They would stop at nothing short of Armageddon to secure their terms.

Extraordinary as these events seemed in the first half of the year, they were to become even more so by the end of it.

CHAPTER 6

Caserma, Switzerland - Wednesday April 9th, 2008

Lieutenant Colonel Ben Fallow swung his assailant to the floor in one fluid yet forceful movement and stepped back to see what if anything his opponent's next move would be. There was no indication that the man on the floor, easily a foot taller than him, was intending to move.

"I suggest you make a slight effort to get up, NCO Roell, even if it is to signify defeat, otherwise I might have to fail you on your levels of fitness."

The winded man on the ground groaned, rolled on to his back, pulled his legs up to his chest then used the momentum putting them down to sit up. He slowly stood, turned to face Ben, bowed and said "Oss", as was proper dojo etiquette, before retreating back to the half-dozen spectators.

No one smirked. None of them wanted to be next. The Lieutenant Colonel had been instructing them for a good three hours in the finer points of advanced Japanese Karate. He had yet to pause for breath.

Seconded to the Army Reconnaissance Detachment 10 of the Swiss Army, his job was to sort the wheat from the chaff. The Swiss Army wished to swell the ranks of this controversial counter-terrorist unit. Grow it into a fearsome taskforce designed to eliminate threats to Swiss nationals at home and abroad.

That the ranks were yet to reach sixty since the detachment had been formed in 2003 was, in no small part, down to Ben Fallow's exacting regime. It was the cause of many an applicant to drop out during the training process.

"Gentlemen, I suggest that you take a moment to consider exactly what you are signing up for. Prepare yourselves for the life you are about to choose. For the past three hours I have been defending myself against your feeble attempts to put me down. Not once have I had any cause to feel threatened by your actions.

"Now consider this. I have been using purely defensive actions. Yet all of you have managed to end up on the floor within thirty seconds of bowing."

He made a lurch forward to the six in front of him and all flinched to a man.

His eyelids tightened, his eyebrows lowered into a frown and his fists went to his hips.

"My god!" he snarled. "What a pitiful bunch of girlies they let in this year. Heaven help you if someone actually intended to do you harm. It's a good job you and your families qualify for that Swiss Army insurance plan, is all I can say. Honestly, what am I going to do with you? I'm not relishing the prospect of submitting my report in six weeks' time about your performances, that's a fact."

He checked the clock on the dojo wall then looked back at his applicants.

"I suggest that you all go for a run right now before I decide that perhaps the best way to get you motivated is to start breaking some bones for real. With a mental attitude like that, if some terrorist nut were to come in and give you a pounding right now, he'd kick your buts and your Mothers would feel it. Out!"

Quick as a flash, the men bowed, shouted "Oss!" and fled before he had the chance to change his mind.

Ben stood for a moment then smiled. It was the same procedure every year. Break them down, build them up and then ship them out.

The truth was, today was the first day he'd felt a lasting twinge in his back. He'd been seconded here for five years now. Several years before that he'd seen much more gruelling action. Ben finally felt deep down it might be time to find something else to occupy his time.

He wasn't getting any younger. It might be time to quit. He still had a nigh-on straight nose, both his ear lobes, a full complement of pearly white teeth and mousy blond hair. At least the majority of the scars on his body were between the neck and his thighs. In most circumstances and European climates that meant they were generally easy to cover up.

He stretched, arms high above his head, heard a few pops. Flopping from the waist down to the ground, he pressed his hands, palms-down, flat on the floor.

Standing up, he glanced at the clock again. He decided that he might go and surprise his recruits half way around the cross country route. Give them another going over before knocking off for a shower.

He grinned to himself.

He was always thorough when it came to his work. He knew however that whatever he was doing was in the best interest of his trainees.

God forbid that they'd ever meet someone like Ben in theatre in a one-on-one scenario. He'd never lost. He knew he was a lucky bastard.

He'd always felt blessed, relatively. He just seemed to be in the right place at the right time. Even landing this job after his time in the SAS had given him a huge boost. He was now one of, if not, the best instructors in the force. He'd been connected to the right people just at the right moment.

The job was great. Punishing, but great.

He met his targets every year. He got rid of the time wasters and beefing up the mental and physical fortitude of the ones that would join the ranks of the elite ARD 10.

The money, in Swiss Francs, was fantastic. His food and lodging had been covered in full for the past five years. Granted, he only had four weeks off every year. But there was only so much he could do to amuse himself before he started pining to be back in the training grounds.

But this year he felt different. A phase of his life was passing and he needed something new.

He felt excitement, rather than terror.

Having trained for virtually every eventuality, Ben was always enthusiastic to embrace change. Its constant attendance in life comforted him. Then again, he'd always seemed to land on his feet when things happened. He'd never really experienced what it felt like when things went wrong. Yet.

14

CHAPTER 7

Near Mayak, Crimea, Ukraine - Wednesday April 9th, 2008

The Historian had retired into the cabin of his boat and was currently seated at the small table in the kitchen diner area.

A single gas light shed a warm but limited glow around the place. Shadows of the coffee pot and mug flickered against the steps up to the hatch leading to the outside.

The smell of a recently finished meal of macaroni and cheese still lingered. Perhaps it was an odd choice for the time of the year and the heat. With limited rations in tins, sometimes it was difficult for one to dine appropriately for the season.

The Historian stirred himself from his internal reverie. He swallowed another gulp of strong, grainy coffee and again picked up the Dictaphone to continue the story he had spent the last six months telling.

"It's important to state that The Watchmen is a name that I have given those I'm telling you about. I'm not aware of anyone else in the world that feels the actions of these people ripple out into their consciousness. This is because I am not aware of anyone else in the world that concerns themselves with events in the same way that I do. Or at least, I am not aware of anyone still alive that has experienced their reach and lived to tell the tale.

"I do not know specifically who these people are. I could not tell you *where* they are. I cannot tell you for certain whether they are young or old, male or female, local to each other or geographically dispersed. I cannot even tell you if they like or detest each other.

"All I can say for a fact is that these people exist. They are combining their skills to force outcomes that I can only assume enable them to retain power or control over others. They number around a twenty, if one averaged out the strength of their skills and the resulting force it seems to deliver. I could be wrong."

Another sip of coffee, scalding hot, then the mug went back on the worn, varnished surface.

"How do I know this? You will no doubt soon read about a computer that predicts the future by analysing millions of digital texts. Its name is Nautilus. It was designed to understand and compute the types of words used and, from that, to predict what might happen in the future. You know the kind of stuff. Economic downturns. The prediction of stocks. The location of terrorists. That kind of thing.

"Well, I am a Culturomicist. I employ the same methods as the computer, the computational lexicography, but with a difference. Firstly, I happen to do it with my mind."

His face cracked into a grin before he continued.

"Secondly, I'm a damn sight better at it than Nautilus. Why? Because I do not limit the texts that I consume, and thus have a far broader archive to work from. I can make more connections. I am allowed to leap without the creation of a new algorithm. I can also understand much better the nuances and tone that comes from the state of mind in which every piece of text, whether long form or news snippet is written.

"I am blessed or cursed depending on your perspective with a photographic memory. I have never been formally diagnosed, but I present at a very low level Asperger's. This, as you can tell by my ongoing monologue, focuses my fascination on works of non-fiction. And my almost exclusive focus on one, if broad, topic. That of human life."

Another sip, the cup clinks down.

"My 'condition' would be quite obvious to you, were you to observe me in my work. So, I have unusual talents, a strange focus, unending research material and years of practice. I quickly saw that the intent of Nautilus and Culturomics was of potentially huge import. In its implementation though, its results at best are a fluke and the project is a dud. It lacks the intelligence to empathise, associate or infer. I believe this is critical in the analysis of the intent of a vocabulary that changes in meaning and use in a relatively short time.

"I have made discoveries using similar but enhanced techniques. And I discovered something about the source material also. Across

16

the ages, in the writing of articles about certain events, there was a lack of tone that was eerily unique. It was as if the authors were required to write the articles but there was nothing behind the style. The words rang empty, as if produced by a machine themselves. The lack of, for want of a better word, soul was disturbing.

"I scanned the articles in question, across all publications. More recently, I gained sources from independent bloggers and untrained citizen journalists. There was no doubt. Meaning was missing. Subtext was absent. There was no mass to the subject matter. Something was influencing their writing. They wrote to describe the situation but said nothing at all.

"Time and time again I saw it. And it has been going on for years. Hundreds of years."

A sudden splash outside of the boat made The Historian snap his focus up to the port hole and pause, his finger over the stop button.

Nothing followed. Just a fish jumping for flies perhaps.

He felt the final sentence of the night slip out of his mouth as a harsh whisper, escaping through his lips.

"These people are manipulating luck and you have to stop them."

CHAPTER 8

Vienna, Austria - Saturday August 30th, 2008

He often sat in front of his screen contemplating how one three syllable word could carry so much potential for destruction.

Collision.

It was an oily word. Close to collusion, a word Karvorkian enjoyed more vicariously. Collusion was so much more... friendly. Collision was a nasty, aggressive, brutish word. An incredibly powerful word when employed by the wrong type of person.

Physicists.

He grimaced, rolling his tongue across his teeth and made as if to spit out some poisonous taste.

It was not the normal definition of collision that set him on edge, nerves jangling, sending shivers of electricity through his muscles. The normal definition sat fine with him. Indeed, he and his like had employed tactics such as 'the act of colliding', or 'the violent coming together of two entities in a crash' many times to sustain their status quo.

No. It was the scientific application of that word which he detested. He had committed its word for word definition to memory since physicists had managed to persuade those in power to begin investing in the understanding of the microcosmic make-up of the universe.

"The meeting of particles or of bodies in which each exerts a force upon the other, causing the exchange of energy or momentum," Karvorkian hissed.

That's what was fucking up their happy existence currently. Physicists stupidly about to bash things into each other at high velocity to see what would happen and then analyse it. Fucking clueless.

It was fine when they confined themselves to the poorly-funded, feebly-powered Electron-positron colliders of the latter half of the previous century. Faffing about with circular devices a few kilometres in circumference was fine.

18

Oh sure, the likes of DORIS and then PETRA at DESI in Germany had led to some landmark discoveries in the structure of matter. They had had nowhere near the amount of power that would enable them to stumble across the truth of things. But it had provoked an urgency that seemed to capture the imaginations of politicians, and that was dangerous.

In the early 1960s, countries had begun to divert their attention up to the heavens. Fine, he had thought, so be it. Let them seek out the mysteries of the universe in a voyage to the stars. A big goal. Good luck to them. He knew there was nothing there that would enable them to find whatever it was that they thought they were seeking. It was just a smoke screen, in more ways than one.

Far more dangerous was the desire to look at the small.

To look down, to take notice. Down right into the microscopic and then some.

He didn't know where this sudden urge had come from, but to his mind it must have been stimulated by the invention of the atomic bomb. The power it had created and the change that a few explosions had made on the world he knew all too well.

Perhaps it was just perceived to be prudent to spread the bets. Focusing down as well as up meant that scientists could cover the whole table when mitigating the risk. That of losing, a nations pride dented in the face of the international scrutiny.

Regardless, it had made the job of his generation's circle to protect their birth right that much harder. Super colliders and particle accelerators began springing up around the world. It was a bloody bugger to keep sabotaging them. They had to keep throwing problems in their way until the respective funding bodies and oversight committees suggested it was time to close that particular vanity project down. Or simply bump off those with talent.

But they bloody well kept on building them. Bigger and more powerful each time.

As every new machine came along, it made the job of keeping the status quo even trickier to maintain. Too much action on one side of the fence and the chaotic equilibrium might tip. So they had to counter their actions with equal vigour to make sure the force on both sides of the equation smoothed out.

One scientist dies. Another genius destined to shuffle off this mortal coil sooner rather than later inexplicably continues to live and releases a significant piece of work. It develops some emerging field of science by leaps and bounds, unrelated to the one now castrated. Focus is diverted.

It was exhausting. What on earth was the point of having this privileged position if all he could do all day was worry about maintaining it? Where was the opportunity to lavish his wealth on yachts, wine, women and song?

So now, there was one of particular concern that appeared to be succeeding where others had failed.

It had a particular resilience that none of the other projects had shown before.

It was puzzling. They thought they'd cracked it when they'd managed to shut down a much bigger threat in the form of the US's Superconducting Super Collider. SSC, as they loved to drawl it in a three letter acronym.

When it closed in 1993, after ten years of construction and at a cost of two billion dollars, it was due to a choice between continuing that project and building the International Space Station. Up, not down, a delicious irony for sure. The power of that machine if completed would have dwarfed his current problem child. It would also have secured America's continued dominance in the world, essentially forever. To the exclusion of all other nations. Most probably within a couple of months of them switching it on.

True, the US still had the second and third-largest colliders in the world. But frankly, they just didn't seem to have the heart for this type of work. As he knew, if you weren't searching hard enough, you just wouldn't win the game.

No, it was the Large Hadron Collider, and the team leading the project, that was his biggest pain in the backside.

The reports he heard were disgustingly positive. The team was uncompromisingly determined. They constantly seemed to defy the counter-measures thrown at it.

His hand balled into a fist but it was left impotent.

20

There was nothing near that he wanted to punch.

How could it be that these scientists could be so moronic? Blundering around, trying to prove the existence of one thing, their actions causing a fundamental effect on another thing they didn't even know existed?

They should have known better.

After all, Einstein and Heisenberg had argued enough over the course of the last century for them to have at least registered some of it.

Nothing can be observed at a quantum level without that which is being observed, whether all of it or some of it, seen or not seen, changing.

The physicists were acting like moronic dinosaurs. They were crushing millions of future species under their dumb, fat feet. Destined to become extinct by something they didn't have the capacity to predict.

Whatever the future, Karvorkian thought as he sloped out of the room, it was not going to be quiet or restful. Especially if more of these machines were allowed to be turned on rather than off.

CHAPTER 9

Caserma, Switzerland - Sunday August 31st, 2008

Ben was in the Officer's mess, grabbing a beer with some of the best friends he'd ever known. Others would call them the most lethal combatants the theatre of terrorism had earned the misfortune to encounter. It was without doubt a good thing that those currently present had a moral compass and felt positive about the human race. The world would currently be much more broken than it otherwise was if this were not the case.

He'd known some of the guys for many years. He'd fought alongside them to extract civilians in the most godless places in the world, were there. Others he had known for just a few short months at ARD-DDR-DEE, the official moniker of the Swiss unit he belonged to. That still felt like he'd known them a lifetime.

This was their final official salute to Lieutenant Colonel Fallow before he stepped down from his post as Special Operations Forces Senior Instructor. The 'senior' bit was something the boys teased him about frequently. His special focus on physical fitness and close combat fight training put a limit on how far they went though.

His work was pretty much done. As predicted, around half of the current year's recruits had folded. This was either through lack of mental fortitude, intellectual capacity or the simple guts to be able to get the job done. The other half had steeled up, bucked up and joined up to the cause and were doing brilliantly. Ben thought that a couple of them were possibly the best recruits he'd had in his five years in Switzerland. Not necessarily the best he'd ever seen, but there was still time.

So he was now enjoying a drink. Having a beer with some of the few people in the world he could trust with his life. Putting off going back to his billet to start the tedious but short job of putting his personal items into the few bags and boxes he needed to shift to a storage facility.

Not that he needed their help. Ben was a Seventh Dan in Karate. He'd passed all of the examinations possible.

He'd earned a number of levels through the respect of his teachers along the way, as one must do. Had he not chosen a path that took him into the Armed Forces (something that concerned his teachers considerably when trying to marry the ethos behind karate and Ben's chosen career path) he would probably be a Grand Master himself. A Level Ten, a Karateka helping shape the art using new methods.

Instead, Ben had taken his skills and used them to protect those that did not have the means to protect themselves. He had no doubt that what he did was not counter to the philosophy and required moral code that drove Karateka around the world. Instead, he was one of the few that employed Karate in theatre when it was a life or death situation to minimise that binary decision.

Ben had not killed a single opponent whilst protecting those he needed to free, extract or guard. He had been up against hundreds if not into the thousands of captors, torturers and enemy combatants. For sure, they didn't get carried away from their encounter with him without injury. There was no Vulcan shoulder grip that subdued someone without pain. A couple of techniques came close.

But along with Ben's skill and aptitude came wisdom from years of practice. He conducted himself with a level of control that meant he could minimise the injuries as much as possible in his opponent. Even though they might be the most morally poisonous pieces of shit their greed, religious indoctrination or corrupt leadership had turned them into.

Ben took in all the faces in the mess and grinned as he raised his glass to them. There was a mixture of sadness, gratitude and wistfulness in the eyes of those regarding him respectfully for a moment. It lasted a short time when Ben delivered his cheeky grin. As glasses rose, a shout of "Oss!" in unison and the drinking began.

As the quad bells rang eleven, Ben was staggering back to his quarters, drunk enough to face packing. He tried to dodge analysing his life to date. Spending too much time assessing his past was a rat hole he didn't much like to go down. So the act of packing up stuff accumulated over the years was not something he particularly relished. He tried to keep very few possessions.

His Karate trophies. Gifts from his buddies over the years that, whilst not big, had sentimental value and which it would be rude to toss out.

He had a modest wardrobe. That was something he would need to expand now that he didn't have the luxury of wearing formal, PT or combat uniforms every day. He stopped and swayed a little, wondering if he'd ever owned a suit in his life. He didn't think so. Not in his adult life anyway.

He wasn't much of a groomer either. He washed with soap and water, used a deodorant stick and shaved with the most basic of razors and foam. No moisturisers, and yet, probably because of his mainly outdoor lifestyle, he still had a good complexion. His soft skin belied his years.

Relatively speaking, thirty-five was not that old. Compared to some, he appeared a lot younger. Whether blessed with strong genes or simply because he took care of himself, Ben was a good-looking man. Physically a catch for any woman who could manage to pin him down in one place for long enough. This was a slight fly in the ointment for those potential wives, as Ben didn't like to be in one place for too long. Or at least, that was what he told himself.

Perhaps, he thought, throwing the last of his socks and underwear into the rucksack, it might be time to stop and watch the world turning. Just for a bit.

He flopped onto the bed, flipped the switch on the alarm clock and switched off the light by his bedside. Immediately, he slipped into a dreamless sleep.

CHAPTER 10

Near Mayak, Crimea, Ukraine - Monday, September 1st, 2008

The Historian was up before dawn as always. He always liked to greet the sun, no matter where he was in the world. Besides, he barely slept. There was too much information flying around the internet and then into his brain. It constantly clamoured for attention. It needed acknowledgement and then filing if not directly relevant to his current lines of enquiry. It required categorisation and associated metadata labelling for it to be stored usefully for later access.

His yacht presented itself like a ramshackle tub of junk. But, as with so many things, its beauty lay on the inside. Behind a seriously good special effects job, cutting edge tools were at his fingertips. Super-fast technology hid behind wooden and scratched casings of old radios. Old televisions framed flat screen monitors. Other out-dated nautical doodads hid various routers, filters and power supplies.

The Historian was alone, but he was not disconnected by any stretch of the imagination. RSS feeds, snippets of code built from services that scraped online sources in an 'if this, then that' way, all filtered into a secure and encrypted database in a custom cloud server storage array. The Historian had built these beauties himself with all data securely salted and all passwords hashed for safe-keeping.

He gained access in the form of a typed password combined with a fingerprint scanner and random call-back service. He'd paid a company for twenty-five years to provide him this voice biometric service. They'd created it to unlock the cockpits of US fighter pilot planes by checking the voice and stress patterns of the pilot.

If the system deemed that his fingerprint was too cold or his voice under too much stress, access was denied. If it found unexplained drugs in his system, access was denied.

There was an override protocol.

A one-time use USB providing a two thousand and forty-eight-bit encrypted handshake that could give him administration rights to re-set access terms. He would then have to wait twenty-four hours before trying to re-gain access to the system.

While he was unaware of whom exactly he was hiding this information from, he was in absolutely no doubt about the seriousness of their capabilities. They had a global reach and an almost instantaneous response in which they could resolve any challenges they faced.

Not like those jokers at the NSA.

He logged on to his system and quickly accessed another unique programme that he had modelled himself. It was loosely based on an associative search engine developed from Swedish military-grade intelligence work in semantic analytics. It presented a word cloud of current affairs clustering 'hot spots' which one could then click into, showing associations and related strings. One could circle down rabbit holes without ending if one was not careful.

The Historian had refined this, massively increased the indexation of content and its speed. He'd ripped out and kept the sentiment analysis aspect within the confines of his own 'meat space' super computer. His brain.

The Dictaphone from the previous night's monologue, with a final chapter completed this morning over a fresh batch of coffee, sat next to the computer. He would transfer the content into a sound file, encrypt it and then obfuscate it. He would do this by overlaying an album from a random unsigned band. The completed output would be like a subliminal self-hypnosis package. The monologue would be inaudible unless decrypted and rebalanced.

He would then post it to a popular online music sharing website under a fake profile of a seventeen-year-old Greek student in Athens. He'd then put the URL to the profile in a single file which he would put on a USB key.

That USB key would then find its way to the one person The Historian had identified that might just have enough chance of defeating those who were rapidly sending the world down a sink hole from which it might never recover.

But for that USB key to get to the person that needed it, The Historian had to set foot on dry land in a western European country. He had not done that willingly for almost two decades.

It was not something he relished, given his condition and his self-appointed mission. If they recognized his face from CCTV or a passport flag, the European boarder police would also raise a good few eyebrows.

He was supposed to be dead after all.

CHAPTER 11

Geneva, Switzerland - Wednesday 10th September 2008

It was only after leaving the base that Ben discovered just how alone he felt.

It wasn't as if overnight he'd lost contact with all the people that he'd befriended over the years. He wasn't exactly a loner either. He was more than happy to socialise with small groups. He held a conversation well, especially when it wasn't about him. He had a talent for telling stories, especially ones that put him in a detrimental light. He'd found early on that making others laugh at your misfortunes was not only endearing, but it kept a person humble.

The trouble was, moving around so much, he'd found himself making strong bonds with people in the Forces, but few outside. For one reason or another, he didn't have school friends to fall back in with. He'd moved around a lot when he was growing up and inevitably that made it difficult to sustain friendships over time.

It had also taught him a lesson. Using humour more than violence got you out of difficult situations. Especially when you were trying to introduce yourself into new schools with well-established friendships.

He had been learning Karate since he was a kid, so it wasn't that he wasn't capable of taking care of himself. He simply learned that it was easier to integrate when you revealed some flaws and people didn't see you as a target to be beaten, ticked off some list or used as leverage.

So the majority of his mates were in the Forces. They supported each other. When together, they were good friends, but often they could not talk for months due to the theatre they'd been put in. It was either difficult or dangerous to disclose their locations.

Ben had no family. His parents had died in an accident when he was younger. His Uncle, his mother's brother, took him in. He had held a position in the UN peace keeping forces.

As Ben grew up, they moved from one base to another around the world. Increasingly, he saw more and more countries. Eventually, it felt natural that Ben should consider going in to the Armed Forces himself.

The first week in training in the United Kingdom, Ben received news that his Uncle and Aunt were dead. They had died in transit as they were travelling back from a diplomatic event to their base by an improvised explosive device. He couldn't remember now even in which country it had taken place, it was so long ago.

Truthfully, the person he felt most close to now was the person managing the trust that had been set up in his name after his parents had died and who had provided him with the longest relationship he had sustained. And he was a lawyer. Gerry Bairstow.

It was to him that Ben turned as he mulled over his new life, thinking that perhaps he'd been a little hasty in ending his commission. On the other hand, he was generally a lucky bugger who was still alive after too many close shaves in combat.

He figured it was time to live life off the edge for a little while. One outside the certainties and comforts that a life in the Armed Forces, especially the Swiss Armed Forces recently, had provided him.

As he had no mobile phone, after getting off the bus (which he detested taking), he made his way to the first public call box he could find. Dialling a UK number, he smiled as someone on the other side of the English Channel picked up a receiver.

"Hello, this is me. Is that you?"

"Gerry, it's Ben. Yeah, it has, hasn't it? I'm good, and you? Great. Listen, I have some news. Have you got a minute? You might need a pen too."

They discussed some financial arrangements and the transportation of the personal items he didn't want to lug around with him. After that, they chatted for a couple of minutes about not much at all.

"So, my boy, when are we going to be enjoying the pleasure of your company? Glenda would be delighted to try to feed you up for a couple of weeks solid down here. What are your plans? Can you come over?"

Ben grinned again, thinking of the fine home cooked fare that Gerry's wife Glenda always set down on the table.

"Do you know what Gerry? That sounds fantastic. I'm not too sure what I'm going to do now. Give me a couple of weeks to acclimatise to being a civilian for the first time in my adult life. Then I'll head over from wherever and look you up, if that's okay?"

Gerry growled. "My lad, if you'd have turned me down there would have been hell to pay. I don't know how she does it but Glenda will sniff that I'd been speaking to you in an instant. If you don't turn up sometime soon, I'll be on a diet as punishment. So you'd better not let me down or I'll be sending a tailor's bill to you for all the alterations my wardrobe would need."

Ben laughed. It would take a significant reduction in calories and several padlocked doors before Gerry would make any kind of dent in his portly figure due to a change in his diet.

"I got it. I've heard my orders loud and clear. I'll be in touch."

Gerry grunted, then added softly, "Ben. Listen. Anything you need, any time, give me a call? I don't want anything to happen to you before we see you."

There was a pause, then he was back to his old self.

"After all, keeping tabs on your bloody trust fund is the only thing I've got to get up for these days! Well. That, and Chablis, obviously."

#####

As he neither had a house to register one to or the inclination to burden himself with more property, Ben rented a black Nissan Altima Coupé on a month's usage and a vignette to enable him to drive on the motorways, paying in cash. He knew parking was going to be a nightmare but if he stayed away from the centre mostly it wouldn't be so much of a problem.

Ben couldn't stand not being mobile. Even on the base, he made use of the pool jeeps and other vehicles to get him out and about when he had some time to himself.

Or when he felt a yearning for some female company and headed out on the town. Relying on buses, trams or tubes or coughing up exorbitant taxi fares was just not his style.

When he did take the bus or train, he usually managed to get himself into a situation where he was breaking up a fight, collaring a pick pocket or preventing some tyke from getting themselves into further trouble. He had a knack for attracting that kind of action.

He jumped in the car and took a spin out in the crisp morning air, going nowhere in particular. He noted that the authorities had yet to remove the street marketing boasting of its host status for the Euro 2008 football tournament which finished months earlier but which the country was still proud of hosting. It was like the metropolis was still wearing a festival bracelet, reminding itself of the fun times, months after the bands had packed away and the tents were struck, clinging on to the excitement and memories with a dirty old plastic strap.

Looking past the municipality and instead at the countryside, the landscape was as good as any in and around Europe. After a couple of hours driving around idly, enjoying the freedom, he wound up at the airport, where a university and casino nestled together. Unlikely bed fellows, he thought, and then remembered the story of the card-counting MIT students who almost broke the bank in Vegas.

As good a place as any, he though. He drove up to the nearby hotel, jumped out and gave his keys to the valet. He slung his bag over his shoulder and headed towards the front desk.

"Welcome home," was his first thought. Swiftly followed by a rhetorical, "is it too early for a drink?"

CHAPTER 12

CERN, Geneva - Wednesday 10th September, 2008

At ten twenty-five in the morning, two spots of light appeared as a flash on a screen to signal the beam was all the way around.

They had done it.

The control room exploded in a cacophony of geeky celebration. It was less than an hour since the Large Hadron Collider had been switched on. For the first time in history, super cooled magnets had guided a beam of particles finer than a human hair around twenty-seven kilometres of tunnels in a vacuum, passing through the gargantuan ATLAS device on their way.

Professor Fenkhause's eyes were misty. His team jumped up and down, whooping with delight, hugging each other. The noise made his ears ring. The past hour had progressed through intense quiet and murmuring into claps and ecstatic celebration as they removed each block. He lost count of the beams they purged and re-injected.

There had been huge nervousness a quarter of an hour in as one beam didn't make it through after they lifted one block. The Director-General in his infinite wisdom had suggested that, after testing of the initial stages beyond Point Six, they did the testing blind. In front of the eyes of the world. From that point on, their activities were under the scrutiny of a sceptical and nervous public, waiting for something to go badly wrong.

But it was less than a minute before the next cycle engaged and flashed on the screen, showing it had made it to Point Five. Just one Point away from unchartered territory. A half-hour later and it had made it through to ATLAS. His team's screens were alight with data flashing in all of its glory. It was like a prelude to the replication of the big bang itself, digitally dissected and squirted on to their monitors. ATLAS captured a big burst of muons as the beam passed by. His team was already beginning to collect precious knowledge in anticipation of the scheduled experiments in just a few weeks' time. He couldn't have felt more proud.

Then, just a few minutes later, under the watch of the five remaining living Director-Generals, the hadron beam had made it all the way around. A sprinter running at 99.999% the speed of light, lifted and guided by magnetic forces like a rocket train of matter speeding towards the destination of knowledge.

The journey concluded not with a collision in a vacuum but an explosion of pure elation in the Control Room. This time, the reaction was not in the Collider. Instead it was in the hearts, minds and voices of the men and women who had built it.

Other, unobserved reactions by an external group were altogether different. Those reactions grew as the scientists at CERN proceeded with their testing and circulated a beam around in the opposite direction.

Disgust. Dread. And decisiveness.

This machine was not going to succeed.

They would see to it.

CHAPTER 13

Vienna, Austria - Thursday September 11th, 2008

The secured conference line beeped twice as another person joined the call. Attendees were unannounced. The conference number was seemingly unregistered.

The private conference call company was wholly owned by a subsidiary company and used for these particular calls only. The connections were software and hardware encrypted. Each proprietary handset had two-factor authentication, as well as a serious bit of military-grade voice analysis technology. This was sensitive enough to identify unique breathing patterns, let alone an impersonator.

"I believe that makes us a complete quorum. I welcome you all in the spirit of our shared purpose and thank you for your time regarding this pressing issue."

The calls were always conducted in English, it being the most common language shared between all attendees.

There were few Asian and Northern European representatives within this generation of the group. Representation of regions did change over the centuries. Like a stalactite forming over thousands of years, the group's ethnicity morphed and changed in slow motion over a long time.

Karvorkian paused, and then continued. "Our intelligence predicted the timeline correctly. I am sorry to confirm that the team at CERN yesterday successfully sent a beam around the Large Hadron Collider. In both directions. All indications lead us to believe that, bar any intervention, this infernal machine is going to work."

Silence across the wires. Not because the participants were muted. They were all, each and every one of them, consummate politicians, strategists and game theorists.

None of them let their precise feelings show about such a momentous, life-changing event. Not just for them, but for all those around them.

There were still cards to play.

Karvorkian continued.

"When the project first commenced in nineteen ninety-eight, we agreed a plan of action. Were they to realize this progress, we would proceed to a vote that would establish the appropriate action to take. I am now providing you access to the options on which we will vote in precisely one minute. Voting will be open for thirty seconds only. I will then announce the decision to the group. This will be validated by two randomly-chosen participants. They will have access to the live voting platform from the moment the results are captured. This will preserve the integrity of the decision-making process.

"Depending on that outcome, pre-agreed actions will occur. As is usual, these have been modelled to achieve as close as possible the desired outcome with little or no damage leaking to influence other events. Your options should now be in front of you and the voting system will be live in five seconds. Thank you."

Karvorkian muted his line, selected his choice and sat further back in his chair, scrutinising the votes as they came in. The time limit from when the options presented to the closing of the vote was in place for a very good reason. Gut instinct, foresight, soothsaying, whatever you wished to call it, was as strong a principle in this group. As strong as the belief in the fundamental principles of science were to those at CERN. Too much time to digest the choices and post-instinctual rationalisation crept in, bringing doubt into the equation. This time limit enabled a swift decision without debate. Participants could be confident that they made a choice without the benefit of doubt. Were any of the participants questioning their membership of the group, real-time analytical data sets enabled complex algorithms to spot any potential weaknesses in the group's armour through miniscule hesitations.

"Time, Ladies and Gentlemen."

The voting system froze for the majority of the participants except for two. It displayed a series of bars relating to the options. If there were there multiple answers, several bars would show.

In this instance, there was only one bar. Every single participant had chosen the same option.

"It seems we are all in agreement that the best course of action sabotage, yes?"

"I validate."

"I too validate."

"Thank you for your validations. I will inform the task force. We authorize an operation that will see the experiment suffer a catastrophic failure event on or before the nineteenth of this month. I can only say that I am as disappointed as you that we cannot undertake this intervention sooner, so that it might appear like a direct result of the tests. Our most powerful ground team could not operate under the right conditions until a relevant conference could get him close enough without arising suspicion. That conference is on the eighteenth and should provide the most conducive environment for him to get the job done. He will get in, do their job, get out and leave no trace."

Silence again, then he continued.

"One more thing, if I may. In light of other, how shall I say, elements of unpredictability? It may be wise to withdraw some if not most of your financial instruments around the same time. Combined, this may provide us further, more aggressive, camouflage. It seems prudent also. It should insulate us in case the events of two thousand and seven were to occur again. More importantly, it will also avert eyes that we do not wish to see clearly and give them something else to focus on."

At this, there was a murmur of appreciation at the difficulty of the situation and then the line again fell silent.

"Well Ladies and Gentlemen, as there is no further business today, I thank you for your time. We will reconvene after this course of action has played out and you will receive invitations in the usual manner."

This group had no motto, no greeting, ceremonies or name. There was a membership list but it was itself encrypted and the keys only known to three members.

It could not be called by anything, as no one ever needed to tell another soul that they were a member of this group. It was the closest thing possible to complete anonymity. No one could find it even if they were specifically hunting for such an organisation. Or so they thought.

Their flaw was that they'd not employed that gut instinct to bomb proof against one scenario, however unlikely.

One where someone was devouring information on a massive scale and perceiving dark shadows cast where there should be none.

CHAPTER 14

CERN - Thursday September 18th, 2008

There was an understandably buoyant mood at the CERN openlab Major Review Meeting. So close to the switch on, it allowed the attendees to boast and backslap about having some part to play in that momentous occasion. It didn't matter whether they were a supplier CERN or a bona fide member of staff.

The mood soon settled down to a satisfied level of smugness as they launched into the presentations. Topics covered 'New projects in Controls' and 'Update on Grid Monitoring'. One held special irony for an interloper, complete with identification badge and conference pass, in the meeting. 'The CINBAD Project'.

A passing glance at him would present a man engrossed in thought. He appeared focused on listening to the presenters. They were discussing in detail the process for detecting, or trying to detect, system anomalies on the information technology infrastructure used to collect the vast amounts of data from the LHC experiments.

His eyes were closed, his chin on his fingertips. Elbows resting on his knees, he hunched forward in his seat. His brow furrowed. He looked like he was concentrating so hard on memorizing not only all the words said by the two presenters, but every single sound made in the room, mapped out spatially. A surround-sound, pitch-perfect recording, captured in the synapses of his brain.

Whilst he was indeed listening to the presenters, only a small part of his mind registered what they were saying. He had trained his faculties to such an extent over the years that he needed a fraction of his conscious to memorize their talk whilst focusing on more important matters. If asked, he could recall it word for word, even though he was not directly listening at the time.

His employers would have been interested in what the presenters were discussing. The CINBAD project concerned information leakage, sabotage or any number of exploits that might taint the data of the project.

This was something that they could exploit in future.

The speakers explained that unknown anomalies could not be detected very well. He made a mental flag alongside this fact to report back in his normal reporting activity.

Monitoring of threats had only commenced recently on this particular project. The presenters were proudly walking through a slide of 'First Achievements'. This, to anyone other than a scientist, would have resulted in a sharp intake of breath. A few buildings away, in the restricted session of the hundred and forty-eighth session of council, after the pleasantries of the LHC Inauguration Ceremony and the visiting dignitaries, a few council members shared expressions of horror in subdued conversations over the very topic of these 'achievements'.

From just two days of testing, the CINBAD team had found multiple incidents. These ranged from 'strange Ethernet-to-serial-hub devices which are sending information from the network to the outside world' through to 'external DNS users and strange traffic on port 53'.

The man suppressed a smile as his mind focused laser-sharp on his target.

A week previous, after Beam Two, the anti-clockwise beam, had been circulated for over half an hour, the team had seen the failure of a power transformer on one of the surface points of the equipment. They had taken a decision to switch off the main compressors of the cryogenics for two sectors of the machine and exchanged it.

During the exchange, they put the cryogenics system which cooled the magnets into standby mode for those sectors. The team had been busy re-cooling the magnets for the past few days in preparation for operation of Beam One that day, replicating the previous week's test.

The man focused his mind's eye. He visualised the tens of thousands of components in the LHC, zooming down and in. It was like using an online map patching together high definition satellite imagery. His reach extended further though.

39

Through the ground, into the tunnels and on to the very magnets that guided the beams.

He swooped into one magnet. Further down on to the surface and into the components of the piece.

Then, like in an old car manual, he exploded the machinery. Suspended, he spun it and zoomed around every item until he found what he was searching for.

A weld. One single weld, holding two magnets together. It was marginally unstable. A weakness.

His brow furrowed again and his breathing paused for a moment. He concentrated his focus further. The weld showed signs of increased fatigue. Then a single hair's breadth crack appeared.

The man's eyes snapped open, darting left then right, but he gave no further outward sign of accomplishment.

The presenters were coming to the end of their exposition of CINBAD. The operative listened on with disdain. He wondered how this project had come so far with such a significantly poor understanding of the penetration risks that the experiments were under.

No matter, he thought. He clapped and smiled with the rest of the audience as the two presenters acted out bashfully at the front of the auditorium. After tomorrow's test, they would not need to worry about their networks being penetrated again.

There would be no networks to penetrate and no witnesses to report what the causes were. The LHC would explode in a devastating fireball when the massive arc of electricity surged through the liquid helium cooling the machine. That would make Geneva a little more exciting for the locals, wouldn't it?

CHAPTER 15

US Federal Reserve – Thursday September 18th, 2008

At about eleven in the morning, the US Federal Reserve became aware of a tremendous draw-down of money market accounts in the United States.

Around five hundred and fifty billion dollars evaporated in a matter of an hour or two. Once alerted, the US Treasury tried to stem the collapse in liquidity by pumping one hundred and five billion dollars into the system, but it did not work. Then it dawned on them that a massive electronic run on the banks was happening. They had no idea where or how.

They closed the money markets and announced a guarantee of two hundred and fifty thousand dollars per account to reduce the inevitable panic.

After the event, The Treasury's own evaluation was bleak. Had it not acted, money market withdrawals would have reached five point five trillion dollars that day. The US economy would have collapsed by two that afternoon. Within twenty-four hours, the world economy would have fallen.

The public heard none of this from the President, who was coming to the end of his two terms in office. Yet again, he had no intelligent response to this event. This time, he was not sitting in front of a class of school children reading to them.

Instead, the Securities and Exchange Commission acted on an emergency order. It said it was taking 'temporary action' to 'respond to market developments'.

Then, the Treasury Secretary suddenly revealed a seven hundred billion dollar plan to rescue the housing and banking institutions. This plan comprised five pages. The President gave it a ringing endorsement.

Many representatives of Congress reacted angrily to such a shoddy proposal.

A closed door meeting was called.

After much discussion, described officially as 'sombre', the plan was carried forward.

The truth was that the White House had instructed Congress that, if they did not act on the siphoning of funds immediately, the President would have to declare Martial Law.

Months later, a Democratic representative seemingly slipped up and stated his views on the situation candidly on a television network. "It would have been the end of our political system and our economic systems as we know it."

Much worse was to follow.

CHAPTER 16

CERN, Geneva - Friday September 19th, 2008

Were someone to have had a slow-motion, high definition camera trained on the corrupted weld in that superconducting wire connecting those two magnets together, they would have seen how much importance such a small exchange of energy could have on the progress of the human race towards a higher state of knowledge.

As the energy flowed through it, heating it above its normal operating temperature, it turned the wire into a resistor. The constant relationship between current flow and voltage in the machine changed. This caused a massive eight point seven kilo-amps of power to arc through the liquid helium. It punched instantly through into the surrounding vacuum vessel.

In just milliseconds, the arc slashed out like a whip. It vaporised most of the nearly meter-long connection between two magnets.

Liquid helium that had been maintaining the temperature of the magnets surged through the tiny hole. It accumulated like a possessed sea mist and into the insulating region of vacuum. The void sucked in six tonnes of the cryogenic refrigerant in an instant.

It was here that the crisis almost turned into disaster. Relief valves designed to allow the helium to escape were overwhelmed. Later, the relief valves' tolerances were concluded to have been based around 'incorrect assumptions' on how much helium might escape in an accident. That there had, again, been a 'design error'.

There was no such mistake.

In another second, the pressure of the explosion wrenched magnets off their concrete supports. Magneto would have been proud.

As in the fictional super hero films, however, his desires were he watching, would not met in full.

Something somehow had stopped the explosion from spreading.

Of the ten thousand magnets within the twenty-seven kilometre tunnel, the event only damaged a fraction. Some force or other had prevented the total annihilation of the structure.

For sure, there was significant damage. But there was no hole in the ground.

No CNN breaking news alerts. No day of mourning for the most destructive event in human history caused by scientists experimenting with dangerous, world-affecting prototypes.

Someone had invested millions and months in planning in that outcome. They would be, to put it mildly, fucking pissed off. But then, trying to explode a prototype when you've got nothing to practice on is also a tricky piece of work.

There were, it seemed, no guarantees for anything, even if you had lots of money. Unpredictability was getting more powerful day by day.

####

The Control Room inhabitants stopped talking as one and spun towards the monitors and screens in disbelief.

It was like someone had pressed a mute button. Professor Fenkhause's mouth dropped open. The remains of any colour in his face he'd gained over the summer walking to and from the facility drained away to grey.

It felt to Ebhart like hours passed in those seconds. It generated data that the analysts would spend months looking into.

"Uh," someone said.

Without his eyes leaving the screens, his hand moved shakily to a telephone.

"Shit."

Tapping of fingers on keyboards began in frenzy.

The Professor picked up the receiver and dialled the five-digit emergency number.

"Lindsey, we have a situation. We need to evacuate immediately. And activate emergency procedures in the tunnel. Something's gone wrong. Very wrong."

In a few seconds more, the emergency tannoy system blared.

Everyone to proceed to the exits.

This is not a drill.

As people moved around him, the Professor stood stock still, staring at the screens, willing what he was seeing not to be true.

"Professor, come on! We have to move."

He turned as he felt a hand tugging at his lab coat and saw it was Chenni, as ashen as he was, but still possessing wits that had departed him.

"Yes. Yes," he mumbled, but still he couldn't move.

"Now!"

Chenni yanked him hard, so that he stumbled. He moved his legs simply to regain his balance. Then they were off. Through the doors and following the lines and protocols set out in the training manuals, health and safety sessions and drills they'd all chatted through or skim read in order to satisfy the requirements of their contracts.

None of those sessions had mentioned the feeling of nausea, disorientation and emotional trauma that this kind of event induced. None of the people who wrote the courses or manuals had poured their lives and souls into creating the environment that was now threatened with destruction.

Ebhart's cathedral was in danger of being rent asunder and there was nothing he could do about it. His heart felt gripped with a hand as cold as the liquid helium flowing below him. He stumbled on, guided by Chenni, as people in hazmat suits began to swarm in the other direction.

It was at that point he realised that he was still praying, as he had been since the incident began, that God would step in and save everything. He felt disgusted.

CHAPTER 17

Meyrin, Geneva - Saturday September 20th, 2008

Ben slowly emerged from sleep. A rhythmic thumping noise was interrupting the tranquillity.

He cracked opened one eye and snuck a glance at the digital clock next to him. It confirmed it was too early for the alarm to go off. He swung his arm out and slapped the snooze function anyway, just in case the previous resident had played a joke and set the thing to a thrash metal radio station. It had no effect on the sound.

What was that banging?

"Mr Fallow? Open up please, this is hotel security."

Ah, so that's where it was coming from.

Ben yawned and sat up. The light was barely creeping under the black-out curtains of the room. That suggested that it was sometime after seven in the morning. Given the dreadful weather it could have been later. The alarm clock, which he'd not checked the previous evening when he'd checked into the room, could have been off. Might he have missed the checking-out time?

He glanced at his watch on the bed side table. It's luminous glow confirmed that it was just past seven fifteen. Plenty of time. So what was the emergency?

"Mr Fallow!" It wasn't a question, it was an instruction.

"Okay, okay, I'm awake. Give me a second."

Ben pulled his boxer shorts on. He grabbed the dressing gown from the chair he'd thrown it over after he'd showered and dressed for the evening before. Glancing through the security viewer, he confirmed in fish-eye that indeed, two suited and booted gentlemen with security badges purporting to be from the hotel, were waiting impatiently outside of the door.

The one in front was caressing his knuckles. They appeared a little red.

Ben clicked the dead bolt off but didn't remove the security chain as he opened the door.

"Hi guys. I don't remember ordering a wake-up call?"

There were no smiles to be had.

Courtesy, it seems, was in short supply this morning. Red Knuckles inflated ever so slightly and stared at Ben unblinkingly.

"Mr Fallow, the Manager has requested that you gather your belongings and vacate the hotel within the next fifteen minutes. You will not be charged for the room or any items from the mini bar. Viktor will wait outside the room to assist you with any luggage and your car will be waiting for you at the front of the lobby."

The body language from both of them said there was no negotiation.

Ben paused, glancing from one to the other. Given his experience, he was not intimidated by these messenger boys, although that was not to say that they weren't up to the job. He knew this was not their fight. Ben nodded.

"Thank you Gentlemen. I'll be out in ten."

The suits were momentarily thrown off balance, as if they had been expecting more trouble from this guest than most. Red Knuckles deflated marginally. The slightest smile broke through, acknowledging a minor triumph in the Unwanted Guest Removal Procedure. He performed a curt nod to Ben, turned on his heel and walked back towards the lifts, only reaching for his radio once out of ear shot.

Ben turned back to Viktor.

"Any chance you can make sure there's a coffee when I get to the lobby as well?"

Viktor's lack of response suggested that either he didn't speak English, or wouldn't. Ben suspected the latter. The hotels around here put the phones down on potential guests who tried to make reservations using English, according to multiple disgruntled comments online.

"Right then. Let's get this show on the road."

Ben shut the door and began to throw things into his suitcase.

#####

Ben had been expecting some kind of reaction after his adventure the previous night.

The Casino du Lac Meyrin was one of the few spots in Geneva that opened until late. You could also wear casual rather than formal clothing. That was about the extent of the positives.

It was not by a lake. Instead, it was right by the airport, four kilometres outside of the main town, next door to the hotel that he'd decided, temporarily, to call home. It was close to the Jura Mountains, but then so were many places, as they stretched from France right through to Germany.

On entering, Ben was immediately drawn to the sound of a wheel clacking. He heard a dealer saying "Faites vos jeux". He glanced over and saw that the eight players had different coloured chips. That confirmed this was one of his preferred games, La Roulette Anglaise.

Ben loved the little wheel and, more often than not, the wheel loved Ben. He walked up to the table, acknowledging the dealer and other guests, placed some bills down on the table and collected his chips. He called a waiter over and placed a drinks order, then turned his attention back to the table.

In a couple of minutes, he was sipping a Gin Martini with olives. Ben assessed the collection of thrill seekers around the table.

Several should have gracefully withdrawn a good few spins before. Like so many, they seemed addicted to the desire to see an all or nothing result.

Other, more sociable, gamers were enjoying the events more visibly. Some were up, some down. All could not care less whether they won or lost. This was simply a pass time to drive insomnia away in the company of those with similar physiologies and outlooks.

As the wheel spun, Ben decided to play orphans. Orphan numbers belong neither to the thirds nor to the neighbours of zero. He announced his bet on eight numbers and placed five chips. A straight bet on the one, split between the six and nine, fourteen and seventeen, seventeen and twenty, thirty-one and thirty-four. Just as he placed the last chip the dealer called "Rien ne va plus."

The ball ticked and bounced its final few movements as the wheel spun slower.

And came to rest in the slot market One.

Yes, Ben thought. It feels like it's going to be an odd rather than an even night tonight.

#####

The game progressed and the night drew on. Around half of the participants finally conceded defeat, receding into the banks of slot machines. The lights temporarily hid the greyness of their complexions, made up like clowns in fleeting LED colours.

The table was now left with four players. Two, including Ben, were significantly up. The other two were enjoying their Scotch, conversation and the random placement of chips on the felt from time to time.

The other player with a solid number of chips in front of him was starting at Ben. He slowly stacked and re-stacked some of his chips in front of him without diverting his gaze.

Ben finally focused on him, raised an eyebrow slightly and nodded to him, a collaborator's recognition that the tables were in both of their favours that night.

Instead of returning the gesture or raising a glass, the other man scowled. He coughed with his mouth open, then slowly and deliberately turned his gaze to anywhere but where Ben was.

Asshole. Ben realised that for the most recent plays, the guy had been following his bets, making gains through following his lead. He felt a little wicked spark wake up inside him.

Ben began to deliberately lose. He placed smaller bets, pretending that he was tired, getting drunk, or both. As more and more chips left his possession, the other man's pile also began to shrink. However, where Ben had reduced the value of the chips he was playing with, the other man stuck with his original chip value. Within half an hour, the asshole was down a significant sum of Swiss Francs.

Ben felt that the time was now right to strike.

He gathered up all his chips and placed them on Evens. Sweating slightly, the other man did the same.

The ball fell on 0, meaning that the chips were 'locked in', immediately losing half their value.

In line with the rules, Ben swiftly recovered his chips at half their original value. The other man, too greedy to take that kind of a hit, left his chips where they were. On Even. He sent Ben a glower across the table.

As the dealer spun again, Ben again placed all his chips on the table. On Odd. Right next to his fellow players pile.

The ball travelled around the wheel, its random tap dance, a Morse code message. It tapped out the destination of some intended attack point to whoever could translate it.

Ben sipped his drink calmly.

The ball bounced finally and landed. Seventeen. He was back up to the original value of his chips. His opponent sat silently as the dealer scraped away all his remaining chips.

Ben left his chips where they were as the wheel spun one more time, sipping his drink and staring straight into the other guy's eyes. The rage in this little man's visage was fierce, but Ben was not perturbed. He'd worked out that this man had made himself through the actions and work of others. He knew that this wouldn't be the last word on the matter, as the man pushed himself away from the table and stomped off towards the bar.

"Monsieur?"

"Hm?"

The dealer called his attention back to the table. Not only had the chips been there for the next spin, but also the next two. His original wager had grown eight-fold whilst he watched his opponent march away to the far end of the casino.

Ben happily cashed his chips in, leaving a good tip for the dealer. Definitely an odd evening, he thought, as he made his way back to his room. The odd evenings were always the best.

#####

True to his word, Ben was down in the lobby within the prescribed time and his car was waiting for him. He passed his room key over to the concierge and nodded his thanks. The concierge gave him a rueful shrug, a slight jerk of his head indicating a direction that Ben might be interested in focusing on.

Ben surreptitiously glanced over. His gaze was met again by the chubby, puce-faced man from the evening before. He was standing next to someone. Ben supposed was the Hotel Manager. The manager was tall, dark-haired, with a big roman nose and square glasses. He had an oily complexion, thinning hair brushed in a comb-over. His arms were crossed awkwardly. What a pair they made.

Ben did a visible double-take, pulled a surprised but pleased face, and waved happily at the two across the lobby. He then marched, smiling, to his car. Viktor had already placed his suitcase in the boot.

To Viktor's surprise, Ben gave him with a ridiculously large tip before jumping into the driving seat and zooming off loudly from the hotel forecourt.

Viktor stared open-mouthed at the money in his hand. The direct consequence of one man's misplaced faith in exploitation and another man's generosity in revenge.

CHAPTER 18

Near Mayak, Crimea, Ukraine - Sunday September 21st, 2008

The yacht was steel hulled and around twenty-two years old. It had been built in France but The Historian had purchased it from some boat hippies in Bali. They'd realized that, without money for weed, they didn't actually like living in a confined space with each other. According to the guy with a black eye and arm in a make-shift tie-dyed sling, the enlightening moment had not passed without a distinctly un-hippie-esque punch-up.

He'd maintained the thirteen meter vessel to as good a condition as he was able given his personal and geographic limitations. He was confident that it would withstand the journey of several thousands of miles back to western European waters adequately.

He had filled the two freshwater tanks holding a total of one thousand litres. The diesel engine had a good overhaul. The thousand litre fuel tank was also filled to the brim.

As the sails went up, he felt a sudden pang which disturbed him. For as long as he could remember, he had not become connected to a place. He appreciated beauty in a theoretical rather than emotional manner. He found the chaotic patterns mesmerising, the light and dark captivating. He dissected it to understand, rationalizing it in his mind so that he could stand living in it.

But this place had moved him. The crystal clean water, which turned into a bath in summer, gently stroked white sandy beaches. The peculiar rock formations riddled with caves. The rich vegetation and capes carved their authority out into the sea. Unspoilt bays and fantastic islands, hiding mysterious ravines covered in wild vegetation.

Perhaps it was the echo of a once-dominant culture, the Greeks, which stimulated this sensation. It had a huge number of archaeological remnants. Signals of occupation by this mythological people.

How quickly and to what level great civilisations fell.

Little remained of them but words and ruins. They provided adventure for people that came many generations after them.

Their legacy reduced to a game to try to re-discover and piece together what they knew.

As he moved the rudder, he mused about the success of archaeologist's' abilities to truly understand the past.

Discovered over a century ago, the Antikythera mechanism had only recently become a significant artefact. That was down to the lack of enlightenment and pride blinding academia and archaeologists to the obvious.

It was obvious to the Historian that the Greeks had computers that helped them navigate around the world. The Antikythera was hard evidence for that. Current civilization only had access to computers for around half a century. Experts therefore assumed no previous civilization could possibly have developed that kind of technology. Nor could evidence of that technology disappear so completely.

He realised that he was unlikely to be seen in these waters again, not unlike those Greeks. There would be no memorial or mark of his passing here. The odyssey that he was intending to complete would mean that, hopefully, at least this environment would last a little longer. More adventurers could come and scrape around in the dust and dirt to re-discover their humility and wonder at the past.

He shook his head to rid himself of this line of thinking.

One thing annoyed him most of all. It drove him to withdraw from the world, into his own mind to seek refuge. Man's pride. His arrogance.

As he mentally set his course to navigate around the Black Sea, he closed down his thoughts and focused on his goals for the next few hours. He broke his journey down into simpler goals. He had, he thought without any irony, a lot of water to cover and time and tide waited for no man.

He unfurled the spinnaker and the yacht momentarily leaped forward until it settled to a speed of fifteen knots.

It had begun.

CHAPTER 19

CERN, Geneva - Wednesday October 15th, 2008

The team raised their eyes as Professor Fenkhause opened the door to the lab. They'd been waiting for him.

He paused, taking in their faces one by one, and smiled gently.

"Hello."

Various murmurs came back at him, softly inquiring.

He sighed, nodded fractionally and shut the door.

"Well, it could be worse," he said.

The Professor had returned from the initial investigation panel's briefing on the previous month's accident. He'd listened to its assessment of what caused the reaction and, most importantly, the way forward. The outcome would mean significant impact. On the lives of those who sat before him; on the many thousands of physicists distributed across the world expecting to analyse the data; and the hundreds of thousands of students hoping to learn from one of the most exciting scientific projects ever conducted.

"How much worse, Professor?" That was Doctor Bert Hervey, a French particle physicist from Marseilles.

"They've agreed it's fixable."

"Well that's a fucking relief!" said the ever-brash Chenni Jeng. An experimental PhD student from Manchester University and Ebhart's rescuer at the time of the accident.

The Professor shrugged.

"So what's the bad news, Professor?"

This considered question from Suzi Pelmert, a PhD fellow at the Niels Bohr Institute in Copenhagen.

"We broke it, so we have to pay for it?" Peter Mayer, the joker in the pack, called out from the back of the room. He was a scientist from Indiana University in the United States.

No one laughed. His grin dropped, and he slumped back in his chair. "Well, shit. Sorry Prof, just trying to lighten the mood in here."

"Well, it's going to be expensive. And it's probably going to take around six months, if not more," the Professor acknowledged.

The invisible minibus that his team had all been travelling in just impacted, causing them to whiplash in their seats in synchronicity. Or that's how it looked to the Professor as he shared the news.

Ebhart went on to explain further.

"Sectors three and four lost approximately six tonnes of liquid helium. This was vented into the tunnel. That caused a temperature rise of about a hundred degrees Celsius in some of the affected magnets.

"The magnet quench and the ensuing helium gas explosion had damaged over fifty out of a total of one thousand six hundred superconducting magnets in the affected sectors. The mountings were also affected. The vacuum pipe is contaminated.

"As you know, most of the superconducting magnets weigh over twenty-seven tonnes. Approximately ninety-six tonnes of liquid helium is needed to keep these devices at their operating temperature.

"So we're in shut down for the foreseeable future. The vacuum pipe needs to be cleaned. New magnets and housings need to be installed and we need to get more helium. But we also have another problem."

The Professor scanned around. His team leaned in, as if straining to hear the Gospel for the first time.

"We only have thirty-five magnets in storage, and we need to replace over fifty, so we're short."

"Brilliant."

Piotr Morodov was the most cynical of the bunch. He was also the most qualified outside of Ebhart, having a PhD from the Joint Institute for Nuclear Research at Dubna in Russia.

Ebhart nodded. "But that's not the only issue."

"No? You surprise me Professor!"

"Peter, stop it."

Peter glowered at Suzi, who was red in the face. He slunk even lower in his chair, hands firmly tucked under his armpits.

"It seems that there is another design flaw. We do not have the correct number of valves required to remove the amount of liquid helium released if an event were to occur again. They are also not ideally positioned. The system needs to be re-worked, re-tested and new diagnostics fitted to give us a better warning before, if, something like this happens again. And that, I'm sorry to say, means even more cost and delay."

In different circumstances, seeing his team physically deflate in front of him would have been an interesting observation. It was far from that in the current situation.

He cleared his throat and began his attempt at the pep talk he'd been rehearsing on the way back to the lab.

"We've hit a road bump, nothing more. It's taken twenty years to get us here, but think of how incredibly lucky we are. To be here. Today. Yes, it's hugely disappointing. Yes, it's going to delay our journey. But considering the potential outcome..." He trailed off.

Alf spun his chair left and right. He was inspecting the floor for the good news and inspiration he'd yet to hear from Professor Fenkhause.

Piotr exhaled loudly then, to Ebhart's surprise, stood up and smiled.

He walked over to him, slapped the other Professor on the shoulders at arm's length then peered into his eyes.

After a pause, he nodded.

"Let's fix this thing, find that goddamn particle and stick it up his heavenly arse!"

With that, he left the room.

Which burst out laughing a split-second after the door shut.

CHAPTER 20

Various locations - Tuesday October 21st, 2008

The LHC Inauguration Ceremony was scheduled to take place at Point 18 of the Laboratory.

Some of the highest representatives from the member states of CERN were present. Perhaps more high profile representatives might have graced the facility with their presence had the machine actually been operational. That aside, it was a well-attended affair with an estimated one thousand five hundred guests, press included.

The PR and Events Team had tried to pull out all the stops to fill the void that the machine's inactivity left in the excitement department.

LHC-Fest, as it was dubbed by the PR Team, would commence after the Inauguration Ceremony. It was going to be full of exciting things. A multimedia concert, specially created for CERN by a world renowned photographer and accompanied by a new soundtrack played by the Suisse Romande Orchestra.

A host of international chefs to prepare a 'molecular' cuisine buffet. Popular in the UK and now abroad, wacky television chefs used dry ice and laboratory tools to come up with unreasonably sounding yet surprisingly delicious taste sensations. The price was eye-watering of course.

What really made The Watchmen lean forward in their seats and view the stream of the event with wide-eyed interest though was the small papier-mâché child's toy. The ceremonial gifting to LHC leadership proved to be a moment of painful clarity.

As they watched, the current Japanese Vice Minister of Education, Culture, Sports, Science and Technology filled in the second eye of the Daruma doll with a brush.

It signified the completion of the goal of constructing the Large Hadron Collider. He then passed it over to the LHC representatives on stage.

A veil lifted from their eyes.

No one had given a second thought in 1995 to when the then Japanese Minister for Education, Sciences and Culture gifted a Daruma doll to CERN's Director-General.

It was a small gesture to mark the occasion of Japan becoming an observer state on the project. In accordance to Japanese tradition, one eye was painted on the doll. This marked the beginning of the LHC project. The second eye would join it at the time of its completion.

As they contemplated the event, with its stage-managed artificiality, they began to understand. Something they had dismissed as a gimmick had obviously borne a much, much greater role.

Daruma or Dharma dolls are children's toys. Hollow and round-bottomed, designed to roll back up if pushed to the ground. They are simple things.

But simplicity can so often provide the most powerful reinforcement of symbolism. It also holds the right attributes to be over-looked as a pure symbol of power because of it.

In front of his screen, Karvorkian cursed his operatives' shared lack of insight.

To be fair, back in 1995, there were limited satellite television channels, no widespread use of social media or instant access to information. Few media outlets reported this globally insignificant gesture. They were immersed in the Balkans conflict, the O.J. Simpson trial and Italian corruption cases. It deserved only a passing mention in a routine report. But dammit, they should have sensed it.

In Japan, Daruma dolls are a symbol of perseverance and good luck, making them a popular gift of encouragement. Such a symbol, imbued with the belief systems of a whole country and ancient culture, was kept at the heart of the Large Hadron Collider project. It represented a significant power to protect the LHC from the likes of his group's actions.

If other powerful artefacts were near it which they were unaware of, the Daruma doll could have increased their affects.

Its presence in the building was essentially like having a force field generator at the heart of the facility. It would partially if not fully deflect actions sent its way.

Their agents and facilitators had walked past it for years, not thinking or not comprehending its importance.

Karvorkian realised that millions of dollars had been spent in what they had assumed was a guaranteed destruction of this insane project. That goal could never have been achieved.

No wonder this one monument was still standing. Damaged but not beyond repair, their actions had brought all those other machines down quickly and easily.

Daruma dolls were supposed to be burnt at the end of the year and replaced with new ones to set new goals and objectives. This one had had thirteen years in which to increase its protective power. It channelled the hopes of not only the people who offered the gift, but also the dreams of the recipients. It had also drawn, inadvertently, from the power directed at it from them.

Two beeps on the line.

"Facilitator, I believe we need to address an urgent issue?"

The voice was quiet, the line eerily clean.

"Indeed. I could not agree more. I suggest we make preparations in the next half an hour to postpone whatever events or appointments you had planned. I will have new communication details distributed. I am sure we are all keen to digest this new information and re-form our prognosis."

After a series of beeps, he remained the sole occupant on the line. He pressed the disconnect button and the line was dead.

He had some serious cost-benefit analysis to do in the next half an hour. But he could not draw his eyes away from the Daruma doll's newly created pupils on the screen.

"I was blind but now I see," he muttered.

He switched off the monitor, rocked back on his chair and closed his eyes. He went to work.

#####

The call was re-established and the participants logged in one by one.

It soon became obvious that they could take no decision on further action at the macro level. The virtual meeting was several participants down from a quorum. According to their unwritten charter, they could not agree collective action at this level.

Certain participants had immediately sent their apologies through the encrypted message system. Matters of state kept them. No one questioned their commitment. These individuals, bound together by something more than a simple membership of an elite club, had too much skin in the game to miss one of these calls due to trivial matters.

All attendees had undertaken the same activity that the host of the call had between the two calls. Some required less time than others to complete their contemplations. The years of experience in undertaking the activity brought benefits of speed and mental agility.

As with all other skills, when one had completed enough practice, technique improved. A small number attained a level of skill that might be called virtuoso if a public recognition of their gifts were ever recognised. Of course, this was exactly what they were hoping to avoid.

Karvorkian took his line off mute.

"I sense that there are a couple of new pieces on the board that we should consider the positions of," he began.

A general murmur of consent came back to him across the static-free airwaves.

"The first is associated with our current situation and is a negative charge. This piece requires removal from the game. She is somehow connected to a path that seems to wish to establish itself the dominant event-chain in the coming months. One, I hasten to add, which would be extremely detrimental to our wishes."

Another voice, a woman's, forceful but deep, continued the line of thought.

"She seemed incidental to me until recently and has only just emerged as a person of interest. Her location and focus in her occupation changed status in the past month. It now transpires that her work is drawing her closer to those who might possibly, collectively, lead to a perception-awareness state-change. Was this as unanticipated by others present?"

Murmurs of agreement again.

Another, deeper voice, mellifluous and obviously used to public speaking, took up the thread.

"The proximity of her work in relation to matters of state is within the main zone of conflict at present. Any perception-awareness would not help to progress the cause we wish to pursue. As a result, I propose a motion that we remove her from the stage with immediate effect to dull the event-chain's effect."

Karvorkian's eyes dropped to the left to take in the voting dashboard which lit up in unanimous agreement. There was no requirement for the formal timed voting process and verification for this level of decision-making.

"Proposition granted."

He cleared his throat and stopped his index finger from tapping the desk in front of him.

Was he nervous? He frowned slightly.

"So, on to something a little more macro then."

There was silence on the line.

It felt tense. He was not the only one feeling awkward about raising this particular agenda item.

"It seems that we need to release a positive charge. Relieve some of the pressure that has built up through our recent interventions. One with a degree of strength. Rebalance some of the energy we have disturbed due to the artefact at CERN."

"Yes." Several participants stated in unison, as if saying 'Amen' to the end of a silent prayer.

"It is unnecessary to discuss the event or name of the individual in question. We know what will provide the right amount of force required to provide a global burst of positive emotion. One which would then have the required half-life to gradually degrade over the following four years. This re-balance should allow us to refocus on the required long term plan."

A Chinese accent with a thin reed-like tone, interjected.

"There is a significant risk that this intervention might cause even more of a charge than we would like though, is there not?"

Unobserved, Karvorkian nodded.

"That is true, but it is a risk that we have little choice in making, given the lack of alternatives. In that instance, it would take us slightly longer to re-engage our long-term plan. Essentially though, the effect would be the same."

Another voice, a woman, with a European accent, jumped in.

"We must all acknowledge that at this point, taking no action is not an option. Manufacturing the perfect candidate would be almost impossible in the timescales we have to work with. It would also appear extremely odd were they to suddenly appear on the world stage in this day and age."

Muted agreement again rustled through the participants, a low-level breeze through autumn trees.

The European voice continued. "I propose that the entire group adopt the proposition to enhance the campaign of the gentleman in question. We must use our collective skills to ensure that by any means possible, the people choose this man."

Again, all lights were in agreement.

Karvorkian smiled. Even interfering in the election of the most powerful person on the planet did not warrant the use of the formal voting system. Such was the lack of real power politicians had these days.

He acknowledged the vote. "Proposition carried. We will reconvene after three days and following procedure commit this action to our kin in the usual manner. In the meantime, we will establish a task force to remove the woman from the equation and keep our focus on the CERN situation. If we gain any further reports from our agents inside their team, the reports will be distributed in the usual manner."

No goodbyes were proffered. Karvorkian terminated his line. He leaned his chair back, put his feet on the table and looked up at the ceiling.This would be fun.

Yes we can, he thought. Hope isn't even required.

CHAPTER 21

Geneva, Switzerland - Saturday 25th October, 2008

Ben was coming out of the Caffe de la Presse on the Boulevard de Saint-Georges when he hit her.

The building was a remnant of a bygone era. It extended like a long finger pointing away from the University, a skinny island in a stream parting the road on either side for a hundred meters or so.

The coffee wasn't particularly special. The strangeness of the building had drawn him to it. The smell inside the little café was always pleasant and the welcome warm, even to someone with a basic French vocabulary.

He'd settled on the place after a couple of weeks mooching around different areas of the city. He'd sat in several, scouring newspapers for topics of interest that might spur him to find a new career.

That morning seemed to be shaping up into one of those bright sunny autumnal days all too rare in Europe. The trade winds had shifted subtly north. Ben had decided he'd de-camp to a park and do his research whilst catching some yearned-for rays.

Paper under one arm, coffee in hand, he held a pastry in a paper bag in the other. At the same time, he was trying to open his sunglasses with his mouth. Hands full, he was attempting to exit the coffee shop by shoving the glass door with his back.

He unexpected made hard contact with something else softer.

He heard a squeal and immediately spun around. He caught the final moments of a slim woman fall backwards on the ground.

She had shoulder-length, glossy dark hair. She was wearing a charcoal jacket, white blouse and business skirt and high heels with red soles.

Her attaché case skittered across the pavement, coming to rest on the road near a pedestrian crossing.

Her eyes were closed.

One leg was at an awkward angle.

Ben immediately dropped the paper and the pastry. His sunglasses fell out of his mouth as he opened it.

"Oh my god, are you okay? I mean, ça va?"

He scanned left and right but there was nowhere to put his coffee, so he put it on the pavement close to the wall and knelt down to check her.

The woman's eyes fluttered. She tried to lift her head and groaned.

"Ow. Shit."

"Hey, take it easy, you went down with quite a bang there."

He checked to see if there was any bleeding, broken bones or other damage.

"Did you hit your head?"

There was a frown as if she was concentrating on something. Then her eyelids snapped open. One brow raised as the woman managed a scowl.

"Are you kidding me?"

Ben felt like he'd been winded as soon as he saw her deep brown eyes.

"Esther?"

The woman's eyes focused and for a moment, softness crept into them. Her mouth opened a little as if she were taking a breath to say something. Then she seemed to think better of it, and closed her eyes again.

"Brilliant! Just brilliant! Ben Fallow. On all the days, in all the places, you had to knock me flying because you had an important coffee and pastry run."

"I'm so sorry Esther. Are you hurt? Can you move your leg?"

She made a move, groaned again, and slowly sat up, moving her leg back into a more suitable position.

"Yes, I'm bloody hurt! I'm going to have a massive bruise and a hole in my bank account to replace these shoes, not to mention suit. Oh Ben, why can't you be more careful?"

She offered him her hand and he gently grasped it.

He scooped his other hand behind her back and lifted her up as if she were no weight at all.

In the years since he'd last seen her, he noticed, she'd kept her figure and was as lithe as he remembered her.

"Oh," she said, a little dizzy as he placed her on her feet.

She scrunched her eyes, still seeing stars, and rubbed the back of her head.

Reassuring herself that there was no blood but a nice bump was forming, she drew a deep breath in through her nose. Then she exhaled through her mouth.

This time her eyes opened slowly. She found she was inches away from Ben's concerned face. His hands were still on her waist.

"So, not content with sweeping women off their feet you've graduated to slamming them to the ground now, have you?"

Ben blushed deeply

"I'm so, so sorry Esther. Can I get you anything? Water? Coffee? Something stronger? Do you need to go to the hospital? Is there anyone I need to call for you? What do you need?"

Esther shook her head slightly, put her hands on his chest and laughed lightly, even though it caused another furrow of her brow.

"I've had far worse scrapes than this Ben, as you well know, growing up on a military base. But I think a few minutes sit down inside and a coffee would probably be a good idea. I don't think I've broken anything but I've got a bit of a buzzing going on in my head. It might be best to make sure I won't pass out behind the wheel for a couple of minutes."

Ben picked up his coffee and threw the paper, pastry and his now disintegrated sunglasses into a nearby bin. He retrieved Esther's attaché case from the street, then opened the door to the café. Gesturing Esther to enter first, followed.

Several patrons who'd been gawping through the window moved to fuss around Esther, who shooed them away.

An old lady and gentleman, who seemed to have resident's permits for the place, scowled at Ben over cold espressos.

He ordered two more coffees, a bottle of mineral water and a small cognac. He brought them over on a tray from the bar, insisting to the waiter that it was fine and tipping him respectably enough to keep him back.

After placing it all down and giving Esther the coffee, cognac and water, he sat down opposite and gazed at her.

"Esther, how on earth are you here and what are you doing?"

Sipping the piping hot coffee, she put the cup down, poured a little mineral water in to cool it down and peeped back up at him.

"I could ask you the same thing. How come you're not off somewhere saving the world instead of being in the most boring city on it?"

"Well, if I was, I wouldn't have had the..." He began, but realised that his foot was inserting itself in his mouth faster than normal. "Listen to me! I sound like the one who had a bang on the head, not you!"

"Nothing new there then!" she retorted, more jest than anger. A sparkle was coming back to her eyes and her cheeks were filling with colour again.

They both smiled at each other for a moment, and then began to talk at the same time. Stopped, began again. They both laughed. Ben jumped in.

"You start."

"Well, I'm here on secondment with a Non-Governmental Organisation for a couple of months investigating, uh, certain activities by unnamed individuals or companies that are not for discussion in this kind of establishment with a man like you."

As she talked he appraised her properly.

She was still beautiful, even though her hair was out of place and there were a few tears in her jacket. Her olive skin was back to its usual glow, her rich, dark eyes gaining more and more clarity. Her mouth was full under a small but strong nose, her almond-shaped face ending in a pleasing chin.

Dimples played at the edges of her up-turned lips. He was pleased to see that any make-up she wore accentuated rather than covered up her features.

He noticed there was no wedding or engagement ring on either hand. His heart gave a double-thump in appreciation.

"And you?"

66

"Well, up until last month I was working with the Swiss Army, but those days are now behind me. So I guess I'm scouting for a new career."

"Well, here's some useful advice, Ben..."

Ben leaned forward. "Yes?"

"Don't be a Doorman."

They both laughed.

The espresso maker hissed and cups and saucers tinkled out a soundtrack behind a rekindling of affection, if not more, of two people who hadn't seen each other for fifteen years.

####

Ben had met Esther during the summer of 1990. Three years after his Father had died, although no body was ever retrieved. Two years and six months after his mother had died of a broken heart.

He Uncle was rarely around much given his United Nations responsibilities and so it his Aunt cared for him on the base. She was a nurse.

Ben was fifteen and starting to bulk out into an adult. He'd been practising his Karate for a good long while, beating boys significantly above his age group. Even made a name for himself in the amateur circuits.

When his father was reported missing when he was twelve, it focused him even more on his sport. It drove him deeper into himself until he had a, some might say unhealthy, obsession with perfecting his skills. He'd seen 'Karate Kid 2' the year before and it had captivated him as an eleven year old, so he became immersed in the whole martial arts world.

At any free moment, Ben would be found doing press ups, strength training, meditation and repetitive exercises, often hundreds of times per move, until he had cramp or felt the need to puke. But the focus was paying off physically and he was growing into an attractive kid, albeit with the usual amount of acne for a teenager.

What he didn't have was a mentor for his soul. With his parents gone, his Uncle was barely around. His Aunt worked with the sick and injured much of the time. Without any siblings, he had no one to share his grieving process with.

He felt alone. There was no Mister Miyagi to help him through his dark days, process his emotions and channel the anger into a positive direction.

He got into his fair share of trouble. It wasn't at a level where he might have jeopardised his future.

He still had people watching out for him even if he didn't see it. On some nights where his dark thoughts were front and centre, Ben felt more like one of the recruits of the film's baddie, John Kreese, than the hero. On very dark nights, he willed for himself to be Kreese himself.

However, Ben was strong-minded and had obviously gained some inherent sense of right and wrong from his parents. He eventually snapped out of it. He'd come to the conclusion logically that it was better to help than to harm, and grew into a strong, honest boy.

He was pretty shy though, so was oblivious to the fact that as he was growing up, he was becoming the teenage heartthrob of the base in the eyes of the girls. The mystique, his withdrawal, the loss and his focus on his Karate, all made their hearts go a bit fluttery. Whilst he was polite and courteous, he didn't seem interested in them at all when it came to evenings and weekends.

They were left to fend off the advances of the various offspring around the base, from over-privileged officer's sons to under-developed Neanderthal half-wits. The whole world was represented in that base.

For Ben, Esther was a breath of fresh air when she arrived on base. She immediately made a bee-line for him and, unlike the other girls, seemed to want to get to know him for who he was, not for his muscles.

She was forward, cutting through his shyness like scissors through paper. She made him laugh, had a great sense of humour for a girl.

To top it all off, she really liked running.

They'd train together in the mornings. First thing, when it was just becoming light, a couple of miles around the base, panting in the dawn mist. There was no talking, just a smile and a 'Hello, how are you?' as he picked her up outside her parents' billet. Then they shared a rhythmic and calming partnership of exercise. The air buzzing in the frosty pre-dawn haze, making everything alright.

Esther was three years younger than him.

They had been friends, nothing more. Right up until Ben left to go to university on an Army scholarship. Then they both realised but didn't voice that it had, too late, the potential to grow into something more.

They'd tried to keep in touch but time and distance in an age without affordable internet access meant that they drifted apart. Letters got lost. Dormitories gave way to houses without a shared telephone. Esther's family moved on to another location. Esther left home and went to college.

They each faded in the other's memories, hidden under a pile of new experiences and emotions.

####

"Ben! Shit! I have to go!"

They'd been chatting for about half an hour. Then Esther's eyes went wide and her arm snapped out, shooting an elegant wrist watch out of her sleeve.

"Really? It's Saturday."

"Yes, I know that. But certain organisations follow different working weeks due to their location of origin, if you know what I mean."

"Oh, right. So basically, it's not a weekend to the people you're speaking to? That makes it Afghanistan or Iran then." He checked her outfit again. Undamaged, the suit was business-like, rather than party-town, the exception being the shoes. His eyebrow rose as he thought of the Sharia requirements for women's dress.

69

Esther saw his appraisal and tutted. "Don't be smart Ben. Not all business is transacted face-to-face. And not all businesses in the countries you mentioned are native."

Ben shrugged, acknowledging the point. There was a moment of silence before Esther put her cup firmly down.

"Look, it's been, um, nice. Ish. Most of it. But I have to go. Really."

"Can I drop you anywhere?"

"No, I have a car around the corner, and now I'll need to dash home to get changed."

"Let me walk you to the car at least then?"

"No, honestly, I'll be fine." She grabbed a napkin from a holder, lifted a pen from inside her jacket and scribbled a number on the tissue.

She thrust it at him, a faint pink blush rising on her cheeks.

"To be honest, it's a little lonely here, so even though I'm a little sore, it was nice to bump into you. Call me so we can do this again without the grazes?"

"That would be great. I don't have a mobile at the moment, next thing on the list otherwise I'd give you a number back."

She nodded.

"I'm really sorry again Ezzy, but it was lovely to see you."

He leaned over and gave her a peck on the cheek. It was her turn to blush. She threw her arms around him and hugged him tightly, then groaned.

"Ouch." She sat back, eyed him slyly. "You owe me big time, mister. You'd better call, alright?"

Ben put his hands up.

"I promise. What time do you finish today?"

She sighed. "That I can't tell you as I really have no idea myself. But text me your number if you can't get through and I'll call you?"

"Okay, great."

And with that, she dashed out of the café, swung right and down the road, teetering on her damaged heels. Ben had no idea how she would drive in them.

He sat day-dreaming about their encounter. It dawned on him that the half-dozen customers in the establishment were quiet.

Some were glancing over, others staring outright at him. One of the waiters was idly gazing at him whilst cleaning a steaming cup with a tea towel.

Ben raised an eyebrow. Immediately, conversations sprang up. Newspapers rustled and the cappuccino machine started slurping away on some random cleaning cycle.

He shook his head. The dearth of entertainment in this town that meant that Ben and Esther's encounter would probably form a significant chunk of these and their close relatives, friends and acquaintances topics of conversation for the next few days.

He gathered his few possessions and made sure Esther's number was secure in his wallet.

As he stood up, he finally noticed that Esther had left her attaché case behind.

It was discreet but also the colour of the seats they were sitting in, and it had been half-obscured by a cushion.

She'd been in a rush, flustered. There was still a possibility of concussion, which caused disorientation.

He grabbed the bag and thanked his audience sarcastically.

Carefully this time, he opened the door, turned in the direction that he'd seen her go. And heard a screech of tyres.

Around two hundred meters down the street, he just caught sight of a woman that looked like Esther. She was flopping into the arms of two men standing by the open door of a car. One of them seemed to be removing a syringe of some kind from her arm.

Ben shouted and began to sprint towards them. The men deftly manoeuvred her inside the back and jumped in the car, which accelerated off.

He had just enough time before it shot down the road to get a make and model and a partial plate.

He eased up and stood, wondering just what the hell was going on.

####

He slammed the door to his own car and sank into the driving seat. For the first time in a long time, Ben didn't have a clue what to do.

He started by analysing what had just happened.

He'd visited a café that he'd only recently become familiar with. He'd found it through the recommendation of a local barber who he'd popped into only to get a short, back and sides the previous week.

On his third visit, he'd nearly brained his childhood sweetheart, who he hadn't seen since leaving for university back in the nineties. A completely random chance encounter had almost ended in serious injury.

Everything seemed to be getting smoothed out and Ben felt that his being in Geneva a little while longer might be a good decision. But then Esther gets abducted in broad daylight. For God knew what reason. Driven off by God knows who to God knows where. That left Ben with nothing and with no official remit to act.

He tried to think through his options. He had no access to the specialist equipment he used to back with the Swiss Army. He couldn't trace her phone or otherwise gain access to any security camera footage in the city.

He wasn't really in a position to make a credible phone call to the police. Without further detail on where she worked, what had put her in this position and no witnesses, all leads would lead pretty quickly back to him.

He'd been observed physically assaulting her. She'd been seen running off quickly at the end of their brief encounter. She'd disappeared without taking her briefcase. He'd been watched rushing out after her, chasing her. Luckily, that was where the eye-witness accounts would end.

He checked out the attaché case. It contained nothing that might be immediately of help. There were various items. Unbranded pens. Blank sheets of paper with no insignia and a fresh notebook. Some mints. A compact and a well-used lipstick.

There were no business cards, stationery of any kind or return address details for the case if found.

72

His feeling of loneliness crashed back on him. It reinforced the loss of the positive vibrations he felt in Esther's presence.

It couldn't have been anything other than fate that had sent him crashing into her. There was no other explanation that he knew of.

He started the engine and began to run through a list of things he'd been putting off, when he thought he'd had all the time in the world. First on the list, an unlocked and SIM-free mobile phone. Tri-band, with a couple of spare instant charge packs (or even better, a solar charger).

He didn't know where he was going to end up next, so he'd better be prepared, he thought, as he stared down the street through the windscreen.

CHAPTER 22

Alboran Sea - Saturday 25th October, 2008

Although he had made good progress, The Historian was still thousands of miles away from where his gut was guiding him.

He was travelling under counterfeit papers. His vessel had various aliases to avoid being tracked too closely by monitoring and maritime safety systems. That meant that he had to locate out of the way refuelling stations off the beaten track.

In Eastern Europe, perhaps surprisingly, this was fine. Sidling up to a jetty and waving some cash around usually got him almost everything he required. But as he moved west, his options became more limited and had the potential to arouse more suspicion.

As he journeyed, the weather too began to frown on him. Waters became choppier. Churning green mountains of foamy undulations replaced the relative stillness of sparkling silk sheets.

It felt as if the closer he made his way towards his final destination, the harder the force from something pushing back on him. Trying to restrain his progress.

In the times when the auto pilot was set, he monitored his systems. He noted further patterns of gaps. Tell-tale vacuums that seemed to have sucked in the life of a person here, the existence of a company there. Black holes that swallowed a seemingly inevitable outcome. Popular movements disappeared overnight, with no outrage, surprise or comment of any kind.

Like sea-sickness, which he had overcome relatively quickly, discovering these oddities made The Historian's insides swirl and groan. Unlike sea-sickness, there was no simple panacea to address these symptoms.

As the yacht creaked and groaned around him, sails tight, it sped through the Alboran Sea towards Gibraltar. He shut his eyes and visualized himself back on the Black Sea.

Right now, he needed a calming influence. A place where he knew he was secure. Somewhere he could retreat to find the peace necessary to sleep.

He needed more energy to help him achieve his near-term goal.

One goal at a time. That's what he needed to focus on.

Otherwise he would become too visible to them. He needed to be overlooked as a person of no significance. Otherwise it would all be for nothing.

In his imagination, the cove he had grown attached to slowly formed.

Within a few minutes, he was asleep. There were, however, no pleasant dreams. He did not dare to dream these days.

CHAPTER 23

Domaine Du Lac Saint-Prex, Switzerland – Saturday October 25th, 2008

Esther felt herself lifted by her legs and arms and tried to raise her head.

She was groggy but quickly realized that she lacked even the energy to perform this simple task or even open her eyes. It sounded as if her head was submerged in a bath and someone had left the taps running. All the noises that would have normally been understandable were muffled.

She thought she could hear voices and a car or a lawnmower, but could not make out anything clearly. She felt herself swaying as she was carried. A wave of nausea hit her as she realised that the person who was carrying her top half had their arms underneath her armpits. Hands were grasping her breasts. She was indignant rather than scared but still powerless to do anything about it.

Behind her eyelids she saw the transition from light to dark. A door slammed behind her and then there was a slow brightening again, as if someone had played with dimmer lights in a room. She was carried further through what she suspected to be a domestic building. The rushing noise in her ears subsided marginally to a dullness, the muting more like cloth than water now.

Her mind seemed alert but there was absolutely no response from her body. She felt a deep lethargy. A strange sense that her spirit, whatever, the thing that made her a person, was floating just slightly above her. It was kind of bouncing on her like it was on a spongy trampoline.

Her legs began to ascend higher than her head but then soon levelled out. She had no idea of how long it had been since she had been taken. She was completely disorientated about her current location.

After what seemed hours, she was tipped onto something firm but soft. Her captors manoeuvred her around.

Again, the hands were in places she would have lashed out in response to, had she the ability to.

She was now curled up in a semi-normal sleeping position and a blanket of some kind was dumped on top of her.

In the stillness, the muffled sounds in her ears retreated. Light became dark and she slipped back into unconsciousness.

Not before she heard a door locking soundly and securely. Its precision made her entire spine shiver involuntarily with terror.

#####

Manek wiped his brow as he and his companion walked back down the stair case.

"Are you sick, Manek?"

"What?"

"She was not exactly fat. Are you out of shape?"

"No Fritz, not at all. I am just wearing too many black clothes today. I did not expect the sudden sunshine."

"Hm. Perhaps. I think you're sweating for another reason."

"And what would that be?"

His companion glanced sideways at him, his eyelids half-closed as he perused the other man's face.

"I think you're uncomfortable being that close to a woman."

"Fuck you."

"Yes, I think that is it. You are uncomfortable being so close to an attractive woman."

"Fuck you, Fritz."

"Even if they are drugged, you get all sweaty and nervous, like a teenager."

"Fuck. You."

"I bet you will go home and cry like a baby."

Manek spun around and snapped a fist towards Fritz's face.

Seeing as the other man had instigated the action, he'd been fully prepared for retaliation. He side-stepped Manek, used the momentum of the punch to keep him spinning and swept his legs from under him with one swift jerk of his leg.

Manek was on the ground in an instant, falling heavily on his arm.

Fritz stood there and glowered down at Manek.

He was now mirroring the position that they'd left Esther in minutes ago on the floor above in one of the guest rooms.

He paused, shaking his head in mock disapproval.

"Manek, you really must keep in shape. Mentally. Physically. Emotionally. Otherwise you will be of no use. And then I would have to do what I do best."

Manek stared up malevolently but said nothing. He was seething with impotent fury at the man standing over him. He couldn't stand people laughing at him. Especially those bigger than him. Fritz was almost a foot taller, and a good few stones heavier. He'd been stupid to get wound up, but the red mist had fallen on him quickly due to the adrenaline rush of the kidnap.

He knew that Fritz was right too.

He'd already got angry when he'd seen Fritz with his hands all over the woman's tits and arse. Fondling them with the excuse of getting a better grip when he was carrying her upstairs backwards or pushing her into a good position to sleep.

He'd done what Manek hadn't had the guts to do. And yes, it probably would be the only time he'd get the chance, due to his social awkwardness around women.

Fritz had over-stepped the mark though, and he was going to pay. He didn't know how, but he'd make sure it would happen.

Fritz stood over Manek, seeing his frustration and smiled. Then, offering a hand to Manek's good arm, he pulled him up swiftly enough to bounce Manek off his chest.

"Come on playboy. We've got work to do."

Manek scowled and followed him out of the door.

CHAPTER 24

Lafayette Park, United States of America – Saturday October 25th, 2008

Karvorkian was sitting on the weathered park bench closest to the entrance to the park.

He had some earphones in, giving the impression that he was listening to some music, Debussy perhaps, on his iPhone. Instead, he was scanning the park for signs of his contact over his copy of the Financial Times, which was also a simple prop purchased to blend in to the environment. He never paid any notice to what journalists wrote in newspapers. He had far better sources than they did. He'd rather get unfiltered information than read some politically motivated twaddle.

Another hastily arranged conference call with all in attendance had approved the outstanding issues. It fell to Karvorkian to set the activity in motion. This required a rare physical meeting. Something he did not relish.

The park was pretty quiet for a place so close to the big house. Perhaps it was due to the bitter wind that day. There were the inevitable joggers and dog-walkers doing circuits. But relatively few people sitting on benches like him, which made him feel uncomfortably exposed.

There was so much sophisticated technology in the world. It frustrated him that he still had to traipse out to locations such as this to do a simple deal for some basic wet work.

However, he knew, since the Patriot Act passed, that the NSA was doing its best to intercept every single form of electronic communication it could locate, decrypt and index.

All the criminals he knew, knew it too.

It was just those on the right side of the law that were still living under a misapprehension.

They would never believe their government and its corrupt politicians weren't acting in their best interests.

Instead, they were snooping where they felt they shouldn't be in a free society with abandon.

So, rather than take the chance that the goons in the NSA might stumble across something, Karvorkian's contact for 'this kind of thing' preferred to meet face-to-face. To 'minimise risk'.

The problem with that was, at the end point of every verbal or written transaction ended with a person. That person was as leaky, if not more so, than the technology employed to communicate with them. People could be incredibly porous, he mused. Especially if something sharp is repeatedly stuck into and pulled out of them.

He had become conscious that he'd been more and more reluctant to go outside in the past few weeks.

He'd get a glimpse of shrubbery as he left his apartment before jumping into his limousine. A grey cloud as he went from the first class lounge and up the steps into the private jet.

He felt removed from nature, distrustful of it even. He felt almost a physical pressure change when he went outside. It was like an increasing force around his body trying to crush the breath out of him. It was oppressive.

He knew this was all in his mind. There was no great being in the sky squinting at a miniature Karvorkian through almost-closed thumb and finger, imagining crushing the life out of him. But at the same time, he also knew that there were men and women on earth that had the capability, when combined, to do just that.

The reason why he was sitting here was to do with those people. They were anonymous to him as they should be to the entire group. It was this anonymity that enabled them to operate in a circle of trust. It was a case of security through obscurity. Yet, when this feeling of oppressiveness started, it began to make him think that someone had perhaps found a way around these protocols.

Karvorkian was currently Chair, as he would be until his death. At his passing, Chairmanship would pass to a randomly selected member of the circle who would then take the reins and orchestrate their joint vision.

He knew in his heart that if someone had found out how he had manipulated the 'randomness' of his selection, they too could gain

80

from the position he currently enjoyed.

A pigeon suddenly burst flapping from the bushes. A puppy that had slipped his leash bounded after it, yapping.

Through the earphones, Karvorkian heard the owner calling out fretfully. The puppy had obviously a few more lessons of dog training to go before he would be conditioned to return to his master.

He glimpsed the young woman running after it. His focus changed to see his contact walking towards him on the light-dappled path through the trees.

Over six feet, he wore an expensive suit, a waxed raincoat and held a folding umbrella. As was protocol, he carried nothing else. No briefcase and certainly no form of identification.

Karvorkian was the same. Even his iPhone was a burn phone, illegally cracked.

He stood and began walking slowly as his contact reached him.

"Nigel," his contact said warmly, no emotion on his face.

"David, how nice to see you."

There was no handshake. They continued to walk.

"You have some papers for me?"

"Indeed. Usual place. Usual box."

"Disposal?"

"Something new. On contact with air they will disintegrate into a fine powder within fifteen minutes. Just rip the bag open, digest and then pop them back in the bag when you're done, then put that back into the deposit box."

"Nice. How did you produce that?"

Karvorkian slowed and turned to stare at the man, his head on a slight angle.

"Right. Sorry."

Actually, he couldn't resist. "If you must know, it's a unique printing and packaging method that is in a hermetically sealed unit which operates in a vacuum. The paper is 3D printed from a special solution. It's then transferred to the adjoining printer and then fed straight into the specially-designed envelope. Once sealed, it passes through an airlock into dispatch."

'David' whistled his appreciation softly.

"I know a few governments who wouldn't mind getting their hands on that."

"I have no doubt."

They did not talk about payment, simply a timescale for delivery of the activity.

"David, I needn't tell you about the consequences if what we are asking of you does not happen precisely in the manner that we have outlined, do I?"

'David' motioned his understanding of the situation with a rapid movement of his head. His Adam's apple jumped up and down inside his throat a couple of times as he swallowed to refresh his dry throat.

"David?"

"Of course not."

"I'm very glad to hear it. Now, if there's no other business...?"

"No, nothing more at this time, Nigel."

"Good. Have a pleasant day."

With that, 'David' stepped up a gear and walked off. Karvorkian watched him go, putting earphones back into his ears. He absent-mindedly clicked the play button on the wires.

Wagner blasted into his ears. A gust of wind blew a murmuration of dappled leaves across the path in front of him.

He shuddered, wrapped scarf more tightly around his neck and walked back to the entrance to the park, glancing at the White House in the near distance.

Karvorkian ducked quickly into his limo as the first fat spots of rain began to fall.

CHAPTER 25

Geneva, Switzerland – Saturday October 25th, 2008

Ben had been at a loss to how he could pull together any evidence relating to Esther's alleged abduction. He forced himself to calm down. Using his years of experience, he assessed the potential resources in the area. He switched the engine off and got back out of his car.

The lack of vehicular and pedestrian traffic meant that there were very few people he could rely on as witnesses to the event. The speed at which it had happened meant that, had he not been chasing after Esther, even he might have passed over it. This type of thing just didn't happen in a place like Geneva. Added to that, the city's inhabitants had a reluctance to get involved in anyone else's business.

None of the businesses in that part of the street were remotely close to open at this time of day on a Saturday. There was a cleaner working in a hair salon with their back to the glass-fronted shop. When Ben banged on the window a couple of times to get their attention he got no response. Then he spotted the earphone cord coming out of his pocket and saw the top of a candy bar phone peeking out. He thought he could hear strains of thrash metal coming from the ear buds, even outside on the street. So that was another dead end.

Inspecting the area, he was almost ready to give up when he suddenly saw it.

A CCTV camera on a high pole towards the end of the street.

Of course!

He remembered now. Cameras had been installed for the European football tournament. They were scattered around Geneva but especially in places that visitors would go.

Until then, Geneva had resisted the relentless march of surveillance technology to watch over its inhabitants. It was only approved due to the potential for rioting from some countries' football fans.

FIFA required host cities to do everything possible to rout out the trouble makers whilst documenting these activities at the same time.

It so happened that he'd been involved in some of the training preparations for the security of the event. Some fifteen thousand troops had been made available to enhance the strength of existing police and security forces. Ben was introduced to some of the security detail, including the head of the team, Kevin Daste.

The matches had been long finished, but the camera was still moving over its defined grid. He knew that he needed to get in touch with Kevin urgently. The technology was covered by federal data protection laws. That meant unless there was an on-going investigation or prosecution, they wiped the data twenty four hours after retrieval.

The only way he could access that data would be to visit Kevin in person as he had no phone number or email address.

Kevin was based in the Federal Office of Police, or fedpol as it was known.

In Berne. Over one hundred and sixty kilometres away.

He set off at a pace to his car and jumped in. The race was on.

After navigating his way out of the centre, it took Ben around two hours to get to Berne and then another half an hour to find a place to park.

By the time he'd got to the fedpol Nussbaumstrasse headquarters, it was well past noon.

Without a security pass, he had to wait in line until he could speak to the person on front desk, adding another twenty minutes. He finally approached and waited patiently until the young man had finished his paperwork. The desk clerk drew a clean form and glanced up at Ben with a blank expression.

"Yes Sir, how can I help you?"

"Hello, yes, I'd like to see Kevin Daste please. It's a matter of urgency."

"Your name, Sir?"

"It's Ben. Ben Fallow."

"And what is it relating to Sir?"

"It's about an abduction."

The desk clerk glanced up, one eyebrow arched and his pen paused for a second.

"When did this abduction take place?"

"This morning, around eight thirty, in Geneva."

"I see. But it would not be Mr Daste who would be..."

"I know that. However, I believe Mr Daste would want to see me given our recent history."

"Oh? And what would that be?"

"I trained several of the security team in close combat for the Euro 2008 detail. Protecting several high profile Swiss dignitaries. Mr Daste said if there was that anything I needed in future..."

"Well Sir, that sounds like a fascinating story but it still doesn't qualify as a reason for me to disturb Mr Daste at short notice. He may not even be available as it is a Saturday."

A couple of seconds of silence passed as Ben stared at the desk clerk. He did not move a muscle.

The desk clerk blinked and, still facing Ben, his left hand went to the desk phone and picked up the receiver. He quickly tapped out an internal number. After a couple of seconds, there was a bark at the other end of the line.

"Sorry to disturb you Sir, but there's a Mr Ben Fallow here who claims to...Yes Sir...Of course Sir...I was unaware of that Sir. Would you like me to...right. Thank you, Sir."

The clerk put the phone down and swallowed slightly.

"I'm sorry to have kept you, Sir. Mr Daste will be down to see you personally in a couple of minutes. If you'd like to wait in interview room four I can arrange some tea or coffee?"

Ben smiled back. "Thank you. Water will be fine."

He turned his back and followed the signs to the interview rooms and entered room four.

The clerk meanwhile was standing motionless.

The pen in his right hand hovering over his form, he was staring sightlessly into the distance.

He had never seen eyes like the guy he'd just been up against in a staring match and he'd been doing this job for a couple of years. He thought he'd seen every expression possible on the faces of the people he'd met. Disdain, fury, terror, all of them.

He'd stared into Ben's eyes and he didn't know what he'd seen. He only knew that in the space of a couple of seconds, he'd felt incredibly small. Like a speck of dust.

"Excuse me!"

He snapped out of his trance to see a little old lady around five feet tall tapping her umbrella on the glass partition in front of the desk.

"Someone has been stealing the milk from my step for the past week. What are you going to do about it?"

A couple of minutes later, the door opened and Kevin Daste loped in to the interview room. He was all arms and legs and a large nodding head, like an uncoordinated and excitable Great Dane.

"Lieutenant Colonel Fallow, this is a pleasure!" His hand shot out, his wrist ejecting from his suit sleeve and shirt cuff a good couple of inches. It looked to Ben like a thick hairy tree branch.

"It's just plain old Mr Fallow now Kevin, but the sentiment is shared." Ben wasn't small but Kevin's hand enveloped his in long fingers and a palm the size of a saucer.

Kevin Daste was nearly seven feet tall and completely uncoordinated. It seemed as if balancing to stay upright was a constant struggle. Everything about him, including his brain, was over-sized and he was one of the Force's brightest.

He would have been the best also, were it not for his lack of co-ordination. The management quickly saw that his mind rather than his muscle was what the Force required. So they put him in an investigatory role in which he quickly excelled.

That got him a position of responsibility, which enabled him to earn the respect of his colleagues and peers. He performed exemplary work on a number of high profile, nasty cases.

"So Ben, what can I do for you? I'm under a bit of pressure at the moment, but I'll help if I can?"

Ben explained the events of the morning with as much precision as he could. Kevin perched, still swaying, on the edge of the table, the chairs being too small for his frame.

Every so often he interjected a question which Ben answered to the best of his ability and Kevin nodded and hummed.

"And you've no idea where she works?"

"No, and neither who for. Everything within the attaché case was fresh and blank."

"So, the big question then. How do you think I can help?"

Ben explained about the CCTV camera that he'd seen. He asked whether he could assess the footage to see whether it might have caught the car or abduction taking place.

Kevin stopped moving for a couple of seconds, arms folded and head bowed. Ben didn't know whether this was a good or bad sign.

After a moment of contemplation, Kevin studied Ben and puffed his cheeks out.

"I know I said anything you need Ben, but this is a step that might be too far."

Ben nodded, adding, "Kevin, if there was any other way..."

"I simply can't allow a civilian access to material protected under federal law Ben. Even I can't wriggle out of that one."

Ben deflated. He knew it was a long shot.

"However..."

Kevin was smiling.

"I can of course share it with a freelance security consultant that I have requested evaluate the continued usefulness of the CCTV infrastructure for the city. I trust there is a registered company that I can send an invoice to with relation to that?"

Ben smiled broadly and grasped Kevin's hand in both of his.

"When can Fallow Security Consultants commence its evaluation?"

Kevin grinned.

"No time like the present, is there?"

"That's it! That's the car."

After checking Esther's mobile to see whether they could triangulate her position, they'd come to a dead end.

The phone was off.

Someone had obviously removed the battery, so there was no way of tracing it back. So the next step was to check the CCTV footage.

It hadn't taken them long to identify the camera and the rough time when the abduction had taken place.

Unfortunately, as the camera was on a fixed rotation pattern, there wasn't a shot of the actual abduction itself. But Ben had managed to identify the car on the grainy recording as it came along the street and pulled up ahead of Esther

The shot established itself long enough to see one of the abductors get out. He opened the trunk of the car, as if checking for something, and the camera panned away.

That action enabled Ben to see that the vehicle was one of those where the number plate was on the boot lid that swung up.

"Can we clean that up?"

Kevin sighed.

"If it's a hit of the kind that you've outlined Ben, there's a high probability that it's a stolen car or that they replaced the plates. I'm not sure how useful that will be."

"I know Kevin, but I'm asking you. It's all we've got at the moment."

Kevin picked up the phone and asked for a clean-up on both the number plate and one of the alleged assailants. They then chatted for a couple of minutes about nothing much before the phone rang and they had two files dropped off.

"Good, let's run the plate. I'll also take a copy of the guy and see whether anyone knows who he is."

Ben picked up his copies and pumped Kevin's hand again.

"I'm going to get myself a mobile phone now. I'll call you on it as soon as I have so you've got the number. Hopefully by then we'll have some progress to report."

Kevin patted Ben rather heavily on the back.

"Let's hope so. I've got a couple of other things to attend to but I'll keep abreast of how things are going down here. At least the CCTV crew have finally got something they can get their teeth into. The whole Euro 2008 thing was a complete let down for them."

"Well I'm glad someone's getting something positive out of this. Thanks again Kevin. Expect to hear from me in the next couple of hours."

Ben left the station and went back to his car. Step by step, he thought. Break down the big problems into manageable chunks, we'll get there.

He switched on the engine and pulled out, heading for the nearest phone shop.

Time to get connected.

CHAPTER 26

Domaine Du Lac Saint-Prex, Switzerland – Sunday October 26th, 2008

Esther woke gasping from a dream. She'd been struggling to swim up from the bottom of an ocean with one leg chained to a concrete rock. Just as she thought she was going to drown, a sharp pain in her arm snapped her awake. Sitting upright, she was just in time to see someone pull a disposable syringe from an injection kit and discardg it in a nearby waste paper basket.

The room was light and spacious. She was currently at one edge of a queen-sized bed, with grey, satin sheets, a little crumpled from her occupancy. She became aware that she was also wearing silk pyjamas. She reddened at the thought that someone had undressed her whilst she was unconscious. She scanned around the room for her clothes, struggling to remember what she wore last.

Instead of her clothes, she saw a man in a dark suit. He was sitting quietly to her right, in front of windows that stretched the entire length of the room. Partially obscured by light net curtains, she looked out on a beautiful lake vista.

The person – woman, nurse – who had injected her gave her a plastic glass and gestured for her to drink.

She felt parched but she sipped the cool, refreshing water. Her eyes remained fixed on the man sitting in the chair, still keeping silent.

She did not have a good feeling.

As she turned to place the beaker back onto the low side table next to her with nothing else on it, she felt a tightness around her ankle. Wriggling it a little, she realised that they had handcuffed her leg to a bar at the bottom of the bed, obscured by the duvet.

This was not good at all.

She turned back to the man sitting down and stared at him.

The man nodded to the nurse, who slipped wordlessly out of the door, and then he turned back to Esther.

He switched on a forced smile, putting his hands together under his chin.

"What you are about to experience will not be pleasant, but it is better than the only other option that is open to us in cases like yours."

Esther frowned. At this point she was totally confused. She had little recollection of how she got there, or what had happened in the last couple of days. She wasn't quite sure whether this was a private medical facility, a sanatorium or some other place. Had she had a breakdown? Been in an accident?

"I'm sorry, I don't quite understand. Cases like mine? Who are you?"

The man stood. He turned and lifted the chair closer to the bed, so that she could better see him. He sat down again and scrutinized her for a couple of moments before continuing.

"Who I am and who you were is inconsequential. All that matters now is for us to try to minimise the pain of the procedure that you will undergo. So that you can be fully re-integrated into society."

"Who I was? Who...I was?"

Esther felt panic bubbling up inside her. Fear.

The man peered at her through his glasses, trying to assessing her state of mind through her body language.

Then he sighed, removed his glasses and pinched his nose as if to clear a pain behind his own eyes.

"What is your name?"

Esther opened her mouth then closed it without speaking.

She thought hard. Frowning didn't shift the cloud that was in front of her memories. Nor did shaking her head.

The tears that began to flow from her eyes did not wash the mugginess away either.

She knew something was there, hidden. She could feel her brain full of thoughts, memories and ideas. They just seemed blocked to her.

The man leaned forward.

"I'm sorry, I didn't catch that?"

She must have mumbled something.

"I don't know."

He leaned backwards, looking satisfied. He'd made his point.

"Good. Overnight, we've been working with you to suppress who you were so that we can begin the second phase of who you will become."

Esther felt her spirit deflate even further. Had anyone been searching for her since she had gone missing? Had someone deliberately put her there? Someone she knew? Was she really ill?

The man continued.

"The second phase is truly remarkable, really, if a little risky. We're taking what's being worked on with mice in MIT and are far more advanced in our results to date than they are."

The man became more animated as Esther withdrew more into herself. Whatever they had injected her with was obviously doing something to her.

She felt her strength sapping away minute by minute.

"It's called False Memory Syndrome. It's been known about for years. But it's never been used to completely overwrite a lifetime of memories in someone whose existing memories and knowledge has been chemically suppressed. It's incredibly exciting actually. Much more real than the Manchurian Candidate crap that we've all seen. We can literally turn someone into another person."

Esther sagged back onto the pillow and couldn't restrain a sob.

"Yes dear," said the man, patting her arm in a paternal way. "I know it's going to be quite painful and disorientating. All those electric shocks and everything. But it's better than the alternative, isn't it? Hm?"

Esther had some idea of what the alternative was but wondered in that moment whether this was better than being dead.

The man stood and moved off towards the door, then paused and glanced back. After a moment's contemplation, he gave a shrug and a wry smile.

"I knew your father you know. C'est la vie, n'est-pas?"

He closed the door softly behind him and Esther's last link to her past disappeared to who knew where.

CHAPTER 27

Geneva, Switzerland – Sunday October 26th, 2008

Kevin had been right of course. Expecting a seemingly-professional hit team to have the arrogance to use its own vehicle to perpetrate a kidnap was a stretch.

Having purchased a mobile phone, he called the number in and left his new contact address, another hotel. Ben had received a call first thing the next morning.

"I'm sorry Ben. This mob is good."

Kevin proceeded to relate that they'd run the number plate and had found it registered to a legitimate business man.

He'd sent a team out to visit the property, as the owner had neither reported the vehicle or number plate as lost or stolen.

To their surprise, the car was in the drive.

After phoning the owner, who was out of town on a client visit for a couple of days, they gained access to the vehicle.

They had found absolutely no trace of prints, blood, skin or any type of evidence.

A mechanic specializing in the type of car had accessed the on-board computer and found that the telematics had been tampered with. It was clean after the owner's last official journey. They'd also clocked the milometer.

"It was definitely the same car?"

"Without question. There was a ding on the real passenger door which happened just prior to the owner leaving town. He was going to schedule to get fixed on his return. That was just visible in the cleaned up CCTV footage."

"Anything material-wise embedded in the tyres?" Ben knew he was grasping at straws.

"Nothing. We've had wind but not rain for the past few days. No indication that it's been off-road or to an area of high vegetation. I'm sorry Ben."

Ben sat in the car at the side of the road, hazard indicators softly ticking.

He stared into the distance, unfocused, thinking. Eventually he spoke.

"I really appreciate your help Kevin. Thank you."

"It's no problem, it's what we're here to do. We'll keep searching for her employer as well. It seems strange that no one else has approached us to report a missing person, don't you think?"

"Yes and no. I didn't take Esther as someone who worked for any intelligence outfit. But at the same time, she did intimate that she was working with organisations based potentially in the Middle East region. That can be a tricky business to negotiate."

"Understood. Well, let's keep in touch then?"

"Yes. Sure. I think it's about time I went to the UK and start to get some stuff I've been putting off for a while straight. I'll call or email you once I've got myself sorted."

"Alright. Keep safe Ben. Talk soon."

"A bientot."

#####

Gerry Bairstow confirmed with pleasure that it was more than fine for him to visit. Ben returned the hire car and headed for Geneva Cornavin Station with his kit bag.

He could fly to London in an hour but he wanted some time to reflect on things, see the Alps and also keep his luggage with him. He'd decided to stay for a day in Paris, then spend a couple of nights in London before heading down to Gerry and Glenda's place. The first leg would be Geneva to Paris on a high-speed TGV train.

He picked up some essentials in the shopping centre below the concourse and some French perfume for Glenda. Then he jumped on the train.

As it pulled out of the station, Ben gazed out of the window at the receding skyline of Geneva.

He was surprised to find that his heart was aching. It was not for the city though. It was for what had been found, lost and now deeply, profoundly missed.

He closed his eyes tight against the threat of tears that he'd not shed for more than a decade and pictured Esther's face in his mind.

Where are you?

#####

That night, Esther dreamed. She dreamed of having coffee with a man in a café. He seemed nice, handsome. She liked his face. He was smiling, his eyes lit up.

His eyes. They were so...deep. Like pools. No, like oceans. Like the night sky. Omniscient.

He stopped smiling and his gaze went blank.

Where are you, he said.

Then she woke up, screaming with pain, as thousands of volts of electricity coursed through her spasming body.

#####

The Historian was having a particularly challenging time of it. His yacht was fighting through a gale force storm off the coast of Portugal, when he was struck with what he could only describe as a seizure.

Just before he fell to the ground, he smelled something which evoked a memory from years ago then felt himself go stiff as a board.

As he lay on the deck, shaking and jerking with the convulsion of muscle spasms in the stinging rain, a face he barely recognised emerged, staring at him.

Choking as he struggled to breathe, the face mouthed something that he couldn't distinguish in the noise of the storm, but he could sense the searching behind it.

His journey immediately stepped up a level in its danger, importance and urgency. As the convulsions slowed, his breathing regulated. His lips turned back from blue to a weak pale pink, He lay there, soaking in the downpour.

After a minute or so, he picked himself up, corrected the yacht's course and set the auto-pilot.

His general direction now had a more specific destination.

England.

CHAPTER 28

CERN, Switzerland - Monday October 27th, 2008

Professor Fenkhause sat down with a weary sigh and surveyed the state of his team's laboratory.

The fluorescent lights seemed darker today. The room more cluttered.

It didn't seem the place of joy and excitement that it had been just over a month ago.

He should have known. They all should have. Experiments can go wrong. Theories can be incorrect. For every success, there always was equal and opposite disappointment and uncertainty in science.

So why did he and his team feel so disturbed by this latest accident? Why did they think that they had a monopoly on any certainty of outcome?

He inspected the report from Deputy Head of Hardware Commissioning for the LHC. He refused to believe what he was reading.

The report detailed the flaws in the electrical splices between the magnets the engineers had found. Not just a few. Hundreds. Potentially thousands.

It was almost as if someone had designed them in. A small enough change so as not to be noticed when they were tested. But enough to compromise the system, rendering them useless in the exact scenario that the LHC had just encountered.

The good news was that they didn't need urgent attention. The bad news was that they wouldn't be able run the tests that they wanted to with as much power as they could muster. That meant another delay in discovering the Higgs boson.

They would only be running the LHC at five trillion electron volts, or TeV. Its maximum energy was Seven TeV. This would continue until at least until November 2010 when they could shut it down and patch things up.

Then they would need to maintain that for a couple more years, until they could benefit from the planned upgrade around 2012.

Further delays, millions more Euros and even more egg on the faces of the Board when reporting back to CERN's investors.

That wasn't all though. There was something more troubling.

According to the report, several magnets had 'lost' their training. This Fenkhause could not understand at all.

All the LHC magnets were trained. Programmed how to operate into a stable state where the magnet could reliably work at the current it was intended to handle. This was so that it didn't quench, a reaction not unlike a fuse blowing.

Fenkhause stared through the paper he was holding, as if it were not there.

It was inconceivable. These magnets could not have 'lost' their training between setting and installation.

Nothing, short of deliberate human intervention, could have affected the systems with this outcome.

There was a saboteur amongst them. A heretic in his cathedral.

A chill went through him as he began to comprehend the potential outcomes that this could lead to. He began to question every incident that he and his colleagues had put down to human, computational or mathematical error over the past few years.

Of course he was aware of the fringe lunatics and unbalanced edge cases who thought that the LHC was going to open a gateway to hell. Or suck everyone into a black hole.

But direct action? That would take huge amounts of planning in getting around the security at CERN. The knowledge they would need to integrate into teams who had access to the LHC, the ATLAS experiment and other systems?

No, it was not possible.

It wasn't like you could walk in off the street, get a cleaning job and gain the clearance level necessary to enter these types of environments. That kind of plot scenario was left to dodgy sci-fi films.

There was no other explanation.

He reached for a mug of cold coffee, which he sipped even though it had the consistency of mud and tasted burnt at the same time. He needed time to digest this information. Work out how to address this without raising awareness of his concerns with the person or people responsible.

That was another blow. How many people actually were there? Who could be behind this? What country would possibly want to create a diplomatic situation through the annihilation of a large part of territory that held the head offices of so many international organisations? How far did this network extend? Were off-site suppliers involved? What else should they be investigating?

He was suddenly very aware of the nearby city under which the LHC was sited.

All those lives. All those people. The weight of responsibility crashed mentally on his shoulders. He physically slumped in response as the realization dawned on him.

Not only was he a scientist, hunting for the origins of life on the planet. He was also now a criminal investigator. Searching for individuals unknown who wished to cause harm to tens of thousands of people. Deliberately.

He felt a dull pain behind his eyes as the beginnings of a stress headache began to form.

He needed to rest. It was late and he'd been on the go for hours.

He closed the report slowly and carefully locked it in his drawer. He gently hung his lab coat in his locker and left the lab.

He would sleep on the issue and see if it brought some clarity on any appropriate action he could take in the morning.

Hopefully the cold light of day would enable him to make an informed decision.

As he went into the night, he felt completely out of his league, unchartered territory to him. It dawned on him that he was a little scared.

A part of his scientist's mind couldn't resist commenting, "That's interesting."

CHAPTER 29

Geneva, Switzerland - Sunday November 2nd, 2008

Karvorkian smiled to himself as the private jet made a perfect landing at Geneva Airport and taxied up to Terminal Three.

It was one of the perks of the job. He could access vast resources from various investments made hundreds of years ago by their ancestors. It kept him in the manner he was accustomed.

Another shell corporation owned this particular private jet. It wasn't just the convenience it afforded. It also enabled further information gathering exercises. It was hired out by some of the most powerful men and women in the commercial and political worlds.

Intoxicating alcohol, altitude and pretty women in uniforms. Combined, they loosened otherwise tight lips and un-buttoned buttoned up executives. Senators, royalty and members of various ruling elites were not exempt either.

Karvorkian was smiling to himself.

Not because he had suddenly grown to delight in his gruelling travel itinerary.

He'd just received a coded message which told him that his most recent assignment was complete. The resulting analysis led to only one outcome for the upcoming election.

This most recent course of action was more grounded in real-world action than their usual methods. It had consisted of a number of prongs.

First, teams had focused on the ballot-rigging activities of recent times. They'd restored machines previously designed to favour one party back to factory settings. This ensured the voter's choice was correctly registered. They disposed of and replaced those officials who had resisted this process.

Second, they freed up ballots withheld from overseas force personnel. These would now arrive with enough time to count.

Third, they re-registered those who had been unknowingly disenfranchised.

They reinstated those unfairly struck off the voting register.

They cleansed the electoral roll of fraudulent voters.

Finally, they began the sizzle.

A campaign of subliminal messaging was injected into broadcasts. Editing of copy in newspapers and magazines employed neuro-linguistic programming techniques to reinforce the fact that there was only one real choice to be had, and that was one of change.

The Watchmen knew that this was a risky strategy.

The projected winner of the election was no more or less capable of guiding the country and world through a period of chaos caused by their actions than the jokers in the other party.

However, as a symbol, their candidate represented an idea. It was this idea, held in the hearts and minds of the population, that Karvorkian and his compatriots wished to encourage.

The notion that one man can make a difference.

This was of course a completely false hope. But it provided a controllable and useful force for however long they needed it. It would help balance out the negative actions that they'd be focusing on one place, to utterly destroy it. In doing so, they would secure their own future.

Happy and unhappy accidents, he thought.

His smile waned as the cabin de-pressurised and the doors were set to manual. Out into the bleak cold of a buttoned-up city full of jumped-up pricks who thought they were making a change in the world or a fortune in their pockets.

They didn't have a clue what real power felt like. They were just fame hungry charlatans, gambling with their lives, winning a little but never big. The house was always stacked against them, he thought, as the plane door opened and he stepped out.

#####

Manek, dressed in a chauffeur's outfit, picked him up. He drove an anonymous-looking but top of the range limousine, complete with blacked out windows. They made good time to the lake house.

As they pulled up, Karvorkian found himself thinking what a shame it was that the house and the lake were in Switzerland.

He made a mental note to ask one of his staff to get in touch with the architects. See whether they could build several identical ones in different countries of his choice with a similar aspect.

He very much approved of the lines, décor and layout of this house, but it wouldn't be appropriate to keep it as a residence. Too much evil had been perpetrated within its walls in the short time since its completion. It would hold too much Bad karma to live with permanently.

It didn't bother him that the very convention on human rights that had been drawn up in the city not so many miles away from the house was being broken on a daily basis by his hand. He was ambivalent to it. The actions were necessary, simply a means to an end.

To take someone's humanity away from them and replace it with another, he argued, was better than death. Whilst they had no qualms in choosing death as an option when entirely necessary, it wasn't the only solution. He wasn't a monster.

Indeed, the reason for his visit was to see the advances in a very promising solution to making problems disappear. Without any mess at the end to tidy up.

As he took the steps two at a time energetically, the front doors swung open. Karvorkian was greeted by some of the house staff. Dressed in white medical smocks they lacked badges or other identifying features.

No one in the house had identification. Many of them didn't know their own, true identities. They had been wiped and re-booted in a less well-developed process than the one Esther was undergoing at that moment. He knew this because he could hear her screams.

#####

Karvorkian entered the room a few minutes later. Esther was sobbing quietly, the effects of the sedative only just kicking in.

102

Doctor Charles Damen, the man Esther saw on a daily basis since her incarceration in the house, greeted Adnan Karvorkian warmly. He guided him over to the bed where Esther lay.

Karvorkian examined her face with great interest. His cold, black eyes pierced her somnambulant state. His stare penetrated into her skull like a needle through her retina.

She tried to flinch back.

He put a hand on her arm. She couldn't pull back, the restraints were too tight.

"Hello my dear. And what's your name?"

"I don't know. I don't know."

"Well now. That's fine. It's not a problem. How long have you been here?"

"I don't know. Really, I don't."

"Well, the doctor here tells me that you're doing very well and that you're responding well to treatment. Isn't that right doctor?"

Dr. Damen nodded vigorously and smiled. "Yes indeed. Very well. Remarkably well in fact."

"Do you remember the doctor's name?"

"I. Uh. No...no."

"That's okay. It's alright."

He patted her arm once and then turned to speak to Dr. Damen.

"So the memory loss is permanent?"

The doctor answered with a negative.

"Not at the moment. We still can't be certain that we've blocked all her memories. However, we can repress them chemically. We can manage their suppression through medication and a new implant we've been developing. It slow-releases a formula over time. So it's an entirely manageable situation."

Karvorkian nodded thoughtfully.

"And the new personality and memory layer?

"This is working better than we'd anticipated. With the study from Boston and Japan which you secured, thank you again, we were able to modify the MRI scanner. We stimulate the synapses and generate new memories to construct the personality. We combine that with hypnotic suggestion. These memories should be permanent within the brain architecture. They have a special marker which means that the suppressive implant will not affect them."

"That's excellent. So when will she be ready for me?"

"Well, Mr Karvorkian, I would think around a month or so's time?"

Karvorkian stared at Dr. Damen. He disliked people using his name.

He tolerated the good doctor's usage of it only due to his current usefulness. Once he could replicate the procedure, the doctor's usefulness would end. The doctor was unaware that the house's security system had been recording his every move.

Karvorkian eyed Esther again, and enjoyed another pat on her arm.

"Well, my dear. It seems as if we're going to have a lovely New Year together once you've got your memories back. I'm looking forward to it. We'll be thick as thieves you and I in no time."

To Esther's horror, he then leaned forward and kissed her on the forehead. His lips burned into her skin and made her restrained limbs feel like they were crawling with insects. All she could manage was a whimper.

Karvorkian smiled slyly and stood up from the bed.

"Excellent work again, doctor. I'll see to it that you're compensated adequately for your progress."

"It's a real privilege Mr Karvorkian. I thought my best work was behind me, but you've opened up a whole new avenue for me to pursue."

"Well, as long as you don't publish, our agreement will stand."

"Of course, of course."

Esther watched them as they both headed out from the room, then closed her eyes tight.

Karvorkian. Karvorkian. Karvorkian.

She tried to burn the name into her mind, associating it with the kiss on her forehead that was still tormented her.

She might not know her own name, but she knew that she had to remember this one.

Her life might depend on it.

CHAPTER 30

Lundy Island, off the coast of the United Kingdom – Sunday November 2nd, 2008

The Land Rover's passenger door opened as soon as the helicopter blades had stopped rotating.

Ben thanked the pilot, dragged his kit bag from the seat beside him and jumped down to the soggy ground.

A hum-dinger of a rain storm was pelting down, so he was especially thankful that the pilot was an adrenaline junky. Most normal commercial pilots wouldn't have stirred from their offices on an afternoon like this.

Ben's boots slapped in the wet as he made a beeline for the vehicle, its horn now frenetically beeping like the Roadrunner cartoons.

Just as he got to the door a towel catapulted out and Ben grabbed it before it fell to the ground.

With his other hand, he swung open the rear door and threw his pack on to the back seat, then jumped in the front.

"Good trip?" Gerry grinned enthusiastically, with a glint in his eye.

Ben returned the expression, giving Gerry a playful punch on the chin.

#####

After a relaxing day and night in Paris, Ben had caught the early evening Eurostar to London. He'd checked into a boutique hotel fairly central, then gone for a quick run. He showered then headed out for an early supper at The Wolseley, which he fell in love with all over again. As he walked back to his hotel on Charlotte Street, he finally acknowledged that he was dog tired.

He was asleep as soon as his head hit the pillow.

The next morning he found a swimming pool.

He ploughed through a couple of miles before a breakfast of egg white omelette with ham, granary toast and green tea.

The next few days were spent shopping for some new clothes. He checked out what had changed in the years he'd not been around. Generally he enjoyed the sights and sounds of this surprising lively city.

It was a far cry from Geneva.

On Sunday morning, he reluctantly checked out of the hotel and headed over to Paddington train station. Heading down to Exeter St. David's, the weather turned ugly. Sheets of rain slapped against the window, obscuring the view to just a couple of feet. It kept up for the majority of the two-hour journey.

Ben closed his eyes and tried to sleep, but he kept picturing Esther's face.

In Exeter, he had to run to make his train connection, but it was almost deserted so he easily found a seat. He was at Barnstaple around an hour later, so he texted Gerry to say he'd arrived. His phone buzzed twenty minutes later. A helicopter would be waiting for him at Hartland and that the Stagecoach bus should be there in a couple of minutes.

The 319 did indeed turn up within five minutes. A driver who appeared to Ben to be around forty years over official retirement age angrily opened the door and told Ben to get in. After shouting the fare at him and grating the gears, they jerked off, the rain still lashing down. Ben couldn't help get the feeling that the guy wasn't on a scheduled service trip. Someone must have shouted very loudly at someone else to get him out here. He was the only one on the bus.

At the other end, in Hartland, after thanking the driver who went puce in the face, Ben dashed through the deluge. He got to the small airport. A guy with a sign greeted him. They were up in the air within seven minutes and swaying all over the shop. He stole a couple of glances at the pilot sitting next to him, a huge smile on his face and eyebrows up near his hairline. Ben felt the same way.

With that final precarious mode of transport, Ben arrived on Lundy Island and into the hospitality of one of his family's oldest friends, Gerry Bairstow.

#####

As the Land Rover bounded over the bumpy road, Ben whistled at the sight of an imposing Victorian mansion house that appeared out of the gloom.

"I'm glad you approve!"

"Wow Gerry. How on earth did you get your hands on this?"

Ben had not seen Gerry face to face in several years due to his various placements and postings. The last place he'd visited in England was a relatively small cottage in a Surrey hamlet. This was a world away from that.

"It's a bit of a story but the short version is, recession. Lundy's a protected nature reserve and under the control of the National Trust after a generous old man bought the island in 1969 and gifted it. It's managed by the Landmark Trust. However, times are tough. So, when I heard through connections that they were seeking to raise a bit of money as well as offload some costs, I was in like Flynn, you might say!"

They parked up and collected towels, bags and other bits and pieces. Gerry explained that the house had been built in 1835 for a family called Heaven. It was traditionally the place where the island's owners, of whom there had been several, lived until it passed into public trust.

It had been run as a going concern in the form of a hotel and guest house since the seventies. But fewer and fewer people visited the island, preferring instead the appeal of the Caribbean or other exotic destinations. The number of guests meant it had become more of a liability rather than a help supporting the main purpose of the Trust's activity, conservation.

Gerry added: "It takes a particular type of person to live in an environment like this, but we love it. There are just about enough people on the island at all times not to feel isolated. I get to use the transportation services at a discount and we're good for all the utilities. The only thing we can't get is cable and the fifth terrestrial channel, but that's the last thing I'd have on my wish list. We can always search on the internet for programmes, so it's no loss."

Ben swung his bag over his shoulder, feeling damp all over. "Sounds like you're set up for good Gerry. Just one question."

"Oh? What's that?"

"How is the local brew? And what is it?"

Gerry laughed loudly, squeezing his still-portly frame out of the driver's seat. The diet obviously had not been going too well.

"You know me Ben. Strictly a grape rather than a grain man, so I can't really tell you."

Ben shrugged.

"Ah well. I'm not tied to beer. I guess I'll survive."

"Glad to hear it, old son. Now, come through, change up and let's get something to take the edge off before we eat. What do you say to that?"

"That sounds like a great plan. Lead on, m'lud."

Gerry waved an arm at the pantry door. "No, after you, old chum. I just need to lock up behind you," adding quickly, "not for security, mind, just so the wind doesn't blow a lake inside."

Ben headed through the door and gratefully removed his boots in the porch. He missed Gerry's furtive inspection in the misty gloaming before he slammed the door shut and threw the bolts across.

Lights flicked on in the rooms inside. The wind blew outside, carrying only the sound of some seagulls cackling away like witches boiling bones and a faint crash of waves against rocks not too far away.

#####

Glenda Bairstow was obviously delighted to have company and even more ecstatic that it was Ben. As he'd come down from a hot shower and changing clothes, she'd hugged him with a vice-like grip that was incredibly powerful.

She was a foot smaller than him and barely managed to get her arms around him entirely.

"Oh Ben, it is so good to see you again! I'm delighted that you've finally left the Forces. What you've given over these years obviously is so respected. But personally, I've always worried about you. I'm so pleased you're out of harm's way."

Ben smiled fondly down at her, and put his hands on her shoulders, kissing both cheeks.

"I'm touched that you say that, Glenda. It means a lot."

Glenda tutted and threw her head from side to side, a glassy aspect in her eyes. "Come come, now! I'm being a silly old goat, nagging you after your long journey. Come into the living room. We've got a lovely fire going."

She led him through to a cosy drawing room, kitted out like a Scottish laird's club house. Dead animals adorned the walls, along with landscapes in watercolour partially hiding tartan wallpaper. Deep, well-worn leather couches interspersed dark mahogany occasional tables around the fire. Low-light lamps with red velvet shades and tassels cast a moody light about the room. The fire cast shadows across the walls, bringing the animals to life again to hunt in the flickering light.

They had a brandy to warm themselves up before moving into a small dining room. Ben was force fed a huge meal with a continuous supply of red wine.

Conversation flittered from the happenings in Geneva through to local politics and the state of the economy.

As the night drew on, Glenda excused herself to clear and wash up the dishes, at the protestation of Ben. The two men moved back to the lounge. Gerry sloshed out two more very large brandies before they slumped into settees. They gazed at the embers of the fire in silent contemplation.

Finally, Gerry asked the question.

"So Ben. I can't help unless I know what the problem is. Want to tell me about it?"

"Who's saying there's a problem?"

"Come on. I've known you for too many years. I know when something's off. You're still young and fit. You've got many years of good service in you yet. You wouldn't need to fly a desk for at least a decade. So what made you leave?"

Ben stared into the honey-coloured liqueur and spun the glass slowly in his palm.

Gerry had asked the one question that he'd not dared to ask himself. Why *had* he left?

"To tell the whole truth, I don't know, Gerry. One day I just woke up and it felt right."

Gerry hummed, nodded once and slurped on his brandy.

"I guess it's kind of how I've lived my life to date. I do things because they just feel, inherently, right to do."

"Like a kind of life beacon? An internal sense guiding you along a path or course, you mean?"

Ben thought for a moment, and then shook his head.

"It's not even as clear as that, but it just seems that it's what I'm meant to do. Not in a deterministic way, like I'm compelled to do it. But in a way where I've subconsciously chosen from a number of different paths and the right one has bubbled up into my consciousness."

"So, what's that old sub-consciousness telling you to do now then, old bean?"

Ben glanced sharply up at Gerry.

"That's just it. There's nothing. It's like there's a gap. I'm waiting for it to happen, but perhaps it's not the right time. Perhaps I need to wait."

"Or perhaps you're in exactly the place you're meant to be?"

Ben nodded.

"Yes. Perhaps. But there is more."

"Oh?" Gerry's eyes were sparkling as he enjoyed the conversation and the warmth of the brandy.

Ben explained about seeing Esther again, his surprise at the meeting and his feelings about seeing her again. Then he explained about her abduction.

Gerry listened intently, sipping from his glass every now and again.

When eventually Ben stopped talking, it was his turn to give a little whistle.

"Well, that's quite some encounter Ben. I need to think about this. Promise me you won't mention a word of this to Glenda? She's only just come down from the high about you leaving the Forces. Getting yourself into the middle of some gang of thugs and their power plays will not help her heart one bit."

"For sure, understood."

Gerry grunted as he made his way in stages to get out of the sofa.

"Ben, leave it with me for a day or two. I have a few, ah, contacts that I can press to see whether we can shed any further light on who these crooks might be or what they're up to. I need to make some calls but I think I know a couple of fellas who might be able to help."

"Gerry, be careful, for God's sake. The last thing I want is to mix you up in all this, whatever it is."

Gerry harrumphed. He poured himself another large brandy at the impertinence of Ben's last comment.

"I can take care of myself young Ben, don't you worry. I'm old enough, ugly enough and fat enough to squash any potential threat."

He raised his glass enquiringly. "Join me in one more?"

Ben smiled and wagged his finger slowly back and forth.

"Sorry Ger. I'm out of practice. You'll need to give me a couple of days to get up to speed to match your rate. I'm going to hit the hay if you don't mind.

"Spoilsport. Never mind. Get some rest. We'll chat further in the morning."

Ben grasped Gerry's hand, who then pulled him into a bear hug.

"We'll sort it out, don't you worry."

"Thanks Gerry. For everything."

#####

In his dream, Ben was running with Esther around the base in the early morning mist. They were kids again. Running made them feel good, alive. They ran fast, enjoying the burning sensation of chilled air being sucked into their lungs and forced out with every pace.

Esther kept up with Ben, even though she was three years younger. Ben liked Esther.

She was a funny kid. She was regular height, but lithe with it. Still boyish, which was probably why Ben felt comfortable around her. She had yet to grow any curves.

They were pounding the concrete path around the security fence, running the perimeter of the camp where they had access. They did this most mornings before breakfast when they could.

It was their time. The silent companionship gave them the space to share moments without speaking. A joint sense of appreciation for their environment and their place in it.

Ben remembered this particular morning. The sun came up between the mountains that he'd forgotten the names of. It was like a single beam of light that cast itself in a long, golden path that stopped right in front of them.

It provided one of the few moments where they were stopped in their tracks. Panting with hands on hips, staring at the beauty of it, knowing they were in a minority of human beings to see it. They looked at each other and grinned.

At that point, his dream diverged from his memories. He gazed out at the sunrise and it transformed into an explosion, complete with mushroom cloud.

Bits and pieces of debris were falling from the sky. Shrapnel through to chunks of machinery, artillery and fuselage.

He drew his attention back to Esther, but now she was wearing the clothes he'd seen her wearing in Geneva. Still a child, they were far to big for her. Her mouth was opening and closing, eyes wide with fear. She reached a hand out and he did the same.

No matter how far he stretched, then ran, he could not reach her. She seemed to be in the same place distance was twisted. One of those tricks in a dream.

She started to fade. Just her, everything else was as clear as reality. She just became more and more transparent, until in a final shimmer, she disappeared completely.

Ben finally made it over to the place where she had been standing. All that remained was the attaché case she'd left behind at the café in Geneva. He clicked it open and was blown backwards by an explosion. Booby trap.

Before he landed on the ground, he work up in a cold sweat.

The remnants of a peel of thunder faded into the night.

Ben groaned, turned over and reminded himself never to eat cheese in the evening again, no matter how insistent Gerry was.

CHAPTER 31

Lundy Island - Tuesday November 4th, 2008

Ben was running around the island, sweating out the residual alcohol of yet another boozy night with Gerry the previous night, when his phone beeped.

The morning was crisp and blustery. The chill wind had finally chased away the storm clouds of the past few days.

As he ran along the path, he was careful to take in the terrain as well as the view. A five hundred foot fall of steep cliffs was only a few meters away from the path on most sides of the islands. A strong gust could push him much closer to a fall than he would appreciate this morning.

His head pounded from mixing his drinks the night before. The exercise was a painful but necessary penance.

He'd run one length of the island, which was around three miles long. He was heading back down towards Gerry and Glenda's house when his phone chirped into life.

He slowed down to a pace and pulled it out of his hoodie pocket. It was a message from Kevin Daste.

Target identified by Interpol. Call me.

Finally, a break-through. Rather than fumbling with cold fingers on a device he'd still not got used to, Ben decided to run back to the house and make the call from there. He'd rope Gerry in on it so he wouldn't have to explain things twice. Introduce the two was a wise precautionary measure so they both knew each other, in case of any unplanned emergencies.

In ten minutes and he was back at the mansion. Another thirty and he'd showered, changed clothes and was sitting down to a plate of egg and bacon, black pudding and a even blacker coffee. All served up by a beaming Glenda.

#####

"Kevin? It's Ben."

"Hello Ben. How is Blighty?"

The line was crackly, perhaps as a result of the storm the previous night.

"Good thanks. Kevin, I just wanted to let you know that Gerry Bairstow, who oversees most of my financial affairs over here, is on the line too. Just so as not to blind-side you."

Gerry boomed out, "Hello Kevin, good to talk to you. Thanks for helping out Ben over there."

"Mon plaisir, Gerry, good to talk to you too."

Ben got straight down to it. "So you've made the goon in the CCTV footage?"

"Yes, that's right. It was a bit of luck to be honest. We happened to have a liaison team from Interpol over. Showed us a new facial recognition system they were trialling. More as a challenge than as a specific thought I put the picture we pulled in front of them and asked them to try it. Their system had a match within minutes."

"That means he's on the system? He's already been tagged?"

"Yes..."

"That's great."

"...and no. He was caught in a combined sting operation between Italian and our police forces. Drug smuggling over the border. However, during or just after processing, he disappeared. As did the drugs. We think there was an inside man on the Italian force, but of course it wouldn't do to say such things."

"So what? What does that mean?"

"Well, they'd managed to take his picture and fingerprints, but that's about it. We don't know his name, nationality or other connections."

Ben thought for a moment, and then asked Kevin, "What about the drugs? Cocaine? Heroin? Perhaps something that had come in from Afghanistan that was being shipped into Europe via the Italian mafia?"

It was Kevin's turn to pause.

"No. Not Class A drugs in that sense."

"Then what?"

"Prescription drugs. New ones. Experimental ones."

"Does that make sense to you?" Ben asked, turning to face Gerry who was frowning.

"Without a market, it's difficult to conclude who would want such things and what they are intended for," said Kevin. "It seems strange that we've not heard of this occurring before. We have no knowledge of its purpose or destination. And we've only recently discovered the source of the drugs themselves."

"Wait, you traced their origin? Where were they from?"

"Not the Middle East. Unfortunately, they were produced in a lab for hire, which was leased by what appears to be a shell company. Another dead end."

Ben grabbed some paper. "What's the name of it?"

"What, the drug or the shell company?"

"Company first, then drug."

"Well, the company is called Caradine Pharmaceuticals. It's registered in the Cayman Islands. The drug is called AK-ZM Beta 7, and we have no idea what that labelling means."

Ben repeated the spelling of both and Kevin confirmed he'd got it.

"Kevin, you're a star. Thank you again. I'll do a bit of digging and let you know what I find."

"Be careful, Ben. If this guy can disappear on us with what we confiscated, you can bet he's got some serious friends behind him pulling strings."

"Understood. Will do. Speak soon."

Ben put the receiver down, turned to Gerry and grinned.

Game on.

#####

The automated monitoring system registered the use of two keywords in real-time. It copied then sent the entire audio recording of the conversation to a pre-specified email address. An automatic coded SMS alert was also sent to the Standby Team, which immediately went into action.

Within minutes of Kevin, Ben and Gerry finishing their conversation, the location of both parties had been identified.

Given their use of both trigger keywords and the analysis of the depth of their knowledge, a pre-determined order was put in place around half an hour after they had finished talking.

Two teams were dispatched. One to Geneva, the other to a little island just off the British coast.

At the time, the Commander of the Squad felt it was inappropriate to inform those for whom he worked of this activity. His operations were set up such that he had automatic authority to conduct activities such as these when the time was right.

As there was no mention of Esther in the phone conversation, the Commander was unaware of the bigger picture. He was also unaware that his oversight would have far greater consequences than he had anticipated.

His teams were going out to try to patch up two new leaks in an already punctured inflatable. At least one of the teams would not return.

In hindsight, it would have been better to let the dinghy sink.

CHAPTER 32

Lundy Island - Wednesday November 5th, 2008

"Well David, as you well know, old lawyers don't die, they just go back to the bar!"

Gerry had made a few firm contacts throughout his legal career and with whom he continued to maintain a relationship. He'd spent the previous afternoon and the morning on the phone, calling in favours. As the morning turned into the afternoon, Gerry played telephone tag with a couple of them. He hoped to identify the man in the CCTV footage or uncover any information on the operations of Caradine Pharmaceuticals.

Ben meanwhile felt about as useful as a chocolate teapot. He sat and tried to read the paper but it was full of nothing he was interested in. Events happening around the world that he felt no connection with. Struggling after the first few pages, he threw it away in boredom and instead switched on the television.

Property programmes. Inane chat shows. Reality television segments about common people with common problems. Antique valuation programmes and American rah-rah gung-ho shoot 'em ups.

Ben stared open-mouthed as he flicked through the four channels. No wonder television was described as the drug of choice for the masses.

It was utter shit.

He meandered through the house, taking in the rooms, and came across Glenda polishing silver in a vast banqueting room. He spent an hour chatting with her, buffing off the cream and polishing up the hardware, which gave him a sense of peace.

He realised that this was his own personal opiate. He'd simply replaced his dress boots for some forks and spoons and got lost in the reflections of the past.

Having run out of silver there, they left the room and made some tea.

Glenda reminisced about the olden days when she was a stenographer and when she first met a much slimmer Gerry up in London town.

"He was so handsome, I almost missed two lines of his cross-examination! He was so smart and stern in his wig, I was barely able to stop flushing. I didn't think that he even noticed me. But, at one particular point which he made and which drew a huge laugh from the public gallery, as he was turning round, he winked at me! I nearly fell off my chair and the Judge was banging his gavel like it was an end-of-pier game. That was a lovely day."

She wiped her eyes, almost using the polishing cloth before pulling a handkerchief out of her pinafore.

"That evening, he asked me out to dinner. We had a dance – yes, Gerry could dance in those days – and then he brought me back to my lodgings. We kissed on the step. We were married in six months."

She smiled wryly as her eyes sparkled.

"He's put a pound on for every year we've been together since, silly old fool! But hopefully, with you around, he'll get a little bit more exercise."

Ben grinned.

"I remember meeting him for the first time. I ran and hid behind the sofa, I thought he was so scary. I think he was shouting, re-enacting a court room drama he'd been through that day for Mum and Dad, but I thought it was real. He scooped me up from behind the couch and sang funny songs until I'd stopped crying. Then he threw me up and down in the air until I felt sick from laughing and motion sickness."

The afternoon was filled with reminiscing until they realized it was nearly five. A huge pile of silverware sat gleaming on the long rustic kitchen table.

Glenda made her excuses and began to prepare supper, but suggested that Ben try out the only pub on the island nearby as he had time.

Thinking about how much alcohol he was likely to be plied that evening, Ben decided against it.

As the weather was clear he decided to go catch the sunset instead.

He stuck his head in to Gerry's study as he left, indicating that he was popping out, and was released with a wave and a nod. He had the telephone receiver stuck to his head, writing furiously away.

#####

Ben headed West. Past the church and across country up to the old lighthouse. He crested the hill just in time to see the sun sink into the sea and release a huge splash of red, pink and purple across the cloudy sky.

The view was mesmerising. The sea crashed against the cliffs, huge structures of air and water billowing across the sky like transportation units guided by some unknown force.

Glancing down and to the left, he could just see the southern end of the island. He decided to walk around, down to the landing beach on the South East side and then back up to the house.

There were several people who lived permanently on the island during the tourist season. They ran the guest houses, the pub and performed maintenance on the island and its utilities. This time of year, they were at a skeleton crew level. There were no tourists who generally stayed after dusk in the winter months.

As he walked down to the intriguingly named Devil's Limekiln, which was actually a sea cave, he noticed someone walking towards him. Tall, well-built and dressed in dark fatigues, Ben assumed he was a part of the conservation team. Perhaps on the wildlife side of things which required a certain level of camouflage in order to stalk the island's critters.

Right up until the point that a hunting knife was projected towards him, Ben had not anticipated a threat on the island. His instincts kicked in. He swerved, grabbed the wrist that the knife was in, pulling the arm across his front whilst stepping behind the man. Quickly punching the man twice in the kidneys, his other thumb applied pressure in a spot in the wrist he knew to cause extreme pain.

The man grunted, dropped the knife and tried to kick back at Ben's legs with his feet. He missed completely.

In a fluid motion, Ben tipped the man up, twisted and slammed him down on the ground.

The man expelled the air in his lungs and Ben landed a foot in the small of his back.

He made a sound, expressing his pain automatically. With no air, there was little vocalisation.

Ben checked the man for further weapons and found none.

No ID either. There was a tattoo but not a recognisable one. Keeping force on him and holding both wrists in one hand, Ben reached for the knife and threw it over the edge of the cliff.

"Up you get."

He yanked the man up, quickly moved behind him and forced his hands on his head.

"Listen carefully, buddy. I don't know if you speak English, but any funny business and I'll take you down again, and this time you'll stay down. Understood?"

The man did not react.

"Your call, pal. Come on."

Ben pushed him forward, continuing on the path. His mind was turning over but his first thought was how and when this guy got on to the island.

His second thought, how many others there might be with him, corresponded with a loud explosion from the vicinity of the house. Ben saw the sky, now a deep purple transitioning into a star-studded black, turn fiery red again.

"On no."

The man turned and smirked at him in the twilight. Ben threw one punch, knocking him out cold, and ran back to the house as fast as he could.

CHAPTER 33

Lundy Island - Wednesday November 5th, 2008

He stopped as he crested the slope. His chest heaving, he stood in horror, seeing flames coming from every window of the building.

A bullet ricocheted off a rock, spitting up stone fragments, a foot or so away from him. Ben cursed. He'd been sky-lining. His silhouette was clearly visible against the last purple light on the horizon and the few stars that had come out. An amateurish and life-threatening move. He zigzagged forward, dived down, rolled then crawled to an area of scrubby grass and tried to seek out the other assailants. In a couple of seconds he saw a gleam from a telescopic sight on a rifle just a couple of hundred meters away.

Then a flare went up and a green glow joined the red flames from the fire licking at the sides of the house.

There was a shout from the opposite direction, from neither Gerry nor Glenda.

It sounded like a scout.

Knowing he'd been spotted, Ben jumped up, again ran in a zig-zag and dove into one of the out-buildings of the mansion.

His one chance of survival was close combat, so he'd force them to hunt for him building by building.

As long as they didn't have any explosives left, he'd be fine.

#####

A few minutes later, Ben stood over three bodies in the outbuilding, wiping his hands with a rag.

The first dead man was the rifleman who'd taken a pot shot at him.

For some reason, they'd lacked the foresight to bring any night vision equipment. So when he'd stuck his rifle through the door first along with his other colleague, he'd not seen Ben perching on a beam above them.

As they entered the building, Ben simply dropped, focusing his centre of gravity as low as he could.

He landed on the rifleman's head, snapping his neck instantly.

Using the collapsing body to cushion his landing, he rolled off quickly. He adopted a low position as the rifleman's partner turned to see what had happened.

He held a pistol in his hand. As it came up, Ben spun and kicked it away, a snap signifying that he'd smashed the man's wrist.

Before he could scream, Ben punched him in the throat, then brought a foot swiftly up between the man's legs. As the guy bent forward, the air rushing from his throat, he snapped around again with a high scissor kick. It sent him crashing into a vertical post face first, his nose cartilage and bone splintering into his brain. He swayed momentarily then then dropped to the earth.

Ben felt heat as the door behind him, which had swung almost closed, open again wider than the wind would have blown it. Instantly he sprang back into shadow.

Another man staggered into the building, obviously disorientated. Ben manoeuvred around him, keeping to the shadows. Then he jumped, kicked and dispatched camouflage man for the second time that evening. This time for good.

"Told you I would."

He checked for pulses quickly. Finding none, he turned and ran back to the house.

There was no chance anyone would have survived if they had been in there.

Nothing would have.

As a habit, Ben carried his most important possessions with him at all times, the things he couldn't do without. Additionally, the things that he couldn't carry, he stored in safe places that he knew would survive for decades.Over the years, the things he carried changed. Now, these consisted of his passport, his new mobile phone (with important numbers stored on a memory card, out of the phone's internal address book), a wallet with some cards and his driving licence, a set of keys and a small emergency kit in a flare-sized waterproof canister.

He had the clothes that he was standing in. That was it.

He went back to the outbuilding now being temporarily used as a morgue and checked the men again.

This time, he left with the pistol, several packs of ammunition, another knife, some flares, the rifle with scope, a balaclava, gloves and one of the men's black jackets.

As anticipated, none of them had identification on them. He also checked for similar tattoos to the knife man but there were no unifying marks. Dead end, literally.

It was time for him to go. He had to leave the island.

He couldn't risk being tied up in police enquiries or locked up in a place where the people who'd sent these thugs could get to him quietly.

The only way off that he could see was to get down to the landing beach and see whether the men had left anything that might get him away safely. As he ran off through the trees, the first signs of the locals reacting to the flames manifested. There were shouts of panic and frantic activity to find something nearby that might start to douse the inferno.

Good luck with that, Ben thought.

He was suppressing his emotions with anger out of necessity. He had to be dispassionate until he could re-group.

He had a clear mission.

As clear as the silhouette of the person standing in front of him on the pier beside the yacht. He slowed from a run, to a jog, then a walk. His fists were balled, but not yet ready to reach for a weapon.

The man simply stood there, silently waiting. Ben approached him.

This was no mercenary. This was something, someone, else.

A ghost.

Someone who should have been dead.

"Dad?"

"Hello, Ben. I didn't expect to see you again. It's time to leave. Jump on."

CHAPTER 34

The World – Wednesday, November 5th 2008

Every front page of every newspaper around the world that had a free press (or the time to hold it) ran a picture of the incoming president of the United States of America.

Partial or full phrases from his carefully co-ordinated campaign ran in the headlines, positive and bold. Comments were sought for rolling news channels. Pop and television stars through to coffee street sellers were sought. Voices of previously ignored minorities and the disenfranchised enjoyed their moment in the limelight in this particular political carnival.

The positive outpouring of hope, empowerment and joy at the impossible made possible in America accelerated around the world. It picked up speed due to the viral network effect of social media, something the candidate's team had excelled at tapping into.

It was not just relief that the 'other guy' hadn't got in. There was a real and emotional response to what seemed to be a modern-day miracle.

Aside from the lunatics on the fringes at both sides, the racists, the small-minded and those afraid of change, the world's inhabitants that could read, listen to a radio or television or access the internet felt buoyed by this historic win.

They forgot for a moment that this new hero was a trained lawyer, a politician and a player. They focused on the fact that he was an African American, born to a broken home. And that he'd managed against all odds to win the biggest contest in the world.

They felt that this was a man that they could trust. Someone who understood them. Someone who could change things. Someone they could associate with.

They felt on the edge of an exciting new world, of peace, hope and prosperity.

They dreamed that, if they believed hard enough, good things could come to good people.

They ignored the fact that this was a campaign.

They chose not to remember that the winner had done so through a multi-million dollar marketing campaign.

They overlooked his training as a lawyer meant that, like the out-going Prime Minister in the UK, he had learnt to use words with care. To retain knowledge better than most. To employ strategies that enabled a compelling and winning argument to change people's views.

They completely missed that he was not a super hero, merely human. Like them.

He had no inherent skills to be able to change the world by himself.

No skills apart from a gentle sense of humour. An oratory ability not observed in politicians for decades. A winning smile. And the ability to reach out to people across the world through the internet.

Those four things which the world saw and embraced created a massively powerful outpouring of hope, if just for a few days.

That's what tipped the balance.

One man can change the world. One man can make a difference. Even if he was not doing it on his own.

Others were about to learn this lesson.

CHAPTER 35

Lundy Island - Wednesday November 5th, 2008

The locals were trying to find some way of managing the inferno so that it wouldn't spread to other flammable sources. Ben and his Dad took the opportunity to sneak back into the out-building through a door on the side of the structure not facing the house.

Using as much cover as possible, they dragged the bodies one by one over to a rusting car trailer and dumped them in. They then heaved that over to the cliffs before tipping it into the sea. It was the easiest way to deal with the situation and get out.

This was done with little talk beyond instructions given by Ben and acknowledged by Nathan Fallow. Ben could see his Dad straining with the effort. A wiry and gaunt fellow, he'd never been bulky. Ben noticed that the muscles on his arms, whilst not big, seemed strong as cables and sinewy. He looked like he'd been working out but had a cyclists rather than a body-builder's physique.

The shock of recognition had focused him on doing what needed done, then getting the hell out of Lundy as quickly as possible. Now finished, they raced down to the boat. Ben's Dad stayed behind whilst he jumped on board to untie the ropes securing them to the jetty.

Then they were off.

Ben watched as what seemed like a massive pyre flamed and smoked, sparks flying high up into the night.

He just hoped that Gerry and Glenda had not suffered.

As he gazed back he saw the blinking lights of a helicopter rushing towards the island. No doubt it had a cargo full of water to dump on the building. He shook his head at the carnage of it all.

Then he turned back to his Dad. All he could see was a black silhouette of a figure with his hands on a ship's wheel.

Yet this shape had come from out of nowhere, stood in front of him and spoken, years after he was supposed to have died.

Ben walked, swaying to balance himself as the yacht pushed on through the waves. He viewed his father side-on. He didn't speak in case he distracted him. They were navigating through some treacherous rocks he'd mentioned just before they left.

Underneath a well-worn peaked cap, he saw a leathery face.

Eyes, bright but sunken, with several bags under each. A prominent brow, brimming with bushy white eyebrows. A strong nose and equally strong lips, turned up at the edges, mainly covered by a salt and pepper beard.

His chin was sticking out. Muttered words escaped as his eyes darted from the ocean to the instruments and back. He was in the zone. It was as if Ben didn't even exist, let alone the fact he'd not seen him for several decades.

Ben began to ask if he could help with anything but a hand fluttered in his direction, combined with vigorous head shaking.

He headed below deck and inspected the quarters. This was a serious amount of junk, he thought.

He went through the cupboards and eventually found a half-full bottle of brandy.

Grabbing a small glass, a shaking hand poured a glug from the bottle, re-corked it and put it back in the cupboard.

Dropping down into a cabin seat, Ben raised the glass, closed his eyes and said a prayer for Gerry and Glenda. Then he slugged back the warming liquid.

He sat quietly as the yacht ploughed on through the waves. Ben mentally reviewed the most unusual, sickening and shocking day of his life to date. He briefly explored how he felt about it, then let it wash over and through him until it remained a memory without emotion.

He collapsed sideways and fell asleep.

#####

When he woke up, around twenty minutes later, he found his father sitting in front of him.

It was still a shock.

"Where. The. Fuck. Have you been?"

"Yes, well, it's nice to see you again too, Ben."

"Seriously?"

"Seriously. If I had told you, I would have had to have killed you, or someone else would have."

"What's that supposed to mean?"

"It means, Ben, that I was doing something sufficiently important that I had to give up my life, my wife and my son, in order to satisfy myself that no harm would come to you. That my death would, hopefully, close off an avenue of investigation the people I was concerned with would then stop pursuing."

"So why are you back?"

His Dad whistled, jerked his knee awkwardly and touched his fingers to his thumb on his right hand. His eyes scrutinized something in the air above Ben's right shoulder.

"Is there something wrong?"

"Hm. No, hm, I'm fine. Hm, hm. It's a part of, hm, who I am I suppose. It happens when I start feeling out of control socially, which is quite frequent.."

"Okay...so what is that, like, some kind of illness?"

"No, not so much. More of an amplification of certain attributes. Which has, as a side-effect, some physiological and sociological manifestations."

Ben stared at him, not speaking. After a while, the movements and noises subsided and his father was able to engage Ben's eyes again.

"I've been on my own for an awfully long time, so forgive me. It's especially hard as it's you."

"You didn't know I'd be there?"

His father moved his head rapidly from side to side.

Ben couldn't tell if it was a tick or an acknowledgement of his question.

"I didn't know where, I didn't know who, I only knew the clock was ticking and I was potentially going to be too late."

"I'm sorry, I'm not really getting any of this. What are you doing? What is all this about?"

The man sitting opposite him sighed.

"It's a long story, Ben. Very long. And it now involves you. Against all my hopes, I fear it has always involved you. But how, I can't yet be certain. But we will know soon I think."

He got up, checked the computer which was currently showing weather, tidal flows and a course direction. He flicked a couple of switches, hummed and nodded again.

He turned around and studied Ben for several moments.

"Ben, I'm not the man you knew. I'm different now. I'm still your father, but I have taken on another role."

He turned back to the entrance to the galley, moved and closed the hatch.

With his back to Ben, he continued.

"There are very few people in the world that know what I do Ben. I believe that our role – yours, mine and one other for now – is to restore the balance of luck in this world. Transitioning its control out of the hands of the few and into the hands of the many."

Ben's mouth opened wide.

As he turned, Nathan Fallow said, "My name is now simply The Historian, as will yours be when I'm gone."

Then he smiled wistfully.

"It is good to see you again, Benjamin. What would you like to eat for tea?"

CHAPTER 36

Domaine Du Lac Saint-Prex, Switzerland - Thursday November 6th, 2008

She woke from a disturbing dream that she couldn't remember as soon as she opened her eyes. It was still dark but she could see dawn's first light creeping over the mountains.

Yawning and stretching, she spun herself around to the edge of the bed. Putting her feet on the floor, she felt for her slippers with her toes.

Flicking the bedside light on, a warm glow cast itself across the room. She hopped up and walked lithely across to the dresser. An espresso machine sat ready to squeeze out a perfect wake-up shot for her.

Switching it on and popping a capsule inside, the machine delivered a beautiful aroma of bitter-sweet coffee as it streamed gently into the cup.

Taking the tiny porcelain container over to a white leather seat which faced the lake, she folded herself into it and snuggled down, just as the morning rays began to creep over the crags.

She loved this time of the day. She always had. There was nothing more that she delighted in than sitting in a chair, sipping a hot espresso and taking in the sun rise. New beginnings.

She especially liked it here, with the fantastic views of the lake.

She was really looking forward to today, as she was going to be meeting her new boss.

Her role was an important one to him. She was going to assist him with his important work.

His name was.

She woke from a disturbing dream that she couldn't remember as soon as she opened her eyes.

It was dark but she could see the green of the monitor that was checking her pulse, heartbeat and other vital signs. She couldn't see it but she could hear it.

The scratchy machine that made marks on the paper which rolled continuously and which had something to do with her brain.

She heard a beeping from outside of the door. It continued for a few seconds then went off. About a minute after that, the doctor walked in. He rubbed his face then replaced his wire-framed glasses. He assessed her with a frown and sighed.

"Celine. Celine, Celine. You have to stop fighting this. The alternative will not be pleasant."

"I'm sorry, doctor. I don't know what I'm supposed to be doing. What should I do?"

"Just stop fighting your treatment."

"How do I do that? Can you tell me? What should I do? I want to be better. I really do."

The doctor smiled sadly.

"I want that to be the case Celine. You want to be a better person, don't you?"

"Yes. Yes, I want that. I want that so much."

The doctor brushed some hair back from her forehead and patted her gently on the head.

"Then stop fighting. Just sleep. That's all you need to do. Listen to your thoughts. Enjoy your dreams. Accept them. Then you'll be better."

She nodded.

"Yes, doctor. I'll do that. I can do that."

"Good, that's good. Now, get some rest. Do you need something to help you sleep?"

"No, I don't think so, thank you."

The doctor focused on her with his head tilted.

"Fine. Well, goodnight Celine."

"Goodnight doctor."

The doctor was gone and all that was left were the machines. Celine closed her eyes and focused on the darkness, encouraging it to layer over itself and became blacker and blacker. Eventually, she sank back into her dreams.

Not before a soft voice in her head that wasn't her own said a name that had been committed deep into memory.

This happened every time Celine went to sleep and first thing when she woke up.

Karvorkian.

CHAPTER 37

Vienna, Austria - Thursday November 6th, 2008

Karvorkian screamed at the man standing in front of him, throwing his cup and the contents of it over him.

The coffee had been poured, just as Adnan liked it, steaming hot.

To the Commander's credit, he didn't flinch. It hit him on the cheek, spilling the boiling liquid down his neck, inside his shirt and down his front.

"Why the fuck am I just hearing this now?"

"At the time it was not considered operationally important, Sir."

"And who the fuck made that decision?"

"It was routine, Sir. Textbook. There was no reason to suspect that this was a Code Two, Sir. We were following protocol."

Karvorkian stared at the man, the pulse in his forehead visible from several feet away. He clenched his hands by his side, and tried to pace his breathing.

"You did not think when you discovered that the location of one of the parties was the Head Office of the Swiss Security Forces that this was not a Code Two?"

The Commander continued to stare forwards.

"No, Sir. It's not the first time that someone in a position of security responsibility has been dealt with. I'm sure it won't be the last."

Karvorkian nodded sarcastically.

"But you don't think that it was strange? That the person or persons they were talking to when using the keywords were on a tin-pot island off the coast of Britain? With no hint of a connection between them?"

The man's eyes flipped over to take in Karvorkian for a millisecond and immediately reverted to the space a foot or so to the right of his head.

"It did not Sir, no."

Karvorkian's eyes narrowed.

"You really fucked up this time."

134

"Sir."

Karvorkian paced slowly around the room.

"So, to recap. We have one wrecked office building floor. This contains the bodies of some of Switzerland's best and brightest policemen. That's the positive. We also have one smouldering ruin of a mansion house on an island called – what was it, Lunti? Lundi? Whatever. The remains of whomever was in the house are unverifiable, so brutal was the fire. Not so positive. But the best bit? Three of your team in various states of decay are found dead. Floating in a sea cave with broken necks, spines and other bits. By the British fucking Coast Guard. And what's your response? You followed protocol."

Karvorkian signalled two men in the shadows to step forward. They moved and immediately pushed the Commander to his knees.

Karvorkian pulled a long piece of metal, a little like a knitting needle, out of from his jacket.

He thrust it swiftly into the Commander's left ear, pushing hard and quick.

There was a crunching, mushy sound as the steel punched through the skull. It piercing the Commander's brain and ended up just short of coming out of his other ear.

The Commander's eyes swivelled to odd positions. A single drop of blood fell from his nose.

Then he fell forward onto the floor.

"And that, 'Sir', is my response to you."

Karvorkian removed a silk handkerchief. He wiped his hands, even though there was nothing on them, then threw the scrunched up piece of fabric on the twitching body.

He observed the two men standing stock still in the room with him, barely daring to breathe.

"Clean this mess up. And get me a new Commander. One that has a few more brain cells than that sorry mistake for a soldier."

All this power and he had to do everything himself, he thought, as he marched back up the stairs and out of the basement.

"Adnan, is that you dear?"

"Yes, my love."

"The children want a story, and only Daddy will do. Do you have time to tuck them in?"

"Of course, my love."

"Everything myself," he muttered. He trudged up the stairs, heading towards the sound of young laughter and pillows slapping against pyjamas.

#####

The call later that evening was even more of a pillow fight than his children had performed.

After reporting the outcome of the events in Geneva and Lundy Island, there was uproar.

"Ladies and Gentlemen, please calm yourselves. I can assure you that there is no sign of our involvement in these events."

A Japanese male interrupted him.

"With respect. This is the first time that I am aware of in recent history where an intervention has gone so unfortunately wrong. Evidence of impropriety has been left."

"You are correct. However, one should not read too much into one instance in hundreds of thousands over the past few decades."

A French accent, with a hint suggesting that it was not from France but one of its old colonies, brought up further questions.

"Do you not feel that in the past year a significant proportion of our activities seem to be, for want of a better word, soured in some way? Is it not the case that we expect success from our endeavours? Progress?"

A wave of aggressive acknowledgement swept around the conference call.

"You are correct on that point also," Karvorkian spat. "I am no less frustrated than you are about the extraordinary difficulties that we're facing right now. Please remember, I have as much to lose as you do in the future if we do not continue to uphold our preferred course of action."

The group calmed down a fraction at this statement.

Karvorkian grasped the opportunity to jump in and reveal what he knew would cause further upset.

"What has come to light out of all this is that an unknown unknown has now become a known unknown. We understand that someone called Ben Fallow, ex-military, has somehow become involved within a possible timeline that is becoming dominant. We believe that he escaped our intervention somehow and his location is at present a mystery."

"I must add that it turns out this Mr Fallow is the son of Nathaniel and Alice Fallow."

Shouting erupted on the call and continued for a good twenty seconds until there was silence.

An ice-thin, female Chinese voice asked the question on everyone's lips.

"How did we not know this before?"

Karvorkian agreed.

"A very good question. It seems, until now, that he has been hidden from us somehow, shielding his importance to us. Perhaps the loss of his father at such a young age dulled his importance. Often without guidance this can happen. Something has happened recently to change that and thrust him back into our path."

He clenched a fist.

"But, now we know, we can work to make him a known known. After his performance on Lundy, we should consider our strongest response possible. Out of respect for the people he killed."

There were one or two murmurs on the call, but most were still shocked at the revelation.

Karvorkian sucked in a breath and threw the final hand grenade in.

"Without wishing to ruin your festive period, I have also had reports from CERN that repairs are progressing well. There is a renewed vigour within the team. While there are a considerable number of repairs to attend to, it seems that these will be finished by the Summer. They expect the experiments will begin again in the Autumn."

Cold silence swirled on the call.

If hatred could be visualized, bitter dry ice would have poured from the speaker phone.

"Ladies and Gentlemen. It has been a long, difficult year. An annus horibilis as the British Queen once put it. We are all in need of a holiday, to refresh and replenish our strength and powers. May I suggest the best course of action is to see how our recent success on the world stage progresses? The President will be inaugurated early next year. I may even see some of you at the ceremony although, for obvious reasons, I will not be able to say hello!"

A few participants laughed and Karvorkian noted a slight thawing of mood. He smirked as the belief that they were all in this together re-balanced their emotional investment.

"So. Well. Let me wish those of you who have festive holidays coming up the best of wishes. Those with New Year's celebrations soon, I wish a prosperous future to you. We will reconvene next year unless there are any other unforeseen circumstances in the meantime."

A number of participants said farewell greetings before the call ended. That was unusual.

Karvorkian sat in the silence. He contemplated for the first time whether it would be his generation that would see the end to their power.

The world seemed to be turning up-side-down and anything could happen.

Snapping out of his fugue, he stood up, chomped his teeth together a couple of times and flicked on his intercom.

"Yes, Sir?"

"Bring me a scotch Manek. And find me anything on Nathaniel Fallow."

"Sir."

He kicked back in his chair throwing his feet onto the table, laced his fingers together and cracked his knuckles. It was time to fight.

CHAPTER 38

The English Channel - Thursday November 6th, 2008

Ben and the man who used to be Nathaniel Fallow assessed each other over empty dinner plates silently. It was well past midnight, several hours after they'd left the chaos of Lundy Island.

Whilst cooking, Nathaniel, now The Historian, explained that they had to move to a place of security. A place where technology infrastructure was less embedded in the fabric of society for a couple of months to lay low. This would give them both the time and space for Ben to learn about the recent past as well as prepare for his new future.

The Historian had decided that Funchal in Madeira would be a viable option.

It was quite far off the coast of Morocco in the North Atlantic Ocean, under Portuguese authority,

He also explained that it would be impossible for Ben to understand in just a few short hours why he had lost his father. What he was up to now. How it all involved Ben. Ben was to trust what he said, even though it might seem contrary to his better judgment. Trusting a man who had pretended to be dead for several decades.

Ben couldn't argue with the last part. For some reason though, he felt he knew what his father - The Historian - said to be true.

"So. I guess we get used to this for the next few weeks then?"

The Historian nodded.

"Yes. We'll stop off a couple of times on the way to re-fuel and re-stock, at which point you can get some more clothes and, you know, things. Don't worry about money. I have access to funds."

"How?"

The Historian grinned like naughty child.

"That would be telling! Ha! Not yet."

Then his face dropped slackly.

"Now, it's time for me to document the world. Excuse me. I need to go and search for things that aren't there again."

With that, he stood and went into another section of the cabin.

A mass of what seemed like a bunch of old technology lurked.

With a click, the junk sprang to life and Ben could immediately see that it was state of the art.

"Camouflage," he mused.

His father was sat in front of three screens that wrapped around him like a virtual reality conference centre but on a smaller scale.

What appeared to be a hub and spoke representation rendered on the screen.

The earth at the hub and what turned out to be articles, videos, blogs and other news sources on the outer branches.

He manipulated this with some kind of gesture-based attachment. It turned the whole thing into a hands-free operating system. Additional streams of information ran in various different blocks on the screens.

The Historian pecked at these with his fingers variously, picking what appeared to be algorithms out. Then he'd throw them at different places on the screen.

Ben couldn't be more confused.

This guy had the essence of what he remembered to be bits of his father's traits were he to have met him twenty years later. He had features similar to those of his father from a few old photographs he'd saved.

He remembered his father was slightly eccentric. He never really had the chance to talk to his Aunt and Uncle about that.

A thought suddenly struck him. Did his father know that Alice was dead?

He would wait, he decided, a few days before he raised the subject. He didn't know how he would react.

He obviously seemed to find it difficult to talk about emotions, people and those types of things. Hell, Gerry was one of Ben's father's closest friends. Yet there was little response to seeing the charred remains of the house that burned him to death.

It must be some kind of autism Ben mused. Especially seeing him operate the computer and what was on the screen.

The guy in front of him was the poster child of what a heightened intellect could achieve. Along with many drawbacks, depending on one's perspective.

He looked inside himself.

How did he feel about his Dad being alive? That was interesting. Perhaps he was still in shock but it was difficult to work out his feelings on that on.

He backed away from the harder question forcing itself into his mind.

Instead, he headed towards his bunk and lay on the bedding area.

He'd barely slept since the events on Lundy the previous night. He desperately needed a good sleep to be able to cope with the oddities that the world had thrown at him over the past week.

Remember, remember, the fifth of November. Gunpowder, treason and plot.

Abso-fucking-loutely, he thought, as he sank into his unconscious.

CHAPTER 39

Vienna, Austria - Thursday December 4th, 2008

Karvorkian devoured the information he'd been delivered an hour ago. It had taken some time to access the archives, but the information had finally arrived.

Nathaniel Tristan Francis Fallow was born to a mathematics professor Edward Fallow. At one time Edward held the Chair of Mathematics at Oxford University. He had solved a number of mathematical problems previously thought unsolvable.

His mother, Kristina, was perhaps surprisingly a leading Russian ballerina. When she was in England with the Kirov Ballet, she met and instantly fell in love with Edward and defected.

Nathaniel was their only son. The War intervened before they had a chance to expand their family further. Sadly, Kristina was arrested and incarcerated. Edward, perhaps fearing for his life and potentially being branded a traitor or Communist, disappeared. He left his son with a close friend, Oliver Bairstow, to be raised up as a brother to Gerry.

At some stage in the next few years, it transpired that Nathaniel was different. He was withdrawn and found it difficult to interact with others. At the same time, his capacity for problem-solving was immense.

At seven, he was a chess prodigy. At eleven, he had taken advanced level mathematics. He had even solved Fermat's Last Theorem, decades before it was re-solved in the nineties.

Not only that, it appeared that he had a photographic memory and a voracious appetite for history. Given the relative proximity of the war, this type of history fascinated him the most. He would consume books on battles, military strategy and global politics and commit them to memory like a machine.

He had of course gone to Oxford, albeit having to put up increasingly with comments regarding his politics due to his parents. Studying history, he flew through his degree in two years.

Given the Cold War and other issues of national importance, it was not long before the British Government had heard about him through academic papers that he'd written. He no felt very uncomfortable at Oxford. So Nathaniel jumped at the chance to work within the bosom of a protective diplomatic job. He accepted a position as a military analyst with high-level clearance as soon as it was offered.

His use to the government could not be under-estimated. He spent a happy couple of decades smoothing out some significant issues into only minor creases. Then he was seconded to the United Nations. There were some particularly rough areas of the world that benefited from his expertise.

It was on one of these missions that he met Alice, a field nurse from Australia. She broke through his autistic wall and made him fall in love with her. She was the opposite of him. Physical, beautiful in a natural way and the life and soul of a party. She adored him.

They got married and it wasn't long before Ben came along. They travelled around the world continuing their work with the United Nations. Until one day, Nathaniel disappeared whilst on a mission.

That was where the official record stopped. But Karvorkian knew that the official record was incomplete.

Nathaniel Fallow had got on The Watchmen's radar because he had been working on a side project. He'd been trying to build a better model to map the world's political flares and try to work out how to pinch out flames before they grew too big.

In the course of his research, he'd stumbled across areas of interest to The Watchmen. He became a Person of Interest to them.

It had seemed that the clean-up job they'd done back then was thorough. But if a person disappeared in a desert and failed to ever re-appear? That was not concrete evidence that someone had performed a perfect job, was it?

Karvorkian's recent experiences reminded him. All of them, the support teams that they relied upon, had become complacent.

They had trusted too much on humanity becoming a race of couch potatoes on their own. First radio, then television, then computer games and now social media had all sucked at their souls and energy.

They had relied too heavily in the dismantling of serious educational institutions. The dumbing down of schools and examination systems around the world by successive governments, demotivating and demoralising the population. Make them take menial and un-fulfilling jobs so that they would rush home to consume the next instalment of that nation's favourite reality show.

But with free access to technology, the problem was getting bigger, rather than smaller. Technology was liberating people, not enslaving them. It gave them access to more, not less. It broke down barriers and inspired, rather than depressed and repressed people. This was unacceptable.

A thought occurred to Karvorkian. The internet had made money flow extremely easily. Become more liquid. It had made once difficult tasks of legends - building new, fake lives - easier. And Nathaniel Fallow was a whizz at computers, right from the word go.

The British government hadn't understood computers. They still didn't. Nathaniel must have walked all over them. Using his high level clearance to build his own knowledge and blend it with technology.

In that moment, Karvorkian knew that Nathaniel Fallow was alive. He knew that he was still on their path. And he knew that Ben Fallow was now involved too.

What a fight this was shaping up to be.

CHAPTER 40

Funchal, Madeira - Wednesday December 24th, 2008

They had arrived at the harbour at Funchal in the dark, their red and green sidelights glowing like lonely fairly lights.

It was Christmas Eve and the day that Harold Pinter, the English playwright had died. Ironically, one of his memory plays described where Ben and The Historian felt they'd arrived.

No Man's Land.

The one blessing was that it was at least warm, even in the rain, compared to where they had come from.

It had taken them nearly two months to carefully work their way down the western part of Europe, pretending to be on a once in a lifetime trip. Not rushing.

They re-stocked as they went along, making minor repairs here and there. As promised, The Historian managed to magic up the required funds every time they made dry land. Boys with envelopes stuffed with local currency ran to the piers or down harbour steps. Ben did as he had promised and didn't asked questions.

Having never been to Madeira before, Ben was slightly surprised that The Historian had chosen it. He knew it as a tourist destination and quickly saw that it was a popular one at that.

"Yes," The Historian had acknowledged.

"So why here? Surely there's enough infrastructure and surveillance here to effectively spot us?"

The Historian was coiling rope meticulously.

"It's a tourist destination but not one that's at the top of people's lists. Funchal has a population of just over one hundred and ten thousand people. The next biggest town is around forty-five thousand. In total though, there are just under two hundred and seventy thousand inhabitants. But each year it draws nearly a million visitors. So tourists outnumber inhabitants around four to one."

He moved on to the next rope.

"Most tourists come from Europe, meaning that we'll blend in well. However, an important point to note about Madeira is that it is an offshore financial centre. That means it's one of those places that administrations tend not to want to poke their noses in too far."

He glanced up at Ben and winked.

"Madeira gained political independence a couple of years back from Portugal. It's prosperous, growing, has a diverse terrain in which we can get lost yet still easily sneak back into town when we need to. And of course, it provides ample access to the kinds of funds we may need."

With that, he swung himself over the side of the boat and on to the harbour, with the energy of a man half his age.

As he slung a kit bag over his shoulder and Ben clambered on to dry land as well, The Historian gazed at the harbour wistfully.

"Besides. I thought you might like to see where I proposed to your mother."

There was a little twinkle in his eye, reflecting the harbour lights which sparkled in the water. As he turned, these were replaced by the Christmas decorations that were out in force.

As Ben watched The Historian march off towards civilization his eyes searched further up the hill. Built on to the side of the inactive volcano was a sprawling conurbation. Lights twinkled from tiny windows like stars plucked from the sky and stuck to the rock.

Christmas music floated down through the air. He followed on, musing on whether or not it would be worth going to a therapist after whatever was coming had concluded.

So many mixed feelings about what had happened in a few short months. Ben felt confused beyond anything he'd experienced before. Learning what had happened over these past few months were the result of events put in play decades before staggered him to the core.

And yet, there was his father. Marching off towards a festive setting in a warm climate that seemed to welcome them as strangers. Offering them the protective custody of anonymity. He couldn't help but smile.

That was perhaps the trick. Don't be concerned with what is out of your control, and don't worry about what's under your control, he thought.

"Come on! Let's get some Espada and bananas. You'll love it!" The Historian grinned.

Ben shook his head and laughed. He headed after the man-child who was running into the crowd as if it was already Christmas Day and there were presents to open.

CHAPTER 41

CERN, Switzerland - Thursday December 25th, 2008

The official close for the Christmas period of CERN was on 20th December. Since then, there had been a noticeable change in the noise levels and heat within many of the buildings. The IT Department had requested all non-essential machinery and equipment to be shut down until early January.

It took Ebhart a good few days to acclimatise to what felt like a dead environment. He'd spent so much time at the facility as more and more equipment came online, connected, started processing theorems. Being disconnected from any one of his sources of data felt almost like losing a limb. He had the memory of what it performed and yet could not access it to help him. He was over-dramatizing of course. He would be easily able to reattach himself to it early the next year, unlike the loss of a limb.

He knew that many, both in his own department and related ones, were starting to whisper about him. Some from his own team expressed concerns about his well-being more forthrightly. People like Chenni for example, who made sure to bring him soup and bread regularly. She also took his lab coat and swapped it for a fresh dry-cleaned one on a regular basis.

Today, Ebhart was sitting quietly in his lab, taking stock. It felt somewhat appropriate to be here, in his cathedral, on the day that Christianity had appropriated from more medieval religions. Religions that worshipped nature.

Today, Ebhart did not feel particularly like celebrating. Instead, he was working through his own theories about who was trying to sabotage his life's work.

Over the past few months this had added to the pressure he felt under. He had no idea who inside or outside of CERN or his immediate team that he could trust.

He had doubled down on checks and balances as the repairs continued.

The positive thing was that they seemed to be a good position to be operational mid-way through next year.

But the damage had inevitably led to much stricter contingency plans being drawn up. It had driven down the total power that they could use in order to work towards identifying the Higgs boson. Things would take a lot longer.

This in itself wasn't the issue he was worried about. The issue was, with things taking longer, there was time to experience further acts of sabotage. Opportunities that could present themselves as accidents would continue to be logged as such. Ebhart simply could not risk alerting people to the fact that he was aware that chance was not a factor in these events. There was a deliberate hand guiding actions.

And it was not divine.

For now, Ebhart knew that he needed to continue his pretence. Pretending he was unaware of the subversive activity being directed at his experiments.

He had already discounted that there was anything personal against him in these actions. There would have been plenty of times where, both here in the lab or outside in the real world, he could have been 'bumped off'.

No, this was an attack on science. That meant one of two things. Either a religious organisation, perhaps a fundamentalist one, had no desire to see their power base crumble. The clear demonstration that matter and not faith constructed the reason for humanity would do that. Or that some other unknown group, perhaps of countries not in the CERN alliance, had other designs on the discovery of the Higgs boson.

In both instances, Ebhart had no data on which to base any kind of response. The worst possible scenario would be to alert them to the fact that he knew something was going on but that he had no response to it.

Thus, his best course of action was no further action. Or, more specifically, no further overt action. He was no spy, but he could operate with a political will when it suited him.

Science was also a cut-throat business with only a few prime positions such as the one he currently held. There were plenty of usurpers who would dearly love to get their hands on the resources he controlled.

So this was a dangerous game.

Ebhart needed to steel himself to play it. Against unknown and unmeasurable opponents.

He would have to be careful.

Very careful.

And he would have to remember to feed himself. And wash. And pretend that the world was all right and that people were not trying to create a huge crater in a neutral country in central Europe. And that he was as far as he knew the only one who was trying to stop that.

His mouth went dry for the umpteenth time that day. He sighed, rubbed his eyes and picked up his coat, forcing his arms through it.

Switching off the lights, he moved through the lab doors and trudged his way out of the exit and into the festive snowstorm.

CHAPTER 42

Geneva, Switzerland - Wednesday 31st December, 2008

"Celine, may I introduce you to your new employer Mr Karvorkian?"

Celine's eyes shot up from her Kindle. She immediately put down on the sofa and stood to greet the man. He was impeccably dressed in a dinner suit and bow tie that had been tailored beautifully.

"It's a pleasure, Sir."

The man stared at her for a couple of seconds, searching for any recognition that they had met before. Nothing. His face broke into a smile as he reached out to her hand and pumped it firmly once.

"I'm delighted to meet you Ms Matheson, I've heard great things about you."

Celine blushed. It was more to do with the uncomfortable way that the man's eyes bore into her than any complements coming out of his mouth.

"I do my best Mr Karvorkian."

"Well, Ms Matheson, it's all one can do, after all. I hope you are ready?"

Celine nodded and indicated to the executive suitcase next to the sofa.

"Yes, all packed. Although I must admit I will be sorry to leave."

The man inspected the architecture, admiring the open plan aspect of the living room with the views over the lake.

"Indeed. It is an impressive building."

His eyes crawled back to her face.

She shivered inwardly.

"However, I hope you'll find that a change of scenery will be as enthralling as this place."

The man turned and said his goodbyes to Celine's most recent client. After a moment's disorientation, she remembered that he was a scientist. Yes, that was right. He was pursuing a line of study into behavioural change in mice.

151

It was apparently very exciting.

She'd been recently secured as a research assistant to cover while his existing one was on maternity leave.

"Well, Dr. Damen, let's get Celine's coat shall we? We've got a long journey ahead of ourselves and it would be appreciated if we could miss most of the New Year's Eve traffic."

"Of course, bien sur, Mr Karvorkian, I understand entirely."

Dr. Damen turned and indicated to another member of staff who presented Celine with her coat.

He approached her until he was close enough for Celine to smell his tepid breath. She steadied herself internally, wondering why she was taking so much offence from the attention of these two men.

"Well my dear, I'm sorry to see you go, but c'est la vie!"

He kissed her on both cheeks. His hands squeezed her upper arms gently before he stepped back and admired her as if she were some kind of ornament.

"I'm pleased to have been of help Dr. Damen. I would appreciate a reference on LinkedIn if you feel that my services were of use to you."

Dr. Damen chuckled. "LinkedIn. Of course, my dear. I'd be delighted to endorse the skills of Celine Matheson."

Celine smiled back, confused by why this might be so amusing. Coat now on, she joined Mr Karvorkian who was walking towards the door.

Another man, no less odious to her than the others, brought up the rear with her suitcase. She felt his eyes staring at her rear.

They said their final goodbyes and stepped into the limousine, its doors pinging gently as they closed. Inside, it was warm, plush leather seats provided the ultimate comfort.

"So. On y va."

The car rolled down the drive silently. Celine glanced back at the property, lit up like a lighthouse through the curtain less windows.

Whilst her gaze was diverted, Karvorkian admired her for a moment. He wondering how much of Esther was left in there and what would come out if the medication was stopped.

152

He smiled to himself. If he got too bored, he thought, he might just run an experiment for himself.

CHAPTER 43

Funchal, Madeira - Wednesday December 31st, 2008

Ben and the man he now comfortably associated in his mind as The Historian were finishing off dinner. They had eaten out in the Armazem do Sal restaurant on the Rua da Alfandega.

They'd spent the past few days exploring the island and finding suitable accommodation. They could have stayed on the boat. The Historian insisted that space and stability were two key requirements for their time here. Ben noticed that he mentioned no timescales.

They had found a property in the centre of the island which faced north, high up in the mountains. Scouting the lay of the land, they had confirmed that there were ample places to hide. It had good escape routes and some strong areas to launch surprise attacks if needed.

Additionally, the property benefited from a cellar beneath a false floor. A place for smugglers to stash their hauls no doubt.

The Historian hired a bashed-up jeep with local plates. They proceeded to take the essential computing kit and other goods they'd purchased along the way down to the island.

Within a day they'd created some sense of order out of the dusty and forlorn house. The owner was abroad for several years on a contract in Saudi Arabia. The only people that would be poking around would be the letting agents. They were quite happy to sit back and accept the money, no questions asked.

Ben had pressed The Historian for information pretty much as soon as they had regained their land legs. The Historian would have none of it.

"All in good time Ben. You need to relax for a few days, try to put recent events out of your mind. What is coming will be stressful enough, I promise you."

So they spent what free time they had walking, running and visiting some of the more out of the way areas of the island.

Partly out of interest, partly to find out more about the island they were on in case they needed to move quickly.

New Year's Eve arrived. They headed back into Funchal, hearing of the spectacular fireworks that occurred every year.

It was over dinner that The Historian began to outline the coming months.

Ben's eating slowed gradually to a stop as he listened to The Historian outline what he had recorded on the Dictaphone so many months ago. Ben also explained why he had been on Lundy, about Kevin and Esther, whom his father had never met.

"The identities of the people behind all this are a mystery to me. I believe the key to unravelling this is located at CERN, specifically the ATLAS project. I do not know why Esther is involved in this, or even if she is, but I have some idea as to why you and I are sitting here."

"Why?"

"Because you are my son, as I was my father's, and he the son of his."

"What does that mean?"

The Historian put his own knife and fork down and returned Ben's gaze. He sighed.

"There is no such thing as chance, Ben."

"You mean everything is destined? We're destined to do things?"

"No, not quite. There are actions and there are outcomes. But every action has an outcome and there are multiple actions that might be undertaken in any situation. The combination of these actions with an environment results in an outcome, which then feeds into another, and so on. So the outcome is destined but the action, or combinations of those, are made with either conscious or unconscious decision."

"Okay, I think I get it. But why is that important to CERN?"

"It's not. But the existence of luck is."

"I'm sorry?"

"Chance doesn't exist Ben. But luck does. Luck is very real. As real as the air around you."

Ben stared at the man in front of him. Over the past few days he had grown a little closer to him he felt. He thought he had even begun to start to understand him.

This threw everything out of the window.

"Luck exists."

"Yes."

"Theoretically?"

"No. Really."

"Where is the proof?"

"The proof, Ben, is very much what you're living. Esther's kidnap, the devastation on Lundy Island, people dying, our being here. This is the proof."

"I mean scientific proof?"

"Why do you think people are trying to blow up the Large Hadron Collider? Why do you think every other scientific project at the scale required to see at the sub-atomic level has been shuttered or failed over the course of the last fifty years? These people do not want people to find the evidence, or hard scientific proof as you call it."

"Why?"

"Because they control it, Ben."

Ben sat there, stunned.

"They...control it? Like, ration it? Like an oil cartel?"

"In some ways, yes. In some ways, no. Very few people on earth today know about the existence of luck, even though it's a word virtually everyone knows and uses. They know its meaning, but they think of it as some kind of fairy tale."

"Why?"

"Because they no longer know how to tap into its power."

"You can tap into its power? How?"

"Like anything in science, if you observe it, you change it."

"Say that again?"

"When you observe something, you change its state. When you change its state, you change what it does, what its effect on something else has. When you change its state, you can control it. It applies a force that bends things to our will and shapes a positive outcome over a negative one in the life of the person who is observing it."

"And so they want to shut down CERN because the team is close to observing this Luck... particle?"

"Yes, I believe so."

"How do you know?"

"Well, that is my particular talent. I see outcomes as related to actions and, when you study enough of those, you start to see patterns in things that aren't there."

"So how, if you're aware that this Luck particle exists, are you not able to use that against them?"

"To have knowledge of something is not necessarily the same thing as being able to utilise that knowledge. For example, I know many pieces of piano music by heart simply by reading the music and remembering it. That does not enable me to know how to play the piano. To inject the appropriate amount of virtuoso performance to elicit tears and a standing ovation from an audience at the Royal Albert Hall."

"Fair point. So what are we going to do about this?"

"You're going to manipulate luck."

I really should have seen this coming, Ben thought, and gulped a big mouthful of wine.

"And what makes you think I can do that?"

"I don't think Ben. I know."

"And how's that then?"

"Because that's what our family has working towards for over two hundred years. Actions and outcomes Ben. You're here for a reason."

A thunderous explosion forced its way into the restaurant as the fireworks began.

Happy New Year, Ben thought. He stared dumbfounded at The Historian sitting in front of him, who was smiling kindly and nodding.

CHAPTER 44

Washington DC, United States of America - Tuesday, January 20th 2009

No single event in the Capitol had ever gathered such numbers before.

More profoundly, no gathering of this size in this city had been so positive.

Every single individual in the one million, eight hundred thousand strong crowd had hope in their hearts. Imagery from the GeoEye Satellite captured hundreds of thousands of hearts beating wildly in the late morning. They thronged down Washington D.C.'s National Mall. The Washington Monument in the capitol of the United States of America flooded with people.

That hope even touched the cynical commentators, jaded journalists and outside broadcasters present to record and pass judgement on the inauguration of the forty-fourth and first black President of the United States.

To many, it was a miracle that this man had achieved what had seemed impossible for so long. The day after Martin Luther King Day, commemorating the instigator of the twentieth century dream of equality, now perhaps realized in the twenty-first. Seeing this man sworn in to be the most powerful person on the planet was something many considered to be out of a fictional movie. Reality had been put aside for a day, and anything seemed possible.

Security was intense. In the bars and clubs around the country, whispers of whether he would make it alive to see this day had faded into the bottom of beer glasses. Even those of a Republican persuasion waited to see what this day would bring, glued to their sets.

There was a chill in the crisp air, but it stood no chance against the warmth of the people in attendance. Even those accidentally barred from the ceremony as gates shut early soon overcame their complaining. They were just happy to be in the vicinity, inhaling the same oxygen.

There were some mishaps. It was inevitable. This event was effectively the release of pressure that had built up over the past few years. For that to happen, a little more pressure was needed before the safety valve would release.

In all, the inauguration was a success, albeit with some words stumbled over, leading to a re-run the next day. No one was perfect. It didn't ruin the pomp and celebrity-studded nature of the event. All the pop stars and actors provided just the right amount of dumbing down to keep the population amused by the politicking.

But one man knew only too well that, whilst it seemed that he had won over the inevitable, the challenge that lay before him was almost insurmountable. He stated as much in his speech.

He had been involved in that situation where America almost became bankrupt in a morning.

He knew the regulators had barely any more information now about how it had happened than at the time.

They still didn't know who had done it or whether it might happen again.

There had been frequent reminders of the precariousness of the situation throughout his campaigning. But it was reinforced only the day before. Russia devalued the Rouble for the sixth time. The British Government announced a three hundred billion pound bailout package for its banks after a one revealed its biggest loss in history. Bank shares plummeted again.

No such thing as a bankrupt democracy could exist, he knew. Only anarchy would remain.

He also knew there were powers that the previous administration had clumsily alluded to as the 'known unknowns'. Unrelated to Saddam Hussein, they had crept into that security analysis by ineptitude and carelessness, which were all too real. The NSA, with all its funding and technology, could not give him a simple answer.

There were going to have to be some tough questions over the coming months. He had yet to hear the full story until he officially became the forty-fourth President. Above all, he knew that these things had to be addressed against the backdrop of what had turned out to be an erosion of the basic American dream.

What people believed to be the truth, that anyone can make it if they try, had been exposed as a myth.

He knew that the people knew it, and he had to use his eloquence to try to re-set their perspectives. He also knew that he needed to make them realise that an America that continued to stand alone would not be able to stand against those unknown threats.

He also had a sense that power lay, not in the building of forces, but in the people re-building their hope. They needed to extend their view of the world from their small patch outwards, to encompass a wider understanding of their place in the world.

Ultimately, he was well aware that he was a mere puppet, a marionette being played by party politics. He would fight partisanship as long as he could and use his talents to try to wake up a nation sleepwalking to their own demise.

As he moved into position, he rehearsed his key message under his breath one final time.

"With hope and virtue, let us brave once more the icy currents, and endure what storms may come."

Like a wave rushing towards him, he stepped out into a wall of sound and flashing lights.

There was no turning back now.

#####

Karvorkian sat in the Imperial Suite of the Four Seasons at the entrance to Georgetown. It was twelve blocks from the White House and within walking distance to the neighbourhood's many boutiques and restaurants.

For inauguration, the hotel's cheapest room cost a princely one thousand and ninety-five dollars a night. For a five-night minimum. He was staying only two, even though he'd paid for five.

In the background, he could hear the reporter on the television replaying the events of the day breathlessly.

He too had been in attendance but did not share her sense of excitement and adrenaline.

160

He could not recall being this tired at the start of a year.

Many battles still lay ahead, both personally and professionally.

He was tiring of his current wife.

She had started to nag him about his 'work-life balance'. She claimed her motivation was from a sense of love. His conclusion was that it was from a growing sense of jealousy. He travelled, she did not. He ate out, she did not. And so on.

Then there was the concern about his position within the group and the longevity of his tenure. He had yet to find concrete evidence that someone was trying to oust him, but his gut told him that this was the case. He had not settled on a specific plan of attack but everything led him to believe that the best defence was offence. He had to go out and meet the challenge head on before someone had the chance to surprise him.

He needed to identify the other members of his group and watch them. At the first indication of any wrong move, he would strike hard like a cobra.

He sipped his Champagne and turned his attention back to the television. They were showing highlights from the dance.

Karvorkian sneered at the coverage.

It was like the reverse of the film the Truman Show, where the life of one person was being directed for the entertainment of the masses. Instead, this poor fool was being manipulated by a few people he'd never recognise if he met them. He was their entertainment in the course of events he would never be able to comprehend.

Keep dancing Mr President, Karvorkian thought. The tune will change soon.

"Celine, would you ask for the car to be ready at ten tomorrow morning please?"

"Of course, Mr Karvorkian."

"We'll be heading to Europe so keep your warm clothes in your suitcase. That will be all."

"Yes, Mr Karvorkian, good evening."

"Good night to you. Sleep tight."

CHAPTER 45

Monte, Madeira - Wednesday January 21st, 2009

Ben had been training solidly since the beginning of the year. For what, he really couldn't say.

He'd kick off before dawn with an hour of meditation and then proceed with a fifteen kilometre run. He finished up at Porto del Cruz, where he swam for an hour before running back to the house in the mountains. After a protein-rich breakfast of an egg white omelette with ham and some green tea, he would meditate for another hour then discuss events with The Historian.

After lunch and a brief siesta, he would then practice Karate. Another hour of meditation and then he would start practising some of the techniques The Historian had outlined to him.

It was at this point in the day he would usually get frustrated and let that out on a punch bag that they had put up in the cellar.

Sweating, he would then jog to a high point in the mountains and watch the sun go down.

Dinner would be a light affair at the house and bed followed not long after for Ben. The Historian barely slept, immersed in the world of data within the computer. The next day would be the same and so too the next.

His frustrations aside, Ben understood the power of routine and training, repetitious as it was. It meant that what started out as difficult, requiring concentration, could become automatic, like muscle memory.

He had learnt this firstly through Karate and then through the training process in the Army.

Of course, it felt much better at the end of the process than at the beginning. Additionally, it also helped to understand what the end goal of that practice would be, something on which Ben felt was he fuzzy.

He couldn't get his head around why or how he had been pre-destined to be the person to have to go through this alone. Or why this fact had been kept from him.

162

He was angry.

Some of that anger was aimed towards the Historian. The man who should have been his dad but who also had had a role thrust on him before completing his fatherly duties.

Early on New Year's Day they continued the discussion. After the conversation-stopping fireworks display had squeezed its last gasp from the delighted crowds. The Historian continued to lay revelation upon revelation on Ben.

Each point had stabbed Ben's brain and heart with red hot needles.

The Historian seemed oblivious to the effects his words were having on him. It was as if Ben was a hard drive and The Historian was simply transferring data.

Grandfather. Great grandfather. Great, great grandfather.

Each and every one of them had been part of the line of sons who excelled in their field. Each disappeared after marrying and bringing another son into the world. Years later, they revealed themselves to surprised offspring alive and well but, living 'off the grid'. So that they might be in a position to tell their children about the important role that they would play in the future.

At first, it was not understood at all why this was happening. Some knowledge had been lost along the way about why it was so important that this was the modus operandi of the Fallow family.

The Historian had traced their family tree back to the earliest records.

Instead of farmers which the name indicated, he discovered the original family name to be Franklin. It derived from Middle English Frankelin meaning "freeman". It described a land owner of free but not noble birth, from the Old French word franc meaning "free".

They were from an ancient Anglo-Saxon line. It had a family seat in Buckinghamshire dating back well before the Norman conquest.

How could such a family exist, being able to own land but not call themselves Lords?

Why would they then split the family, disenfranchising themselves?

Changing their family name to something far more common, to hide within the populous masses.

"Obviously, something momentous occurred in the Dark Ages that dramatically affected the family. Their power and wealth diminished. It was eventually taken by the Normans. They became simply wealthy yeomen, according to the research I've done. That is until, of course, Benjamin Franklin, scientist and statesman, became a founding father of the United States of America."

"Jesus, Dad!" said Ben, momentarily forgetting his father's new self-appointed moniker. "Are you suggesting that we're related to Benjamin Franklin, the First American?"

The Historian grinned. "And the inventor of the lightening rod, eh?"

But then his face darkened. "Related we may be, but don't forget, there was a fracture in the family. We do not know why and yet we find powerful people, extremely powerful people, on the side of the family that is not the Fallows."

He let that sink in a moment.

"Through the centuries, we see now that perhaps these people didn't necessarily play by the same rules others did. Perhaps they had access to abilities others did not. A once powerful family, reduced to mere yeomen. The Normans taking that power from them and increasing their fortune. A Franklin suddenly attaining great wealth and fame centuries later on a different continent. Turning that land into the most powerful country in the world. Then, recent events in the last century. The last few decades where America seemed to be losing its grip on its power. There is most definitely a shift going on. The transfer of power is under way."

"But to who?"

"That's the question Ben. The answer, I believe, is that this is no longer about countries and continents, if it even ever was. It is about corporations or, perhaps more specifically, the people that own them. Corporations are the true successors to countries. They are the new feudal lords. There are few people left who can truly call themselves Franklin, 'free men'. We are all, most of us, slaves to corporations."

"That's a bit of a stretch isn't it?"

The Historian turned his gaze on Ben again.

"You think?"

Then he nodded.

"Yes. Yes, I suppose. It is a stretch to say that. Without proof, I sound like a conspiracy theorist, I know. I can demonstrate to you what is going on. I can show you the manipulation and the gaps where evidence should be, but that does not justify my conclusions."

"I guess though if you think for a minute about companies like Enron and the like, you're right to signal the power that they hold in the world," said Ben. "The few at the top soured it for tens of thousands of people and the ripple effect was huge. But surely that was just one bad apple?"

"It's not the operation of the corporation, Ben. It's the structure, the blatant motivation of wealth creation. Sucking it from employees and funnelling it up to the few at the top. It's the aggressive 'winner takes all, loser loses all' approach. Business is war. Creation is for consumption, rather than progress."

"Oh, come on. What about your use of technology? You couldn't do what you are doing without your computers. Surely that's a positive of a corporation?"

"Mass production does not equal progress, nor invention innovation Ben. It is another form of control. I am sure I could have achieved similar results using other techniques. But again, you're missing the point. It is not the output that is of importance, it is the intent. We, the corporation, produce for you to pay us, so we can continue to produce for you to continue to pay us. You then have loads of stuff that needs replacing on a regular basis. Increasingly you need to find bigger and bigger spaces to live in, which in turn fuels the need for more and more stuff to fill that space."

"Well, surely people can just stop buying stuff they don't need?"

"You would think. But then, what would happen to employment? It would drop off a cliff. It would ripple right down. The corporate executive fired for not meeting the quarterly target, who would then lay off their cleaners. The house extension would be scrapped. The new car cancelled. Consumption cut, less rubbish would be left out. The municipal bin men would work fewer hours and thus not meet their rent payments."

"Oh."

"Yes, oh. So those that run the corporations know that they're in control. They have governments by the balls. They negotiate the tax they want to pay and governments say fine. Because governments know that corporations are bigger than them. They're multi-national. They squat in the countries they like and then suck the wealth like a mosquito."

"I hadn't stopped to think about it like that."

"You can see it. Multi-nationals are sitting on vast cash piles of billions of dollars, yet millions of people are living on less than one dollar a day. Governments are left to tax the people and provide a welfare state which is tapping into a small percentage of the world's wealth. Corporations are providing nothing back whilst taking the best days of the world's lives."

"Jesus, way to cheer me up. And so I'm supposed to fight a one man war against corporations? How am I supposed to do that?"

"No, of course not Ben. That's not what I'm saying. I'm saying, change the intent, you can change the structure and course of the corporation. To change the intent, you need to shift the balance of power. To shift the balance of power, you need to show people that they can make a difference. To show them they can make a difference, you need to make a difference."

"And how do I do that?"

"By learning how to see luck and use it to your advantage."

Ben threw his head back and laughed.

It sounded like madness. Utter madness.

CHAPTER 46

Vienna, Austria - Friday February 27th, 2009

In retrospect, Karvorkian acknowledged, what was considered a prudent withdrawal of resources from financial institutions incapable of restraint, completely unrelated to the course of events the group had put in place, turned out to be much more significant and related.

Dealing with a group of anonymous individuals, it had proved difficult to predict the effect that the combined withdrawal of personal and commercial wealth from a global system of finance which underpinned civilization in the twenty-first century would have had. And for how long.

Nothing but an entire country calling in debts would have had the same effect on the balance previously. It proved that significant wealth was concentrated in fewer than twenty key players.

Karvorkian saw that the world was coming dangerously close to a tipping point. It was quite possible that more intervention would be required.

The situation was becoming dire. In the first two months of 2009, Iceland's banks had collapsed. Its prime minister resigned. The British banking system was in tatters. Several large investment banks had been disposed of in a fire sale in the United States.

On the twenty-sixth of February, an Economic Intelligence Briefing had been added to the daily updates prepared for the President of the United States. It acknowledged that the global financial crisis presented a serious threat to international stability.

This was not good.

Karvorkian and his allies wished for a balance to be preserved, not anarchy. A chaotic equilibrium of just enough turmoil around the world to mask the actions of the few with power. Maintained with skill, each and every little incident kept spinning. Plates on sticks, creating enough friction to keep others busy.

One plate spinning out of control and it could cartwheel off, knocking many others down.

Political unrest on a mass scale.

Uprisings overthrowing the decades-old political structures.

Dictators being overthrown where once iron rule subjugated.

All these were real threats.

The mass withdrawal had been the one act that had not been thought through. Why? Because they had forgotten the value of money. They had it, it worked for them, and they never needed to worry. Removing it from a system in such quantities was like removing too much blood from a donor.

The system wobbled, went into toxic shock. It was only a last-minute transfusion and induced coma that prevented complete system shut down. Financial and political death.

Karvorkian had to tell them in no uncertain terms that their actions had impacted the stability of their plans. As such, the group's own systems must change somewhat to make sure that these instances would not occur again.

He would argue that what was needed was the ability to gather intelligence about members of the group. Their personal assets and liabilities. To make sure that no such further oversights could occur through what would have been perfectly reasonable activity were wealth not so concentrated in the hands of the few.

A communication was drawn up and dispatched via dead drops and a new date for conference was put forward.

Over the next few days terse responses confirming participation came in. Karvorkian worked on his position, holed up in his study.

He ignored his wife's increasingly angry calls until they stopped.

He heard the faint sound of the front door slamming, filtering down through the air conditioning.

It was time he did something about that as well. She had served her purpose.

His mind wandered to thoughts of Celine as he saw her analysis of the current financial crisis on his desk.

Even with the conditioning she had undergone, she had a sharp mind when it came to this kind of work.

Perhaps she would make a suitable replacement in the near future.

Perhaps once a period of mourning had occurred after Jecca had died in that terrible private plane accident.

Celine had shown no interest when they had landed at Vienna International Airport after the relatively short five hundred mile trip from Geneva.

For Esther however, this was one further step towards a plan for her escape.

After disembarking the private jet, they had again been herded towards another generic limousine. They drove for around forty-five minutes until they reached a castle-style villa set in lush, dank woodlands.

She had seen very little as it was getting late in the evening and there was little illumination provided on the private road. The villa was well-lit inside. The sound of children running around and the general buzz of polite conversation filtered through the air.

She had been directly escorted to a bedroom by Manek. He leered at her, watching her take her 'medicine' for 'diabetes'. She had to inject this into her arm via a pneumatic pen-type syringe. As soon as he heard the spit of the gas-propelled needle puncture her arm, he nodded and wished her a 'Happy New Year'. Then he left and shut the door.

As a member of staff, Celine had not been invited to the New Year's Eve festivities, even as a welcome gesture from her new employer.

As a prisoner, Esther had been relieved that she would be left on her own in a relatively noisy environment. She could explore her new prison without fear of alerting too many guards to her activities.

In that short time before the drugs kicked in, she repeated her mantra, reinforcing the fact that she knew who her employer was. Her captor.

That in turn enabled her to hold on to the little that remained of Esther that the drugs had not suppressed.

The core of her being that knew that something was suppressing her memories. She knew her survival was solely down to how she worked in conjunction with Celine, her new 'flatmate' as she liked to think of her.

As they grew to know each other, they tolerated this arrangement. Esther had no idea how long that would last.

One of them had to eventually evict the other. Until this dawned on Celine, Esther was safe. But time was short. She needed to understand where she was, what Karvorkian wanted with her, and how in hell she could get away with any chance of survival.

She'd checked out the room as much as she could and what she could see out of the window, illuminated every now and again by fireworks. But then she had felt overwhelmed by the drugs and had crawled into bed, still dressed.

Tomorrow was another year, she had thought.

She dreamed of running, as she did every night. The land moved underneath her like a treadmill, but the scenery never changed.

#####

Karvorkian had 'hired' Celine as a research assistant, which sent alarm bells ringing with Esther.

Her superficial responsibilities seemed to be to keep an eye on the financial markets. Flag up any risk factors that might present themselves. Presumably so that he could make informed investments during one of the most deep but potentially predatory recessions in recent history.

She gained free access to a computer with internet connection, and a range of subscription services. These provided a little more depth and analysis than was generally available to non-subscribers.

Esther was immediately placed in a quandary.

She knew without a doubt that Celine's technology use would be monitored. Her every search analysed and logged, each and every website she visited tracked.

If Celine spent a little too long on one page, she might trigger interest in her actions, and that could lead to her being found out.

At the same time, Celine might inadvertently lose focus and start researching things out of her own interest.

This would inevitably lead to interest being piqued again.

It was a minefield. So, she suggested to Celine that they do what every new employee does.

Focus one hundred per cent on the task at hand. No deviations, no hesitations. So that they could make a good first impression. And not get killed.

Celine complied. After all, she was not a fully formed human being. Just a scared collection of implanted memories. Uncertain how she had been pressed into employment in this manner. But those memories were still dangerous. They could trick her body into doing or saying something that might inspire a reaction neither of them would like.

They dug in. Mostly, the research was conducted on their own. Karvorkian was a busy man, always travelling. Neither of them knew what he did for a living but neither really wanted to find out.

His wife, Jecca, and the children kept themselves to one side of the house generally. It sounded like the relationship was under strain. The children were being packed back off to boarding school. This would leave Jecca to one project or other around the house or gardens whilst she was present. Then Jecca went to stay with friends for several days, returning laden with shopping bags from designer stores.

The rest of the time, Celine was kept company by other members of the household staff. The cleaners spoke little English. This wasn't a problem, but they didn't speak French, German or Arabic either. She assumed it was Polish, but it could have been any number of other Eastern European languages.

Then there was Manek. He seemed to double as a handy man one day, chauffeur the next. Perhaps a little laughably given his level of fitness, he was Karvorkian's muscle man also. He was unnerving though. He was a letch,. He spied on them. She could smell when he was around. A mixture of cigarettes, a dank odour and some kind of cloying product he put on his hair.

If there was going to be any trouble, it was going to be with him. On that both of them agreed.

Karvorkian seemed to approve of their work. He even taking them to Washington D.C. for the inauguration of the new President, though confined to quarters. Still, it had the seeds of trust sown, and they could work with that.

If they could continue to work together.

CHAPTER 47

CERN, Geneva, Switzerland - Friday 13th March 2009

Watching the twentieth anniversary celebrations of the invention of the World Wide Web on the CERN Document Network in his lab, Ebhart felt a profound sense of sadness.

His invitation to the event in the Foundation for the Globe of Science and Innovation in Galileo Galilei Square had not just been lost in the internal mail. It had been deliberately waved in front of him by his superior. Then it was nonchalantly handed to a passing visiting professor from Columbia University in his presence. One who bore absolutely no relation to the day-to-day work that CERN produced.

Repairs were progressing well to get the LHC back up and running as quickly as possible.

That still didn't diminish the strength of blame pouring down. Like a water leak in a top-floor apartment making everything below smell of wet dog.

Management was livid at the position each and every one of them had been put in, especially in the current financial crisis. They felt under threat more now than ever.

Big projects had been cancelled before. Even quangos in the European Union were not immune to budget freezes and shake-ups.

So within a matter of months, Ebhart had been reduced from head of the ministry to what felt like the church warden. Fixing broken windows and trying to protect the church silver.

On the positive side, his team had been incredibly loyal. Everyone was driving hard towards the goal of re-positioning the final magnet later that month, testing and then switching the LHC back on in September.

They were all here working, even though some of them had received invitations to the event just about to start.

This again was a pain.

He had hoped that this event might have flushed out the spy.

It would have been easy to narrow down who it might be even if a couple of them had gone along.

But then, he would also have had to have been sure that the spy would have been invited to the event.

No matter. There was time. He needed to play the long game. And for those that were loyal, he felt a deep sense of gratitude.

He turned his attention back to the monitor and watched the event being streamed.

Listening to the presenters would have probably been something that, if bottled, would have been a best-selling remedy for insomnia to the person on the street. To Ebhart, it was enthralling.

The ability to create something new that had never been imagined before was profoundly exciting. To have it used by over a billion people on the planet, was enthralling.

It was a system that allowed scientists to model new theories and share points of commonality around the world. It created huge databases of real-time information sharing. It was a demonstration of all the good that could come out of the work they were doing.

And yet, it was a side-note. Almost accidental. Serendipity.

He began physically shaking at the potential that the discovery of the God particle could have if this is what the effect on civilization was with a mere side project.

He pulled himself together.

His excitement in his work was bubbling up again. The anger at the snub from the top was driving him forward. After months of hard work without thanks, hiding the real reason for the delay, Ebhart finally felt enthused again.

2009 had been declared the Year of Creativity and Innovation by the European Union. He'd damn well show them what creativity and innovation really looked like.

For the first time in months, he smiled to himself.

He was too wrapped up in his own thoughts to notice one of his team taking marginally more interest in him than a moment ago.

CHAPTER 48

Sunday March 15th, 2009

"Doctor, he's awake."

His first sensation was of an incredibly dry mouth, followed by the recognition that he was unable to open his eyes.

"Alright, thank you nurse. Please stand by."

His hearing was a little tinny, as if he were listening to the world around him with the bass range turned off. Dulled.

He tried to lift his head and opened his mouth to speak.

An arm gently but forcefully pushed it on to the bed, or whatever it was he was lying on.

"Just wait. All in good time. There's plenty of time."

He felt that wasn't entirely the case. He knew there was something important that he should be doing.

He just couldn't remember what.

As he lay there, he felt a blood pressure strap hug his arm, hearing the tell-tale sound of a hand pump increasing the pressure. A pause, and then air hissed out. The process was repeated a couple of times.

Then a cold disc was placed on his chest and he was told to breathe in. Hold. And out. And again.

A short hum escaped the person performing the activity and the disc was removed.

"Thank you. Now, can you tell me what you remember?"

"I'm sorry?"

"What's the last thing you can remember?"

"When?"

"Right, let's try something different. Can you tell me your name?"

He frowned, struggling to mentally reach for something. No. There was nothing.

He felt his heart speed up. He didn't know his name.

Again, an arm reached out and patted his.

"No problem, no problem. It happens, especially in situations like this."

He swallowed and croaked: "Situations like...this?"

"You've been in an...incident. Quite a bad one I'm afraid. You've been in a coma for quite some time."

"I see."

There was a pause.

"I'm afraid you don't."

"I don't?"

"Or, more succinctly, you won't. Your eyesight was damaged in the, ah, explosion."

"Damaged?"

"Beyond repair I'm afraid."

He suddenly noticed that he couldn't 'feel' his eyeballs.

"Oh God."

He felt blood racing around his body and his temperature felt like it shot through the roof.

The nurse moved next to him and put a beaker of water with a straw to his lips. He sucked some cool, tepid water into his mouth and swilled it around before swallowing. There was a faint taste of dried blood. He licked his lips then couldn't stop himself from checking if all his teeth were in place with his tongue.

They weren't. That was not a relief.

"So tell me doctor. Am I on my last legs?"

He felt the nurse move quickly away from him, set the beaker down, and exit the room hurriedly.

The door swished closed behind her and a gentle clunk signalled that there were just two of them in the room.

"Ah, yes. I mean no, no! You'll live, of course. I mean you were messed up, but you're on the road to recovery now."

He felt himself slipping back into sleep, with a growing sense of unease.

"Well, that's good news at least."

The tinny sound was receding into his head, and the doctor's words were getting faint.

"But I'm afraid, as to your legs..."

Darkness. Floating. Sleep.

176

CHAPTER 49

CERN, Switzerland - Thursday 30th April, 2009

Professor Fenkhause read the press office communique about the day's activities and sighed. It was an incredibly terse piece of writing compared with the materials put out for the celebration a little over a month ago.

There was no one else in the lab. Everyone was exhausted from the frenetic work to get the last quadrupole magnet underground and connected.

His marking of the occasion was about as far from a celebrated event as one could get. It had the air and respect of a ceremony thrown together at the last minute. Those that deigned to turn up did so with seconds to spare. They listened half-heartedly to his comments and left almost immediately as he had finished.

He read the statement out loud, to see whether it sounded better. It didn't.

"The fifty-third and final replacement magnet for CERN's Large Hadron Collider was lowered into the accelerator's tunnel today, marking the end of repair work above ground following the incident in September last year that brought LHC operations to a halt."

He flinched as he read further down the page. His superiors were really sticking the knife in. He mouthed the quote.

""This is a milestone in the repair process," said CERN's Director for Accelerators and Technology. "It gets us close to where we were before the incident, and allows us to concentrate our efforts installing systems that will ensure a similar incident won't happen again.""

He continued on, forcing himself to reach the end.

The release outlined some technical aspects about how other repairs would run and to what timescale.

At the bottom, the standard boilerplate about CERN, its member states and observers was included. Next to that, the twiddly CERN logo that was an artist's simplistic impression of whizzing particles.

He flicked the page over the desk. It swooped, banked and landed on the floor by his foot.

No mention of how the team had worked around the clock for the past couple of months. Trying everything they could to come in under budget and meet the back-breaking deadlines that had been imposed on them.

No, this was a clear message. This type of mistake would not be tolerated in future. The mission of the organisation was bigger than individual human lives that might be put at risk in order to achieve its goals.

This was science at its coldest. This was a clear signal that the motivations of the countries behind this project were not the betterment of human existence. Instead, political one-upmanship designed to give the leaders a place in the history books as being the ones that shaped conditions for the discovery of the Universe's origins.

Ebhart was low. He could not think of a time when he had been lower. But for the sake of his job, his team and his sanity, he had to pull himself out of his funk.

His life probably depended on it.

He rubbed his eyes with his finger and thumb, pulled his hand down his face until it flicked his bottom lip and slumped down at his terminal.

Where to begin?

He composed a short but heartfelt email to his close team members thanking them for their work. He reiterated his excitement at getting a second chance at exploring the microscopic worlds within the tiniest parts of the matter that made up the universe.

He re-confirmed his vision and belief in their hard work, reminding them of their goal.

He re-emphasised his belief that the Higgs boson would be within their power to prove by the end of the year. He encouraged them to visualize that moment and keep it within their hearts. So that, through good times and bad, they could remember what the light at the end of the tunnel was.

He signed off, "Yours faithfully in science", and pressed send on the email.

He shut his terminal down, dragged his lab coat off his tired frame and swapped it for his overcoat. Bending down to pick up the press release from the floor, he made to throw it in the bin.

Pausing, he then decided to fold it, put it in his coat pocket and keep it as a reminder that things couldn't get much worse.

As he closed the lab door, he tried to visualise his own light at the end of the tunnel.

It looked so very far away from where he was standing.

#####

Karvorkian read the short report from the person that had infiltrated Professor Fenkhause's team.

His associates had hoped that the events they had put into play would have taken much longer to fix. They knew from previous research that there were not enough magnets to replace the entire load. They had not factored in the delight with which the engineers, their suppliers and superiors held in rebuilding, reconditioning and basically cannibalising parts from left, right and centre. Jimmying together a solution to patch up a multi-billion dollar microscope.

It was their own Apollo 13 moment.

Fuckers. Fucking irrepressible scientists, always screwing things up with their experimentation.

And doing it joyously.

Well, maybe not completely. The one positive that his mole could report was that this had hit Fenkhause badly, even though he was trying to cover it up.

Added to that, he still had no idea that all this had been caused intentionally. His plant had tried time and time again to find evidence that Fenkhause was aware of any foul play but there simply was no proof.

They'd installed key-logging software on his terminal. At no stage had he even attempted to begin a search on other accidents, suppliers or security details of employees.

His phone at home had been tapped (he didn't own a cell phone) and his mail and other belongings searched through when he was out. Once a week, regular as clockwork.

Nothing.

Karvorkian smiled thinly. For a scientist, he had hoped that he would have asked more difficult questions.

It would have made him easier to remove. It would have justified more deliberate action.

As the report disintegrated, he threw it into the fireplace. He knew without a doubt in his mind that the penny would drop at some stage. There would be more incidents.

Fenkhause would eventually be eliminated. So too would Nathaniel Fallow, the loose end they had yet to tie up.

He frowned as saw some of the residue of the report smudged on his dark jacket.

The main repairs were complete. That meant that they would probably have to act sooner than they had hoped, and this might affect the balance yet again. Their huge assault on the global balance with this new POTUS was still creating ripples in the chaotic equilibrium, and it had yet to settle. That meant that certain regions of the world were still highly unbalanced. Certain factions, industries and individuals were see-sawing wildly.

A little more time would have those fluctuations settle back down to a less violent rocking, but it seemed like activity at CERN would be full steam ahead before too long.

The lack of any sighting of Fallow meant that they needed to re-double their efforts in that area also. Perhaps cause an event that would make that particular flea jump so they could see it.

"Sir?"

Karvorkian glanced up.

"Yes?"

"The car for the funeral is here."

"Fine, thank you Celine. Would you go and get the children for me?"

"Yes, of course."

Karvorkian moved away from the fireplace, where the embers were dying. It had been cold this year, even in April, but everyone was anticipating a change in the weather.

He buttoned up a black overcoat over his black suit, licked his thumb and wiped a bit of ash from his patent leather shoes.

It was time to go and say goodbye to the wife.

CHAPTER 50

Monte, Madeira - Friday May 1st, 2009

Ben was now so deep in his routine that the days and weeks were merging in to one. He had surprised himself with his ability to kick into an even higher level of fitness. He had thought of himself fit when he was in the Army, but this was awesome.

When he ran, it felt like the most natural thing to do in the world. There was no burning in his lungs. It was like all he needed to do was to open his mouth and as he ran, the air went through him.

He was lean but powerful. Rather than bulk up, he'd managed to concentrate a huge amount of strength into his muscles whilst keeping them a reasonable size. He had virtually no body fat on him. He could still pass as a normal human being when he and The Historian went into town for supplies, blending in so that they weren't seen as outsiders.

His meditation was progressing well too.

He could switch on and switch off at a moment's notice. Everything was going well, except for the main event. The luck training, as he called it. He was frustrated beyond belief at his lack of development.

It seemed an impossible task. Like building a submarine with no materials, plans or tools and without any idea what a submarine was in the first place. The Historian would encourage him to not be too hard on himself, but that would make Ben even more frustrated.

"I just don't know what I'm aiming for."

"That's just it. You can't know. You will understand once you are connected."

"Connected with what?"

"With the world around you."

"Bullshit. That's hippie talk."

"I'm not talking about hugging trees Ben, I'm talking about understanding that you're made of the same stuff. At a basic, molecular and sub-molecular level, we're all the same stuff."

"For sure. But connected? How?"

"Everything is energy when it comes down to it. Energies flow, collide, collaborate. At a miniscule level, everything that is around and in us is a part of that. At this point, all we do experience the parts that we are conscious of. What you need to do is to learn to connect with it. Once you feel it, you can interact with it. Once you interact with it, I assume you will be able to learn to influence it."

"You assume?"

"Of course. I told you, we really don't know what we can do once we are connected. That knowledge was lost to the majority of the human race back in the Dark Ages."

"But if you're assuming all this, how did you come to discover this in the first place?"

"Let's walk, Ben. It's a nice evening and I think it's time for a history lesson. That's best done on an evening stroll rather than inside this shack. Come on."

They stepped out into the early summer evening. The Historian pointed in one direction.

"There's a lot of mystery surrounding Madeira, did you know? That's part of the reason why I love it. It's a place that really demonstrates how luck works."

Ben said nothing, encouraging The Historian to fill the silence with his non-participation.

"Over there is a place called Machico. There's a legend that it's named after two lovers, Robert a Machin and Anna d'Arfet, who fled England in the fourteen hundreds. They were aiming for France but got caught in a huge storm. Eventually they found themselves cast on the coast of Madeira, right over there."

Despite his mood, Ben asked, "Why did they leave England?"

"Not sure. It seems in most of the stories, of which there are several, they were of different classes. He was either a knight, a merchant or an aristocrat. She was of higher social standing apparently, but it's difficult to say as she was known by a number of different names."

"Alright, so what happened to them?"

"Well, again, it's a little difficult to tell. Some tales say that they both died shortly after they were cast ashore. One tale tells that Robert survived, built an oratory over Anna's grave and left the island, ending up in the court of Castille. What is known for sure is that the story indicates that Robert discovered Madeira before the Portuguese. His story endures through time."

"So, good luck or bad luck?"

The Historian smiled. "You tell me. But before you do, what do you see over there."

Ben turned and examined the view.

"The mountain? What about it?"

"Not surprisingly, it's called Monte. It's the final resting place of Emperor Charles the first of Austria. Also known as Charles the Fourth of Hungary, the last of the Habsburg rulers of the Austro-Hungarian Empire."

"When did he die?"

"In nineteen twenty-two."

"Wow. There was an Emperor in Europe in the last century? How did I not know that?"

"He died here in exile. Charles became heir presumptive after the assassination of Archduke Franz Ferdinand in Sarajevo in nineteen fourteen. The event which precipitated World War One after the death of Emperor Franz Joseph. He ruled Hungary from nineteen sixteen for two short years until its occupation by the allies. He abdicated in all but name in nineteen eighteen from both Austrian and Hungarian rule. Then he tried unsuccessfully to gain his throne back twice as political turmoil, allied occupation and ethnic unrest ravaged Hungary."

"And?"

"He was unsuccessful, betrayed by people he had trusted. He was sent here after a decree passed that he and his wife Zita should never return. In nineteen twenty-two, he caught a cold walking into town which turned into severe pneumonia. He suffered two heart attacks and died of respiratory failure on the first of April. In the presence of his again pregnant wife and nine-year-old son, former Crown Prince Otto."

"Bad luck."

The Historian nodded.

"Yes. But. The Catholic Church subsequently beatified him and he is now known as Blessed Charles of Austria."

"Huh. So what are you saying? That his legacy is more important than his life?"

"To a certain extent. But more importantly, those with power have the ability to re-write the history books."

Ben was quiet for a while as they strolled in the cooling air.

The sun was beginning to set, casting swathes or red across the sky and sea.

Eventually he sighed and worked his shoulders, stretching his neck to ease the tension that had built up.

"I'm still no closer to understanding any lessons from what you've just said in terms of luck, sorry."

"Don't be sorry, Ben. It's important to recognise when you see limits. Embracing that is the first step to understanding how to break those barriers down. You will understand soon. But I can't tell you how."

He put a hand on his shoulder.

Contact was still a difficult thing for The Historian, but in his own way, he was developing his skills to grow closer to his son.

He would never be a father again, he knew that, but he could try to be a mentor.

The next thing that came out of his mouth surprised Ben again.

"Next week, I'm going to take you to see a friend I think who can help you."

"We have friends here?"

"Yes, of course. I told you I'd been here before."

"Yes, but.."

"Well, I'm not a complete imbecile! I can talk to people, even with my, hm, condition."

"Sorry. So, why haven't I met this friend yet? We've been here for months."

"Because you weren't ready."

"Me?"

"Yes, you. Now, as I said, we'll go and meet him next week, and I think you'll find that things become easier from thereon in."

The sun set, the entire sky a candyfloss pink.

CHAPTER 51

The Swiss Paraplegic Centre, Nottwil, Switzerland - Friday May 1st, 2009

Even with the medication he was on, sometimes the pain would make him wake screaming and soaking with sweat.

He could not fault the care that he was getting. The doctors, nurses and other ancillary staff were nothing short of amazing.

They could not grow his legs or eyes back. They couldn't stop the phantom pains in his feet, the shin splints and stabbing pains in his knees that weren't there.

They couldn't help him rub his eyelids to stop the sore feeling in his eyeballs that his tired eyes were experiencing. They weren't there.

Kevin Daste didn't feel pity for himself. He felt rage.

Of course, there had been moments where he considered his situation pitiful.

He'd cried, although his tear ducts had been seared in the explosion. He'd apparently not been able to lift his arms for some reason, which was why they were still useful to him and his eyes were not.

Much of his face had been lacerated in the blast and reconstruction was on-going. The force had slammed a desk into his legs and continued to push him back into a wall, smashing his bones to splinters just below his crotch.

He was lucky he still had his manhood. If he'd been sitting down, he would have been crushed just below his rib cage. That would have been lights out for sure.

It had taken him another week after he'd initially come out of his induced coma to return to a level of consciousness that allowed him to start accessing his memories and truly understand his situation.

Other doctors with better bedside manners had explained the situation again, with more sensitivity this time.

They had also outlined what the future might hold for him, in the short- and the long-term.

The Force was covering the cost of his care. His superiors were being kept informed of his progress. He had messages of support in the form of cards he couldn't read all around the room. Being male-dominated, there were very few flowers from the department. Ironically, he would have been able to smell those, as that was one sense that had recovered pretty quickly.

A serious blessing was that his mental faculties were still fully operational. His memory, right up until the explosion, was intact too.

He knew what had happened in the run-up to the incident. He guessed the reasons why it had happened.

He had been investigating who was behind it when the explosion had taken his entire team.

His anger was for them.

There had been no warning. Nothing indicated that a threat of that level should have been anticipated. All it seemed to be was a case of abduction and drug running, nothing more. A little bit of underworld activity creeping into Switzerland across borders. Minor extortion from an organisation for the return of a key member of personnel. That's all it had seemed to be.

Right up until a courier had delivered a package to the front desk, asking for it to be delivered to Kevin Daste personally. Evidence in an important investigation, the he'd said. They must have had a jamming device as the close circuit television footage of the time that he was in the building was just static.

They had learned to be more careful about cameras since.

One of his team, Jérôme, had gone down and picked it up. It had exploded a couple of minutes later according to all accounts, no one knew how. Whether radio controlled, voice activated or whatever, it had devastated the third floor.

To all intents and purposes, the entire team died that day officially. Kevin was now under witness protection, amusing as it sounded to him. He had to learn to be a new man. He was pretty much getting a new face anyway.

What was driving him through the pain was his need to find out what had happened to the one other person who he knew must have been targeted at the same time. The person he hadn't taken seriously enough to warn him about being more careful.

Ben Fallow.

He had heard about events on Lundy by asking subtle questions about anything he'd missed whilst he'd been in a coma. All he knew was that there had been an explosion on the conservation island and some people had been found dead. It gave him little concrete evidence either way.

He decided that he'd have faith in Ben that he'd survived. That he'd found a way off the island and gone somewhere safe, even though there was no evidence for, and strong evidence against that stance.

He had to believe it. He needed to have someone he could talk to who understood after the long months of rehabilitation, excruciating pain, surgical procedures and eventual prosthetic training.

It wasn't enough to have an imaginary friend. That would not get him through.

He needed to talk to Ben. The one that was alive, unharmed. The one who was pursuing the same evil cocksuckers that he would also pursue once he had the strength and ability to focus.

At first, he would talk to him in his head. Ben would help him push himself in his rehabilitation. Then, he would talk to him on the phone, or on email, or some way in the real world. Finally, he would talk to him face to face. They would meet each other in person, and they would go and kick the arses of those that had transgressed against them both.

In the meantime, before that, he had work to do. He had to re-start his research. But this time, with a great deal more care than he had done before. He didn't consider himself stupid. He had never begun to think that he would have been a target deserving to be destroyed by such substantial fire power in his relatively safe country, running around after diplomats and corporate types.

Now, however, he knew better. All of his research on the computer might have been destroyed, but the majority of his memories remained intact.

They had tried, but they hadn't taken his memories away from him.

CHAPTER 52

Vienna, Austria - Thursday May 7th, 2009

Only a week into the month and Esther knew that her situation was beginning to deteriorate.

Since the funeral of his wife, Karvorkian's mood had changed.

The children had quickly been sent back to boarding school, much to their distress at a time when what they needed was emotional support from their father.

He had dismissed them and told them to grow up. He hadn't even seen them to the car.

Whether he was covering his own grief in work or he had managed to get over her completely in a matter of a few days she could not tell.

What was disturbing was the level of attention that he was now lavishing on Celine.

Where she had once been left alone to get on with her research, she was now being called on to spend more time with Karvorkian. He had started to ask her opinions, her analysis of situations and guidance on recommended strategies.

This was awkward. She was not aware of why Karvorkian required detailed analysis of geo-political activities over and above strategic investments for his various portfolios. She had no great understanding of why he required diplomatic options.

He didn't seem to be aligned with any particular government. He wasn't a member of any trade delegations. Neither was he advising any large corporations with regard to their strategic positions in different territories from what she could surmise. She had no idea whether Celine's advice was useful, on target or laughably naive.

The problem was, the more time Karvorkian spent with Celine, the less time Esther had to figure out a way of escape.

What was worse, Celine seemed to be growing to like Karvorkian's attention. At some points, she even caught her flirting with him.

This was not how it was supposed to go.

If she lost control of Celine, she'd be in serious danger.

What Celine didn't seem to understand was that it was extremely likely that she would be too.

The problem was, Celine's personality was not rounded. It was child-like.

It had all the appearance of a grown woman, but it was not grounded in years of experience.

Her implanted memories, Esther could see, were shallow, more like puddles than pools.

There were scant few of them when she compared the hole that her own had left and the ones implanted to make her believe that Celine was the real 'her'.

That hurt Esther the most. She couldn't access her own memories, suppressed by the drugs. She could see where they should be but it was as if they had been stored away in locked boxes. Placed on top, in little parcels with their lids off, were inadequate, plastic, one-dimensional moments. They were obvious to her. She couldn't understand why Celine couldn't see that.

All she could do was hide away as Celine spent more and more time with Karvorkian.

He was not pleasant to be around, especially this week. It seemed the world reports of continued low interest rates in the UK and Europe combined with money-printing antics particularly annoyed him. Added to that, there were protests in Germany, Greece and Turkey on May Day that descended into pitched battles with the police.

Then there was swine flu and freak weather in Brazil, all contriving to have an effect on multiple markets.

Karvorkian was drinking more, and eager for Celine to drink with him. As an employee, she resisted as much as she could, then drank only sparingly when pressed.

She was asked to stay later and later each evening. They began to eat dinner together. Conversation would turn away from business to the kinds of things she enjoyed. Esther couldn't listen to that, so she turned inward and reflected on the things she had learned about the house, the staff and the location.

She tried to analyse everything she could about what she had learned but it was difficult sharing a brain with two functioning personalities. Eventually, Celine won out. Esther was reduced to meditating whilst Celine talked about the merits of the South of France over Greek island beaches.

The next thing she was aware of was Karvorkian kissing Celine on the cheek outside her bedroom door, a hand on her arm, the other on her waist. She hesitated and he moved his lips towards hers.

Esther mentally head butted Celine, who pulled herself back and lifted a hand to her head.

"Are you alright?"

"Yes, I - I'm okay. I have a bit of a headache. I'll be fine."

"Are you sure? Can I get you anything?"

"No, honestly, I'm fine. I just need some sleep I think. Sorry. Thank you for a lovely evening."

"I'm glad you enjoyed it. I hope we can do it again soon?"

Celine smiled. Esther groaned.

They turned, opened the door, went into their room and said goodnight to Karvorkian as they closed it.

Then the argument started and didn't stop until the early hours of the morning.

The honeymoon was well and truly over.

CHAPTER 53

Monte, Madeira - Wednesday May 13th, 2009

"Ben, may I introduce you to Xiang Ming, or Pete to his friends."

They were outside a small house high up in the parish of Monte, in the mountainous region on the north east corner of the municipality of Funchal. The house itself did not suggest any Chinese inspiration from the outside, but the garden certainly did.

"Pleased to meet you, Mr Xiang."

The old Chinese man in front of him stared for a moment, then raised an eyebrow sharply.

"Fuck you."

"I'm sorry?"

"Mr Xiang make me sound old. I look old to you?"

"I.."

"I not old. I seventy-four. You call me Mr Xiang when I a hundred. Not before. Fucker."

He held his scowl a moment longer, making Ben feel unusually uncomfortable.

Then his face cracked into a thousand laughter lines as he bent forwards and backwards, shoulders jiggling in an exaggerated manner with his hands on his stomach.

"I keep forgetting you guys no have the long history of humour like Chinese. You children when it comes to funny. Give you a couple millennia more to catch up."

He stopped laughing, winked at The Historian who was smiling absent-mindedly, then slouched into a more relaxed stance.

"Yeah, also, I can talk perfectly Western if I want to."

He picked a soft pack of cigarettes out of his jeans pocket and tapped one out onto the back of his hand, lighting up in a fluid motion.

"So, you're Ben, huh?"

"Yeah. That's me."

"Okay Ben, enough with the introductions. Let's chat, shall we? I understand you're having a little trouble loosening up, is that right?"

Ben scowled at The Historian.

"Oh, I'm fine physically, I don't need a massage."

It was Pete's turn to glance quizzically at The Historian.

"What've you said to him about me?"

The Historian shrugged.

"Not much."

"Actually, nothing. Just that you're a 'friend' who he just happened to mention last week after us being here for nearly six months."

Pete winked at The Historian and tapped his nose then pointed to him.

"I get it! Smart."

Ben tutted and stared at him. Pete turned back to him.

"You're a serious kid, aren't you? Why? Lighten up a little."

Ben felt his neck prickle. He was getting annoyed.

"Now listen..."

"No, Benny-boy, I'm not going to listen. Are you going to make me? Because the last person that tried, ended up over that cliff there. I'm going to ask you again. Why are you so serious?"

"Look, I don't know how much my Da - The Historian - he has told you about what we're up against, but I was under the impression that we were here for help of some kind, so that I can.."

"Bub, the only thing you're going to get from me is a face full of smoke while I laugh at you if you keep going."

Ben was red-faced now. He was not used to people talking to him like this. He felt his fists balling themselves against his better judgment.

He turned to The Historian. "I think it's time we were off, before something happens that I'll regret."

"I think you're fucking wrong about that, boy. I think you're scared of getting the crap beaten out of you. And I say, you can't leave until I say you can."

Pete stood there, all five foot four of him. Scrawny, arms crossed in an awkward fashion.

He puffed away on his cigarette which he held between his middle two fingers. His index finger parted and his little finger went down, effectively flicking Ben a slightly fatter V sign.

Ben turned and made to leave. Moments later, a stone hit his head, drawing blood. He spun around to see Pete, gazing up in the air, slowly exhaling a grey stream of mist, as if admiring the sky.

"How old are you?"

Pete turned his head back to Ben and regarded him with laughing eyes.

"I told you. Old enough to beat the shit out of you."

"Jesus, you have a death wish."

Ben turned and again, seemingly from nowhere, a stone hit the back of his head, almost in exactly the same spot, making it smart even more.

With a roar, Ben spun around and charged at Pete. With impossible lightness, Pete jumped over Ben just as he was in front of him. He delivered a sharp smack to the back of Ben's head with the sole of his foot as he passed, the force pushing him to the ground.

Still not registering that gravity-negating move, Ben jumped up. He adopted a Karate stance and began to throw move after move at Pete. Who stood there, with cigarette in hand, simply pushing Ben's limbs away as if they had little more force than a some annoying fabric blowing in the wind.

Ben stopped.

Pete, standing sideways, taking him in with one eye slightly shut. The cigarette was now a butt which he dropped and stamped on.

"Now, my turn."

Ben had backed away a couple of feet.

Pete simply twisted his right hand, palm facing front, and moved it gently across his body towards Ben, no more than a foot away.

A force slammed into Ben, sending him sprawling towards the edge of the garden, a good five meters, just a few feet away from a sheer drop.

"Fuck. Me."

196

Pete bowed, relaxed and sauntered over to Ben.

He put a hand out which Ben reached for. In a second, he was on his feet, Pete's strength pulling him off the ground as if he were picking up a stick.

"Now, Mister Fallow. How old are you? Are you an old man? Have you forgotten what life is about?"

Ben was silent, observing with wide eyes the old man in front of him.

"Are you too old to know what it is to enjoy life? To live it to its fullest? To embrace new experiences?"

Pete was walking around him, poking him with his finger.

It was an intensely unpleasant experience. Ben knew that he was back in the dojo and was now in the position of the men he'd trained not one year ago.

"Oh sure, you've been conditioned to do a job, to ignore the nasty parts, get on with life after that. But you've lost your joy. Dare I say, you've lost your humanity."

The poking turned into tickling, surprising Ben. He flinched.

"All is not lost though. If there is feeling, there is still the possibility of re-learning joy. And once joy is back, it will be a short step to opening up your soul to connect with the world."

The Historian was again by Pete's side, who was now tapping out another cigarette.

"Do you think you can help him?"

Pete hawed and wobbled his head, jiggling his shoulders and arms again like floppy scales.

Then he laughed, a light, tinkling sound.

"Sure. He's really fucked up, but I think I can do it."

He lit a cigarette, closed one eye as he got smoke in it, and thrust out a hand to Ben.

"I ain't no Mister Miaggi and this ain't Karate Kid son, but I think we can bring some joy back into your life. God knows you deserve it from what I've heard."

Ben accepted his hand and gave him a sheepish smile. At least whatever was going to happen was going to be interesting.

CHAPTER 54

Vienna, Austria - Wednesday May 13th, 2009

Truth be told, Karvorkian was beginning to suspect that he was starting to go a little mad.

He couldn't settle. He felt agitated all the time. His investigations into some of the other members of their hallowed calling were starting to bear fruit.

On the most recent call, he'd discretely employed the use of a simple digital recorder and captured the voices. He then commissioned a number of specialists he had screened to compare those voices using the millions of hours of news, commentary and political footage freely available online to identify the participants.

Of course he could not be shocked by anything regarding whom these people might turn out to be. What would be more shocking was if any of them were not in positions of power, whether through a legacy of history, family or democracy.

Still, it did not satisfy him when the first identities began to reveal themselves. When he concluded that any one of these could be a potential adversary, his brain started its buzzing.

A fuzzy, mechanical type of sound, almost like a fly trapped in his inner ear.

He had to shut his eyes and hum for a little while to make it go away.

It was all well and good when these people were on your side, all rooting together for the team. All protected by anonymity so that they could collectively manipulate events at will.

But when someone could so easily penetrate that cloak of invisibility simply by recording a voice, he experienced a cold sweat.

Were an infiltrator to ever break into their secure conference calls and do what he'd done, that would most certainly be the beginning of the end.

Then again, why consider the worst case?

Why not someone closer to the fold, so to speak?

What if one of the other participants had indeed come up with the same thought as he had?

What if he or she was, right now, conducting a campaign of intelligence to unmask Karvorkian himself? Wasn't this what he'd been afraid of? Were his fears not often a prediction of events that were to occur?

Wasn't he always right?

Shit.

He needed to speed things up.

Given the instability of the situation, it would not appear intentional if one or two of the people he most suspected of plotting to have his job were to experience accidents, coups or exposure of previously unknown corrupt activities deserving punishment.

It was time to get to work.

And if he had a few successes under his belt, perhaps he'd start to feel better.

Once his mood improved, he decided, he was going to enjoy screwing that living doll of his. She'd never have experienced anything like it. She was going to love it.

He just needed to get rid of that buzzing in his head first.

CHAPTER 55

Monte, Madeira - Wednesday May 13th, 2009

"So, Ben Fallow, what do you know of luck?"

They were inside now, Ben and Pete. The Historian had said his goodbyes and left them alone.

Pete had welcomed Ben into his house, which was showed much more of the Chinese beliefs of articulation and bilateral symmetry than the outside. Pete had built the property himself two decades before. He had situated the property so that the back of the house was against the mountain and there was water in the form of a pond in front of it.

As they walked in, Ben had noted the artwork on the two front doors, depicting what he supposed to be Chinese gods. Just inside, there were screens directly in front of the entrance. To prevent people from seeing straight through the house, Ben thought.

Once fully inside, it was just as Ben had imagined a Chinese house would be. China was one of the few countries he had not visited in his life, officially or unofficially. He noted a sudden desire to correct that in future.

Everything inside contributed to making the space feel comfortable. Unusually, there was a glass ceiling in the middle of the property to make it seem as if the property was built round a covered courtyard.

Pete had fussed around him, apologising for the harsh lesson. Ben had admitted to dolling out the same treatment to his trainees and expressed regret for rising to the bait.

"Ben, it's fine. If you hadn't, we wouldn't be standing here together, now, about to drink some rice wine. You would have been too far gone."

"Oh?"

"Yes. When all passion is lost, there is nothing to fight for. You proved to me there was enough passion for you to be pig-headed, and that was enough."

They sat and Pete poured them both a drink, which they then toasted each other with and sipped in silence for a while.

That was when Pete asked the question about luck.

"Well, I suppose it's like chance. I'm lucky when it comes to the roulette wheel, or that I haven't been seriously injured when others have on missions. I'm unlucky when it comes to meeting the right woman. It's about things that happen to you, outside of your or anyone's control."

"Hm." Pete said, nodding as if Ben had said something sagely. "Bullshit."

They both laughed.

"Yeah, tell me about it. I can guess that it's a little bit more than that. Now that I've seen what you can do and now you're asking me that question, it's got me thinking. I thought my Dad was crazy when he started going on about it when we met up again. Now, well, I must be crazy too, because you guys have got me believing in it."

Pete suddenly changed the subject.

"Do you like what I've done with the place?"

Ben scanned around the room again.

"Yes. Yes, I do. I've never been to China, I don't really know about interior design, but I like it. It feels, uh, laid out right. Comfortable. Homely. Welcoming."

Pete chuckled.

"Ah Ben, only a Westerner could brush over thousands of years of knowledge built up in Feng Shui and dismiss it as interior design which feels 'homely'. Fucking brilliant!"

"Sorry."

"Nah, don't worry about that. You'll learn soon. I'm going to have to give you a bit of a crash course. Have one of these."

"What is it?"

"Traditional Chinese biscuit. Generally given to new house guests."

Ben ate the small, slightly bitter biscuit Pete had proffered while listening to him continue his education.

"Feng Shui is all about the balance of ch'i, various energy currents, and manipulating how it flows. In Japan, this energy is known as Ki and in India it's called Prana."

"Really? Forces? Like molecular forces?"

"If it's real, it must be, right?"

Ben felt that information clunk into his head.

"Second hit. Ch'i always moves in spirals. Just like your man Yeats outlined in the weird automatic writing stuff he did with his wife as told to her by spirits. You gotta keep the ch'i flowing. If it stops, it becomes stagnant."

Ben felt a little strange.

His toes and fingers were tingling marginally.

"Third. The opposing forces of yin and yang need to be in balance. You've seen the symbol right? Wonky teardrops with dots in them in a circle. Remind you of anything science-y?"

"Like, a molecule or something?"

"A diatomic molecule. Right. About 99% of the Earth's atmosphere is composed of two diatomic molecules. Oxygen and nitrogen. Still with me, Bub?"

Ben nodded, his mouth open, his breathing a little unsteady.

"So the final reveal. The Five Elements. The core energies present everywhere which shape and transform all life, are all made of naturally occurring materials. Fire, Water, Wood, Metal."

"But that's four."

"Psh. You ain't never seen that film? 'The Fifth Element'? The human is the fifth, dummy."

"Oh. No, I've never seen it."

"Man, you are sad. Anyway, by combining the elements with a compass, knowing how each element relates to the other and so on, you can understand how they work together in the world."

"To do what?"

"Now what did I ask you at the beginning?"

"About luck?"

"Not about luck. What do you know of luck, I asked."

"I don't know anything about luck. Nothing."

"So, Feng Shui is all about understanding how the Five Elements work together in the world to create good and bad luck, and to start to influence them. It's science Ben, just expressed as interior design because it's got lost in translation. It's all about science. Always has been."

Ben's head was swimming now.

"So you know how to manipulate luck?"

Pete shrugged.

"In a sense, Ben. But in a very weak way. Feng Shui is a mere representation of a skill that was once used and practiced daily thousands of years ago. Same goes with Tai Chi. Think of it like someone in the audience of a Shakespeare play that was performed once trying to dictate it to someone who doesn't know many words to write it down ten years later. That's how much I believe the practice has been weakened. That some of it works is in no doubt, but its power has been greatly diminished."

Ben's balance was off so much he felt the sudden urge to lie down.

"I'm sorry Pete, that rice wine must've been strong. I don't feel too good."

Pete chuckled.

"Nah, that wasn't the wine. That was the opium biscuit I gave you. I told you I had to give you a crash course. This is one of the old ways. I'll see you when you wake up."

With that, Pete seemed to swirl out of his field of vision, transforming into strange shapes, then colours, sounds and smells. He closed his eyes and drew it all in.

CHAPTER 56

Vienna, Austria - Monday June 1st, 2009

Karvorkian woke up screaming.

It was not the usual scream that lasts a fraction of a second and stops once you wake and become aware that what you had just experienced had been a dream. It was a shriek the like of which a madman would give under the misguided belief that insects were crawling under his skin, munching him away from inside.

It continued until he had forced out his last breath. Then, after inhaling another good lungful, out came another.

Thumping footsteps came down the hallway and a determined knocking battered at the bedroom door.

"Mr Karvorkian Sir! Are you alright?"

Karvorkian opened his eyes wide and stopped screaming. He was panting, his silk pyjamas were damp with sweat and his brow was coated in a fine sheen. His skin was pallid, even though he had a Californian tan almost permanently all the year.

The door opened a crack and eyes peered in over the muzzle of a hand gun.

Karvorkian panted.

"Do I sound like I'm fucking all right, Manek? Get the fuck in here and get me a towel."

Manek stepped into the room, grabbed a hand towel and passed it to his boss, who patted his face as he calmed his breathing. After patting his neck, he paused and regarded Manek. Its coldness made him quickly stop staring at his boss and instead inspect at the floor. The view out of the window. Anywhere but in his boss's eyes.

"Manek, why did it take so long for you to get your ass in here?"

"I..."

"You're supposed to be protecting me. That's your job. It is your job, isn't it?"

"Yes, Sir. Of course."

"So what in fuck's name were you doing just then?"

"I... The area was secure, the morning rota was just about to come on, and so I thought I'd just..."

"Yes?"

"Get a piece of toast from the kitchen. I was hungry. I was, uh, losing my alertness, so I..."

He stumbled to a stop.

"You were asleep Manek, weren't you?"

"No Sir, I wasn't. I..."

"There's no way you could have heard me from the kitchen Manek."

"I was on my way back."

"Had you finished your toast?"

"No, I was just about to start it."

"So it will be somewhere on the carpet in the hallway, yes?"

Silence.

"Manek, you're a lying, dumb shit. Worse, now, you're good for nothing. I can't trust you here."

The colour was draining out of Manek's face now.

"Sir, I..."

"Do I seem like I'm in the forgiving mood to you? I'll help you there. No. I am fucking not. You put your beauty sleep over my protection. That in my book is unforgivable."

He stared at Manek hard. Again, Manek couldn't return his stare, choosing instead to assess the state of his scuffed shoes.

Karvorkian sighed.

"I am, however, short of an idiot or two in Geneva to do some grunt work. So it's your lucky day. I'm not going to fire you. I'm going to cut your pay, dock your holiday and you can make your own fucking way to Geneva. I'll be in touch once you're there."

"Thank..."

"Oh fuck off."

#####

When Manek left the room, Karvorkian gave a gasp and fell back on to the bed.

"Shit."

It wasn't insects that he'd felt crawling around under his skin. It was something crawling around in his brain.

Creeping into his dreams.

Watching him.

Had someone invented something that he had yet to hear about? Probing people's dreams in real time? And what good would that do? Better to probe someone when they were conscious so you could read their sentient thoughts rather than get the crazy bullshit sub consciousness broadcasting its bile from its playground of horrors.

No, this was not an intelligence exercise. It was an exploration. A probe. Like an alien, studying everything around it, seeing what was what and how things operated.

It was chilling.

He had felt it reach out and gently pluck a synapse, as if it was strumming it like a guitar string to see what sound it made.

It felt fucking awful.

Karvorkian grabbed a glass of water from the side table and gulped it down.

He'd been harsh to Manek. It was a fight or flight reaction.

He couldn't show weakness to his employees, nor could he have Manek spreading rumours about him to the rest of the staff. Besides, Manek really was a first class fuckwit.

It wouldn't have been long before he'd get someone killed. Better to put him out in the field with the other meat heads.

He got out of bed, moaning and putting a fist in his lower back to ease the muscles that had been in spasm. He plodded into the bathroom, opened the cabinet and popped the lid on a tub of tablets, chugging a couple into his mouth.

As he shut the cabinet door he stared into the face that swung around at him.

They were his eyes, but they weren't.

When he lifted a hand to his waxy cheek, so did the mirror image.

He didn't recognise himself.

206

He stepped into the shower, switched it on and stood fully two minutes under the needle sharp sting of freezing cold water. Then, he turned it on as hot as he could stand it, and cried.

#####

That had been a couple of weeks ago.

While the feeling had not occurred again, Karvorkian had not forgotten it.

He'd scheduled a visit with his physician who confirmed that he had suffered a mild case of swine flu. The high fever had invariably caused some hallucination. With all the travelling Karvorkian was doing, his doctor had said, he was very lucky that he'd not got it worse.

That provided Karvorkian with some respite from worry. Perhaps the buzzing and the ill feelings were simply down to the effects of the pandemic.

At least it made him feel a little better.

His doctor had also taken his blood pressure and the news was not good on that score. It was way high. Laughably, his doctor had suggested taking things a little more easily. Perhaps do a little more exercise, eat less salty food, cut back on his responsibilities.

He used his special look reserved for people he felt were particularly idiotic. The doctor retreated hastily, putting his stethoscope away and suggesting a course of medication that was not yet available on the open market.

"That sounds...perfect", he had said, his enunciation as sharp as steel.

#####

From that point on, whether it was the new tablets or just the reassurance that it was just swine flu, June seemed to improve somewhat.

He was delighted to hear from his spy in CERN that, without even a single intervention, the switch on had been delayed.

207

From June to September at the earliest.

He laughed out loud when he heard that due to this unfortunate delay, a certain star of that vapid film depicting the God particle nearly blowing up The Vatican would no longer be available to switch the LHC back on.

Thankfully, the damn thing would not get more oxygen of publicity than it warranted. He didn't blame the star not wanting to be associated with failure.

He reported this positive news back to his fellow cohorts. His delight quickly turned to fury when they were less than enthusiastic hearing about it. The lack of joint celebration almost felt like a personal attack.

It was time to act. He had a couple of names to choose from and some choice information to leak to the right contacts.

"Celine, I have a couple of letter for the post. Would you be so kind as to take them down to the box by the main gates please?"

"Of course, Sir."

"Celine, please. Call me Adnan."

#####

A couple of days later, Karvorkian was unsurprised to see the news that a certain ex- U.S. State Department official and his wife had been arrested on charges of spying for nearly thirty years on behalf of Cuba.

Karvorkian knew it wasn't really Cuba that this professor had been spying for. But spying is spying all the same.

One down.

CHAPTER 57

Monte, Madeira - Monday June 15th, 2009

The morning after his first journey, which had lasted well into the early hours, Ben sat in the dim light of dawn contemplating the events of the past few weeks.

It was almost impossible to understand how he had got here.

He felt fundamentally changed.

As Pete had said, he felt joy like he'd never felt before, even in the current circumstances.

There was a power that flowed through him now that made him feel impossibly tiny, yet also full of incredible energy.

He didn't feel in control of that power. At that moment, harnessing it was something that he felt he still lacked the skill to do, some knack waiting to be unlocked.

What he did feel like was a conduit. A switch. He could depress that switch ever so slightly and make the power flow in a fractionally different direction, but that was it.

When he'd woken from his dreams stimulated by the poppy, he'd sworn at Pete for five minutes until the air turned blue for feeding him drugs. Pete's laughter grew and grew until Ben spluttered to a stop. He joined him in laughing for a good half an hour, discovering muscles that he hadn't realised existed. He couldn't remember the last time he had laughed like that, truly.

They talked for a long time, Ben accepting cups of green tea and nibbling at more non Opium-based dishes.

Later that morning, The Historian returned and was delighted to see the progress that Ben had made.

"What did it feel like?"

Ben frowned, thinking.

"It's difficult to describe. I felt...yeah, connected. With everything, inside everything. I couldn't see everything all at once, but I could move around and dip in and out. I could see it all so clearly, more than clearly. I can only say that it reminds me of that line that the band the Doors were named after. Like opening the doors of perception."

"Ah, yes. That was taken from Aldus Huxley's essay of the same name. It was about him taking mescaline, which derives from a cactus that Native Americans. It's been used in religious ceremonies for thousands of years."

"Back to religion again."

"Yes, but don't you see Ben, religious experiences of that nature are nothing but chemical reactions? They're absolutely real, they're just not interpreted correctly. There's no deity directing them. Just an incredible collection of forces within the universe all working together to create a chaotic equilibrium."

"I thought the doors of perception was from a poem?"

"Yes, that too. Much older. It's from something called 'The Marriage of Heaven and Hell', by the mystical poet William Blake. He was more than a poet though. He lived in fascinating times at the beginning of the industrial revolution. People were seeing the rise of heavy industry and the decline in the fortunes of the lower class, used as fuel."

"Sounds familiar."

"Yes, to a certain extent. At the same time, as people lost meaning in their day to day lives, new religions were springing up. Blake dabbled in a load of them, perhaps with the use of freely available drugs. He came up with some beautiful writing and illustrations. Most of it tried to educate about the social and moral aspects of the pace of change at the time, but written in parables."

"Where is this going?"

"Ben, patience! You know what else he wrote?"

"Go on."

"'Without contraries there is no progression.'"

"Right."

"Remember back to yin and yang? The guy writing in the seventeen hundreds was writing about the balance of forces. He wasn't just writing parables, he'd seen behind the curtain. Good and evil without morality become simply the positive and negative flow of the same force that act on our realities. Blake knew about the universal forces and he saw that people had lost their ability to shape their ends..."

"...'rough hew them how they may'...That's Shakespeare isn't it? Hamlet?"

"Indeed."

"You're not saying...?"

The Historian and Pete smiled at each other.

"It's long been the case that important artefacts have been handed down through generations encoded in the works of poets and playwrights. Creating first an oral and then a written account for those that had the wit to understand it. It had to be hidden in works that would stand the test of time. So Shakespeare was an obvious choice, and one of his most successful plays the vehicle for that message."

"But divinity is about divine intervention, a god interfering, isn't it?"

"That's what Shakespeare would have wanted the religious leaders to think, to make sure his plays were approved of and kept on the stage. But we all know he was a subversive. Think about the situation Hamlet had just described. He happened to stumble on a letter that was basically giving orders to two people to kill him. Divine intervention or luck?"

"I guess we'll never know. There is a danger here of generating a conspiracy theory linking every important person back until creation together who are all in on this, isn't there?"

Pete laughed.

"For sure. Not everyone was in on it but you can see bright spots along the course of history. Yeats, Blake, Shakespeare, Plato, Hermes Trismagistus, the list goes back and back through time."

Ben raised an eyebrow and Pete shrugged and grinned again.

"But you've experienced it now. You know it's real. And you must see that it's an incredibly valuable secret?"

"I've experienced it, for sure. I'm still trying to get my head around the reality of it though. And I've yet to see how it can be used."

The Historian spoke up.

"Well Ben, that's where I come in. Your training has reached about as far as it can without direction. The training I've committed to over my lifetime has all been to direct your skills towards re-balancing the flow of luck around the world."

"How will you do that?"

"I see the places where luck does not reach. Where it's weak or is being prevented from flowing. The injustices, inequalities, corruption and monopolies. I see the lobbying, the back room deals, the glass ceilings and the caste systems. I see the events and predict the most likely outcomes. Most of all, I see the gaps where none should be, and that is where we need to direct your skills most, but not right now."

"So where do we start?"

"We start small."

Small was subjective, Ben thought, when The Historian revealed the target a day later.

"You've got to be kidding me!"

Pete agreed with The Historian.

"Kid, we need to pick something that will show you that this isn't all just something we've drugged you into believing. It has to be something that in the grand scheme of things is not a massive impact that would turn every eye on to us. But it has to be something of a scale that makes you realise how much the world is relying on you to re-balance it."

"What if it goes wrong?"

Pete was earnest.

"Then we'll have some shit to deal with. We'll probably be seen as terrorists."

There was silence. Then Pete's high-pitched laugh broke the suspense.

"I'm shitting you, Ben! Come on, lighten up! You only have one life. Well, that's not entirely true, but still, you only have *this* one life, so don't worry too much!"

Ben shook his head. "Pete, it's all well and good, and it's a fantastic experience, but these are people's lives we're dealing with."

The Historian put his hands on Ben's shoulders and eyeballed him.

"Which is why, Ben, it has to be you. You did exactly the same in the Army. That was people's lives too. You acted carefully, with discipline, restraint and with the knowledge that you were right. Just because we're dealing with an incredibly powerful person here, doesn't mean to say they are right."

"Yeah. Okay."

Pete jumped up from his chair.

"Great! Now, let me get you something to make you more comfortable. Don't worry, it's not Opium-based. It's just a little relaxant."

#####

Minutes later, he brought Ben a cup of steaming liquid. Ben sat in front of the screens on a mat, with small tables either side burning incense, looking out of the door overlooking the garden.

He raised a quizzical eyebrow at the brew.

"It's a lotus flower-based drink. It'll help you relax."

Ben sipped it. It didn't taste too bad and had an instant warming effect.

The Historian stepped into his view and crouched.

He gave him a quick once over and then nodded.

"Now, you have to balance the ability to focus and be guided at the same time. Focus your thoughts, follow the energy. When you're near, don't press too hard. You need to float through their mind and place that thought there gently. It will seem to them that they've come to a decision that they must have been deliberating for some time."

Ben inhaled and blew out air between his lips until there was none in his lungs, then breathed in slowly from his nose.

"Wish me luck."

Pete laughed. Ben smiled lackadaisically.

"Yeah, whatever."

He closed his eyes and sank into the dark, until he landed in a pool of colours that began to form a stream. Then it turned into a series of branches which suddenly shot out over land.

He was up and floating, the next minute drawn towards one which he attached his conscious to. Then he was off, shooting across land and sea.

#####

On 15th May, The United States released Lakhdar Boumediene. A charity worker for the Red Crescent, he'd been held with no trial on no evidence for nearly eight years in Guantánamo Bay Naval Base Detention Centre in Cuba.

At the same time, the President announced that military tribunals for the detainees at the base would resume.

Small.

A few days later, The Association of Southeast Asian Nations expressed "grave concern" about National League for Democracy General Secretary Aung San Suu Kyi's trial.

On 25th May, nine United Kingdom Cabinet ministers were implicated in Parliament's expenses scandal after a newspaper investigation showed endemic illegal defrauding of the public purse by hundreds of members of Parliament. Multiple ministers began to resign, putting pressure on the Prime Minister to do so.

On 2nd June, The Community of the People won Greenland's parliamentary election, overturning more than thirty years of rule by the same party.

The day after, Indian Member of Parliament Meira Kumar became the first female Speaker of the House of the People.

On 8th June, Gabonese President Omar Bongo died of a sudden heart attack. Gabon was officially one of Africa's richest states due to oil earnings, but most of the country's one point four million people lived in poverty.

June 10th saw thousands of people demonstrate in solidarity with victims of child abuse in Dublin as hundreds of victims were invited to meet with the Irish President.

The Pope had been stunned into silence when briefed about the endemic child abuse uncovered in Ireland by members of the Catholic priesthood and had been seen to be visibly moved. Given his previous responsibilities in investigating and meeting out justice on these crimes, his reaction was noted.

On 11th June, two Japanese citizens were detained in Italy. They were allegedly attempting to take one hundred and thirty-four billion dollars-worth of U.S. bonds over the border into Switzerland, starting the Chiasso financial smuggling case. The two possessed two hundred and forty-nine U.S. bonds worth five hundred million dollars each. Among other securities, they also had ten "Kennedy bonds" denominated at one billion dollars each.

The large denominations on the securities, along with accompanying bank documentation, was what attracted the Italian police's attention. What urge attracted them to choose to stop them in the first place was unclear. Notes of that size were not available to the general public. Only nation-states handle such amounts of money.

Finally, in the middle of the month, on 15th June, huge but peaceful protests broke out demonstrating against the re-election of Iran's president. The loser claimed massive electoral fraud. So disturbed by the uprising, the strength and conviction of which had not been seen for years in the country, Supreme Leader Ayatollah Ali Khamenei called for an enquiry.

#####

Pete, The Historian and Ben were sitting in a bar in Funchal. It was early evening, and they were enjoying the breeze coming in from the sea and watching the news. An American cable network was reporting on the growing unrest in Iran.

When the package was over, they contemplated each other and raised a silent toast. It had begun.

CHAPTER 58

CERN, Geneva - Tuesday July 14th, 2009

While the press had been kind enough to point out that the engineering complexities of something the size of the LHC were akin to those of building the International Space Station, Professor Fenkhause now understood why there had been no celebratory champagne popped when the last magnet had been lowered in April.

It had been known internally for some time, but it was only now that news was filtering about additional faults in the LHC. New leaks meant new delays.

The good news was that these had been identified by the new systems that the Professor's team had been diligently putting in place. The bad news was that the LHC would not be switched back on in September.

The Large Hadron Collider was now currently a full two and a half years behind the schedule CERN had outlined in its 2005 annual report. A schedule that he had written.

The senior management at CERN could barely acknowledge him without grimacing. He'd become a pariah, an albatross on the deck of what should have been a glorious project.

The delays could mean that U.S. physicists using the Tevatron at Fermilab outside Chicago might have more time to discover the Higgs boson. It was an insult that such a device was being trumpeted as a contender to discover the secrets of the universe. Compared to the LHC it was positively Heath Robinson.

But there it was, in black and white in WIRED Magazine.

"If that long postulated but never observed particle is as heavy as scientists suspect, Tevatron scientists still have a shot at spotting some signs of its existence."

The Professor flung the magazine across the lab, narrowly missing Alf. He immediately held his hands to his mouth and gasped.

"Alf, I am so sorry. I have no idea what possessed me."

Alf shrugged and stuffed a marshmallow into his mouth.

"Don't worry Professor. Most people throw chairs at me."

The Professor didn't laugh.

"Do you know Alf, I'm not feeling myself. I think I will take a couple of days off. I surprise myself to say it, but I think I need some fresh air and sunshine."

"Wow! That doesn't sound like you at all. I like it! Have a good time."

The Professor removed his lab coat and patted Alf on the shoulder a couple of times on the way out. He proceeded to human resources to fill in a last minute request for absence. The Administration did not seem sorry to see him leave.

#####

A couple of hours later, Ebhart had retreated to the one place he remembered outside of the lab that he had enjoyed. He'd gone home, thrown some clothes and a wash kit in a rucksack he'd had stowed away in his wardrobe for goodness knows how long, and had jumped on a train.

He'd ended up in Château-d'Oex in the Alps. It was a skiing resort but he had loved to visit in the summertime, when the mountains were verdant and not a flake of snow was present.

It was still magnificent. The plus point was he was early enough to avoid the family vacation season.

The views were simply stunning. If this place couldn't get him out of his funk, he mused, there was something seriously wrong with him.

He checked in at the delightful Le Vieux Chalet Hôte bed and breakfast then headed out for a late afternoon stroll around the Pierreuse Nature Reserve.

The pre-Alps landscape was gorgeous. Mountains and valleys, streams and calcareous rock faces. Wild fauna mixed with sub-Alpine vegetation, traditional meadows stretching across thirty four square kilometres.

As he watched a wild ibex, obviously a male given the size of its majestic horns, bound around in front of him, Ebhart knew this had been the right thing to do.

He had to step away. For nearly nine months he'd been playing the role of a double agent in his own mind, worrying about every little move that he made.

He had to find some space, if only for a few days, where the pressure could be relieved, even if for a temporary period and this was the place. Here, he could watch chamois and marmots whilst basking in the beautiful sunshine. A lack of vitamin D for such a long time had obviously not been good for him.

He didn't know what vitamin was in the cheese that they made up here but he remembered it was superb from his last visit.

As he marched around in the late summer afternoon, only the backpack with some rations, water and other minor goods weighed him down. Everything else was uplifting.

#####

"No, nothing to report. He's stomping around like a fully paid-up member of the European Ramblers Association. No, there's no one with him. No, he doesn't have a mobile. Of course I've checked his room. There's nothing in there. Look, it's obvious isn't it? He's having a breakdown and he's come back to a childhood place where he feels safe. That's got to be it. I reckon he's composing his resignation letter in his head. If he isn't, he might as well go and head butt one of those stupid mountain goats and get it over quicker. Yeah. Speak to you tomorrow. And don't tell me anything about the Tour de France, got it?"

#####

When Ebhart got back, ten minutes from the centre of the village, it was a little after seven in the evening. He had just missed the dinner sitting, so he went up to his room, showered and shaved and stepped on to the balcony to enjoy the last of the sun.

He had made the right decision, he thought. He berated himself for not stepping out sooner, or at a more appropriate time. He recognised that his superiors back at CERN would perceive this jaunt to be a weakness. It was completely out of character for him.

It was what it was. He was re-charging. Re-programming his own magnets, he chuckled to himself. There was only so much a machine can take before it needed a service, and his was well overdue.

He dressed, went downstairs and decided to try his luck in town. If not for a full-blown meal, then at least a beer and some of that wonderful Alpine cheese.

CHAPTER 59

Nottwil, Switzerland - Thursday August 6th, 2009

Kevin Daste ached. He would have said from top to toe, but that would have been anatomically incorrect.

He'd amazed the medical staff by his poise and sense of humour. He didn't make them aware of his desire to seek revenge on the people who had killed innocents. He was lucky to be alive. He enjoyed every day.

He could have been paralyzed. He could have resurfaced from his coma with no limbs at all.

At least, with no eyes currently, he couldn't see the extent of the damage. However, much of that had been transformed already.

They had worked wonders on his face. Most of his hair would not grow back, so he'd decided he'd shave it all off.

That way, he thought, he could get a choice of wigs or simply just wear a hat.

They'd managed to cover up most of the scars. They'd re-attach one ear and reconstructed some eye lids, popping in some false eyeballs as well until his new state of the art prosthetic eyes arrived.

He could still smile. He now had a bridge that filled in some of the holes where teeth had unfortunately fallen out due to some of the reconstruction. He could feel that they were well made and he wouldn't be too self-conscious opening his mouth.

So the rest of it was sheer hard work, bringing his body back into operation. Training in the gym on his upper body strength, getting his arms into a state where they could have been his new legs, until his prosthetic limbs were fitted.

He was also swimming a lot, which he loved. It had been weird at first, getting used to the balance, trying to move legs that weren't there.

What they had done was find some fantastic flipper extensions that fitted to the stumps of his legs, and he'd found a whole new way to swim. It was exhilarating once he got used to it.

He felt like a fish, but sometimes he forgot that he had to surface to breathe. That gave his rehab staff a few scares.

The hard bit was learning to walk again.

That was the painful, slow and crushingly dull part.

But he was starting to get there.

He'd walk listening to the news bulletins, getting up to speed on what had been going on in the world whilst he'd been asleep.

He'd been surprised about how much was changing.

Banks in crisis, the political sphere shifting, emboldened people around the world beginning to remember what it was like to protest.

But it all paled into insignificance when he remembered the people he had worked with.

His focus was on getting justice for them.

He'd been pestering his Secret Service contact for help pretty much since the first meeting.

For a long time, they'd resisted.

It wasn't until he'd threatened to expose the cover up that they'd caved, but there were conditions.

Finally, they'd sent a female Agent as a permanent liaison to try to placate him.

Special Agent Anderegg attended his gym session that day.

"Anderegg, this isn't about me, don't you get it? This is about the stability and security of Switzerland and its people. If a terrorist organisation can walk into the unit designed to protect and defend some of the most prominent civil and military installations of Switzerland and its partners, blowing it to smithereens, we're all completely fucked."

Special Agent Anderegg sighed.

"I get it Sir, I do. But you're in witness protection for your own good. If you start sticking your nose in asking questions that a dead man asked, your cover will be blown pretty much straight away. We're doing our best to protect you here."

"I'm not asking you to do that, Agent. I'm asking you to find someone for me."

"Fine, I'm listening."

"He goes by the name of Ben Fallow. He was on Lundy Island, just off the coast of the United Kingdom, when that disturbance happened last year."

"And?"

"I need for you to find out whether he died there or not. Check the bodies. Test their DNA. His records will be with the Swiss Army. Army Reconnaissance Detachment 10. He was Lieutenant Colonel."

"And if it turns out it's not him?"

Kevin smiled, with his new teeth.

"Then we go on a man hunt."

CHAPTER 60

Vienna, Austria - Tuesday August 11th, 2009

Karvorkian was sitting in his study, nursing a brandy glass the size of a fishbowl. In it, gently warming by the heat of his hand, was a 1993 French Colombard brandy by the Tishbi Family. It was a new acquisition that he'd been saving for a special occasion.

Karvorkian was glowing with pleasure. He'd not been this happy for a long while.

His latest scalp had been fun. It had taken not inconsiderable resources to sway the balance of power away, but those resources were monetary rather than specialist.

In the end, money was often as useful a tool as the forces that they controlled.

The Premiere of The Turks and Caicos Islands in the Caribbean had just had his power taken away from him. The territory had been put back under direct rule by the United Kingdom. It emerged that he'd built up a massive fortune since his presidency began in 2003.

Karvorkian had made it so that any support for the ex-premiere had trickled away over the past month, leaving him completely exposed. He was now watched like a hawk and it wouldn't be too long before action was taken. Most likely by the people he had done business with who didn't want connections to be made.

It had also raised interesting questions on transparency with regard to the financial services industry that the Islands had built up. For a small set of islands in The Lucayan Archipelago, thousands of businesses were registered there. Many of them belonging to some of the names he'd identified as being his partners in crime.

His net was closing in.

He was also celebrating a happy accident. It seemed that the month previous, another of his distant telephone acquaintances had suffered an unfortunate loss in the form of some bonds. Quite a substantial proportion of bonds in fact.

They'd been discovered somehow when they were being transported across the Italian boarder into Switzerland.

It was a clear demonstration of when luck turns bad.

He couldn't see any other explanation for it.

Sipping his brandy, he flicked television channels absent-mindedly, the volume off.

There was a knock at the door.

"Come."

Celine entered, holding the latest analysis for him in a plain folder. There were no logos on the paper, simply a watermark identifying the material as confidential on each page. He switched off the television and put the remote down, signalling her to come closer.

"Ah, Celine, my dear. Good to see you. Will you join me in a brandy? It's absolutely superb. It won an award as a three year old in nineteen ninety-six, but as a sixteen year old, it certainly grown into adulthood. Well. Almost."

Celine smiled as she approached, bent down to pass him the report, and he breathed in her perfume.

"Oh, I'm delighted you liked my gift!"

"What's not to like? Chanel Number Forty Six is a collector's item. I'm intensely flattered that you gave it to me. It's beautiful."

"Not at all. A beautiful and rare perfume for a beautiful and rare lady."

Celine's laughter tinkled in the air. She stepped over to the sideboard, poured herself a smaller glass, then moved back over to seat herself opposite Karvorkian.

She raised her glass.

"Your good health, Sir."

"Please Celine. Adnan. How many times must I ask?"

"I love that line from that pirate film, 'At least one more time.'"

"I haven't seen it."

"No? Oh, but it's such fun."

"I'm not convinced. Anyway, anything interesting in here I should take notice of especially?"

He tapped the report. She quickly sipped the brandy and nodded before speaking.

"General market uncertainty, in a nutshell. Turmoil seems to be growing and there's contagion into other regions."

Karvorkian nodded. Not great news, not entirely unexpected.

"Nothing stand out?"

"Not right now, Sir."

"Okay. Good."

He paused.

"Well, business is over. What say I take you out to dinner?"

Celine blushed.

"I don't really have anything to wear."

Karvorkian smiled.

"I think you'll find in your room that you do."

Celine smiled again and stood, taking her brandy with her. She moved over to him and kissed him lightly on the cheek.

"Well, in that case, 'Sir', I'd better go and get dressed. What time should we leave?"

"Is forty-five minutes enough time?"

"Plenty enough. I will see you then."

She sashayed out of the room.

Karvorkian gloated for a while then went to take a shower and change.

He was going to be a lucky boy tonight, he felt sure of it.

#####

It had all been going so well.

And then, just like that, it hadn't.

Celine had floated down the stairs in a stunning gold Elie Saab sequinned gown. They had drunk champagne in the car before arriving at the Silvio Nickol Gourmet Restaurant Palais Coburg.

It was busy but intimate.

They sat in an alcove and ate truffles, foie gras, venison and cheese. They washed the food down with various wines from the specialist wine menu which accessed the vast cellars below.

225

Celine laughed at his jokes, was attentive to his more self-indulgent reminiscing over trips and held his hand gently when he spoke of the loss of his father.

And then it had happened.

"Esther?"

Both of them stiffened and turned to see who had spoken.

Standing over them was a tall, blond American man, sharply dressed in a grey designer outfit.

His face cracked into a grin.

"I thought it was you when I saw you come in. Your dress is stunning! What on earth are you doing in Vienna and who is this lucky fellow?"

Karvorkian's face turned thunderous. Celine's neck flushed.

"I'm sorry. I think you have me mistaken for someone else. I don't know you."

The man's face flinched slightly and a puzzled expression replaced the smile.

"Jamie. Jamie Dennington? From The Bureau? We worked on the Afghanistan situation together a couple of years ago?"

Shit. The Bureau. This couldn't get much worse.

Celine's head was moving side to side, vigorously.

"No, I'm sorry. You really do have me mistaken. I've never worked with any bureau, and my name is Celine. Celine Matheson."

"Oh. I'm so sorry to interrupt your dinner."

He turned to Karvorkian.

"Please accept my apologies for this rude intrusion. I must admit, the similarity is so close that your companion must be a Doppelgänger."

Karvorkian stared dully at the man and made no attempt at conversation.

"Well, I'll leave you to the rest of your evening. Apologies once again."

He gave curt nod and then was gone.

Karvorkian diverted his cold eyes at Celine who smiled weakly.

His next question was quiet, yet penetrated the general noise like a stiletto blade.

"You've gone very pale, my dear. Are you alright?"

"I seem to have developed another headache, Sir. Would you mind awfully if we skipped the aperitifs and went straight home?"

"Not at all. Waiter? The bill please."

They left swiftly. There was no talking on the ride home.

He walked her to her room, saw her in and made sure that she took her medication along with a sleeping draught.

He walked to his basement and cursed at the top of his voice for several minutes. Then he started researching Jamie Dennington of the Federal Bureau of Investigations.

#####

Esther was struggling against the sleeping draught as hard as possible, panicking.

She'd not been strong enough to take advantage of the best opportunity to escape presented to her in months.

As Celine grew stronger, she was growing weak.

Celine's personality was dominant. She had everything to live for. Her work, the attentions of her powerful employer. The beautiful dresses, the perfume, the whole emerging lifestyle.

To have that taken away from her due to someone recognising Esther made Celine mad. It would ruin everything.

For Esther, the situation was again in flux. She knew Karvorkian would begin to doubt the treatment she'd undergone, to turn her from Esther into Celine. She'd been quiet. Avoided him, allowed Celine to be front and centre in his presence. Calming him, making him forget she was ever Esther.

But the man from the FBI's recognition of her brought it all back to the surface. The uncertainty was back.

That she'd been saved from almost certainly having to sleep with the man was not a positive at this point in time.

Worse, she still couldn't access her memories.

She honestly didn't know or recognise the man claiming to be Jamie Dennington. She couldn't remember working with The Bureau on anything to do with Afghanistan. She didn't remember what she did before 'becoming' Celine.

All she knew was that she'd blown it

The headache had come on due to the swift internal struggle between the two personalities.

One wanted to stand up and shout and be protected by this new man.

The other forcing that urge deep down, wanting to stay. To see how things progressed with this rich, entitled man with whom marriage meant never having to work again.

Fight won over flight.

It was not going to be as easy for either of them to achieve what they wanted from now on. The lock was back on the door.

Esther knew she needed to think more seriously about escape. Time was running out.

CHAPTER 61

Nottwil, Switzerland - August 26th 2009

"Special Agent Anderegg, good to see you."

"Uh, yeah. Good to see you too."

"To what do I owe the pleasure?"

Kevin Daste was sitting in a chair by the window in his room, which overlooked the shores of Lake Sempach, with a hardback in his lap. It gave the illusion that he was there because it cast the most natural light to read in.

The book was in braille. Kevin was teaching himself. The chair was in that position as he enjoyed the heat of the sun through the window. He still had some wounds that required him to be in as sterile an environment as possible, so his time outside was limited.

Agent Anderegg had been pre-announced by a call from reception alerting him. He loved putting her off balance, projecting the image of an able-bodied man in full use of his faculties.

"The research you asked us to do. We got the information."

"And?"

"Nope, it's not him."

"So. Ben Fallow is alive somewhere."

"Well, that's speculative. We did find blood that matched his DNA which had been lifted from the site."

"Could have been anything. He'd been there a couple of days. He could have scratched himself on something."

"Yes, it's possible."

"So, Mr Fallow left the island not by no scheduled means of transport. He must have done so prior to any security forces gaining access to the crime scene."

"That was around twenty-five minutes after the explosion. It was called in by the pub landlord to the Coast Guard."

"It wouldn't have been a helicopter, so it must have been a seaborne means of escape. Were there any boats missing?"

"None that the locals could confirm without reasonable doubt. All the regular vessels were accounted for."

"Hm. So somehow he gets off the island in a boat unknown to anyone and goes - where?"

"We can check for unidentified boats in the area on that night?"

"Good plan. Thank you Agent Anderegg."

There was a minute hesitation which Kevin Daste picked up. He inwardly congratulated himself on the development of his senses which seemed amplified since the loss of his sight.

"Something else?"

"Yes. The woman. Esther."

"Go on?"

"Lead came in from a guy from The Bureau."

"The FBI? How? When?"

"A day or so ago. Said he'd bumped into her in Vienna with an angry guy at dinner. He'd worked with her before a couple of years back. They'd almost had a fling, or so he claims. He was sure it was her, knew her moles and earlobes, that kind of thing."

"Okay. And?"

"She seemed highly agitated, claimed to never have met him, called herself Celine. The man she was accompanied came across as extremely controlling and was spitting feathers to say the least. He thought it might have been some kind of cover, made his excuses and left. Then, when he thought about it, he realised Esther was an analyst. Not an undercover operative, a contractor to the security forces when he was working with her. Albeit with fairly deep security clearance."

"So?"

"So he checked the systems, ran across our missing person report, called it in."

"Great work. Nice to see those guys sharing finally. What's his name? Can I speak to him?"

"No. I'm afraid that he was over for a little vacation and he's now returned to duty. He's on deep cover for a couple of months. Wanted to check up on her before he went back, feels he's done his duty."

"Shit. Okay. Well, we have a place to start. Austria, Vienna. Don't suppose we got a description of the guy?"

"No. He said the purple lighting made it difficult to identify him or get a good look at his features. He'd only recognised Esther as she caught his eye in a fetching gown in the light, before they moved to their table."

"Damn. Well. We can start profiling and work from there."

"Um."

"Yes?"

"Look, to be frank, we don't have any resource for this."

"What?"

"It's not our concern."

Kevin Daste was silent for a few moments. Outside his room, the buzz of the hospital crept through the closed door.

When he finally spoke, his voice was soft.

"Agent Anderegg, listen to me very carefully. If you don't believe that the safety of someone abducted in our own country whilst a guest here is a matter for us, then the terrorists have already won and your job is redundant. When I had a job, regardless of resources or not, I made bloody well sure I did the best that I could with what I had. The moment you stop caring about one life, you may as well stop caring about every life, do you understand? Now, if you don't have the resources in the balls department to speak up and get someone up the chain of command on to this sharpish, I will use the resources at my disposal to make sure someone with appropriate spherical jewels in normal operation replaces you. You'll get bumped to traffic duty for the rest of your life. Do you understand?"

"Yes, Sir."

"Now get the fuck out of my sight and get moving. I want to find her and soon."

Special Agent Anderegg moved to the door. Kevin Daste shouted after her, making her flinch.

"And find fucking Ben Fallow. He'll kick seven shades of shit out of you if you find Esther and he's not around. That I can assure you."

CHAPTER 62

Monte, Madeira - Tuesday September 1st, 2009

They had watched the bizarre spectacle that was Colonel Muammar al-Gaddafi's fortieth anniversary celebrations on the television in the bar in Funchal. They were shocked at the ostentation on display and disgusted by his image-makers depiction of him.

Ben vowed to make him pay. Neither The Historian nor Pete argued.

Once back in Pete's house, the inevitable conversation occurred.

"Ben, I think it's time we went back to Switzerland."

"Really? Why now?"

"It seems as if the they're going to switch the Large Hadron Collider back on in November. I'm pretty certain that there will be another attempt to shut it down soon after it goes back online."

"That's a pretty safe bet, I agree."

"It will take us a while to get back, establish a base and prepare. We'll need to create a new identity for you, get you some papers along the way, so that you can get a car and so on. So I'd prefer to get started before the weather begins to turn."

"Fair enough."

Ben turned to Pete who put his hands up.

"No way you're getting me on that boat. Fuck no! I didn't even take the slow boat from China to get here. Planes all the way for me. Anyway, I'm sticking here. I have a feeling you'll be back, and you'll need a friend."

Ben grinned and fist-bumped Pete.

"Well, I can't say I'm going to look forward to getting back on that boat either, but I guess that's life."

"She's been primed and scraped, so she should be in good condition. I've upgraded some bits and pieces as well, so she'll be as comfortable as she can be. We just need to get my equipment back on board, stock up on supplies and we'll be ready to go."

"How long?"

"Three days I guess should do it."

"Three days it is then."

Pete brought three beers out from the kitchen and they toasted their future.

A little later that evening, Ben sat down on the mat. He no longer needed any aides to help him achieve the right state of mind. It came quickly to him.

His mind whispered to a few people about a certain military dictator who had perhaps overstepped his mark one to many times. Just a little nudge here and there.

As he was getting up, Pete stepped out of the shadows and picked the mat up.

"Take it. It's yours."

Ben smiled, clapped him on the back, rolled the mat up and slung it under his arm.

"Thanks, old man."

"Ah, fuck you!"

He registered Pete's tinkling laughter as he walked away.

#####

Ebhart's holiday may have been a distant memory since he had returned to CERN, but it had put a spring back in his step.

He wondered why it had taken him so long to understand the condition he was in and what remedy was required. The Alpine air, food and hospitality had done wonders, even in the few short days he'd been there. But he was more than ready to go back to the challenge of getting the Large Hadron Collider operational.

Summer sped by but thankfully there had been no more significant hitches. All the systems were reporting normal functionality. Everything was back down to the temperature it needed to be tested at, prior to the switch on.

It was amazing to think that, when cooled to the required temperature and switched on, the LHC environment was colder than space.

The pressure was ten times less than that experienced on the moon.

Stick that in your International Space Station and smoke it, Ebhart thought.

His mojo was definitely back.

His team also seemed to be refreshed and raring to go. The excitement was building again, just like the first time it was switched on. This time, all the fail safes had been checked and double-checked.

There were engineering faults, but those were in hand and would be addressed in the future. They weren't something to worry about running at the levels they were intending to operate at for the next few months of testing.

He was still getting the cold shoulder from his superiors, but he was less inclined to be concerned about that. His philosophy was, if they were going to push him, he would have been let go already. They were still smarting and would continue to until the project was back up and running and delivering data again.

And that's what he was focused on. Espionage was on the back burner for the moment. His logic was, if he focused on making sure that everything underground under his responsibility was in one hundred percent working order, known issues aside, he would be doing his job in preventing anything from stopping them reaching their goal.

Happy days were here again.

#####

Karvorkian had hardly been back to his house in weeks since the episode in the restaurant.

He was bitterly angry that the trajectory of his relationship with Celine had suffered a seemingly fatal curve. Crash and burn territory. His great project of creating himself the perfect wife now seemed doomed to end in failure.

He'd chosen the perfect memories to put inside a fantastic body, hung the best dresses on her and made her feel special. He'd wooed her. He hadn't needed to. He could have just programmed her to wake up one morning, in his bed, roll over and give him a blow job. Just. Like. That.

But that wouldn't have been fulfilling.

He would have found that too easy.

If he'd wanted that, he could just as well have hired a prostitute.

No, he had to make it difficult for himself. And that challenge had now blown up in his face. He'd lost months of work, dreams and money on someone that he now grew angry just thinking about, let alone seeing.

He couldn't decide what to do with her. Kill her? Wipe her completely? It was consuming him.

She really was stunning. He thought he was actually falling for her. How the hell could he? Then again, he'd aimed to create the perfect partner for himself, so why not?

So he travelled to take his mind off her.

He'd pursued his leads on the Bureau guy and located him easily. He was under cover, but it didn't take long for Karvorkian to discover his whereabouts.

He was used to working with people who could keep tabs on the likes of Jamie Dennington and his kind. Whether on their own side or the other.

He'd leaked his identity to the right people and the guy had ended up beheaded. Job done.

What he didn't know was whether Mr FBI had pursued the matter further.

That was a risk. Could he have been identified? Would he have checked into the disappearance of Esther? If so, who would have been alerted? Was anyone searching for her?

He hadn't noticed when precisely, but the buzzing in his head had returned. It was louder now. He had to hum for twice as long before it disappeared, and it was the only thing that would make it go away. It was starting to intrude on conversations. It would wake him up.

It was painful.

So he travelled around, had a day or so of rest and relaxation before getting so frustrated he jumped back on his jet.

He circled the globe almost three times in as many weeks, stopping here and there.

Checking up on his business interests.

Investigating leads on new identities of his fellow journeymen.

Meeting key informants and operatives with new instructions.

Busy, busy.

Putting off the inevitable.

Returning to Vienna.

One more day, he kept telling himself.

Just one.

CHAPTER 63

Nottwil, Switzerland - Saturday October 10th, 2009

Kevin Daste could not believe what he was hearing.

"You didn't? Tell me you did."

He heard Special Agent Anderegg shift from one foot to the other in excruciating discomfort.

"Just how stupid are you?"

As a professional, Kevin had expected more of the secret service. As a citizen, he was shocked at their lack of thoroughness.

"You didn't think to ask which restaurant they were in? You didn't think about visiting all the restaurants and show them a likeness of her? You just decided to, what, go house to house? Snoop around until you might see someone matching her description through a window?"

The agent's head was bowed.

Inside, she was cursing the day she'd offered to be a liaison for this guy, thinking that it wouldn't be too much of an effort.

"Jesus Christ on a bike. We've lost so much time I can't even begin to say it. Get on the phone. Call around the restaurants. You know the rough dates. Ask if a man and a lady in a gold sparkly dress came in and left in a hurry one evening. Start at the most expensive and work your way down."

"Yes, Sir."

"Don't call me Sir! I'm not a Sir. I'm a legless, blind man who can do your job better than you could every single fucking day, even on pain meds. Now get out and come back to me tomorrow saying you've at least found the restaurant they went to. Now!"

Anderegg left. Kevin picked up he coffee mug and threw it as hard as he could.

The sound of it breaking against metal gave him the satisfaction. It had broken against the door handle. Right about where Special Agent Anderegg had been standing moments earlier.

He frowned. He really needed to control his temper.

Otherwise people might start to suspect that all was not rosy in the mental garden in his mind.

The other bad news was that they still had not located Ben Fallow. A boat had been in the area, but it had sailed to France. And there it was lost. He suspected they'd changed the vessel's identity, frequencies and so on, to hide from the usual tracking systems.

That meant that it was almost certainly up to no good, and no good meant smuggling of one kind or another. With the boat in that area at that time, in full view of the events going on lighting up the sky,

Kevin had no problem believing that Ben Fallow had been on board.

It was highly likely that he was still in possession of that vessel. He had to figure out a way of first finding and then contacting him, to let him know that he was alive. Then together, they could narrow down their search for the bastards that caused all this.

#####

Anderegg did return, although it was not until two days later.

There was positive news to report though and he noted a new determination in her.

"You found the restaurant?"

"We did. Two Michelin stars, as you suspected."

"Well I didn't think they'd be slumming it in a place frequented by the FBI with Esther wearing what appears to be an autumn collection dress that's not yet out in mainstream outlets."

"Right."

"So?"

"I spoke to the front of house manager. He remembered them as they left in a hurry and didn't leave a particularly good tip. The bare minimum in fact."

"Did he pay by card?"

"Unfortunately no. Cash."

"Shit, shit, shit. No way we can trace that as it's been way to long."

"Right."

"Reservation?"

"It was made through a concierge service that specialises in reservations on behalf of clients who do not wish to use their names."

"They exist?"

"Indeed so."

"Right. So what about the car? Valet parking?"

"Again, no luck. The chauffeur, dropped them off, drove around the block, came back and picked them up. Must have been nearby in the line of sight, scooped them up and drove away."

"CCTV? In the restaurant?"

"No. I quote, 'We value the privacy of our guests'."

"Street?"

"Some, but no help. The quality is really poor, and the network is due for an upgrade next year. All but useless blobs of colour getting into a black limousine."

"So. Nothing then."

"Not quite. A waiter happened to hear the conversation whilst he was serving another table nearby. Actually, he thought the woman was stunning and kept trying to sneak a look down her dress every time he passed."

"Get on with it."

"He said he heard her say her name was Celine Matheson."

"Great. And you found her?"

"Yes."

"Really? Where?"

"In the cemetery."

Kevin waited.

"Same age roughly. But she died five years ago. And she had blonde hair, was a good five inches taller and, uh, only had one hand. From birth."

Kevin's toes tingled again.

"Well done Anderegg. She's definitely our girl. Now we've got to find her. Quickly."

"Yes, s...Agreed."

"What was the name of that concierge service?"

"I have it, I just don't have it with me."

Kevin threw his hands up in mock exasperation.

"Come on, come on, you've got to keep up with me, Anderegg! Every detail, every single one. Get on them, tap their phones, crack into their databases, their invoices, whatever it takes to get that location. Time is running out, I can feel it."

She turned to go.

"Wait. Anderegg. Thank you. For what you're doing."

The Special Agent paused.

"It's like you said. Forget about one life, you might as well forget about them all."

She closed the door behind her.

Yes, Kevin thought. Good girl.

CHAPTER 64

Geneva, Switzerland - Thursday October 15th, 2009

It felt strange being back in Switzerland after so much time away.

The atmosphere seemed entirely transformed, he realised. He noticed an elevated energy level flowing around the country.

In Madeira, it had been a low, rich hum, a beneficent and benign swirl that encouraged a sense of relaxation and timelessness.

Here it was completely different. It was as if there were different poles affecting the flow, but he knew that was not the case. Even though Feng Shui practitioners had laid a compass over the forces and states, luck didn't abide by a two dimensional representation.

In Switzerland, in Geneva, energy rushed around like the wind, constantly shifting and blowing in different directions, pushing and pulling. It felt noisy somehow. He could almost hear it in real life.

It was unsurprising. Ben remembered all the powerful organisations headquartered in the area. And underneath it all, the most powerful machine on the earth, shooting the stuff that made everything around in a gigantic circle.

No wonder everything was heightened here.

The Historian and he had moored the boat somewhere safely anonymous in the South of France and taken a train into Geneva. After a day or two of checking out various places, they chose and paid for one. They hired a van, returned to the boat and proceeded to remove the computing equipment.

They had chosen a semi-isolated property close to Lake Geneva which made Ben feel as comfortable as possible given the situation with the energy flow.

He spent some time moving furniture, adding in some Feng Shui elements that helped the energy flow even more smoothly around the place. He also identified the best place for him to use his skills when the time came.

It wasn't long before they were set up and ready.

Ben found and purchased a second hand motorbike for cash. It was nearly new.

The owner was happy to off-load it as it had been a spontaneous purchase. To try to avert a mid-life crisis. Its speed scared the current owner. Ben was delighted with it, the owner with the sight of cash.

He purchased a helmet and full black leathers, and some small but capacious panniers.

The Historian meanwhile found a fairly decent second hand BMW in a neutral colour. A popular car in the city and one which would blend in well.

Then they waited.

Switch on of the Large Hadron Collider was not imminent. But, as The Historian said, there was a significant chance that an act of sabotage might occur before the allotted time came. Ben had to be ready.

He was surprised at the openness of the information available about CERN's schedule and the LHC. Pretty much everything was online and open on its website. He guessed it was in the spirit of scientific collaboration. Or just arrogance.

Whatever, it was helpful to him to be able to see potential times of weakness. When and where visitors outside of the core scientific community were there. When there were significant events for key country sponsors.

His other less structured line of enquiry was open to him of course, and he took it. He spent an hour or so a day visualising the energy flows, identifying those around CERN and the huge campus above and below ground. He floated through minds, not able to read them but getting a sense of their emotional state. He noted the negativity in many of them. It would be difficult to identify a single saboteur from that bunch, he thought.

Other minds were full of awe and wonder and excitement. Visitors, children, journalists not too jaded by the daily grind, bloggers, enthusiasts. It was pleasing to see.

The Historian continued his dance with data, his fingers twiddling in the air, leg jiggling under his desk.

He too could sense something was about to happen.

Through it all however, Ben had not forgotten why this had all started for him.

Esther.

He knew somehow that she was still alive. He sensed, although he could never find her on his journeys. He felt that she was still somewhere in Switzerland.

She could have been around the corner, in the next house, for all he knew.

For many months, he'd not dreamed of her. Since returning to Switzerland, he dreamed of her every night. They were no longer running. She was instead sleeping. Floating and sleeping.

He could see her breathing, through her nose, the tiny hairs in her nostrils trembling at each breath in, and out.

After a time, who knows how long in dream time, her eyes would fly open and a silent scream would come out. He would wake up then.

That was not particularly joyful. Not a bit.

He knew somehow that all this was related. He would see her again. He didn't know when or where, or how but it would happen.

Then, who knew?

CHAPTER 65

Lake Geneva, Switzerland - Saturday October 24th, 2009

It didn't take Ben long to settle into his new routine.

He quickly reacquainted himself with the smells and sounds of Switzerland. He went running by the lake and sparring with huge tree trunks to keep his fitness levels up.

However, this now made up a minority of his day, and he dedicated around an hour to washing, training physically and eating.

The rest of his waking hours were spent in a trance. He tracked the flows of energy, gently unblocking restrictions and obstacles that prevented luck from flowing to those places that needed it.

Most of all, he kept watch over CERN for as long as he could. Not physically of course. That wasn't required and in fact would have been detrimental.

CERN had its own special glow around it. It had everything it needed to attract positive vibrations and yet it was virtually devoid of the stuff. It was as if a dome had been placed over the whole place which repelled the particles. It was very strange and Ben thought that he'd never seen the like of it on his travels.

He'd sunk into the ground and dropped into the LHC tunnels. He glimpsed inside the sterile vacuum and identified no further evidence of luck there either.

He could only assume that some extremely strong force was impeding the ability for luck to penetrate here. It wasn't like scientists who didn't believe in the stuff had the same impact on luck that not believing in fairies did, snuffing them out of existence. It wasn't their fault that they'd yet to re-discover it.

There was only one specific and weak source within the whole of the complex that he identified generating positive energy. A Japanese Dharuma doll, in a glass case. As he observed it, the power seemed to get weaker and weaker, like its batteries were running low.

He pondered this absence as he stood virtual guard over the facility.

He'd have to come up with something to break down those barriers, but for now it felt too big for him alone to crack.

As the days passed, he spent less and less time working on the insights drawn from The Historian's analysis and focused more on making sure that all was well at CERN.

As November crept closer, Ben felt a heightened sense that something was about to happen. He couldn't put his finger on what, but he felt the need to test his capabilities in case he needed to act.

He slipped into the lab buildings and floated through until he came to one.

As he entered, he felt a particularly strong force from negatively charged luck and investigated.

In the back of the lab, he saw something glowing darkly. It was a solid state miniature camera, carefully hidden behind some old equipment.

He moved around and saw a late middle-aged man in a white lab coat sitting at a bench close by.

Ben gently pushed with his mind. The equipment hiding the camera teetered then fell to the floor with a crash, making the man in the lab coat jump. He turned, saw the equipment on the floor, tutted and moved to put it back on the shelf.

As he straightened up, his eye line was directly in front of the camera.

There was a microsecond's pause.

Then the man, instead of putting the item down and picking up the camera, placed the item back on the shelf, as if he'd not noticed the espionage equipment.

He moved back to the bench and continued with what he was doing.

Well at least I know I'm fully operational, Ben thought, as he floated back up through the ground.

He was still puzzled by the man's reaction, even though he'd placed the item to directly obscure the line of sight of the camera.

Strange.

245

Professor Fenkhause could not believe what had just happened. His blood was racing and it was all he could do not to visibly shake.

There it had been, in plain sight; a physical manifestation of his fears. Before, he'd thought that everything he'd believed about sabotage was all in his head. That he'd rationalized events that he didn't want to believe could simply be down to negligence. Now, he knew that someone or group was out to personally destroy him.

Now he knew.

Even if it was not personal, there it was. In his own lab. How it had got there goodness only knew. But it was there.

It wasn't just about the LHC. It was about his work. His mind. His theories.

How long had it been there?

He'd seen it almost straight away as he was standing back up. He had virtually no time to make his mind up as to what to do.

If he reacted by picking the camera up, whoever was watching would know that he knew that security had been compromised. That someone was watching them work. That was one easy way to be dead by tea time, he thought.

Instead, he'd done the only thing he'd felt natural. He hoped that the camera was not of sufficient high definition to notice the tiny pause. He'd put the oscilloscope back on the shelf in a position that blocked the camera's view.

Those on the other end of the camera, wherever that was, would analyse the footage. Hopefully they'd conclude that poor old Professor Fenkhause was tired. That the old duffer hadn't noticed the one thing in the lab that shouldn't have been there.

At least, that's what he hoped they would think.

He would still need to be extremely careful. But now, he also needed an insurance policy. Something to let people know what had been going on in case he was a target and didn't make it to the end of the project.

He needed time to think about what that might be.

But switch on was a mere couple of weeks away. He needed to think fast. He strolled casually out of the lab and down to the cafeteria to get a cup of tea. He suddenly had a terrible thirst.

#####

Karvorkian ran the footage that he'd been sent backwards and forwards, frowning.

There was Professor Ebhart Fenkhause in super slow-motion. Bending down and up, up and down. Then putting something in front of the camera lens that obscured it almost completely whilst seemingly oblivious to the camera.

He tapped his finger on the desk.

"So, what is your assessment?"

The voice on the other end of the line coughed gruffly and then said: "He doesn't know."

"You're sure?"

"I'm one hundred percent sure. He's so focused on protecting his backside with all the board breathing down his neck, he can't see his hand in front of his face. Unless it's something directly related to getting the LHC back up and running, he's pretty much a zombie."

Karvorkian ran the footage backwards and forwards one last time, then closed the window on his computer.

"Okay. Well, on your head be it."

"Yeah, well, that's what you're paying me for."

"I am aware of that. Now, I need you to do something else for me."

"Always. For a fee."

"Christ, you scientists. It's really all about money, isn't it?"

"Of course. Money and fame. So, what's it to be?"

"Nothing big. I just need you to hack into the right systems to accredit someone to join the education tour coming up. Make sure he's got the right credentials. He only needs a guest pass and access the museum area."

"No problem. When is it?"

Karvorkian tutted.

"Have you not heard of Google? Do a search, for fuck's sake. Or just visit your own damn website and find it there. Now, get rid of that phone the way you were told. You'll get another one when you're needed to report in."

He put the phone down.

He shuddered. Working with scientists made him feel dirty. The thought made him laugh, a short, percussive bark.

He rubbed his face. Christ, he needed to get a grip.

He scheduled a conference call in order to finalise the official rubber stamping of the actions that he'd all but signed off on himself. Then he sat deep in thought.

There was nothing for it. He'd put it off for too long. He was going to have to go back home and make a decision about Celine.

If she was indeed Celine.

CHAPTER 66

CERN - Tuesday November 3rd, 2009

The programme for the visiting Russian teachers was in full swing.

Since they had arrived on November the first, excitement levels within the group had been high. Like kids in a zoo, it was nigh on impossible to keep them together as a group. Individuals ran here and there, pointing, exclaiming. Snapping pictures and generally regressing to an age where sugar highs resulted in wall-bouncing levels of energy.

They were in the superconducting magnet testing centre. The facility itself, which also housed a visitor's centre nearby, might be compared to a busy tube station. With its futuristic art installation which changed colour depending on the amount of cosmic rays hitting the earth, it was like a swarming interchange to a potentially ground-breaking future Earth.

One amongst them was still.

Eyes closed. A slight frown.

It was an unusual sight in amongst the other teachers rushing around. Like one of those accelerated motion films where someone is standing stationary and the world seems to rush past them.

Stock still, his frown increased. To the casual observer, one might have concluded that he was perhaps having a brief but intense migraine headache. His actions, or lack of them, designed to mitigate the symptoms.

This was not the case. Indeed, what was occurring was not painful in the slightest. Instead, it required complete focus to achieve the goals that had been set out for him.

After about a minute, the frown eased slightly and the man's shoulders dropped a fraction. At the same time, he tipped his head marginally. His neck cracked audibly, as if re-setting itself after being out of joint, and his eyes snapped open.

A faint smile passed his lips for a second.

Then he was off.

As animated as the rest of the group, intrigued by the technology around him.

His mission concluded, he went back to his day job of a Russian teacher.

Visiting CERN so that he could pass on his experience to those that would never have the opportunity to visit.

At the moment his inactivity ceased, an owl dropped a piece of bread over an electrical substation.

It supplied power to Section 81 of the LHC's cryogenic systems. The discarded food caused several busbars to short.

As a result, temperatures in part of the LHC's circuit quickly climbed to almost eight Kelvin. That was significantly higher than the normal operating temperature of one point nine Kelvin. Dangerously close to the temperature at which the LHC's niobium-titanium magnets were likely to quench.

#####

Synchronising almost to the second with the man tens of kilometres away, Ben's eyes also opened. He felt a bead of sweat trickle down his temple and a needle-shaped pain at the back of his head.

He was sitting by the edge of the lake. It was quiet, a few ripples on the water glinting in the wintery light.

Around a half hour before, his heart had started to thump in his chest and his breathing became shallow. Something was about to happen. He had felt the gentle thrumming of the invisible threads, like a spider's web sending information back down to the hub about a fly trapped on its extremities, even outside of his trance state.

He'd been monitoring the environment around CERN almost constantly for a few days, like a background program running on a computer to prevent it from virus attacks.

He had dashed over to the lake, the quietest place he could find, and settled quickly into a trance.

He zoomed in on Geneva, then into the CERN campus. He was drawn. Sucked into the centre of a vortex.

He identified the man and, without knowing how exactly, sourced the object of his concentration.

And diverted it.

Just a small mental nudge.

A suggestion of the vaguest movement.

Nothing too much to alert the perpetrator of the interference that he had failed his task entirely.

But just enough.

As soon as he felt comfortable that the agent had also moved on, Ben jumped up and made his way back to the house.

Things had changed.

The balance of power was beginning to shift. Those behind these acts of sabotage would not take this sitting down. He knew he would have to get to CERN as soon as possible and quickly locate the team that was being targeted.

He jumped into the BMW, spun the wheels on the gravel and shot out through the trees towards Geneva.

CHAPTER 67

CERN - Tuesday November 3rd, 2009

They stared at each other. Stunned, waiting.

Were it not for the significant amount of technology humming quietly in the background, the lab would have been silent. Silence in a CERN laboratory most probably would not have been present since just before the first spade dug the first hole in the ceremonial breaking of the ground on this immense international collaboration.

Eyes darted from person to person. Alf Vertigung sipped a bottle of Evian, a dribble of water escaping the side of his mouth, quickly wiped away by a dirty white sleeve. His leg bounced as if in training for a new career as a drummer practising a particularly syncopated rhythm on the bass drum.

"For how long?" Professor Ebhart Fenkhause stood by the workbench, a telephone handset pressed hard to his ear.

Whilst temperature regulated, it felt to him that all the air had been sucked out of the room. His throat was tight. A pressure in his chest felt like a band had closed around it, twisting aggressively tighter. His kidneys ached.

It was impossible to tell what time of day or night it was. The team ought to have been weary, but instead the atmosphere was charged. The by-product of nerves and adrenaline.

The phone eased ever so slightly as Ebhart's shoulders slumped marginally as he swayed. "I see. Well, please keep me informed the moment you have any further information."

The phone handset slowly dropped back into the cradle. The Professor's hand staying on top of it momentarily. His finger tapped it twice as if passing a signal to it to tell it to sleep. To provide no further bad news for the moment.

Still with his back to the rest of the team, Ebhart raised his head to the ceiling of the lab, as if trying to see the heavens through thousands of tonnes of earth piled above them. Then he exhaled audibly. Long and slow, his shoulders sinking even lower.

"How bad is it?"

He did not register who had asked the question.

He turned and saw them all as one unit, a collective brain, a mass of cognitive geniuses. It didn't matter who asked the question. It wouldn't change the answer he would deliver.

"They're still investigating, but it could be months, like last time. It might even put us back another year."

Reinforcing the group's synergy, everyone gasped together. Then one gave an involuntary, swallowed sob. Another groaned.

The bottle of water Alf was holding by his side fell to the floor and he scrambled to pick it up, his leg still agitating.

"Oh Christ."

"How? Why?"

"I don't fucking believe it. I really don't fucking believe it."

"I need a drink. And a smoke. Fuck it."

"I think we all do, Peter," Bert said. "I think we all need to get out of here, now."

"What if there's an update?"

"Cell phones work above ground and in bars, Chenni," Peter snapped back. "There's no point waiting in this fucking bunker. Let's at least get some real air."

"Perhaps I should stay?" Suzi cajoled, "in case, you know...?"

It was Chenni's turn to be adamant now.

"No. We all go. We all need to get through this. With vodka, preferably. Lots of fucking vodka."

Piotr Morodov swung and span back, almost tipping his chair over, and moved to grab his coat, as did his namesake Peter. They didn't need to be told twice.

"Do we even know what caused it?" That was Bert Hervey, always asking why.

Ebhart slumped against the workbench and tried to stifle an incredulous chuckle.

"A bird," he said.

Eyes swung back around to focus on him.

"I'm sorry, I think I misheard you," said Peter, coat halfway on one shoulder. "I thought you said 'a bird' there for a moment."

"Oh, I did. It gets better though."

"What? Better? In what reality can it get fucking better?"

"It was a bird with a baguette."

"Is this someone's idea of a joke? It's not the first of April already is it? You have got to be fucking kidding me!"

"It's no joke, even though it's bizarre enough to be, I'm afraid."

Ebhart reviewed the team in front of him, wondering at the elemental forces that shaped the world. The myriad randomness of circumstance, cause and effect.

He drew a deep breath and quickly rattled off what had just occurred.

"We're talking about the most expensive machine on earth, worked on for decades, built to understand the sub-atomic structure of the universe. It now sits, currently broken, by a piece of baton-shaped baked produce which a feathered descendant of the dinosaurs took a fancy to. But which was, conclusively, too big for it to carry. And which, subsequently, dropped into our power supply connection, effectively causing a power cut of monumental impact."

He once again stared into open mouths, accompanied by the gentle hum of technology.

Then, quietly, Suzi spoke again.

"Well, I've always said it. Mankind should never have begun to plant wheat. Total disaster, arable farming."

Finally putting his coat fully on, Peter shook his head.

"Nah. Wheat's fine. It's the bloody French and their protectionism over baguette baking. It has to be a certain bloody size or it's not a baguette. It's discrimination against birds and people who don't eat as much as them. If in doubt, always blame the French I say. No offence Bert."

"Almost certainly offence taken Peter," Bert Hervey said, the only Frenchman in the group. "But quite frankly, at this point, I do not, how do you English say it Chenni, give a fuck."

Alf finally stood up, ramrod straight.

"Right then. If this has all gone to the birds, I for one agree that it's vodka 'o' clock and we should go and get mightily trolleyed. After all, we've got at least a few months to get over the hangover."

Again, nods all around the group reinforced the collective.

Ebhart took them all in. Watery eyes misting and blurring his sight. A doleful smile played at his mouth.

With a resigned sigh, he nodded again.

"Okay, first round is on me. Piotr, get the lights and lock up for the day...night...whatever."

They all filed out of the lab, crocodile-like. The room was left once again to hum to itself. The fluorescent tubes ticked off as the Piotr flicked off the switch.

This couldn't be sabotage, Ebhart thought, as he closed the door. Could it?

#####

"The cat sneezed three times."

Karvorkian paused momentarily, not anticipating the code words for failure to come over the line from Geneva.

"I see."

"Instructions?"

There was no hesitation this time.

"Take the owner to the vet. Have him put down. We can't risk contagion."

"Understood."

The line went dead.

It was time for the Professor to be removed from play.

Karvorkian also decided to put the other matter taking up too much of his valuable time to rest also.

He had been too lax with Celine.

It was, regrettably, time his little experiment was shut down too.

CHAPTER 68

Geneva, Switzerland - Tuesday November 3rd, 2009

They had an articulate yet heated debate about the most conducive venue in which to get 'rat-arsed' as Alf put it.

The majority vote finally concluded that the twenty-odd minute trip into Geneva was the best course of action, even though it was somewhat out of the way for at least half of them.

Split into two taxi vans, they navigated the end of working day traffic and headed over to the south bank in the centre of town.

Arthur's Wine Bar on the Rue de Rhone won as the least worst option for this particular sorrow-drowning scenario. Filled with more corporate suits and office types during the week, it was a favourite hang-out in a central location. Close to the higher end fashion area of the city.

It was too cold to sit out, as was normally the case in Switzerland at this time of year. The view of the Lake barely registered in the light anyway, so they headed inside to monopolise the comfortable sofas.

After an obligatory round of vodka shots and a toast to the futility of wishing for a speedy recovery of the LHC, the team finally began to show some individual traits through the choices of their drinks.

Ebhart decided to opt for something that would gently dull the ache in both his head and stomach rather than aggressively chase it out. He chose a glass, albeit a large one, of Sauvignon Blanc.

As he sipped, he surveyed the group in various postures.

He assessed them with both analytical regard and, except for who would turn out to be the spy, huge compassion.

Piotr and Peter immediately started discussing what, if any, food they might eat, as was their want as they launched themselves into standard litres of continental lager.

There was not much imagination shared between them. Unless it was the infinite possibilities of food combinations.

Ebhart glanced at Suzi.

She was sticking on the vodka, like Chenni.

Hers however was with some tonic and lime. She had a habit of crunching the ice in her drink using her front teeth, like a chipmunk gnawing relentlessly on a branch. He shivered as he thought about his own sensitive teeth and wondered why in this climate ice in drinks was necessary. She was drinking quickly, but to be honest, most of the team were.

Suzi was quiet, tending to shy away from being the one to jump into a debate in a large group. But on occasion, she could stun the team with a specific insight that would pivot the debate substantially. This was one of her quiet moments.

Chenni, the other female of the group, was almost the polar opposite of Suzi.

Born in England of Asian descent, she was effervescent, fun-loving and, whilst considered attractive, very much a tomboy at heart. She had lungs like a member of the Welsh Male Voice Choir and the vocabulary of a character from Chaucer. She was brash, opinionated but bloody good at what she did when she needed to focus.

What she was focusing on currently, between an expletive-ridden diatribe at their current predicament, was demolishing a line of Lime-flavoured vodkas without choking.

Alf had a white beer and was taking long, slow gulps of the cloudy liquid.

A native of Geneva, Alf was the most likely one out of the team to turn up during the week with stories of a late evening of beer drinking. This was usually delivered with the wearing of a particularly dark set of sunglasses that were perhaps once in fashion twenty years ago. Which, by the same token, were more than likely to be in fashion again relatively soon.

Much like the rest of his wardrobe which, Ebhart realised, he hardly ever saw due to the lab coats that most of them turned up and left in.

Apart from the fairly dramatic item of clothing here and there, most of his clothing was composed from dark tones.

Fairly standard for scientists.

Alf was nice enough though, pretty social. Brighter than he came across. Which, on most days, was Forrest Gump-esque.

Bert of course was outside, smoking a roll up. His glass of red wine sat next to both some sparkling water and a cup of black coffee.

Bert seemed incapable of just doing one thing at a time, regardless of whether it was drinking or working. It wasn't so much indecision as a desire to experience everything at once, trying to digest and correlate new experiences or see patterns in combinations.

His drive for discovery sometimes led him to adverse reactions, such as one might get when combining Oysters with Whisky. But generally he bounced back. Nothing a quick ciggie wouldn't fix, he'd say, and stalk off, either to the closest medical station or for a quick puff.

When he eventually returned, getting way-laid by a colleague from another department who was peppering him with questions about the rumours going around CERN, the group was well on its way to achieving intoxication.

Ebhart's investigation had failed to reveal the traitor in his midst. So he decided to give up for the evening and have another glass of wine.

#####

The night closed in, wrapping itself around the buildings. The illuminations dimmed as a fog crept up from the lake.

Even though the heater was on, the observer in the car outside the bar pulled the collar of his coat up and a little tighter around his throat. He settled in for the evening, wishing he too could have a cigarette.

Not yet, but soon, Manek promised himself. He reached for another piece of fine Swiss chocolate, thinking about how on earth he had got himself into this position. Whether he'd survive to see the next Olympics scheduled to be in London in 2012.

CHAPTER 69

Geneva, Switzerland - Tuesday November 3rd, 2009

A couple of hours later, everyone was rolling drunk.

For once, Ebhart's mind had stopped thinking about life at the sub-atomic level. It was now swimming in a haze of brandy-infused warmth. Chenni had convinced him somehow that this would be a wise course of action, considering the weather outside and the inevitable wait for a taxi. He'd even begun to smile, listening to Peter and Piotr sing rock ballads. Currently, they were singing one from some long-haired eighties rock band that would inevitably, if not already, re-form to do a world tour. It seemed that things from twenty years ago really were back in fashion.

Twenty years. It was a long time in a man's life but such a short time in 'the grand scheme of things'.

Ebhart scarcely remembered what music he'd liked and what clothes he'd wore when he had first come to CERN, excited and daunted by the huge undertaking that was at the very start of its creation. His smile faded as again the situation and its impact on the delivery of their work hit home. He tried to make sure his reaction was hidden from the rest of the team.

He wondered now whether he would even see the discovery of the God particle in his lifetime.

One person had been watching him closely and came up and put an arm around his neck.

"Professor," Chenni said, "now is not the time for wallowing in sorrow. The night is young. How about we hit another venue and continue this debauchery where the closing times are less authoritarian?"

But Ebhart had had enough.

The night may well have been relatively young for the rest of his team, but none of them were approaching retirement age. His head shook slowly. A yawn escaped. The hand holding the brandy came up to cover his mouth and, momentarily forgotten, he poured the remainder over his lapel and the top half of his shirt.

"Oh drat!"

"Here, let me get that for you," Chenni giggled, grabbing a couple of napkins and dabbing at him randomly.

"I think that I have demonstrably made my point, Chenni. I'm no longer fit to be out in public. Knowing my luck, some reporter will be watching and there'll be another article about scientists in charge of the God machine getting drunk in charge and causing the end of the world. Either that, or I'll embarrass myself with a ridiculously un-scientific quote that the other teams will laugh at and pin on the lab door. No, I think it's best that I gracefully retire. After all, it seems our two songbirds are going through the entire back catalogue of this particular band and, I must admit, I'm not a fan of a capella rock in the key of off!"

Ebhart got up, unsteadily, with Chenni's help. She then proceeded to give him a tight hug, getting some of the brandy on her top also, and gave him a peck on the cheek. Suzi repeated the motion, although carefully making sure she avoided the brandy.

Bert was next to get up.

"No, no, please, enough kisses for today," Ebhart chuckled, and Bert play-acted the spurned lover. He couldn't keep it up for long.

Alf waved. It was also quite possible that he was incapable of getting up. There were a healthy number of empty glasses he had in front of him, the leftover froth of white beer patterning the sides of them.

His eyes seemed slightly more crossed than usual.

As he weaved out of the sofa area, Peter and Piotr together slapped him on the back, still booming out another old favourite. It was difficult to tell whether they were meant to be singing the same tune or they were attempting harmonies. By the glances of people around them, Ebhart was not on his own in trying to work this out.

He finally made it to the door. Passing through it, gasped as a particularly sharp gust of unseasonably cold wind slammed into his open mouth.

Pulling up the collar of his coat, he made it to the pavement and began to walk in the direction of a taxi rank that was a short distance away.

Predictably, it was empty, so he decided to try some of the streets away from the bars and hail one.

The bitterly cold wind prickled at his exposed hands, face and ears.

He barely noticed the tiny dart that incapacitated him a few hundred yards on as he was just rounding a corner into a side street.

CHAPTER 70

Geneva, Switzerland - Tuesday November 3rd, 2009

As the Professor slumped to the floor, Manek caught him to slow his final descent to the pavement. His instructions were clear. The Professor should not be harmed and was simply to be apprehended and brought to the lake house.

Content that he had performed the first part of the task admirably, he quickly deconstructed the blowpipe he had used to administer the pacification formula. He snapped it back into its case along with some spare darts.

As soon as he had done so, bright stars appeared in his vision and he felt his own legs collapse from under him. Uh oh, he thought, as he too slipped into unconsciousness.

#####

Ben pulled the man's car to the front of the street and proceeded to put the Professor in the back seat and the other guy in the boot.

He'd been waiting a long time outside the bar, as had Ebhart's attacker. He'd followed the taxi that the Professor had occupied into the town. Then, after struggling to find a parking space in the vicinity, had walked back. Finding a relatively secluded spot with a view of the wine bar street, he hunkered down to watch what happened.

It had not been long before he'd seen a car pull up and felt that something was awry.

This was no parent coming to pick up an errant teenager from a party.

There was little light coming from inside the vehicle, indicating that the person driving had no reading material to while the hours away whilst waiting for that last, hopefully non-alcoholic drink to be consumed by their son or daughter. He could of course have been listening to some dull discussion on the radio, but there didn't seem to be a light from the dashboard.

The fogged up rear window was difficult to see through.

That also meant that his position was similarly masked to the car's occupant. Ben himself didn't want to move and reveal his position, so instead he focused on the bar that the Professor and his team occupied.

He took a little time to slip into a waking trance just to check the flow of things around CERN. From his cursory check, he was relieved to see that they had assessed the damage. They were coming to the conclusion that it would not have any significant threat on the planned re-start after all. Hopefully that would cheer the Professor up when he returned with a hangover the next morning.

As his focus returned, he was just in time to see the Professor exit the bar, wobbling slightly. His breath puffing out vapour in the cold night air.

He glanced back over to the car to see its occupant get out.

Instantly, he recognised the man and his heart beat faster.

It was one of the men from Esther's abduction.

As the Professor carefully made his way along the street, Esther's abductor crossed. Careful to act casual, he removed something from his pocket.

Waiting until there was real distance between him and Ebhart's stalker, Ben too crossed the road and moved in what little shadow there was. Whilst the street was noisy with people in bars huddling together to keep warm around candles and spirits, there were very few out on the street itself smoking. That was good.

The Professor turned into a side street and Ben knew instantly that he'd need to get a lot closer.

That had been a bad calculation for Ebhart.

As Ben got to the turning, he saw the man finish laying the Professor down on the pavement then stop to put some kind of weapon back into a case. That was his mistake.

As soon as Ebhart's attacker had one hand in his pocket, Ben stepped in. He threw a well-practised manoeuvre starting with a punch at the base of the man's skull followed by a jab with his fingers behind the ear.

It ended with his thumb underneath the man's jaw. It was over in seconds.

Ben checked both of the men's pulses and was satisfied they wouldn't be moving quickly.

As it was closer, Ben jumped into the assailant's car and swung it around to the side street. He made quick work of the two unconscious bodies. After taping the attacker's hands and feet with a roll of gaffer tape he'd fished out of the man's boot, he tipped him in then drove off slowly and quietly.

The whole operation had taken between two to three minutes.

For the first time, Ben felt real hope that he would find Esther.

He dearly wished that he'd find her alive. If not, the man in the boot was going to be on the receiving end of what a grieving, professionally trained 'problem solver' would describe as therapy.

CHAPTER 71

New York - Midnight, Wednesday November 4th, 2009

The news on the television was talking of the successful third mayoral term that the city's residents had rewarded the incumbent with.

Karvorkian did not appreciate the irony.

There was the mayor, s man who had built his empire on information. And here was he, more powerful than anyone could imagine, being treated like a mushroom. Kept in the dark and fed shit.

Karvorkian gritted his teeth as the phone number he'd been trying to reach rang through to voicemail for the twentieth time that morning.

The buzzing noise in his brain was back, worse than ever.

That damn fool Manek was not responding. He'd had no word about the success of the action to take Professor Fenkhause out of the equation.

He rubbed his forehead harshly as he re-dialled. Why the hell had he thought that Manek would be able to perform without supervision on a job like this?

It was his fault. How many times had he reminded himself that if he wanted something doing right, he should do it himself?

Now, he had no idea where the Professor was, where Manek was and what level of shit he was going to have to wade through to set things right.

And that bastard buzzing was back. What the fuck had he done to deserve that?

Well, apart from the obvious.

He'd checked various sources. There was no news of any arrests. No persons matching either Manek or the Professor's descriptions being brought into hospitals. No dead bodies lying on morgue tables beyond those identified as being pensioners who died of cold. Or terminally ill patients having their life support systems turned off by grieving or greedy relatives.

So, they were out there somewhere.

Either Manek had performed admirably or, as he suspected, things had gone tits up, as the quaint British saying went.

The phone rang once more to voicemail. Karvorkian screeched, threw his mobile across the room and saw the glass screen on the phone shatter.

A knock at the door just a second later showed the difference between that amateur Manek and Fritz. The other person who'd been involved in Esther's original abduction.

"Sir, can I get you anything?"

He was calm, his steel blue eyes showing no emotion. His gaze indicated the correct level of respect that Karvorkian required from his support team.

Karvorkian swallowed, counted to ten and rubbed his forehead less vigorously than before.

"Fritz, I am afraid I think it's time to return to the house in Geneva. There is a. Mess. Yes. I'm pretty sure a mess that your erstwhile colleague Manek has left for us to clean up."

"I'm sorry to hear that, Sir. What are your instructions?"

"I'd like you to take the jet and Celine to the house and get everything ready. I'll follow on. I need to make some further arrangements and some more calls. Make sure that we have everything we need at our disposal to proceed, ah, appropriately."

"Understood, Sir."

"Fritz?"

"Yes, Sir?"

"Celine. I'm afraid that she won't be with us too much longer, so please don't tell her too much. Only enough for her to perform her duties. Her contract will be ending in Geneva. She will be seeing the good doctor she was originally under the care of once I get there."

Fritz nodded. Nothing more.

"Be careful with her Fritz. You need to watch her."

"I will."

"Thank you. Now, could you get me another cell phone and some codeine? And a glass of brandy."

266

"I'll arrange it immediately. See you in Geneva, Sir."

"Indeed."

The door closed and Karvorkian was left alone with the buzzing in his head. An invisible chainsaw cutting through his sanity.

He felt his grip on reality loosen fractionally. For the first time, real fear coursed through him as his sense of entitlement and power was shaken.

He knew he was going mad. He just needed to hold on a little while longer, consolidate his position and then, when all was set, he could be as mad as he wanted.

He just needed to hold on, just a little longer.

Not long after, a pristine cell phone was surreptitiously delivered to the door, along with the drugs and brandy. Karvorkian gulped both the pills and the liquid down and fired up the mobile device.

He rang a number from memory. This time it was picked up within a few moments.

"Yes?"

"The lose wire needs cutting."

"Red or Black."

"Red. Most definitely red."

"Affirmative."

The line went dead. That was better. The buzzing was easing slightly. Karvorkian liked working with professionals. He was happy to spread the work around. This particular one was brutal, but delivered amazing results. He knew that particular problem within CERN would be corrected before he'd brushed his teeth in the morning.

He turned back to the television to see the news had moved on to the continuing and growing opposition to the regime in Iran. The Green Revolution it was being called by some.

Karvorkian stared nervously at the coverage.

The world was changing around him, he could feel it. It was time to get some quick wins under his belt and shut that damn machine in Switzerland down.

Then he could at least have a little time to go mad on his own terms.

267

CHAPTER 72

CERN, Switzerland - Wednesday November 4th, 2009

Suzi's eyes snapped up as the door to the lab groaned open. Funny, she thought, I never remembered it making a sound like that before. She was about to make a mental note to call maintenance when the noise occurred again. This time, the door did not move.

"Hello?" she said, quite loudly. She was alone in the lab, and her nerves had not settled from the previous day's events.

She heard a groan. Someone sounded very ill.

"Hello, can I help you?" She moved over to one of the lab benches, her hands searching for something long, hard and purposeful. Just in case she needed to look visibly threatening, something that did not come naturally to her.

A hand snaked around the door and groped for the light switch. Now that was not normal behaviour.

Then a voice.

"S-Suzi?"

She frowned. She knew that voice.

"Alf, is that you?"

"Yeah."

"Alf, what the fu-?"

The hand found the light switches and flipped most of them off.

"What are you doing?"

"Suze, it's five in the morning. What are you doing?"

"Have you forgotten where and how we work? After the bar I came back here. I wanted to make sure that we hadn't missed any updates whilst we were out. As it happens, we did, and I can't wait to tell the Professor the good news. What's your excuse?"

"Suzi, I am always here at five in the morning regardless of whether I've been out on the piss all night or not. If I have, it's the only way I would make it into work the next day. Usually, though, my eyes are not assailed by all the lights being on at this time, which is not conducive to a Weiss bier hangover, I must say. So, I need to dial it down a little, if that's okay with you?"

"God, Alf. You scared the shit out of me."

"Well, for that I apologise. I would really like my beauty sleep though, so is there any chance that you'll be sodding off until your normal office hours? Pretty please?"

Rough was an apt term for how she would describe his current look. He didn't smell that great either. Suzi was not inclined to be pushed out of the lab to wander the corridors for two hours. Nor did she want to go home.

However, spending time in the lab with Alf snoring was not a lifetime ambition of hers.

She sighed, shrugged and tilted her head to indicate he should find his nest and hibernate.

"Go for it. Be my guest. Just please tell me you've got a change of clothes, a toothbrush and some deodorant somewhere."

Alf shrugged, smiled blearily and hiccupped.

"Maybe two out of those three. Or one. I forget."

Suzi grimaced.

"What did we do to deserve you Alf?"

Alf gave her the full shot of teeth this time.

"You decided it would be a good thing to work in a goddamn rat hole in the ground the rest of your days. You were bound to come across at least one nocturnal creature that doesn't like the light, smells bad and is protective of its home!"

Suzi huffed.

"You're a wise ass. Even when you're drunk. Go sleep it off, but you owe me several coffees."

As she walked out of the lab, she saw Alf fall like a tree in the forest behind one of the lab benches. As there was no resulting crash, she could only assume he'd fallen on something soft. That, or as she had not observed it, he had fallen with no sound. She shook her head as she shut the door and headed off in the direction of the cafeteria.

She didn't see the person slip into the lab after she had left.

Or remove the camera.

Or inject a fatal air bubble into the neck of the mole as he slept.

Or drag the body to a discrete corner of the lab where it might lie undisturbed until a more thorough inspection, brought on by the smell of decomposition.

CHAPTER 73

Geneva, Switzerland - 6.00 a.m. Wednesday 4th November, 2009

Ebhart was puzzled. Lying in bed with his eyes closed, he felt sheets that were too soft for his own, yet did not remember booking himself into a hotel. The bed was a double, if not bigger. Certainly it was bigger than the slightly rickety single bed in his apartment.

He was in pyjamas which had been slipped over his vest and pants.

He tried to remember what had happened the previous night but all he could recall was leaving the bar. After that, everything was gone.

He heard the gentle ticking of a bedside clock and knew for sure that he was not at home.

He swallowed, a dry scratchy operation, and decided that he'd need to open his eyes to see whether there was any water nearby.

Also, to find out whether this was going to be his last day on earth.

He cracked one eye open just a little and darted it around.

The room was not completely dark. A column of light was coming through a gap in the curtains. It didn't strike him like a prison cell. It was nicely ordered, not to big but not too shabby. It had a wardrobe, bed side table and a couple of chairs, both of which were occupied.

He couldn't prevent both eyes from opening wide.

"Hi."

The man in the chair closest to him leaned forward and grabbed a beaker from the bedside table with a straw in it, and passed it over to him.

"You're probably thirsty. Sip some of this."

Ebhart inspected the beaker under his nose, then back at the man.

"It's okay."

Ben took the straw out, drank a little of the water, nodded and popped the straw back in.

Ebhart took it and sucked a little of the water.

"Um. What's going on?" Ebhart croaked.

The man stared back at him.

"Do you know your name?"

"Of course. Ebhart Horatio Fenkhause. Professor."

"And the date?"

"I'm assuming as it's light, it's the fourth of November, two thousand and nine?"

Ben nodded.

"Great, no lasting damage it seems."

"D-damage?"

"I'm sorry Professor, I'm going to have to leave now, but my - the, ah, Historian here, will be able to take care of you. I'm sure he'll be delighted to answer any questions you might have."

With that, the man stood up, patted Ebhart on the shoulder and strode out of the room.

Ebhart took another sip of water and placed the beaker back on the side.

He then turned towards the other man, who was beaming from ear to ear. His knee was jiggling up and down as if he was pumping an old fashioned sewing machine trying to break the world record for a garment stitched in a sweat shop. Just like Alf's, Ebhart mused.

"Hello Professor. It's an honour to meet you."

"A historian? A journalist?"

"No, no, nothing like that. I'm not here to interview you. I'm here to help you understand."

"Okay, well that's good. At this precise moment, I'm at a complete loss about what is going on here."

The Historian sprang to his feet and dashed over to the bed. He grabbed Ebhart's hand and pumped it.

"It truly is a pleasure to meet you finally, after all these years watching over you."

"Well, that doesn't sound creepy at all."

"Oh don't worry about me Professor. I just have a condition. There are far more concerning people to worry about outside of these four walls, believe me."

Ebhart gaped. "You know?"

The Historian smiled and nodded.

"You're not alone. We're here to help now."

The Professor puffed his cheeks out and blew a sigh across the room.

"Are you hungry? How about a bacon sandwich?"

The two men grinned at each other.

#####

Ben's discussion with their other house guest was much less jovial.

Manek was secured to a chair, plastic ties on his arms behind the seat back and ankles secured to the legs. He was sitting in nothing but his pants in the unheated cellar basement of the house.

The chair was aluminium. It was fucking cold.

He had a cracking headache, had drunk no water in the intervening hours since his capture.

The door to the cellar opened, the bare bulb switched on and a man came slowly down the stairs. He looked vaguely familiar. He also looked hard.

Shit. This was going to be bad.

Ben stood in front of Manek, who had bowed his head.

"Do you know who I am?"

Manek said nothing.

"Let me tell you who I am. By the time I have finished, you will probably want to re-assess what your natural reaction to a situation like this would be, were it not me standing in front of you.

"By the time I have finished, I would be very surprised if you were not leaking out of at least one of the holes that nature has provided you with. Your body will soon recognise the significance of what my words mean. The pain it will be about to endure on your soul's behalf.

"You might wish to spare your physical body that senseless pain once I've finished talking. You'd be mistaken in your belief that it will be possible to subdue your this pain. You might think that you can withdraw into yourself until the punishment is over.

"You might think you'll save whoever it is that you are protecting under your misplaced sense of loyalty.You might think that you're hard. You might think that you're brave. You might even think that if you died, which is a strong possibility, that your name will be remembered as a good and loyal professional who died doing what he was destined to do.

"It won't. No one will know where you are or will end up."

Ben crouched down and lifted Manek's head so that they were eye to eye.

Manek's heart thumped as he tried to avoid Ben's glare.

"You are looking at the person who has been tracking you for a year. The person who has made it his life's mission to find the woman that you abducted off the street. Under the mistaken assumption that you could not be found. That justice would never catch up with you."

Manek's eyes widened in recognition briefly and his pulse thrummed. Oh shit, he thought.

"Well. I have found you. I have been trained to work with men like you. So that your body and mind cannot be separated during interrogations. That both are as equally tormented if the answers that you deliver are not to my liking."

Ben kept his unblinking eyes on Manek. No emotion came from them or his voice as he continued his explanation.

"When I did this for a job, I was the best that there was. I was motivated by nothing stronger than a desire to seek justice, protect those that needed it and make sure the world was a better place.

"Now, I have no employer but myself. My motivation is a desire to cause you more pain than you can possibly comprehend. To find where you hid and what you did with my friend Esther."

Ben stood and faced away from Manek.

"I want you to think about that for a couple of minutes. Let it sink in. Know that I am telling the truth. Then ask yourself. Do you really want to deal with all of that just to pretend to yourself that I won't ever get the information I want from you? Because believe me, as soon as I start, within five seconds, you will be regretting your decision."

He turned and stared at Manek.

A tear rolled down from Manek's left eye. Ben nodded and walked slowly up the cellar steps.

The light went out and Manek's pants became warm and wet.

CHAPTER 74

Geneva, Switzerland - November 5th, 2009

Fritz had picked Celine up from the house in Vienna with no notice.

Esther knew she was in trouble the moment he told her the location they would be travelling to. Her conclusions were only reinforced by the fact that Fritz told her that there was no need to pack a big bag. She'd be required to open up the house and get it in order. Karvorkian would then stay there for a couple of weeks whilst on business in Geneva, supporting him with his research as before.

Fritz wasn't a very good liar.

In the car, Esther tried to explain her fears to Celine. But Celine was now vehemently opposed to giving Esther any space or dominance in their use of the body they co-habited.

Celine blamed Esther for the degenerating relationship with Karvorkian. She was bitter about the incident at the restaurant which she concluded was the cause of that deterioration.

It was all Esther's fault.

The one positive was that Celine had understood what both of their fates were if Karvorkian were to ever find out that Esther remained in some form within that body. Esther now knew that this trip meant that the ruse was up. That meant only one possible outcome for both women.

The flight was short but particularly bumpy.

Fritz seemed on edge. Esther had not travelled with him that much in the past, so didn't know whether this was down to him being a nervous flyer or whether there was something more on his mind.

He kept on trying to snatch glances at her without her noticing. He wasn't very good at that either.

Without doubt though, Esther knew what he was good at.

And that was why he had been sent by Karvorkian to accompany her.

276

Esther was truly scared.

Not only did she have this hulking great thug watching her every move. She could not guarantee that if there were ever the slightest chance of escape, she would even be in control of her every move.

A double captive.

The plane was buffeted almost every second of the flight, rocking up and down, juddering with an angry syncopation. As they descended, the pilot had to make one aborted landing attempt. He circled for another few minutes and then successfully touched down on the second attempt.

Everyone seemed to be on edge.

Fritz unlocked the limousine remotely and the side lights flashed. With Celine in tow, he opened the doors and abruptly shoved her in the back seat, putting the child locks on. They were back under lock and key conditions. All pleasantries were off the table.

Even Celine started to understand finally that things were heading towards a bad outcome. Behind the facade, inside, she began to cry.

The car started and Fritz pulled out of the airport in the wind and rain. Leaves whipped up into a frenzy of sodden dancing, like some kind of tribal ceremony before a sacrifice.

Esther remained quiet, focused. She tried to remember the trip to the house; the driveway, the trees lining it. She visualized the entrance, the hallway, anything of use to be able to help create a disturbance or use as a weapon to subdue the giant in the front seat.

There was little that seemed to jump out at her. The minimalist decor led to few items that she felt she could lift, let alone wield, against a strong, trained thug like Fritz.

The journey, even in these conditions, was rapidly progressing. She was running out of time. Once fully in the house, she knew she'd be under lock and key until whatever fate she'd been dealt was brought to bear on her.

She had to somehow overpower him between the car and the front door being shut. That was all there was to it.

Finally, she spoke with Celine, who was cowed and broken, and explained what she thought she needed to do.

Celine was quiet.

It had finally sunk in that their only chance of survival was escape.

She also understood that neither of them might make it out alive.

Esther re-focused on the outside world and was alarmed to see that they were turning into the driveway already.

She'd missed precious minutes of preparation whilst conversing with Celine. Now the adrenaline rush kicked her in the stomach.

Her. She felt Celine cede control to her, hoping that Esther would be their saviour.

The car bounced along the gravel driveway and up towards the house. This time, she saw it as cold, uninviting. Hostile.

Fritz swung the car around in an arc that left the rear door as close to the house as possible. He switched the engine off. The bonnet steamed in the cold rain, the engine ticking as it cooled. Fritz sat there, glancing at Esther in the rear-view mirror for a moment.

"Well?"

He opened the door and stepped out in the rain. He shut the door firmly and walked around the back of the car and up the steps to the front door.

He opened up, switched the alarm off with a few taps and turned a couple of lights on.

Esther strained to see something, anything that she could use to her advantage in the few seconds that Fritz was preparing his ground. There appeared to be nothing.

She clutched her purse. She then remembered a small atomizer of perfume, which Celine had filled with the perfume that Karvorkian had given her. She reached in and palmed it with the lid off.

Fritz was coming her way, heading to open the door.

It clicked and swung open.

Esther swung her legs out and he grabbed her by her elbow, guiding her out of the car then quickly up the steps.

He pushed her through the door swiftly then turned to shut it.

As he did so, Esther noticed a small statuette on the hall table.

An ugly metal thing.

How could she have forgotten that?

The door shut and Esther spun around, preparing the spray in her right hand and grabbing the statuette in her left.

Fritz turned his face straight into the stream of perfume. He staggered back towards the door, his hands flying to his face. Partly to protect them from any more vapour, partly to wipe the tears away.

With all her effort, she brought the metal artwork across her front and into his right temple.

He was much taller than her so it didn't have the total effect that she'd hoped for, but he did lose his balance.

That was all she needed. She opened the front door and ran out.

Straight into the arms of someone else waiting to grab her.

CHAPTER 75

Geneva, Switzerland - Thursday November 5th, 2009

Ebhart was back in the clothes he had left the bar in two nights ago.

The Historian had kindly washed and pressed them. They were certainly a good deal cleaner than they had been when he'd worn them last.

He was sitting in the front room of the house that Ben and The Historian had rented. He contemplated the discussions over the previous twenty four hours that he and The Historian had engaged in.

He was flabbergasted.

At first, he had felt anger at the odd man's desire to ridicule his work by rambling on about a Luck particle.

At one stage, he thought that these people were part of the conspiracy themselves. Perhaps they'd been sent to detain him from getting on with his work so that he would again miss the pressing deadlines hurtling towards him.

But as The Historian went on, Ebhart slowly settled into a position that what he was saying was less and less ridiculous and more and more grounded in theoretical science.

It was a total shock. As if someone had conclusive proof that God was a scientific fact.

It was world-changing.

He finally understood at a deep level why he felt so strongly about the importance of his work. And why there were some amongst their kind that were trying to prevent it from being realised.

Ebhart concluded that The Historian was in fact a genius and not mad at all. He just seemed like it.

The Historian had shown Ebhart the computer programme that he'd created. Even now it was ticking away, generating new information about the state of balance.

Highlighting the strange gaps where manipulation of knowledge was occurring.

It was fascinating, deeply so.

Until he remembered that at an individual level there were people who were focused on destroying him utterly to meet their own aims.

And then there was Ben Fallow. Here was another scientific curiosity. One that had saved his life, not once, but twice that week.

How this was possible, how Ben could do what he did, could in itself be a project of study for a lifetime.

Thoughts were physical. They manifested themselves. People were connected to nature, to all things. They could influence and be influenced by the world around them at an atomic and sub-atomic level. Everything was connected.

The particles that had been discovered paled into insignificance when compared to the particles that scientists could predict, isolate and then prove.

It was now more than ever so important for that scientific work to go on, knowing that the repression of that knowledge meant that it resided in the hands of the few for the benefit of a small number rather than the entirety of humankind.

Ebhart considered his life to have changed significantly over the past year. He had dealt with the challenge of knowing that people were targeting his work and his reputation.

But his life had been turned on its head by the revelations of the last few hours.

He was once again full of wonder, excitement and passion for the thing that he had dedicated his life to.

He desperately needed to get back to work.

CHAPTER 76

Geneva, Switzerland - Thursday November 5th, 2009

The man held her arms across her chest with one strong arm to prevent her from struggling and with his other he picked her off the ground. With surprising speed and agility given he wasn't particularly tall and it was still blowing a gale, he dashed off down the driveway and stopped behind a fairly large tree.

He spun her around.

"Are you okay?"

Esther stared at him, surprised.

"Esther. Can you hear me?"

"M-my name's Celine."

Ben shook his head.

"No. No it's not. It's Esther. You're Esther Raccolta, you've been missing since October of last year and I've been searching for you ever since."

Esther was still breathing heavily from the adrenaline of the scuffle with Fritz.

"H-how did you find me?"

"One of the men who abducted you? I found him. Manek?"

Esther nodded.

"The other one. In there?"

She nodded again.

"Do you remember me?"

Esther shook her head marginally.

Ben's heart sank a little. But then Esther said: "I think I dreamed about you though."

Even in the growing darkness, he could see Esther blush a little. Ben grinned, and was about to say something when powerful floodlights lit up around them.

"Lie down! Lie down now! Get on the ground! Hands on your heads! Lie face down! Don't move or we'll shoot!"

Ben and Esther did as they were told.

Within a couple of seconds felt their hands roughly being tied with similar plastic ties to those that Ben had used on Manek the previous day.

They were hauled up. Ben briefly saw men in balaclavas before bags were placed on their heads.

"Esther, are you still with me?"

"Don't talk!"

They were pushed and shoved down the driveway until they were slammed into the side of a van. There was a sound of a door sliding and then they were tossed unceremoniously inside.

"Lukas, Silvan, take two teams to check out the house. Make sure that there's no more than the two of them in there. The house was dark before they pulled up, but that could have been a security measure to make it seem unoccupied."

Ben began to say something but he felt a sharp smack to the back of his head.

"Shut up! Don't speak or else you'll regret it."

The van door slid shut leaving Esther and Ben in the dark as to whether there was someone else inside with them.

They kept quiet.

After a few minutes came the sound of several people approaching the van.

The door slid open again and it rocked.

What sounded like a half dozen bodies piled in. Then a commanding voice reeled off some orders.

"We're on the move. I want round the clock surveillance. Lukas, take first watch. Report back every hour. Silvan, you'll relieve him after four hours. Fabio next, then Linus and finally Lars. Understood?"

There was a chorus of "Yes, Sir", then the door slammed again.

Whoever they were, military training had been well instilled, Ben thought.

They couldn't be related to the owners of the house unless this was some kind of elaborate deception.

They would just have to wait and see where the van would take them.

Then Ben would have to remember how to fight the remaining men with both hands tied behind his back if it came to that.

The engine started, revved and they lurched forward, tyres spinning on the gravel.

He couldn't stop smiling though.

He'd finally found Esther.

The rest he could deal with.

CHAPTER 77

Geneva, Switzerland - Thursday 5th November, 2009

As soon as he'd seen the floodlights which he knew the property did not own spring into life, Fritz ducked into the panic room and hunkered down.

Within a few minutes, boots came storming into the house. Calls grew progressively closer as the teams of men moved from room to room calling areas clear.

The panic room was well concealed behind a huge floor to ceiling picture. An oil painting depicting angels appearing to men. Not being an art critic, he would have said that the style was medieval rather than modern, although it was Pre-Raphaelite. It was quite out of place with the rest of the decor. But as such an obviously ostentatious and eye-catching installation, it kind of slipped by as a place behind which to hide.

He touched his swollen temple and cursed silently. It was wet with blood. If there was any intelligence in the team outside, they'd work out eventually that neither of the two people he'd seen through the porch windows were bloodied.

He hoped that they wouldn't arrive at that conclusion until they were well away from the property.

There were cameras in the panic room but the system was still in hibernation as he'd not yet switched it on when he'd entered. There was however a scrambled telephone system.

He eyed it nervously as he heard the men move around the house. He wouldn't risk calling Karvorkian until they'd gone, just in case the shouting from the other end of the line alerted them to his hiding place.

He was up Shit Creek.

He felt along the shelf and found a half-finished bottle of brandy and a slightly dusty glass.

He wiped it on his shirt then poured a healthy slug from the bottle, flopping into a chair and putting his feet on the table.

He raised the glass silently, toasting his failure.

Well done Fritz. You've done it this time.

How could he have let such a little slip of a woman outmanoeuvre him so spectacularly? After he'd taken so much care in planning the transfer from car to house? What had he done to alert her to the fact that she was going to be in trouble?

And how the hell had that man he'd last glimpsed in the rear view mirror of the car they'd used to abduct her over a year ago managed to find them? Today of all days? And grab her?

He didn't know whether the team currently clearing the house were on his side or not, but either way, they weren't on his.

No one was now.

After another gulp of the brandy he began to feel its warming effect. He anticipated another source of warming effect once Karvorkian had ripped him apart and tossed him in to Hell.

Still, he was a loyal fool, so it was without question that he would tell Karvorkian everything. Mad as the guy was, he deserved a little respect as he'd been good to Fritz.

It wasn't his fault that things seemed to have gone downhill since he and Manek had grabbed that girl.

Manek.

Oh you little fucker, Fritz thought, *it was you, wasn't it? You were out here. Karvorkian said you'd made a mess which we had to clear up. This was it, wasn't it?*

He reached for the bottle again and emptied it into the glass.

Finally, he heard the front door shut.

He picked up the phone and waited for the secure dial tone. He keyed in the number he'd committed to memory then sipped some more of the warming liquid. The line connected.

"Yes?"

"We have a problem."

Silence.

"I'm with the angels."

"I see. And are the trumpets sounding?"

"No, Sir. There is a bugle playing the Last Post."

286

There was silence on the line again, then a laboured sigh.

"What is your condition?"

"I'll live."

"Fritz, listen to me very carefully. If you're still alive when I see you next and you don't have her, that will be a temporary situation."

"I understand. Sir?"

"What?"

"The man she met, before. It was him."

"You're certain?"

"Yes, without a doubt. And with Manek missing, I think..."

"Don't think Fritz. Just. Find. Them."

The phone line clicked dead and Fritz stuck a finger in his hear to shake out the shouting that had made it ring like a bell.

He sipped the glass until it was empty then moved to the cot in the corner to get some rest.

He'd need it before trying to evade the guards that they'd inevitably leave watching the house. Then he'd have to somehow find the bitch and bastard who'd effectively signed his death warrant.

The Angel of Death. The name of the painting suddenly popped into his head. Also known as The Plague of Rome. A fake was hanging in the Musée d'Orsay.

He wouldn't mind if he never saw it again.

CHAPTER 78

Nottwil, Switzerland - Thursday November 5th, 2009

The van came to a halt with all the grace of a bull running through the streets in Pamplona and suddenly confronting a Matador.

Whoever the guy was that was driving was either paid double to get there faster or he'd missed his vocation as a racing driver.

The engine turned off and the door slammed open.

"Out! Both of you! Now!"

Ben shuffled to the door, guided by a not particularly helpful shove every so often and felt Esther get out at the same time.

They were pushed and prodded into a building that immediately smelled like a medical facility.

There were vague sounds from behind closed doors. Beeps and puffs of monitoring and ventilation machines backing up his theory.

After being escorted down several corridors, a hand finally brought Ben to a halt by jerking the scruff of his neck.

"Stop."

A door in front of them opened and someone brushed past them to enter the room. Through the weave of the bag, Ben registered a light click on. There was a whispered conversation and the person came back out. The leader's voice again.

"Move forward. Slowly."

Ben shuffled forward until a hand pulled him back again.

The hood was suddenly jerked from his head and Ben immediately turned to look for Esther, checking if she was coping with all she'd been through.

Her face was white as she stared straight ahead at the man in front of her.

"Esther?"

He heard a man's voice cry out, cracked and breaking. "Oh, thank god!"

Ben turned back to take in the person who had spoken.

The man on the bed raised a hand.

"Hi Ben. Long time no see."

"Kevin?"

"I'd get up, but as you can see, my legs aren't what they used to be. How are you?"

"Shit, Kevin, I thought...I thought we'd lost you."

Esther's glassy gaze was bouncing backwards and forwards between the two of them. "You...you know him?"

Ben nodded.

"We were searching for you together. Esther, this is Kevin Daste. Formerly, I assume given you're not supposed to be alive, of the Swiss Police."

Kevin stopped smiling.

"Ben, Esther, please forgive me. I've only just woken up. Anderegg, you said they were tied up? Untie them at once! Get them a chair. Esther, do you need medical attention?"

Esther swayed and Ben, his wrists newly freed, rushed to catch her.

"I think that will be a yes, Kevin."

One of the men left the room and returned within moments joined by couple of nurses and pushing a wheelchair. They helped Esther ease into it. Ben made a move to go with her, but Kevin called out to him.

"Ben, I trust these guys with my life, so I think you can her, just briefly, whilst we catch up on a few things."

Ben quickly assessed Esther. She was showing signs of shock and exhaustion. Then he looked at the man observing him expectantly. He sighed, waved them off and then turned back to Kevin.

Kevin indicated for the others to leave the room.

"I can only apologise Ben again for the way in which you were brought here. Once again, I've underestimated your talents. You see, we weren't expecting you."

Ben sat down by the bed, taking in his friend's scarred but reconstructed face, bald head and then his missing legs. He was shocked.

He put his hand on Kevin's shoulder and squeezed gently.

"That pales into insignificance compared to the joy I've had, not only finding Esther but finding out you're alive, my old friend."

Kevin reached out searching and then put his hand on Ben's.

"Less of the old, thank you. It is indeed a great day. And of course, you know what day it is?"

Ben felt a psychological slap in the face. It was a year to the day since the events of both Lundy and Kevin's attack.

"Christ, I'd forgotten. How could I?"

"I'm sure you've had some significant distraction today Ben. So tell me, how did you come to be at the house?"

"As you say, a lot has happened over the past year. I was back in Geneva on a, um, how shall I put it, protection mission, and I came across one of our two friends from the surveillance footage."

"Indeed? And in what condition is this friend of ours in after you came across him?"

"Oh, you know. He hasn't lost too much. Nothing that won't grow back. Eventually."

"I see. And he gave you the location of the house?"

"Yes. And that's where your men found me. Very good by the way. I had no idea they were there."

"Nor they you. They assumed that you were the driver of the car they'd seen turning in to the property. And they had no idea that Esther would be the passenger. They just thought it was some hood and his floozy making use of the house for a quick dalliance and she'd had second thoughts and stormed out. They made a snap decision to take ownership of the property and grab the people in the way."

"Understood. But how did you find it?"

Kevin smiled.

"It took a lot more time and finesse than your method. Someone spotted Esther in Vienna. She was ID'd in a restaurant eating with a man by a contact she'd met in her previous line of work. It's a long story but we eventually traced the reservation back to a concierge service. After hacking into their systems, we identified a number of transactions. They were conducted on behalf of an unknown individual linked to the same bank account used to book the restaurant. One of those transactions was to pay a year's rent for the lakeside property."

Ben nodded appreciatively.

"Nice work."

"Thank you. Ben, is Esther..?"

Ben deflated a little.

"No. I don't think so. She's lost her memory I think. She thinks she's a woman called Celine."

Kevin nodded.

"Yes, that's the story that she gave the man who identified her in Vienna. I think an urgent assessment is required before we do anything else."

Ben agreed.

"Happily, this place is a medical centre of excellence. They've done a fantastic job on me, even though it might not seem like it at the moment. She's couldn't be in better hands."

"I hope so. Look, Kevin, I really appreciate everything you've done, I mean that. But I'd like to go and see if she's okay now. Perhaps we can talk in the morning?"

"Of course. No problem."

Ben headed out to the hall to try to locate a nurse. He stuck his head back in as an afterthought.

"Oh, by the way, my Dad's alive and is with Professor Ebhart Fenkhause from the LHC project at CERN. I'll give you the address. Could you get a couple of men over there to watch out for them? Manek's in the basement as well, he might need a drink of water or something."

Ben heard Kevin laugh incredulously as he went down the corridor towards the nurses' station.

CHAPTER 79

CERN, Geneva - Friday 6th November, 2009

The Professor looked down forlornly at the body of Alf Vertigung, shaking his head.

"Oh Alf, what did you do?"

The room was off-limits to all but the Professor and the CERN security team, supplemented by some of Agent Anderegg's Secret Service colleagues. As a crime scene, they'd cordoned it off as soon as Ebhart had walked into his superior's office along with the agents and explained what had been going on.

The cordon initially was set up in order to secure the camera device that Ebhart had told them about. On finding it had disappeared, a more thorough search of the lab revealed Alf Vertigung lying dead behind a pile of cables. His face and hands were swollen and his belly was already distending. There was a clearly visible puncture wound on his neck where a needle had been inserted.

Early that morning, after a call from Ben to pre-warn them, a couple of agents turned up at the house. One took Manek away to a more secure location.

The other, a woman, remained to make sure that the Professor and The Historian were safe.

As soon was as viable, the Professor requested they go to his apartment, where he could get a change of clothes. Then to CERN, so that they could pursue the work he so desperately needed to get back on track.

He said a fond farewell to The Historian who once again thanked him for the work he was doing and expressed a hope that they could remain in contact. Then Ebhart jumped into Agent Anderegg's car.

Once they'd checked the apartment was secure, the Professor checked the frustrated then angry messages from his superiors.

They wished to discuss his lack of attendance for the past two days.

He immediately called them and passed them over to Agent Anderegg.

She informed the shocked member of the management team that they'd be on campus within the hour and that there were some very serious aspects of security they needed to address.

Once at CERN, Ebhart delivered a short, focused presentation to a few key members of the management team. Leaving out his discussion with The Historian, it covered the various events of the previous year. The Professor then joined the security team in accessing the lab.

On the way, he passed Chenni. She smiled, waved in a confused manner and then worried at his lack of acknowledgement.

His heart dropped again at the betrayal from at least one member of his team.

On finding the camera missing he sensed an odd smell that in all the years working in this lab he'd not encountered before. A search of the room exposed the source.

The first incontestable murder on campus at CERN had happened.

Finally.

Evidence that something more than just accidents, human error and experimentation were to blame for the delays that the LHC had encountered.

Acknowledging this evidence meant that those watching events at CERN would know that their actions had been exposed. Those in charge at CERN now knew that someone or some group was actively engaged in acts of espionage and effectively terrorism.

Ebhart's superiors were magnificent in their response to these revelations.

He was quietly praised for his stoicism in the face of severe challenges even his peers were unaware of. There were profuse apologies and even talk of some award nominations he'd recently been overlooked for.

The relief to finally share his burden was overwhelming, but all he wanted to do was to return to the work he loved.

Once Alf's body had been removed from the lab and his team informed, questioned and statements taken, that was exactly what he would do.

He knew that whoever had killed Alf was still out there.

He was relieved to know that it couldn't have been anyone on his team given the time of day and the fact that the only other person, Suzi, had been seen by several people around the time of death. But now it was 'out there', as one director put it, security would be a lot more vigilant.

There was a risk that the media might find out, exposing the story internationally. He was assured that, as a Secret Service matter, measures would be put in place to make sure that the media suppressed it. It wouldn't stop a few die-hard bloggers from trying to post it online, but they could be contained through various legal instruments.

All that was left to do was for him to get the team back on track. Get the LHC up and running to get the best out of the old girl before the Christmas shut down. Ramp her up to the Seven TeV they were aiming for to get those particles accelerating at a decent speed.

Recent traumas aside, Ebhart didn't think that he could be any happier. Even with the loss of Alf, he felt they had turned a corner.

CHAPTER 80

Nottwil, Switzerland - Friday November 6th, 2009

Ben silently opened the door and walked in to the dimly lit room where Esther was asleep. He took a seat by the bed and scanned her face.

Even sedated, her eyes dashed left and right beneath her lids. Her breathing was shallow. She was running in her dreams, desperately searching for a way to escape some nightmare house.

A doctor, young, smart with an inquisitive face and blue eyes, stepped in and shut the door.

"We had to give her something to give her some decent rest, I'm afraid. She'll likely be unconscious until the morning. She's had a bit of a traumatic time of things it seems, not just in the last few hours of her captivity."

He waved some papers.

"Initial toxicology reports. Our patient has chemicals in her body that we've not seen before. I've sent the results off to a specialist I know, and..."

Ben sprang up and hissed. "Whoa! Hold on there. Who did you send them to? You didn't say who Esther was, did you?"

The doctor took a startled step back before composing himself.

"No, of course not Mr Fallow. These were couriered by Special Agents who will be with the specialist whilst the work is done to identify these chemical compounds and their potential effects. It will be conducted in a secure lab, on technology with no connection to the internet and the facility is swept for bugs regularly. The computers have their own mainframe database of information."

Ben eased back into the chair again and nodded at Esther.

"So, what's her general condition? Why can't she remember who she is?"

"Ah, well, that does seem to have something with the drugs. But until we get the analysis back, we won't know how to counter the effects and whether there will be any residual issues later on..."

"Residual issues? You mean that this might be permanent?"

"It could be, but I'm not saying that. I'm saying that while her memory may return, there may be lapses, breaks or episodes where it leaves her again, for a short or long period. We simply won't know until we get some results of what it is we're going to have to deal with."

"Synthetic?"

"Yes, and in a form we've never encountered before."

Ben glanced back at Esther.

Her face was coated in a light sweat and she was obviously feverish.

He reached out and stroked a strand of hair away from her face.

"As for the, ah, additional personality, Celine. Again, we're at a loss to how this could have manifested without some kind of physical trauma to the brain. Before we sedated her there were definitely two distinct personalities, both very upset. The one identifying itself as Celine had a full knowledge of what day it was and where she was, and had at least a partial history of her life. Esther however..."

Ben glanced back up.

"Go on?"

"Well, she was disoriented to put it mildly. She had no access to any memories of her name, who or where she was. Yet strangely, she was not hysterical. She was upset, for sure, but she seemed in control of her emotions."

"You think she still has emotion?"

"Oh yes, I think her emotional core is intact."

"Well, I guess that's something."

"But the problem is again, what to do with Celine."

Ben tilted his head, trying to understand where this was going.

"What do you mean?"

"Without a doubt, Celine is a distinct personality. The question is, how did she get there?"

Ben shook his head.

"No doctor, it isn't. The question is, how does Esther get her own body back from what is effectively a body-snatcher. Celine is not a part of Esther, never has been."

"How can you be so sure? Maybe she had a history of..."

"No." Ben said firmly, standing up. "I'm sure. This isn't some construct that she's created to cope mentally with abduction. Think about it."

"Well, if you're sure."

"I am. There are some big reasons that I can't tell you about why I'm confident. So the real question is, how do we evict this parasite and get Esther back?"

The doctor sighed, well into an eighteen-hour shift.

"Well Mr Fallow, as soon as I get the results back and see what we're dealing with, I'll be sure to let you know."

Ben backed down a little, realising that he'd stood up again at some point, getting much closer to the doctor than he'd realised.

He put his hand on the doctor's shoulder and patted it a couple of times.

"Thank you. I appreciate everything you're doing for her doctor. Let me know if I can help in any way."

The doctor nodded. "You can stay if you like. I'll tell the guard on the door. There's a fold-up cot in the corner which you can pull out. Not the most comfortable of beds, I can tell you, but at least it's flat and relatively soft.

Ben thanked him again and the doctor left. The door swished shut with the smallest of clicks and then the room was silent again but for Esther's breathing.

Ben sat back down and held Esther's hand, stroking it gently.

"Esther, honey, if you're in there, I hope you can hear me. I'm here, I'm with you."

He brought her hand up to his lips and kissed it gently.

"Remember when we were younger, we used to go running?"

Ben talked to her well into the night, telling her about how they met.

How she had broken through his shyness with her brash, tomboy attitude.

How she had asked him to train her so that she could stand up to the bullies that teased her about her appearance, her slight frame, her slightly protruding ears.

How they'd begun to run together in the cold, dark mornings before school. How they'd spent time together as they grew up as fast friends. Playing tricks and pranks, getting into trouble without it being too serious.

Then, as they'd both grown, they'd avoided discussing their growing feelings for each other. They'd had a couple of huge arguments that split them apart a couple of times. Running always brought them back together.

They'd meet accidentally one morning and run silently together. Then one of them would start talking, usually a wise crack about the other. A couple of smart comments thrown back and forth until one of them buckled and laughed, then they both laughed. Neither one apologised to the other. Arguments at that age could be brushed aside easily.

Ben then opened up to her about how one day he'd seen her and knew that he'd had a crush on her. How overnight she'd developed some kind of glow in his eyes. How he couldn't tell her.

He paused.

"I see now that was ridiculous. I was afraid if I said anything that it would ruin everything between us. I'd seen it happen to other people around the base. They'd start going out together then it would all fall apart. I didn't want that to happen to us."

His gaze dropped down to his hand on hers.

"That was stupid. All that happened was that we said goodbye, I left the base and never saw you again. How could that have been worse?"

A breath escaped Esther's lips and he admired her face. A light sheen still covered it but she appeared less feverish than she had done before.

"I'm so sorry Esther. I should have told you. I hope it's not too late."

He let go of her hand and leaned back in the chair and sighed.

His eyes closed gradually and his breathing settled into the rhythm that Esther had set.

Before long, exhausted, Ben was asleep.

For a long while there was silence.

Then, in her sleep, Esther said: "I love you too."

CHAPTER 81

Vienna, Austria - Sunday November 8th, 2009

"Ladies and Gentlemen, please. A little decorum would not go amiss."

Karvorkian's voice cut across the chatter of outrage on the conference call, which to his ear sounded like seagulls fighting over a fish. The voices gradually faded into sounds of shuffling, huffing and tutting, which he supposed would have to do.

"You are all aware of the information that has come to light in the past few days regarding the situation at CERN."

Murmurs of acknowledgement travelled across the stereo speakerphone.

"What you are perhaps not aware of is that we have a new threat to add into our calculations. This threat not only is one of the gravest that we have faced in our time of strength. It is one that could quite possibly tumble our positions of privilege back to those we enjoyed in the Dark Ages."

This time there was silence. Karvorkian waited for a piercing question but there were none. One participant simply said: "Go on."

"It seems that a blood line from our past has come back to life, one that possessed the innate abilities that we have worked so hard to cultivate over the centuries. Time has caught up with us. Nature and nurture have conspired against us and the strands that we worked so hard not to let touch our future have integrated into the fabric of our reality outside of our will."

An angry voice said: "Stop being so cryptic, Sir. We are all busy people. Tell us what you know."

Karvorkian frowned.

"Well, Sir, I am surprised that I am the only one that has knowledge of this information within our set. Have you not felt the shifts over the past months? Did you not question why it was only now that our actions have started to have wider consequences? Did you not stop to think that our strength was diminishing at an accelerated rate even in this age of technology and connectivity?"

The angry voice, slightly more subdued, cut in again.

"Of course we had. But there's a limit to which our power extends. We can't address issues which arise due to the distributed knowledge that comes from information flowing freely at all levels of society. As technology becomes pervasive, breaking down the barriers to sharing knowledge and information. We all know that some calamitous shifts must occur over centuries so that civilizations can crumble. We have to destroy to reset an emancipated population. This is the payment required to secure our families' interests. We've seen it before, with the Mayans, the Egyptians, the Romans and we'll see it again, most probably in our lifetimes."

Another voice, female, interrupted.

"You say you have identified a bloodline? When did this happen? Why were we not told before?"

Karvorkian sighed.

"Madam, you were. It appears, again, that this relates to a matter we thought long closed. It is the bloodline of the Fallows, direct descendants of the Anglo Saxon Franklins."

Shouts of anger again filled the line. This time Karvorkian let them ride. He could wait.

Once they had settled, knowing that their disquiet would get them nowhere, Karvorkian spoke again.

"Friends, I feel as strongly as you about this information. We all know the history of Nathaniel Fallow and of his father before him, and his before him. Now, it seems, there was not only a failure on the part of our operatives to deal with him, there was also a son."

He carried on quickly.

"This person is the one who caused our most recent intervention to fail to achieve its anticipated outcome. He also seems to have caused threads to join through his highly unanticipated, uh, rescue of another of our corrective measures."

A cold silence met his latest pause. Boy, he thought, if this were face to face, he'd be seeing steel flashing in every single one of their eyes.

"He is strong. Believe me, he is as strong as any one man we've encountered. But he is only one man. And we are many."

A British voice, clipped and authoritative, joined the discussion.

"How did he find her and where are they now?"

Karvorkian shook his head, forgetting he couldn't be seen.

"It's too early to say but, given his skill set, we must assume that he will be careful and we must put our best assets on this as soon as possible."

"I see. Forgive me, Chair. It does seem that certain non-core activities undertaken on the, ah, groups behalf recently, by you have somewhat, um, muddied the waters, shall we say?"

There was a general murmur of agreement to that comment.

Karvorkian had been waiting for this moment.

"I see. I hear a shared amount of agreement with the sentiment expressed by our advertising mogul, am I right?"

There was a gasp of shock as Karvorkian tipped a metaphorical bucket of ice water down the Brit's neck.

The man spluttered.

"How did you...? How dare you!"

"Oh, I know who you all are, don't you worry. Anonymity can no longer afford the protection of our group in an age where technology and individual stupidity can go hand in hand. Whilst seeming to acknowledge the power of anonymity, you dismiss the threat of it being destroyed as our plans come to fruition. You rely on historical precedent. If something has happened before, it will happen again. What you ignore is the shift in luck that has never been a factor before.

"Mankind has never seen this level of individual greed before in so many. Civilizations in the past in general pursued a level of morality that was clearly defined in the structures of society. Hierarchy, law, community, knowing one's place.

"This civilization has lost that. Instead of gazing up at the stars in wonder, it pores over them for signs of wealth. It wishes to understand the stars not to enrich the souls of the people on earth, but to enrich the pockets of individuals.

"A new breed of influencers has sprung up, championing the cult of the individual. Society no longer looks after its elderly or poor. Instead, it pursues the excesses of youth, greed driving a consumerist focus on fashion. Consumption for the sake of it.

"This is the fundamental difference. The human mind has shifted from one that desires to live well with others to one that will fight tooth and nail to protect its own possessions and wealth. It has lost the collective understanding that working together brings success for the species. It would rather have its soul sucked out and dropped into a computer game where it can go on killing without fear of reprisal, day in day out."

There was stunned silence on the line.

"I see all these traits in you all. That is why, for the sake of binding the group together, to remind you of what it is that is so important to us, I made the decision to know who you are. I see the politician, the Vatican banker, the spiritual leader of a fanatical Muslim country. I know the mining executive, the matriarch of the diamond dynasty and the Russian software executive. I do not need to name you; there is no use in everyone knowing everyone's name. I need you to know that I know, so you will not do anything rash. Anything that might have its own consequences on our combined vision through your own personal greed and corruptability."

Karvorkian drummed his fingers on the desk a couple of times before proceeding.

"Now, let's get back to business shall we? I will be circulating actions as usual and we will proceed with the formalities as we always have done. But before I do, know this. I have always at heart had the mission of this group at the core of my actions. Everything I have done is to secure that mission to the best of my abilities. I believe that in this time of uncertainty and instability, it would be unwise for any of us to divert away from this mission. If any of you do think that you have any uncertainty in the path forward, it might be an opportune moment to abstain, in case it affects our vote on the matter."

The next few moments were spent sending and reading the options, at which time the simultaneous vote took place.

Karvorkian assessed the outcome, unmuted his phone.

And sighed.

"People, it seems we have an issue with authority here. I stand by what I said. If our mission is compromised, I will be forced to make sure that any deviation from that by any individual is dealt with. The collective will must be obeyed. You may have noted on the past few calls we have been a few members down. This is a permanent situation. One I personally dealt with. They were well off course from our collective agenda. At the moment, there are one or two other members whose hearts do not quite seem to be in this."

His voice dropped to a whisper.

He was enjoying this moment.

"There is only one way off this team, people. Then the baton passes to your offspring. Think very hard whether that's what you want to happen right now."

His voice adopted a jaunty tone.

"Right then! Let's try that again."

This time the vote was unanimous, albeit with a couple of abstentions.

"Much better. I suggest we all go and gird our loins and prepare for battle. This one's going to be epic."

CHAPTER 82

Nottwil, Switzerland - Thursday November 12th, 2009

"It's a match."

They had to wait a couple of days for the toxicology report to come back but when it did a significant piece of the puzzle fell into place.

Ben had joined Kevin in the gym where he was acclimatising himself to some upgraded new legs. He was yet to have the cutting edge artificial retinas that a German company was developing implanted so that his vision could be partially restored.

Ben admired his strength and determination, even after his life had been shattered. It simply did not strike him that the same thing, albeit without any physical manifestation, had happened to himself.

Agent Anderegg was present again, having brought the results back personally. Kevin talked as he walked on the specially-adapted treadmill, slowly and methodically.

"This is truly something Ben. It's audacious, damn dangerous and potentially worth billions."

"What's that Kevin? Are you going to tight walk across the Grand Canyon?"

"Wise guy," Kevin smirked. Ben thought it was good to see him smile, scars and all. "No, the toxicology is back and it is interesting to say the least."

Anderegg nodded to him and handed the documentation over. Ben flipped through a couple of pages, passed it back to her and shrugged.

"I'm not really much of a graphs guy to be honest Kevin. You'll have to explain the lines."

Kevin slowed the machine down, warming down his routine, and rubbed the back of his neck with a towel.

"This is an incredible story Ben. It starts in the nineteen seventies, but actually really kicks off in nineteen eighty three. A guy, a fire fighter called Mitchell, saw a horrific accident once. He couldn't get out of his head until he talked it through with someone, which helped him deal with it.

"In eighty-three, he goes and writes a paper on his experience. Turned it into a process. It's published in the Journal of Emergency Medical Services. Thing is, over the past few decades of research, scientists found out that you can't just erase memories and the subsequent emotions they provoke. They both change whenever they're recalled."

Ben found that interesting.

"So this use of what they called Critical Incident Stress Debriefing or CISD? It's been around for decades, gets people to talk about their memories. Turns out, it doesn't really help get rid of the emotions associated with them."

Ben picked up. "Because they change every time they discussed. Add that to the fact that memories are real, physical things, I guess you're chasing something around your brain that keeps morphing like a flu virus."

The treadmill had stopped and Kevin stepped off, with Anderegg's help. He sat and gratefully drank from a bottle of water that she put in his hands.

"Now, it turns out neuroscientists actually have a map, a molecular explanation, of how and why memories change. The thing is, a memory is maintained only if it is accessed. Whenever it's accessed, it's modified. Whenever it's modified, it changes."

Ben felt a shiver run up and down his spine.

Kevin put up a hand. "Now Ben, before you jump to any conclusions, don't forget that scientists are at the very beginning of their studies here. We haven't even begun to explore the issue of genetic memory storage. Who knows if they're the long term storage units and the brain is the short term one?"

"I think I get it. But if it means that Esther hasn't been able to access those memories for, we don't know how long, will they...survive? How long?"

Kevin was sombre.

"I don't know. But back to the research. Independently of the CISD paper, there was a guy at Columbia University, a neuroscientist. He discovered that there were relatively few chemicals in the brain that helped form memories. What he discovered is that a form of protein kinase C called PKMzeta – yeah, I know - hangs around synapses, the junctions where neurons connect, for an unusually long time. Without it, stable memories start to disappear. Without those proteins, long-term memories don't exist."

Kevin chugged the water and Ben waited impatiently.

"So some scientists, under the auspices of helping people with trauma, started developing drugs that targeted specific memories. Inhibitors that attacked the proteins that caused memories. And voila, memories started to disappear."

Another sip.

"But the issue is this Ben. All of this is years away from application. It's still highly experimental, at the lab rat test stage. Inhibitors being synthesised and injected directly into the brain. What was in Esther's blood work was far in advance of that."

Kevin paused.

"And?"

He nodded.

"Yep. It matched the drugs we found being shipped across the border. The ones we talked about when..."

"Shit."

"Yeah."

Right then, the doors slammed open and another agent ran in, panting.

"Sorry Sir, I thought you should know. Esther, I mean, Ms Raccolta, is awake. She gave us a name."

CHAPTER 83

Nottwil, Switzerland - Thursday November 12th, 2009

Esther smiled weakly at Ben as he came in.

"I'm sorry I don't have any flowers."

She blushed and pulled her white towel dressing gown a little more tightly around her neck.

"I'm sorry I don't remember you."

Ben sat on the end of the bed.

"How do you feel?"

"Odd. Strange. I've still got Celine in here but she seems to be less interested in, well, everything since I came here. I feel stronger I guess. In myself."

Ben grimaced, moved up the bed and squeezed her hand briefly.

"I can't begin to think what that feels like."

There was a silence while they studied each other and glanced off each other's full gaze. It was neither comfortable nor awkward.

Eventually Ben said, "So I understand you remember something about the man who's behind all this?"

Esther snapped up on the bed, her back straight, suddenly animated.

"Something? I remember everything about him. He was a monster wrapped up in the merest layer of humanity. Rich. Unbelievably rich. Smartly dressed, the most expensive clothes, perfume, food and drink. But underneath it all, a mad man. I'm not sure but I think he was quite insane. I think he had his wife killed whilst I was there."

Ben's face must have been a picture, as she leaned back away from him a little. She dropped her gaze to see that she'd grabbed his wrist in the moment, and let go.

"That must have been incredibly scary, being there."

Esther thought about it for a moment, then shrugged.

"To be honest, I was distracted. In the background. I was trying to find a way to get out. Celine was the one that was in most harm's way. I think had it not been for her, I wouldn't be here today."

She paused, then started crying. Ben moved up the bed and hugged her, so her head was over his shoulder. After a couple of moments, she put her arms around his neck and was bawling, her body shaking with the force of her crying. He rocked her gently and shushed her in her ear, stroking her hair every so often.

Eventually, she calmed down and he passed her a tissue from the bedside table. She snuffled into it, saying thank you behind her hand, then leaned back on to the pillows. Ben couldn't help smile at her upturned face, red from crying and streaked with tears. He felt like his heart would burst.

She scowled at him and then stopped, confused.

Then something came to her.

"I think..."

"Yes?"

"That's really odd."

"What?"

"It was more of a feeling than anything. It wasn't a memory. Nothing specific."

"What did you feel?"

"I felt like you were telling me the truth."

"When?"

"About you knowing me. I think it's true."

Ben smiled.

"Well, that's a start."

Esther frowned again.

"But then there's Celine. She seems real, but she can't be. Can she?"

Ben shook his head.

"The Esther I knew wouldn't even entertain the thought of someone else in her own head. She had too much to live for."

"When was the last time you saw her...me?"

Ben closed his mouth.

"The day you disappeared. We had coffee together."

"And before then?"

"Not for years unfortunately."

"And why was that then?"

Ben paused before he answered, then drew in a deep breath. "Because I was an idiot."

A faint smile crept at the edges of Esther's mouth. This time, she reached out to Ben and touched the back of his hand.

"Well, we can't all be smart arses all the time, can we?"

Immediately her eyes widened and she gasped, putting a hand to her mouth.

"I am so sorry. I don't even know you!"

Ben laughed.

"You don't even know yourself, but you're you. And am I so relieved to hear you're back."

He ruffled her hair even more.

"It's good to see you again, Esther Raccolta, even though you don't know who you are. That won't last long, I can tell."

He stood up, kissed her on her head and she wriggled slightly, not knowing whether to enjoy it or feel confused by it, then moved to the door.

"You're going?"

"Not for long. There are some things I need to do, about your Mr Karvorkian, and some preparations I need to make. I'll be back tomorrow."

He turned back to the door and then, over his shoulder, said: "Unless you don't want me to come back tomorrow?"

She sprang up from the pillows, hands behind her.

"You better be here buster. Otherwise I'm reporting you for dereliction of duty or something."

He grinned and winked and she flopped back down on the bed.

She felt odd. Peculiar. And nervous that he wouldn't come back. She needed him to.

#####

Ben sat in silence, patrolling the space around CERN in his mind. The Historian had told him that Ebhart planned to turn the Large Hadron Collider back on as scheduled. That meant an increased risk of attack.

Now that the threat was overt, there was a visibly heightened state of security around the campus.

Badges were checked more thoroughly.

Guest lists doubly verified. Access to the secured areas guarded more heavily.

All seemed quiet tonight.

Ben let his focus wander over and around the city, checking for any convergences. He was amused to see that there was very little luck focused within the casino he had enjoyed the entertainments of before all this started.

He meandered back mentally to the facility, and swooped over those residents sleeping and those with insomnia and night terrors.

He couldn't help it; as he passed, he wished luck on everyone who had suffered so much without cause, without need or without thought for themselves.

All of them.

#####

Esther woke with a start. A phrase floated in the air, as if burned into her retina from watching a child's sparkler writing in the air on a dark night.

Of course!

She jumped out of bed, pulled on some jeans and a jumper, and stumbled out of the room, turning to the surprised guard.

"I need Kevin and Ben in the lab with my attaché case. Right now!"

In five minutes, Ben was there, joined by Kevin and Agent Anderegg.

"I don't know how. It just came to me."

She grabbed the case which Ben had kept safe and had brought to the medical facility.

She popped open the lock., Then, from inside the lock catchment, she pulled out a micro USB key, to her onlooker's astonishment. Grabbing a laptop, she plugged the USB in and then typed in a phrase.

A folder with over one thousand documents popped up.

Everyone stared at the laptop.

Then Kevin cleared his throat. Ben remembered his current level of vision was less than ideal.

"Shit, sorry Kevin. Um. She's in. We're seeing hundreds and hundreds of documents. It's going to take some time to go through them."

Anderegg pointed to one in particular and said, "It might, but doesn't that ring a bell?"

Ben read out the document name, which had a string of letters and numbers, then a dash, then 'Classified Trial Results'.

"That's the same drug we confiscated crossing the border. Again."

They both turned to Esther, who shook her head. Then, quietly, Ben asked her the awkward question hanging in the air between them.

"What was the password Esther?"

She contemplated her feet for a moment and then her eyes lifted. *"'Whistleblower2007'."*

Kevin puffed out his cheeks then whistled through his teeth, stopping a moment later as the irony sank in.

"Sorry."

CHAPTER 84

CERN, Switzerland - Friday 20th November, 2009

The switch on had gone without a hitch.

Professor Fenkhause was both relieved and satisfied. The team was ecstatic and cheers rang around the control room, echoing the mood of the first switch on so many months ago.

It was so successful in fact that the team decided to start shooting some hoops, as Chenni put it.

Two stable proton beams, made up of bunches of millions of particles, had been circulated in opposite directions around the machine. The results were flooding into the network's databases.

The Historian had joined him as his guest, albeit incognito.

A temporary identity provided to him by the Swiss Secret Service. For once, he was still, mesmerised by the data being presented on the screens regarding this massive machine. It truly delighted him.

Now, Ebhart's superiors were happily chatting to the world's media. Boasting about how they might try over the weekend to exceed the operational energy levels that the Tevatron particle accelerator in Chicago. That would stick one point two trillion volts up the Americans.

Others, including Professor Fenkhause, were more circumspect. He advised keeping the beam circulating at low energy and try for the machine's first proton beam collisions.

He had his reasons, his superiors knew. They also knew that something might happen at any moment to throw the project into chaos yet again, or worse.

Ebhart could see both sides. As happy as he was with the LHC being up and running, he worried about its safety.

Something The Historian tried to reassure him of.

"Ben will be here for you, Ebhart, don't worry. It's his life's mission. He's an expert. He won't let you down."

Ebhart absent-mindedly patted The Historian on the shoulder.

So immersed in the data being represented on the screens, The Historian did not flinch at all.

It was close to midnight, so they decided they would drive with a security detail back to Ebhart's apartment.

Then The Historian would go on to the rented house he shared with his currently absent son who remained with Esther and Kevin in the medical facility.

The Historian waited with the Special Agent in the public area while Ebhart went back down to the lab to change his coat and pick up some papers. As he was leaving, the phone on his desk chirruped. Perhaps they'd changed their minds, he thought, as he picked it up.

"Hello?"

"Professor Ebhart, listen very carefully."

"Who is this?"

"My name is unimportant. It will soon be as memorable as yours in the grand scheme of things."

"This is an internal line, how did you get access to it? What do you want?"

"Professor, you should know by now that we always get what we want. And right now, I want you to shut this project down before someone gets seriously hurt."

"Someone already has got seriously hurt. More than one, in fact. You think I don't know that? Do you think I'm stupid?"

"I don't think you're stupid Professor, I know you are. You have no idea what you're dealing with here."

"Well then, perhaps I know something you don't. Because I know that what I'm dealing with is something so extraordinary it will cause all the structures that we have spent centuries building to be re-assessed. I know that what I'm seeking is not what you're referring to and I know that, by exploring for it, I'm forever changing the nature of what you're referring to by continuing. Is that what you think I don't know?"

A faint crackle indicated that the line was still open.

"Stop now Professor, before it's too late."

"I'm afraid I can't do that. It's not within my power."

"Then I am sorry but I cannot prevent what is about to happen either. You were warned. You were all warned."

The Professor, shaking with adrenaline, shouted into the phone.

"Well, good luck to you, that's all I will say! We're ready and we're not afraid of you. We've got science on our side. And luck. Try fighting both of those together."

The person on the other end of the line had disconnected without listening to any response.

CHAPTER 85

Nottwil, Switzerland - Saturday November 21st, 2009

"And you're sure that the person knew that you'd be in the lab at that time?"

Ebhart was getting debriefed by Kevin on the call that he'd received just prior to departing CERN. Being a scientist and thinking about his work first and foremost, it had taken him almost until the end of the drive with The Historian and their security team before he mentioned the 'funny thing' that had happened to him in the lab.

The car immediately swung around and proceeded towards the medical facility. Kevin had given strict instructions that a face-to-face meeting should occur after any activity that even merited the label 'strange'.

Ebhart, The Historian, Ben and Esther were in the cafeteria. It was gone three in the morning, so it was almost deserted.

They'd commandeered a coffee machine and made some espressos.

"Yes, I'd almost swear that a camera was still in the lab somewhere had the place not been swept. I was just leaving. I hadn't been there for longer than around a minute."

Kevin nodded.

"But the walk down from the control room to the lab would have afforded enough time for someone watching to place a call or send a message, knowing how long it would take for you to get there."

"Yes, I suppose that's true."

"Anderegg, get CERN security to run through the CCTV again. See if they can spot anyone."

"Will do."

Kevin sighed.

"Listen to me. The cat is well and truly out of the bag on this and the best people are on the case fighting your corner, Ebhart. If anything – anything – happens like that again, please let them know immediately. Like your life depends on it. Right?"

"I understood."

Kevin gestured more broadly.

"And the rest of you, listen up. I'm starting to think it's a bad idea that we're all here together. I think it's far and away time we spread out and made ourselves less of a potential target. So here's the plan.

He turned to where he thought Ben was standing.

"Fallow family and Esther. Back to Madeira. It's an unknown to our adversaries as far as we're aware and you were able to travel around incognito before, so it's a strong option."

Ben glanced sideways at Esther. She nodded briefly without acknowledging him.

His heart jumped.

"Anderegg, stay on the Professor. Keep me posted. There are some things that I obviously need to finish up here before I can be fully useful to everyone. I don't foresee that taking more than a couple of months."

Anderegg acknowledged her orders.

"We don't know what, how or when the next attack is going to spring out at us. Or who will be targeted. But everyone in this room has, directly or indirectly, been a target of this group. At this point, we're the lucky ones. Let's keep it that way, Okay?"

Everyone agreed at that.

"Right. Lukas, please take everyone back to their respective homes. Ben, Esther, hang back for a moment please?"

Kevin said his goodbyes to Ebhart and The Historian.

Once they'd left, he turned his sightless eyes on the two of them.

"I had the computer read some of those documents to me, and it's not pleasant. You need to know this. Esther, whatever you were involved in, it's got implications that span out to the United States Department of Defence and beyond. Higher, even. It seems like this drug was tried out on people who were tortured and killed by the Special Operations forces out in Afghanistan. These documents allegedly are part of a dossier that's going to hit the headlines next year. Esther?"

"Yes?"

"Would you mind me keeping these documents? For safety?"

"Of course, Kevin. I have no reason now to have them. I've no idea what I was doing with them in the first place."

"According to Anderegg who's been through a lot of them, there's no indication or implication of that either. So if they do land up in someone else's lap, you're clean."

"That's good. I think."

"However. Ben, you need to be aware that the group that we're fighting may be made up of people we currently perceive to be good guys. Let's face it, we're talking here about the involvement of organisations under a President who next month is going to be receiving the Nobel Peace Prize, not far from here. Which is why I think it's best that you go incognito again."

"That's a sound argument."

"We'll make sure we keep in touch this time though. I'll try to establish some links with trustworthy people on the island and we'll agree a code, dead drops and exit plans. Okay?"

Ben frowned, an itching sensation at the base of his skull had started. "Very much so."

"I know that you're on some kind of a mission and all, but now you've got people to look after, you need to start think..."

There was a faint rumble and the glass walls of the cafeteria buckled inwards slightly then re-aligned.

A strange weak red glow lit up some of the corridor closest to the entrance to the building.

"No. NO!"

Ben sprinted towards the entrance, a sick feeling in his stomach. He heard Kevin shouting after him but didn't hear the words.

As he slammed through the side door of the front entrance, avoiding the revolving ones which were switched off and locked for the night, he saw across the clear car park the remains of a vehicle. A mushroom cloud of petroleum burnt away on the shell.

Ben stopped in his tracks, his chest heaving. A moan escaped his mouth.

"They...they went to bring the car around."

Ben turned and noticed Professor Fenkhause to the right of him, by the pick-up area. He was shaking like a leaf.

"They?"

The Professor nodded dumbly.

Ben ran over to the smouldering wreck.

There was no sign of anyone waiting outside the vehicle. He tried to see inside but the blaze was just too strong.

Anderegg, who had guided Kevin into a wheelchair and sprinted out with him, and Esther found him, sitting with his legs crossed, staring at the burning pyre.

It took another twenty minutes for a fire crew to turn up, by which time the fuel had almost burnt out. There was nothing to see inside the vehicle except for some mangled metal and the loss of two more of their own.

The Historian and Lukas were gone.

CHAPTER 86

Sicily - Saturday November 21st, 2009

Karvorkian put the phone down and sat with his eyes closed, relishing the call he'd just received.

Finally, something had gone right and that old bastard Nathaniel Fallow was dead. This time, Fritz had performed adequately, showing at least an ounce of professionalism.

Their mistake had been to drive from the house they were watching over to the hospital where they'd most obviously taken Esther. He had expected to dispose of her. But instead, he felt, he'd neutralised one of the more potent elements that was guiding luck away from his hand.

After waiting it out a few days, Fritz had sneaked out of the safe room just before midnight. He'd left the house via a hidden exit and crawled all the way down the drive, over a period of hours in the cold and wet mud.

He'd proceeded to attach a remote controlled incendiary device and tracker, part of the armoury from the safe room, to the vehicle. Then he'd hidden himself under a pile of leaves and logs. And waited.

At two in the morning, another car had pulled up alongside. A torch shone out of the first, now booby-trapped vehicle's window, the beam hitting two identity cards held up against the passenger side window of the other car.

The beam had flicked off and the doors of both cars opened.

As the changeover shift conversed, lighting cigarettes, one taking a piss against a tree, Fritz had crept away and over a section of the wall bounding the property. He sprinted as quickly as his cold legs would allow him away from the direction that the car had come from for four hundred meters. Then he'd dropped into a healthy run.

This had lasted for a couple of miles until he was clear of the immediate vicinity.

He had then targeted a house, broken in and dealt with the inhabitant, a highly surprised octogenarian who couldn't sleep. He no longer had that problem.

He had sat in the kitchen with a hot steaming cup of tea.

The cooling body sat at the table, an odd angle to its neck, an odd companion whilst he had monitored the progress of the car.

It hadn't been long before it had stopped.

Fritz had made another coffee and then waited for the motion sensor to alert him to someone getting back in the vehicle. From the size of the motion triggered, he had suspected that several people had gotten in. His thumb had connected with the switch and, on his third count, he had activated the explosive device.

He'd then reported in to Karvorkian and asked for further instructions.

It wasn't until Karvorkian had seen the local news about an explosion in which two males had been killed that he had known just who had been taken out of the game.

He visualized the flow, using his rusty skills. He discovered that he could see a gap that once had been there illegitimately, now not there legitimately.

Nathaniel Tristan Francis Fallow was now, officially, out of the picture.

That just left his son and the troublesome contact of the whistle blower to deal with.

He'd spoken again to Fritz and told him to keep an eye on the medical facility. He didn't expect any luck in intercepting Ben and Esther there. However, all information was useful.

The phone buzzed and he checked the clock.

Time for the charade again. He picked up the receiver.

"Ladies and Gentlemen, I have some good news for a change. It seems at least one mess has been resolved."

CHAPTER 87

Madeira - Thursday December 10th, 2009

Esther opened the door to Ben's bedroom and saw him thrashing around on the bed, seemingly battling with his own demons. Hers had diminished significantly since stopping the enforced drugs and starting some new ones.

So much had happened since the passing of Nathanial Fallow.

There had been no ceremony. After all, Ben's father had been officially dead for several years. Not only that, there was little left that was identifiable, such was the destructive power of the explosives used.

After seeing to Kevin first, Agent Anderegg had quickly moved them to a safe house. She'd then brought all the belongings from their previous rooms across. The plan was the same.

Ben in obvious shock but he had a job to do.

He was still the prime defence against The Watchmen and their on-going campaign of sabotage on CERN's brightest and best. Most of the time he was focused, trance-like, watching over CERN like a hawk.

There would be no more owls delivering bad news to this particular institution. A decision was quickly made to fly them under special protection back to Madeira using Secret Service transportation. To spend as little time and minimise disruption to Ben's mission as possible.

The boat, moored back in the South of France, and the other vehicles they'd picked up along the way, were disposed of.

The Historian's computers were of no use to Ben. But he requested and watched the agents reluctantly magnetise the disks and then destroy the hard drives. He doubted that they would have been able to work The Historian's programs anyway.

So Ben had yet again left Switzerland with nothing but a few bags. Esther had done the same.

There were no ashes to scatter.

All there was were a few pieces of personal effects, a USB, a Dictaphone for which the batteries had run out and some dog tags.

So little of a life to remember someone by.

Within twenty four hours they were out of the country and back in Madeira. Ben had managed to get a message to Pete and the place he'd rented with The Historian was still available.

They picked up a few provisions in town and moved straight in that evening.

Ben had then focused in on himself, seeking, searching for the activity that he knew The Watchmen would be conducting. Small acts of sabotage were quickly highlighted and corrected. Leaks, both human and computer, were identified and closed. One drew amazement at the level of the person within the organisation identified.

And then, on the sixth of December, the pressure had fallen away. CERN shut down the LHC for the Christmas period and Ben's duties were on hiatus.

Suddenly drained of the energy that adrenaline had supplemented, he dropped into bed and slept for a few days. Pete came over and helped Esther around the house, cooking and cleaning and generally providing company for her. He also recommended some herbal infusions to help her ease her transition back to a whole person again, for which she was grateful.

That evening, after watching the news and shaking her head at the President of the United States of America's speech to the Nobel Peace Prize Awards guests, she had gone to check in on Ben.

He was extremely agitated in his sleep.

Esther wasn't yet strong enough to help him with his, but she felt herself falling in love with him all the same. It was something that she couldn't seem to stop, feeling almost like muscle memory rather than a new process. She was re-learning a certain feeling that she'd had around Ben in a previous life not yet remembered.

Wondering yet again whether she ever would recover her memories, Esther shut Ben's bedroom door and went back to her own room. She climbed on her bed and hugged her legs, gazing at the stars outside her window.

What now?

#####

Ben's dreams were action-packed. Like a scene out of a horror story, his thoughts and dreams had merged and were forging a physical change in the world.

No claw-like hand scraping along a blackboard, ready to gouge a path across the flesh of a screaming teenager. His dreams were instead like drones, flying through the landscape, bent on reconnaissance.

In his dream state, Ben's subconscious was free to roam, actively searching for the opportunity to exact revenge. Seeking out the perpetrator of events that fell into the category of inhuman.

He was pursuing a monster, not a person. He was fighting an evil.

It had to be stopped and would require all his strength to do it. But for the moment, he needed to do what his father had done for so many years. He had to learn and understand the nature of the beast.

He had to track it and trap it before avenging it.

#####

Professor Fenkhause put the phone down and picked up his jacket.

Kevin Daste had been relieved to hear that all had proceeded to plan with the LHC shut down for the winter and that experiments were progressing well. He would make sure that Ben and Esther were kept up to date with progress and try his best to keep them all safe from his somewhat restricted position within witness protection.

Ebhart was back to his normal self.

His standing in the department was even higher that it had been before the acts of sabotage.

Things were progressing better than ever. The LHC had become the world's highest-energy particle accelerator achieving one point one eight teraelectronvolts or TeV per beam.

They had hundreds of collisions with millions of data to analyse over the coming months.

There were still some limitations that needed addressing. Little acts of terrorism were still being discovered on a daily basis.

Magnets were 'forgetting' their training again, for one thing. Of course, explaining this to media outlets like the BBC was easy enough, but there was absolutely no logical reason for it to happen.

The winter shut down now would allow for them to make further modifications to some of the magnets. Fit more early warning systems and protect against the work of The Watchmen.

The frustration of having to stick to a power limit until there was no shred of doubt that nothing they could control was going to go wrong was going to be significant. But it would still allow for them to work towards that one final objective of identifying the God particle.

Sometimes, Ebhart thought, as he turned out the lights, the journey is more enjoyable than the destination.

This time, there were no cameras to capture his exit.

#####

Karvorkian drained the amber liquid then threw his crystal tumbler into the open fire. The logs crackled and spat sparks in the hearth.

Then screamed at the top of his lungs, head in his hands.

Moments ago, he had been staring at the television. He tried to bore his eyes into the skull of the man standing there, radiating warmth and eloquence, reading a speech with mesmerising skill that insulted the gift that Karvorkian had given him.

How could this man, this puppet, have created such a strength of feeling around the world? He was only meant to have created a re-balancing back to the status quo.

Karvorkian and his associates had completely underestimated the total repression of hope. The strength of the wishes millions of people who had not dared to think positively for hundreds of years. The possibility of change that this man represented, however weak on his own, had enabled them to catapult this man into virtual sainthood within a few months of his office.

That message of hope and change was not limited to African Americans. Many countries deferred to the United States and followed whatever they did, in fashion, technology and art. Karvorkian's friends were completely out of touch and had lacked the finesse to understand this.

As he sat there shaking his head, he listened to a man argue the case of a just war in front of a Nobel Peace Prize audience.

A small, needle-like pain invaded from the base of his skull. Then, like a lightning bolt, it shot up and into the rest of his brain, just as he was draining his brandy.

His scream lasted until his lungs were empty and he sat gasping with the pain.

His eyes closed, it was as if a message was burning into the back of his eyeballs.

He saw it, even though he wished he didn't.

Found you.

CHAPTER 88

Madeira - New Year's Eve, 2009

The first night she had crept into his bed, Esther and Ben had simply lain together, enjoying the feeling of companionship.

The next, he gently stroked her hair. The third night, he woke to find her snuggled in his armpit. On the fourth night, they had their arms around each other.

On the fifth night, tonight, he kissed her on the head and she sighed and lifted her lips up to his. Their tongues touched gently as she stroked his cheek. As her arm moved away and down, she moved her wrist past his boxer shorts as she was turning, accidentally acknowledging his stiffness.

She paused in the dark and then rested her hand on it. Ben groaned and laughed, and she chuckled and snuggled back in, kissing him lightly on the cheek.

As the fireworks exploded outside, they began to explore a new side to their relationship.

New lives, new experiences and a New Year.

CHAPTER 89

Funchal, Madeira - Friday 19th February, 2010

It was unusually cold, Pete thought, as he shopped for groceries in the small Chinese specialist store in the harbour town.

He was having a rare moment of home sickness. He had decided to cook a traditional Chinese meal for Esther and Ben who had become fast friends with Pete, just as Ben's father had decades before.

He'd start with bō cài miàn. Noodles made from spinach, topped with a spicy tomato-like sauce combined with egg, potato, carrots, beef and chili. Nice and warming for a day like today.

He'd then do some fried dumplings with a black vinegar dip, mixed with a chili sauce, which added a unique bitter, sweet and spicy flavour.

Finally, he'd finish up with Peking Dust. A chestnut and cream based dessert that he remembered from his childhood. Most likely the cause of several of his missing teeth.

As he bagged the ingredients, his mobile buzzed away in his pocket. He ignored it, chatting happily away to the young Chinese lady on the till about her Chinese New Year celebrations on the fourteenth of that month. She'd especially enjoyed this year as she was born in the year of the Tiger. He passed on his congratulations and left the store, walking into a particularly strong gust of cold wind.

Pete frowned.

In all the years he'd been here, it had not felt this cold in February. He pulled the collar of his jacket closer around his neck and leaned into the wind

The sky was a moody grey. The weather prospects were not boding well. His focus on the climate distracted him from his usual alertness. He missed the tall frame of Fritz browsing through a newspaper rack opposite the store he'd just vacated.

#####

Fritz had been traveling almost constantly since he left Geneva, following up leads to find the whereabouts of Ben and Esther. He'd had little success with phones. Obviously Ben had somehow twigged that they'd been monitoring for keywords and phrases, as these had almost become non-existent.

Mobiles had been swapped. Hard lines had been encrypted. It meant that it was a good level of difficulty harder to intercept anything. Not impossible, but difficult in the timescale he'd been given.

Instead, he'd worked through other, less concrete sources. Informants here, a break-in there to steal official records.

He'd gone to France where an unusual item, a boat, was being auctioned off by authorities related to the secret service in Switzerland. Allegedly seized as a drugs sting. It had raised Fritz's interests as nothing had seemed to have been reported about the original seizure. This was strange given the celebratory nature of announcements around these types of things when they went well.

He had noted the details of the yacht and searched online for its log history and another alarm bell went off. Its passage history was incomplete. Turning up here or there randomly, as if it had teleported rather than sailed there. It suggested an illegal nature to the vessel, but something was still off.

As he investigated, he managed to tie together a patchwork of other missing vessels that had sailed the logical routes that this one should have.

It soon became clear that this was a ghost ship in more ways than one.

He followed a path and in early February found himself on the island of Madeira.

He'd checked in with the Harbour Master and heard of a boat matching the description of the one in the South of France. It was piloted there several months ago by an older man accompanied by his son.

Fritz tipped him heavily and asked for him to watch out for anyone he recognized in town.

A couple of days later he got a call on his mobile.

The Harbour Master had seen Ben with a Chinese guy and they were in Funchal.

Fritz rushed to the square, grabbed a table by a window in a cafe that had a good vantage point and waited.

An hour later, there was Ben with the old Chinese guy, carrying a couple of bags of shopping, walking briskly through the square.

The corner of his mouth lifted slightly in a sneer. Fritz gulped his coffee and went back to the hotel room where his satellite phone was waiting.

#####

Pete scrambled to retrieve his mobile whilst he was driving his battered old van back to his house. He glanced at the text message he'd received and sighed.

It was a link to a BBC article stating that the LHC would be switched back on at the end of the month. That meant Pete's meal would probably be the last thing that Ben and Esther would enjoy together for a good long time.

He felt for them, truly. To be thrust into the middle of something like this, with no support structure. Nothing from which to learn and try to meet the expectations of nature in re-balancing what was intended to be a force for all was an impossible task.

Even with his years of experience, his training and the activities of his youth in pursuing a democratic mission within his own country, he could not begin to comprehend the size of the task and the effort of will required to do this.

No one would blame them if they turned their back on their ancestors. The price to be paid was significant. The chances of them succeeding were so very small.

He switched the radio on in the car as the first few spots of rain fell, heavy on the windscreen, and heard the music transition into the presenter talking about the weather.

As the rain fell more heavily and the gloom descended, he switched his headlights on.

The car following him at a distance did not, but the visibility was now so bad that Pete didn't notice.

#####

Even though the rain was bucketing down, Ben and Esther laughed and joked with Pete as he prepared his dishes with incredible skill and care.

He'd shown the text to Ben surreptitiously whilst Esther had gone to powder her nose. Ben's only reaction was to nod and toast his host with some rice wine.

It had been an inevitable. At least he knew he had around a week to prepare and get himself focused. With the goal of Seven TeV to hit this year, this was above and beyond anything any scientist had experimented at previously. Ben was certain the threat from The Watchmen at the end of last year had not been an idle one.

This was a whole new level.

Esther re-joined them and they had a great meal, even though the pudding was as sweet as pure saccharine.

Eventually, it was time for them to leave. Pete stuck his head out of the door and closed it quickly.

"Are you sure you don't want to stay?"

Ben shook his head.

"Thanks Pete, but we need to get back. We've obviously got some things we need to make sure aren't floating away in this storm."

Esther kissed Pete on the cheek and thanked him softly.

"Okay kids. Well, drive safely. I'll speak to you soon."

They pulled their coats on, not designed for this type of deluge, and dashed over to their jeep. Within seconds, Pete could not see them until a weak set of headlights flashed on like the doleful eyes of a bedraggled animal.

It roared as the engine came alive then slunk off, bouncing along the track road, to find shelter.

Pete smiled and waved although no one would see him.

"Stupid old man," he berated himself and shut the door, wiping the rain from his hair.

He didn't see the cudgel slam into the side of his head. He did see an impromptu fireworks show as further blows rained down on him from above and he slipped into unconsciousness.

#####

"Ladies and Gentlemen, I hope you are ready?"

There was little reaction across the conference line. Karvorkian sighed.

"It is now time to stop this man from fulfilling his family's desire for intifada against us. With our collective strength, we can break this upstart once and for all. As one, we can resolve this threat quickly. Once removed, there is nothing that can stand in the way of our goal. We can, we must, we will destroy that which seeks to reveal the understanding of our power to all."

Karvorkian slammed his hand down on the table as he emphasised each word, shouted across the line.

"Luck. Is. Ours. We begin at midnight. Destroy the island and we destroy the man. Destroy the man and CERN will fall."

CHAPTER 90

Madeira - Saturday 20th February, 2010

"Ben, what's wrong? What is it?"

He'd sat bolt upright in their bed just as a clap of thunder echoed around the surrounding hills like a bomb going off, waking Esther up.

The thing was, Ben was not awake.

His eyes were open, but his pupils were high in his head, underneath his lids, giving him the characteristics of some extra in a ghoulish body snatcher movie.

He was shaking.

Esther gasped for air, feeling like she couldn't breathe. She moved towards Ben and hugged him, hard, as if trying to give him moral support through her physical presence.

Another bolt of thunder and a thin, low groan escaped him.

His body became marginally more supple, but still vibrated with a tenseness that scared her.

She eased him gently back down on to the bed and scrabbled around for the phone.

Pete was not answering. She tried several times but the lines must have been down.

A whimper escaped her briefly then she stopped, slapped her face hard and began talking to herself.

"Snap out of it. Come on. It's just a storm and he's just. Just. Well, he'll be fine. Get up! Sort yourself out. Make yourself useful."

She wriggled into some clothes, all the while glancing across at Ben who was shivering in bed as if electricity were coursing through him. She'd not seen anything like it. Not that she could remember. She found some more blankets and threw them over him, thinking to keep him warm.

She stroked his hair and felt it was damp to the touch and hot.

She went into the kitchen and put a pan on the stove. Just as she eyed the candles in the pantry cupboard the lights went out.

She edged her way across to the cupboard in the light of the gas on the stove and grabbed the candles.

She melted the bottom of one and stuck it on a saucer, then lit the other end with the gas also. She now stood in a weak but flickering flame with new shadows dancing all around her and a cacophony of sounds slamming, creaking and moaning outside the house.

She grabbed a sponge and put some cool water in a bowl and brought it, with the candle, back into the bedroom.

Ben was in the same condition as she had left him in. Something was happening in his head, she knew it.

She dampened his forehead and watched, watching him closely, waiting for any change in his condition.

A tree crashed down outside the house, making her jump.

She climbed back into bed with him, still wearing the jeans and jumper, and prayed to whatever was out there to watch over him, her, both of them, until all this was over.

That was going to be significantly longer than she was hoping for.

CHAPTER 91

Madeira - 20th February 2010

Ben was unaware of the extent of the freak weather conditions battering the island that he had sought refuge on.

He was very aware that something was happening however.

His trance had occurred seamlessly whilst he slept, his normal dreams taking up opacity and then revealing the thrumming lines of luck.

Unlike most of the times he'd experienced them before, where they pulsed, they were like sound waves now, creating friction as if someone were strumming them, like stringed instrument.

It was not pleasant. He experienced the sensation of stabbing pains in his head as he saw the violence in the action.

He flew higher mentally and saw that this disruption was focused on and around the island, and instantly knew that he and Esther were trapped.

They knew where he was, where they were.

As he observed, he noticed that this violence was not aimed at him, but at the entirety of the island. They didn't just mean to target him, they were trying to cause a catastrophe across the whole geography.

This was an end-game move. He'd seen enough of those in his time in various conflicts to understand that.

His confidence wavered for a moment, replaced by a steely resolve forged by the knowledge that, were he not to act now, neither he nor Esther would escape to tell the tale.

It was refined by his desire to see his father avenged.

So be it.

If those wishing him harm were being proactive, he would need to fight fire with fire.

As flood water began to race down the hills and on into Funchal Harbour, Ben reached out with his mind. He began to explore the places he'd been in his subconscious mind, identifying those that were ripping and shaking the lines of luck.

At the same time, he sought out natural defences.

Areas of resistance, streams of wind, all nature's forces that could be used to counter the incredible storm being forced on the island and its surrounding areas.

As always, where bad luck was being forced, there were areas of good luck being created elsewhere. Ben grasped and held on to these. He pulled them together to form a strong cord that compressed as it tightened, brightening as it went.

Ben gently undulated the cord until it took on the movement of a jump rope. It began to hum at a low, almost inaudible level, like a moaning wind but one which had a warmth to it.

He felt the energy come from it and into him, energising him and enabling him to ascend higher, seeing more.

As he rose, he tried to shape the strands into some kind of a mesh. To shield the island from the worst of the waves from the vibrations of negativity coming from the oscillating threads. It partially worked. The waves were cut, shortened by the mesh, leaving them with less power than their original form.

This continued for some time. Attacks thrummed from different threads and Ben would divert the mesh across to the areas that seemed to be most at threat. This inevitably meant that he couldn't cover all the areas he wanted to. Some waves found their way through. But it was enough to stop total devastation.

Eventually, after what seemed like hours, that part of his conscious that had gone out found its first target. Ben turned the full force of his mind's eye on it and shot one word in its direction like an arrow.

Karvorkian

The word had been formed with sorrow, rage and vengeance, built up over months of grieving, anger and malevolence towards the person responsible.

The word was made real, given energy, momentum and purpose.

The word was a weapon. And it pierced the mind of the target instantly.

There was a pause. Like hitting the eye of the storm, everything stopped for a moment.

The lines of luck thrummed more gently as what had just happened sunk into the consciousness of the others.

But that was not the end of it.

Suddenly, the lines thrummed again as whatever motivations those others drew from his actions drove them on.

Ben saw in the distance a handful of words, from all corners of the world, floating towards him. At first, they moved slowly, as if created from a soap bubble.

He easily burst them and they disappeared.

Increasingly, they too grew harder. More spear-like, flying at him more quickly. He had provided them with the lessons in a new and more powerful weaponization of their talent. Something even they had forgotten, not passed down through their own families.

As their words gained more force, the thrumming lines becalmed themselves.

In the real world, daylight had finally won and the scenes of devastation in the harbour were revealed.

More rain had fallen that night than the island normally experienced in three months.

Houses had slid down the mountain.

Cars were floating in the harbour streets.

Over ten people were dead and several, including Pete, were unaccounted for.

But the island still stood.

Ben had deflected the attack from it and on to him.

Now, he needed to keep The Watchmen occupied until Ebhart could hit his objective. If he could not, he would at least try to hit some of those attacking him in the same way that he'd dealt with Karvorkian. Without knowing who they were, it would be difficult to wound them in the same way.

This had become more dangerous than he had ever thought. He could no longer operate consciously whilst deflecting this kind of attack.

He was trapped inside his own body for as long as this was going to continue.

He required all his strength to combat his unknown attackers.

Ben gave himself one brief moment to drop back to reality and see Esther's face. He said one word before soaring back up into the stratosphere for however long it would take.

"Sorry."

CHAPTER 92

CERN, Switzerland - 30th March, 2010

Standing in the control centre at CERN, Kevin Daste beamed with pride as he watched Professor Ebhart Fenkhause and his team. Through his new artificial eyes, he watched them achieve their goal of colliding two beams of particles at Seven TeV. Four point five in TeV each direction. Finally, they'd reached the marker of the official start of the LHC research program.

Champagne flowed. Lots of sweaty hugs and kisses were shared. Kevin dreaded to think how many brainy but unattractive unplanned babies would be born into the scientific community in nine months' time.

Across the room, Professor Fenkhause caught his eye. He was being hugged by one of the few fairly attractive young lab assistants. He raised his glass in a silent toast.

Kevin knew to whom that was directed and returned it.

Ben.

As soon as he'd heard the news of the devastation on Madeira, Kevin had sent Agent Anderegg over there. She had reported back that Ben was in a coma-like state and that Esther was going to need some help too. Reluctantly, Kevin had agreed that she should stay over there and find some more appropriate accommodation for Ben.

According to Anderegg, Ben didn't seem to be in any physical pain. There was no immediate threat as long as his limbs did not atrophy. He just needed to be regularly exercised. Mentally, there was a huge amount of brain activity.

He just wouldn't wake up.

Kevin had no idea what Ben was going through, but made sure that any strings he could pull with funding were pulled. Making Ben's care more comfortable whilst funding any research into the causes and possible solutions to the coma-like state he was in.

Deep down, he knew that it all had something to do with where he was today.

He worked his way over to the Professor and took his hand.

"Congratulations Professor."

"Thank you, thank you, Kevin. Now the hard work begins. We'll be running full tilt until December this time and we've got a lot of work to get done. But I am relieved and delighted that we've managed to get here today."

They clinked glasses and Ebhart asked if there was any update.

"I'm afraid that things are still the same, Professor. Of course, you'll be the first to hear if anything changes."

Ebhart sighed. There were so many things that he wanted to say but which felt foolish at this point.

"I appreciate that."

Kevin allowed himself another sip of Champagne.

It was the first alcohol to pass his lips since his accident. He didn't want to fall over on his new artificial limbs. Otherwise he'd have to blame the gyroscopes in front of a crowd of rocket scientists.

"Well, I'll keep a close eye on your progress Professor. And let me know the instant you feel if there's anything wrong?"

Ebhart smiled and nodded.

Kevin put his glass down on a table. He said his goodbyes to the Professor and made his way through the crowd slowly but purposefully. He came alongside the special agent who was temporarily standing in for Agent Anderegg.

"Come on, let's leave these eggheads to party like it's nineteen ninety-nine."

"Yes, Sir."

Kevin sighed. He missed Agent Anderegg more than he cared to admit. It even crossed his mind to find out her first name, before he embarrassedly put that thought to the back of his mind.

CHAPTER 93

Hospital Dos Marmeleiros, Monte, Madeira - 30th March, 2010

In the relative darkness of the ICU, no one would have imagined the battle raging inside the man lying dormant on the bed, a drip feeding him moisture and vitamins, and the various representatives of The Watchmen. Leaderless, fighting an insurgent's war in the ether.

Every now and again, a twitch here or a jerk of a wrist there would indicate that there was a person still living within the confines of that body. Unless studying the ECG machine, an observer would have considered a person lying so still to be in a vegetative state.

On the contrary, the activity on the ECG showed someone with an immense amount of activity going on. More than was thought humanly possible.

Ben fought on as The Watchmen threw everything they could at him.

His one blessing was that, as a group, they did not seem to communicate or coordinate their actions very well.

He had removed the head, whether permanently or temporarily. The actions of the group after that seemed to imply that this was a significant blow to their strength.

He drew power from the luck around him. He remembered he was connected with everything. He seemed to be able to withstand vastly more than some of those that were raging against him.

It appeared that they could not dedicate themselves to their fight wholeheartedly.

At times, there were few attacks, at other times he felt at least a dozen of them, all lobbing words at him.

These words were misshapen. Fragments of language snapped into bits over the distance they travelled, bounced off other words directed from a different origin.

Many were weak by the time they got close and he was easily able to deal with them.

One particularly potent one however managed to slip through when he was low.

Historian

It was not his name, but it was close enough to wound. He was surprised by their knowledge of it. He dropped his guard.

Like a knife slicing off a portion of his brain, there was a spike on the ECG and his body convulsed for several moments in the dead of night.

He felt a part of him slide off and did not know whether it would grow back.

He immediately parried with several words of his own in that direction and felt no resistance to the second volley he sent over.

There were no more ripples from that direction.

One slip was one too many, he cautioned himself. He rose as high as he felt he could without losing his consciousness into the white stream that seemed to be projecting the universe on to their physical plane. Higher up, closer to that source, he felt the beams to be much more powerful. He spent a little time there, wrapping himself up in strands of luck that seemed to have no direction or destination. Then, suitably armoured, he sank back down, just in time to prevent an attack on CERN.

Ben stopped thinking of 'time' and 'space'. His purpose was singular.

He concentrated on defending his position and his causes whilst continuing to scout for the enemy.

Over time, one by one, they dropped in numbers. Then there were fewer than the fingers on his right hand.

And finally, the attacks stopped altogether.

CHAPTER 94

Madeira - December 6th, 2010

Ben opened his eyes and slowly turned his head to his left.

Esther was there, just as she had been when he went to sleep.

He reached a hand out to stroke her hair, but immediately noticed the needle inserted into his hand connected to the clear plastic tube.

He sat up, as did Esther whose eyes snapped open when she'd felt the vaguest sign of movement.

She immediately put her finger on his lips, shook her head and started crying silently.

Ben pulled her in and hugged her, noticing that she too was in a hospital gown.

She pulled back and kissed him lightly several times, then whispered in his ear.

Ben's gaze slid across to the small carry cot sitting on the table just past the end of his bed.

Just then, a tiny hand appeared over the side, its fingers curling as if waving at him.

He swallowed and tears came to his eyes.

"I am The Historian," he said, and hugged Esther to him tightly.

EPILOGUE

Bahçesaray, Crimea, Ukraine - December 2010

Fritz shelled the pistachio nuts one by one, tossing them into his mouth as he stared at the bed's occupant.

The person stared dully back at him with weak blue eyes, mouth hanging open and with saliva dribbling down the side of his face.

His arms were secured to the hospital bed. Mainly for his own protection.

Sometimes not.

Fritz had finally found him after months of travelling. That's all he seemed to do. He didn't know where home was these days.

He had had no idea where Karvorkian had been the last time he'd spoken to him. Most of his network of homes and properties, along with businesses, were unsafe or insecure. The Special Forces investigation had roped in Interpol's huge resources.

The drugs factory and all documentation relating to it had gone up in smoke. The connections they'd had with the military had dissolved as quickly.

They'd been cut off, pretty much completely.

So he'd found his way back to Karvorkian's homeland, more in the hope of finding some leads than finding the man.

But such was the depth of his fall, it didn't take long for Fritz to locate him.

Gossip about a madman sectioned in the sanatorium was news around these parts.

And there he was.

The dribbling wreck in the bed in front of him.

Fritz finished his nuts, wiped the detritus from his knees and then carefully picked up his bag.

He fished out a case and opened it.

Inside was a syringe.

Humming a vague tune, Fritz added a fresh hypodermic needle to the instrument and then selected a small vial out of his bag.

He looked at the man in the bed, looked at the label on vial then tipped it upside down and inserted the needle.

Flick, flick, squirt.

Fritz injected the fluid into the man's arm then sat back and waited.

-- THE END --